The
War
Orphan

BOOKS BY ANNA STUART

The
War
Orphan

ANNA STUART

bookouture

Published by Bookouture in 2024

An imprint of Storyfire Ltd.
Carmelite House
50 Victoria Embankment
London EC4Y 0DZ

www.bookouture.com

ISBN: 978-1-83790-229-3
eBook ISBN: 978-1-83790-228-6

For the real-life Natasha – my astute, passionate and all-round amazing editor. And my treasured friend.

PROLOGUE

AUSCHWITZ | JANUARY 1945

It is snowing on Auschwitz. The flakes whirl in the searchlights, sparkle on the barbed wire, and catch in the ears of the guard dogs. They fall in a thick blanket that covers the mud and the corpses and the broken remains of the crematoria. They deaden the cries of the dying and the panicked shouts of the guards. But they can do nothing to soften the last throes of Nazi violence.

'Raus! Raus!'

Tasha Ancel starts from sleep, curled up tight with her mother, and looks into the thin light creeping through the open barrack door. An unnatural star-glow is shining off the snow onto the prisoners huddled beneath their meagre blankets. It lights up the kapo who is going from bunk to bunk, banging the uprights with her club as if it were dawn.

'Up! Get up, you lazy Hündin. Time to go walkies!'

Outside, an Alsatian barks feverishly.

'Walkies?' Tasha's mother grabs her, her eyes alert in the half-light. 'Get blankets, Tash, all you can.'

Lydia Ancel snatches up their meagre covering and swoops on another, left behind by a woman hastening blearily to do the kapo's bidding.

'Where are we going?' Tasha chokes.

'Out somewhere. The Allies must be coming.' Lydia pauses in the tumble of bodies and grabs Tasha's shoulders. 'The Allies are coming!' She kisses her, even leads her in two steps of a jig before the kapo swipes out with her club, knocking her sideways.

Lydia laughs in the woman's face. 'Your petty power will soon be gone,' she tells her, tossing her slowly regrowing hair. The Nazis stopped shearing them last November, around the same time they knocked down the crematoria. It has been one of Tasha's greatest delights to see her mother's red hair start to return; and one of Lydia's great delights to see Tasha's.

'You see,' she's said every evening, stroking the determined growth. 'They cannot put us down. Every knock, we get up again; every cut, we heal; every bit of their hate, we fight with our love for each other.'

And now – now the Allies are coming and they, it seems, are leaving. As Tasha and Lydia shuffle towards the door, blankets wrapped tightly around themselves, they can see line after line of prisoners hunched beneath the still-falling snowflakes, the thin breath from their wasted lungs hanging in an orange haze above them. Tasha puts a hand to the barrack wall. The hard, mean room suddenly feels like a sanctuary.

'It's cold out there.'

'It's free...' Lydia whispers. She points to the stark gates in the distance. 'Once we're out of those, who knows what can happen. We just keep our heads down and stick together and—'

'You – back!' An SS guard in a thick coat, stands in front of Tasha. 'No children on the march.'

'I'm not a child,' she tells him, panicked. She's sixteen. She's been working as an adult for these cruel masters, so how can they now decide she's a child?

Lydia is being hustled out of the door, pulled away from her on a thin tide of humanity.

'I'm sixteen,' she protests, desperately trying to get past.

'Ha!' the guard says and pushes her so hard she falls to the floor.

Another girl pulls her to her feet.

'It's warmer in here,' she says. But although that's exactly what Tasha was thinking a moment ago, it no longer feels that way, for Lydia is outside and all Tasha's warmth comes from her. It is how they have survived this hellish place – together.

'Mama!' she cries.

'Tasha!' Lydia is trying to fight her way back to her. 'She's an adult,' she shouts. 'She's sixteen.'

'No children,' the SS man repeats.

'But–'

'And no buts, Jew. Save this one.' He hits Lydia around the head with the butt of his gun and laughs uproariously at his own joke as she staggers.

'Mama.'

He turns on Tasha, gun lifted again, and Lydia grabs at his arm.

'Don't hurt her!'

His eyes harden, the laughter draining out of him, and he slowly, deliberately, rotates his gun so that the tiny, vicious mouth of it is pointing straight at Lydia.

'No!' Tasha screams, but an officer marches up, snapping for speed, and the guard contents himself with shoving Lydia towards the terrified lines of prisoners.

'You have every drop of my love, Natasha,' Lydia calls, still defiant.

It's what she's told her throughout the dark, cold months since they lost her little sister. Every drop of her love – it's been enough to sustain them both and, although her words tangle in the prisoners' cries of distress, they ring into Tasha's ears, loud and clear.

'You have every drop of mine too, Mama.'

Lydia smiles. 'I'll see you soon,' she calls as she's shoved into a line. 'Stay strong, Tasha, and we'll find each other. We'll meet in—'

But her words are cut off by the snow, and the barks of the dogs, and the lines of people forming rapidly behind her, until Tasha can see her no more. She tries, again, to reach the door but other children are being shoved inside and she is fighting against a driving tide. The kapo lifts her club to strike her again and Tasha instinctively cringes back, but a big arm reaches out and takes the blow. Surprised, Tasha looks up into the dark-brown eyes of a boy of about her age. She hasn't been near boys since she was brought into Auschwitz last October and this one is tall, with broad shoulders.

'Georg Lieberman,' he introduces himself, as if this were a normal situation in which to meet.

She can only stare. 'You're a child too?' she asks incredulously.

'That's what I told them,' he says. 'Better in here than out there.' He nods to the door and the bitter night beyond.

'It's not,' Tasha wails. 'It's not for me.'

She tries, again, to reach the door but as she gets close, it's slammed shut. She hears the clunk of a heavy wooden plank being rammed into place and hammering on it does nothing but make her knuckles bleed. Looking frantically around, she scrambles up to the third tier of the bare bunks, where a thin open strip provides a sliver of light. The prisoners sleeping up here always complain when the wind and rain blows in on them, but Tasha presses her face to the tiny gap, taking the sting of the snow as she squints through it.

Far across Auschwitz-Birkenau, she can hear the shriek of metal as the gates crank open and the first of the prisoners begin to shuffle forward. They've all dreamed of stepping out of those gates, but not like this, not on a march into hell. A shot rings out as some unfortunate fails to step forward and is disposed of as casually as an ant on the pathway.

'Mama!' Tasha calls desperately.

And then she sees it – a flash of auburn hair, snowflakes caught within the tufts but still fiery in the glare of the search-lights. Her mother looks round, her blue-green eyes searching frantically, then the pace picks up and she has to turn forward. She pulls the blanket over her head and she is lost, gone.

'Mama,' Tasha whimpers.

Her fingers claw at the mean strip of window and her tears frost on her cheeks as she is left, alone, to freeze into oblivion with what remains of Auschwitz-Birkenau.

PART ONE

LIBERATION

ONE

TASHA

'Have you seen this woman?'

Tasha flinched back against the rough wall of a falling-down townhouse as a wiry man waved a photograph in her face. The picture was small and dark, the edges frayed and the image creased with too much looking, but the big eyes stared clearly out at Tasha.

'Please? Have you seen my wife?'

She forced herself to take it. Survivors had to stick together, if only to remind themselves they'd truly made it out of hell. She'd been here in Theresienstadt, a strange ghetto-town turned refugee camp, for nearly a month, but part of her still felt locked into Auschwitz, and she replayed her last days in there over and over in her mind when she struggled to sleep at night.

After two desperate days locked in the barrack, she and the other 'children' had been released by a brave midwife called Ana and her kindly nurse friend, Ester. Together, their little band had foraged the ruins of the camp for food and fuel to keep themselves alive until the magical day when the Soviets had marched through the gates bringing liberation. After 'recovering' in the Auschwitz main camp, they'd been brought to this peculiar Czech town just as the snow and ice of Tasha's worst-ever winter had given way to the warmth of spring. She was still stunned that she was alive.

If alone.

Tasha looked at the photograph, as she had looked at a hundred similar ones since arriving. Everyone had someone to find and here, in this transit city full of the lost, photographs were top currency. She stared at the young woman, seeking something she might recognise, but the photo was from before the war when people had looked fresh and rounded and not the skeletal waifs they'd become.

'I'm so sorry but I don't recognise her.'

The man snatched the photo back, tucking it in against his heart. It was all he had left of his wife and maybe all he would ever have. Every day more news came out about the scale of the Nazi killings, and every day the odds of your family surviving dropped. And yet also every day, even four months after the first camps had been liberated, more refugees flooded into Theresienstadt. Some people had survived, so why not *their* people?

Why not *Tasha's* people?

She watched the man limp off and pounce on another woman further up the narrow street. She saw her take the photo, study it, and shake her head sadly. Then she saw her produce a photo, just to have the pantomime reversed. Yes, everyone had someone to find.

Instinctively, Tasha's hand slid into the little leather bag she wore across her chest. She'd found it in the remains of Kanada, the great warehouses of Auschwitz where the Nazis had sorted through mounds of goods stolen from the Jews. The guards had tried to burn them down before they ran away, but the snow had choked the flames and, in the days after liberation, the survivors had been able to pick through the remaining goods.

Others had searched for gold or jewels, but for Tasha this bag had been treasure indeed, for it would keep safe the one possession she'd clung onto through her four terrible months in the camp – a single lock of her mother's hair, as red as her own. It wasn't as precise as a photo, but there weren't that many red-headed Jews so perhaps it would get her further than all these blurry, run-into-each-other images of lost loved ones. Plus, it was the only piece of Lydia she had left.

Until she found her.

Stroking the lock, Tasha thought back to the terrible day in October 1944 when she'd bagged this paltry treasure. They'd been newly arrived in Auschwitz, reeling from seeing Tata shot down in front of them in the ruins of bombed-out Warsaw, and dazed from days in a dark, waterless cattle truck. They'd found themselves in a long line snaking around a stark, empty barrack and been so desperate to keep her little sister close that their sole worry when they'd been stripped naked had been that it would be apparent Amelia was only twelve. No one, however, had paid much attention to the shape of their bodies, wanting only their arms to carve anonymous numbers into. And then they'd got to the clippers.

Tasha clung to the wall behind her as the memory swamped her once more. She didn't know why, amongst all the horrors of Auschwitz, this one had stuck so sharply in her heart. She didn't know why, with all the disease and misery she'd seen later, she was most upset by the moment they'd taken the shears to her mother's hair. It hadn't been the darkest time, that had been when sweet Amelia, ravaged by hard work and emptied out by typhus, had slid, with a sad smile, into the afterlife. But after weeks of suffering that had been almost a relief. Tasha and her mother had got down on their knees and thanked God for taking the poor child into His care at last. The sorrow of her sister's loss had torn at Tasha's heart, but it had held none of the shock of those initial shears.

Something about the memory of the rusty blades running across Lydia's scalp, sending a curtain of her glorious red hair falling to the filthy floor, brought all that was harshest of that hellish place into sharp focus for Tasha and she stroked the remaining fragments now. This was the hair that had brushed her face when her mother kissed her goodnight as a child. This was the hair that had shone in the sunshine at lakeside picnics, and blown in the winter air as they'd chased around Łazienki Park. This was the hair that Tasha had brushed out at the hearth in their home in Warsaw, loving the way the light of the flames caught in the fire of her mother's locks. The Nazis had cared for none of that. In a few harsh cuts, they'd turned her mother from a beautiful, unique individual into a bare-headed replica of every other wretch in the camp. Tasha had hated it.

They'd shorn Amelia too, but perhaps by then Tasha had got over the shock, and her own shearing had felt more like an act of solidarity. Her hair was growing back now, finally becoming more than ridiculous flaming tufts. Her mother's must have done so too and everywhere she went, she scoured the crowds for this beacon of hope. So far, nothing, but she wouldn't give up. The Red Cross said there were thousands of people in camps all over Europe, for the Nazis had dispersed their prisoners with careless cruelty. It would take months – maybe years – for everyone to find their way back to where they were meant to be, so every day Tasha searched as hard as the rest. They'd all made it out of the killing zones alive, but until you found someone to whom that mattered, it was hard for it to matter to yourself.

'Tasha?!'

The voice came from the next street, high-pitched and

needy, and Tasha instinctively slunk into an archway as a pair of younger girls ran past looking for her. She wasn't strong enough to play with them right now and she cursed the bad luck that had condemned her, once again, to a children's barrack. She liked playing with the youngsters and she wanted to help. She knew if she'd died instead of Amelia, she'd have wanted someone to look after her little sister, so she did her best, but it was exhausting. They couldn't understand that sometimes Tasha wanted to *have* a mother, not to *be* one.

Georg, her fellow survivor, had managed to blag himself a place in a man's house, but that was Georg all over. From the moment he'd put up his arm to protect her from the kapo on that dark, snowy day in Auschwitz, he'd brought drive and positivity into her life.

'We'll be rescued,' he'd assured her as they'd lain side by side in the barrack, trapped for two cold, hungry days and rapidly losing strength.

Then, when that first, blessed knock had come on the door, he'd been up, finding reserves of strength to help the nurses outside, and that had given Tasha strength too. It had been Georg who'd fought his way into Kanada to get them warm clothes and fuel, and Georg who'd picked the locks on the crates of food Tasha had found in an abandoned railway carriage. It had been Georg who'd kept her going in those dark days and Georg who found them the little extras that made life as a refugee just about bearable.

That boy was able to charm his way in with every person of influence. Not only was he in an adult house, but a house in Mecklenburg, the smart area of Theresienstadt where the Nazis had housed the 'privileged Jews'. He was sharing with a pianist from the Vienna Philharmonic, a philosophy professor from the University of Berlin, and a well-known Czech artist, so was awash with culture. More to the point, he had his own little bedroom, a bathroom shared by only ten men and a tap with actual running water. Tasha was so envious.

'How did you do that?' she'd asked him when he'd first brought her to see his new lodgings.

'I said I was nineteen. And that my dad was the chief of police in Krakow.'

'Was he?'

'Course not. He saw the inside of a few police stations, but not from that side of the desk! But how were they to know? I've got no papers, so I can be whoever I want to be.'

Tasha had shaken her head, unable to believe he could even make the best of being robbed of his identity. She, in contrast, had been quite happy being Tasha Ancel, daughter of Lydia and Szymon, sister of Amelia. A bedroom of her own, however, would be very nice, as there was little chance of rest in the children's dorm.

The majority of the kids had been in Theresienstadt throughout the war, looked after by women who took pity on them when their parents died or were sent away. They'd only survived because of their PR value to the Germans, who'd filmed this barren place, plastering flowers, vegetables and bread on top of the usual deprivations to try to convince the world they were treating the Jews well. And they'd succeeded – until the Russians had forced the Wehrmacht into retreat and the gates of Auschwitz, Bergen-Belsen and Buchenwald had been thrown open.

Mr Dunant, head of the International Red Cross and care-taker of Theresienstadt, had played them a BBC film telling the world about Belsen the other day. The man had been reporting on starving prisoners, cruel living conditions and pits full of corpses, his plummy voice run through with emotion. Some people had laughed, manic with the bitter humour of the British man's clear shock, but Tasha had just felt sad. If only someone had cared enough to come looking sooner, she'd thought, they could have been spared this nightmare. Tasha would still be in her comfortable home in Warsaw with her loving family and her future ahead of her, instead of in this gaping hole of a present in a barren ghetto-city in Czechoslovakia with Tata shot in ruined Warsaw, Amelia dead in Auschwitz, and Mama who knows where.

'Tasha?'

This time the voice was warm and deep and sent a pleasing ripple down her spine.

'Georg! What are you up to?'

'Looking for you, gorgeous.'

Tasha flushed instinctively, but then reminded herself that Georg said things like that all the time. Flattery came easily to him and he used it on everyone. He didn't really think she was gorgeous; how could he? She was skin and bones with strange, bulging flesh sitting on top from the last month of being fed cheese and chocolate by the Swiss Red Cross. Her hair stuck up like a burning bush from her gaunt face and her skin was grey and flaky. Even so, she couldn't help smiling at Georg as he bounced up to her. His dark hair was growing back into tight curls she longed to twist her fingers into, and, although his body was as wasted as hers, his brown eyes burned with life.

'Here I am,' she said. 'What's going on?'

'Someone just came in through the gates.'

'So? There are always people coming in.'

'Yes, but not usually on horseback.'

That caught Tasha's attention and she let Georg pull her down the rough street towards the big square at the centre of the ghetto-city.

'What sort of horse?'

'A grand white one, like in the fairy stories.'

'With a prince on its back?'

'Better than a dumb prince – a messenger in a fancy

uniform. He rode up to the town hall, leaped down and strode inside, handsome head held high.'

Tasha laughed; Georg certainly knew how to tell a story.

'And then what?'

'And then I don't know. He's been with Mr Dunant for ages and everyone is gathering outside. Rumour has it there's going to be an announcement. Rumour has it...' He stopped and reached for Tasha's other hand, pulling her so close that her breath caught embarrassingly in her lungs and she had to gulp for more. 'Rumour has it that the war is over.'

'No!'

He nodded eagerly and she gazed up into his eyes, trying to see if he was pulling one of his usual tricks, but he looked totally in earnest. The German surrender was to be expected, she supposed, but they'd been living in limbo for four months and had got used to it. They were urged not to leave Theresienstadt because fighting was still raging outside the walls, so the idea that the whole world might one day become safe enough to travel felt impossible.

'It's been so long.'

He squeezed her fingers. 'It's nearly over, Tash, I'm sure of it. Come on, let's join the rest and find out.'

He pulled her down the road and into the main square where many of the twenty thousand refugees crammed into the city were gathering. There was a buzz of excitement running through the crowd and, for once, no one was fighting or searching or arguing. Myriad emaciated faces were turned up to the balcony on the first floor of the town hall and, when Tasha looked up, she saw a curtain twitch and a door open.

'There!'

The word rippled through the crowd and hundreds of fingers pointed as Mr Dunant stepped out, a piece of white paper in his hand.

'That's it,' Georg said, clutching Tasha close. 'That's the armistice. It has to be.'

Tasha fixed on it, but her eyes were so dimmed from years of poor eating that the man might have been holding a dove. And, to all intents and purposes, it seemed, he was.

'Ladies and gentlemen!' Mr Dunant's voice rang confidently around the square and a hush fell, broken only by footsteps in the side streets as others came running. 'I have in my hand official notification that Grand Admiral Karl Dönitz, German Head of State since Hitler's death last week...' He paused for a dark cheer to tear through the crowd, then raised a hand for quiet once more. 'That Grand Admiral Karl Dönitz has signed the armistice. Germany have surrendered and today, May the eighth 1945, the war in Europe is officially over.'

He smiled and looked around expectantly, but the massed people below him just stared back. Someone near Tasha sobbed, a few began whispering to each other and then slowly, nervously at first, but with growing certainty, a rumble of excitement built in hollowed-out chests and wasted lungs. At last, the first cheers rang around the ramparts of Theresienstadt and Mr Dunant smiled and waved the paper like a flag.

'You are free, my friends – free of tyranny, free of bonds, free of fear.'

Tasha looked around as the cheers grew. Free? What did that even mean?

'We thank you for your patience and I personally assure you that, although it will take time, we at the Red Cross will work tirelessly to help all of you who have been ripped from your houses, your families and your countries by this evil war, to finally go home.'

'Home!'

The cry was taken up by the crowd and bounced between them like a ball as people leaped up and down, embracing each other and crying. Tasha felt Georg throw his arms around her and liked his closeness, but her own arms were rigid, her heart cold. Home sounded wonderful but she, Tasha Ancel, had no house, no family and no idea where home was or could ever again hope to be.

Turning, she slipped out of Georg's hold to let him dance with the others and slid away through the crowd, searching – always searching – for the glimmer of red hair that might offer her a way forward once more.

TWO

ALICE

'Yesterday morning at 2.41 a.m.... Grand Admiral Dönitz, the designated head of the German State, signed the act of unconditional surrender of all German land, sea and air forces in Europe to the Allied Expeditionary Force...'

Alice Goldberger stared at the radio, picturing Churchill's florid face speaking the astonishing words. She ran her fingers through her greying hair, tugging on it to be sure she was really alive and listening to this, but then tutted at herself for her silliness. They'd known the end was coming. Berlin was taken and Hitler was dead, so the full surrender had only been a matter of time. Even so, it was a thrill to hear the prime minister speak of peace.

Alice looked to the nursery children, gathered cross-legged around the old set, mesmerised by Churchill's steady voice, even if his words were a little convoluted for their young brains. One cheeky lad caught her eye and winked.

'He's saying the war's over, right, miss?'

Alice smiled. 'That's right, Charlie.'

'Does that mean my dad will come home?'

'It does. It might take time, but he should come home safe now.'

Even as she said it, Alice crossed her fingers behind her back, shocked at her boldness. Here at New Barn – one of Anna Freud's War Nurseries – she made a point of never lying to the children, or promising things that she wasn't certain she could deliver. Hopefully Charlie's father, an infantryman in the Allied Expeditionary Force, was now safe but anything could happen. The last few years had been a bitter lesson in the fragility of life. Everyone who'd made it out of the war was blessed, yes, but not necessarily safe.

It was easy, here in leafy Essex, to imagine the whole world laying down their guns and enjoying a convivial cup of tea together, but Alice had seen the chaos in Europe when she and her brother, Max, had fought to leave Germany as the Nazis gathered power, and was pretty sure it would be similar now. So many people had been uprooted by this vicious, vast-ranging conflict, and it would take a long time to get them back to where they belonged. Some, too weary or wounded by the war, wouldn't make it. She prayed every day that her Max was safe somewhere, his wife and daughter too, but she'd heard nothing since she left Germany and thoughts of what might have happened to them tore her gut every morning when she woke.

'We must pray that everyone's daddies come home safely,' she said now.

Several of the children instantly put their hands together and Alice was touched to see it. She was Jewish and most of the children Christian, but surely it was the same God up there and He must be very pleased his most sophisticated creation had finally found peace. They'd all heard rumours about camps with gas chambers and mass crematoria, they'd all listened in horror to Richard Dimbleby's report from Belsen, but it was still

impossible to believe that the Nazis had actually been extermi-
nating people.

And that she'd escaped.

Alice had fled Germany in late summer 1939, catching one
of the last boats out before the Nazis had clamped their iron fist
around the continent. She'd hated leaving her homeland, and
hated even more that it was being torn apart by evil, but there'd
been no choice.

'We have to get away,' her brother had insisted. 'Germany is
no place for Jews any more.' They'd spent days at the embassy,
begging passage to Great Britain, but in the end it had been
only Alice who'd been granted her papers. As a registered carer,
she'd been deemed useful to the British, whereas Max, his wife
Lilliana, and their three-year-old daughter Ruth-Gertrud were
merely a burden. It had been a bitter blow. All her life Alice
had cared for Max, and he for her. And she loved Lilli and little
Ruthie as her own.

'We should stay together,' she'd insisted.

But Max had shaken his head and said, 'We should stay
alive, Alice.'

The emigration official had assured them that once Alice
was established in England, they would have a far better chance
of applying to join her and so, in the end, she'd agreed to go to
save them all.

She'd failed.

As soon as she'd set foot on the docks at Southampton, she'd
been met by a policeman and a polite, 'Can you come this way
please, ma'am.' The British authorities, it had swiftly emerged,
had been less keen on accepting German citizens, Jewish or
otherwise, than the German authorities had been on getting rid
of them. Alice was designated, with a polite but firm apology, as
an 'enemy alien' and transferred to an internment camp on the
improbably named Isle of Man. Although held in relative
freedom on the pretty island, her movements had been

restricted and, more importantly, she'd been unable to secure authorisation for Max and his family to join her.

Alice swallowed, thinking of her bright, caring brother. Her parents had been kind enough people but, both academics, had been rather formal with their children. It was with Max that she'd known true affection and with Max that she'd spent her childhood in happy, made-up adventures. Where was he now? Had he made it through the most hideous of real-life adventures? Had Lilli? Or little Ruthie? If Alice's niece had made it, she'd be nearly nine now and Alice ached to see her, but felt with a razor-sharp fear that she never would.

'Just do your best, Alice,' Max had said, kissing her on both cheeks with the train puffing out steam behind them. 'And if it doesn't work, at least one of us will have made it out.'

Well, she'd done her best, but it hadn't been good enough. Not by a long way, even once she'd been freed. That had been down to Anna Freud, daughter of the famous psychologist Sigmund Freud and making a name in the field of child psychology herself. Searching for relatives on the Isle of Man, Anna had heard about the kindergarten Alice had set up in the camp, and petitioned Parliament to let her out to help in her Hampstead War Nurseries.

Alice would always be grateful to Anna for that and she loved her job, running New Barn in Essex for children whose parents were either away at war or busy with vital work, but it hadn't helped Max. By the time she'd been released from the Isle of Man, Germany had been closed, and it was only thanks to a brave letter from a family friend that she'd learned her brother and his family had been sent to the Theresienstadt ghetto. She'd had no word of them since and could only pray they were still there, still alive, and that Max, like Charlie's daddy, would somehow find his way home.

'Almost the whole world was combined against the evil-doers, who are now prostrate before us,' Churchill boomed out of the radio.

Alice looked uncertainly to her friend, Sophie Wutsch, New Barn's smiling, caring cook with a talent for turning even the humblest ingredients into a royal treat, usually with several eager children 'helping'.

'Listen, Sophie,' she said, 'Churchill is calling Germans "evil-doers".'

'Churchill is calling *Nazis* "evil-doers",' her friend corrected her. 'We know that better than most – it's why we left.'

'I'm still German and you're Austrian.'

'By birth, not by choice. We're just people, like everyone else – people of the world.'

Alice sighed. It was all right for Sophie, a cheery blonde, with a sunny smile and easy disposition. She was accepted wherever she went, whereas Alice was slight, dark-haired and awkward with strangers.

'Tell that to anyone who hears our accent,' she grumbled.

Throughout the war she'd been subjected to strange looks whenever people heard her German accent in shops or on transport. It was, perhaps, one of the reasons she liked working with children – they didn't care what you looked or sounded like, as long as you gave them your love and attention.

'So, work on your English!' Sophie laughed. 'Stop dwelling and let's take these little ones out to celebrate. Who wants ice cream, kids?'

There was a predictable roar of approval and Alice laughingly pushed herself up from her chair and clicked off the radio, forcing herself to silence her misgivings with Churchill's steady voice. Sophie was right – the war was over and it was time to be happy. Taking the hands of two of her younger charges, she let herself be danced out of New Barn and into the streets.

Lindsell was a typically English village and, in typically English fashion, the residents were collecting on the impossibly green cricket square. Efficient housewives were setting up a tea urn and producing cakes from who knows where. Someone had dug out bunting to string around the rope protecting the precious wicket, and several older men were carrying jugs of frothing ale from the nearby public house. Two more were striking up a tune on a guitar and a fiddle, and a buxom young woman began singing something about bluebirds over the cliffs of Dover to much applause. As the grocer wheeled his ice cream cart out of his shop, the children let out a loud cheer and Sophie dug for her purse.

'It'll cost you a fortune,' Alice hissed as their twenty charges crowded eagerly around.

'So? It's the end of the war, Alice – live a little!'

She was right, of course, and Alice forced herself to accept a vanilla ice from the beaming grocer.

'Half price today,' he told Sophie. 'Thank Churchill!'

Sophie sent Alice a broad grin, which she was forced to acknowledge with a smile. The ice cream really did taste delicious, the sun was shining and, as the children sat round with their treats, Alice allowed herself to relax at last. It was over. The war was over!

The musicians moved into a jig and she felt the tune pull at her limbs. At forty-seven years old her dancing feet might be creaky but she'd always loved music and it called out to her now with clear, simple joy. She'd learned the piano from an early age and, working in a Berlin nursery for deprived children in the struggle of the 1920s, she'd found it was one of the few things to cheer everyone up. But then, in 1933, the Nazis had come to power and she'd been deemed unqualified for her job on the basis of her 'tainted blood'. She'd had to take more erratic work, helping children in Berlin's Jewish community, and there had been no more piano.

Missing it, she'd taken up the harmonica and Max had bought her a lovely little instrument for her fortieth birthday in

1938. She felt in her pocket for it now, but she was far too shy to play with these English musicians, so contented herself with clapping along with the rest. When eight-year-old Charlie got up and offered her his arm like a gentleman twice his age, however, she took it gladly and let him lead her into an impromptu dance. The war was over, she was alive, and so were the lovely children in her care – if that wasn't worth a jig, she didn't know what was.

Later, as the sun went down, Alice and Sophie led the weary children back to New Barn for cocoa and scones before bed. The rotation dictated it should be bathtime for the seven- and eight-year-olds but it was late and they made do with a quick flannel-rub.

'I wish it was VE Day every day,' a little girl called Doris said to Alice, rubbing with careless lack of success at her grass-stained knees.

'At least every day is a day of peace now,' Alice told her, turning a blind eye to the still-green skin and tucking her into bed before she fell asleep where she stood.

'I don't remember peace,' Doris said sleepily and then her thumb went into her mouth and her eyes drifted shut.

Alice stood looking down at the little girl, considering her words. How terrible that a generation of children had grown up knowing only war, only bombs and separations and black-edged telegrams. Doris, she realised, was about the same age as her niece, Ruth-Gertrud. What had Ruthie's last five years been like? Alice shuddered and, dropping a kiss onto Doris's fore-head, walked down to the kitchen for some much-needed supper. On her way, she instinctively glanced in the hallway mirror, then wished she hadn't. The dancing had pulled her greying hair from its bun and flushed her cheeks in an unbe-comingly mottled way. She looked like what she was: a spinster travelling all too fast towards her fiftieth birthday, made even gaunter and dowdier by the privations of war.

'So what?' she told her reflection. 'You're not here to look pretty; you're here to care for children.'

Besides, it wasn't like Sophie would care, so she headed, untidied, into the kitchen.

'Alice!'

Oskar Friedmann, one of the Hampstead War Nurseries' top psychologists, leaped up and, taking her hand, dropped an ostentatious kiss upon it. Alice felt herself flush.

'Oskar! What on earth are you doing here?'

'Alice!' Sophie scolded from the stove.

'Sorry. I mean, it's lovely to see you, I just thought you'd be partying in London with your, er, your family.'

'I was earlier,' Oskar agreed easily, pulling out a chair for her. 'But then I thought I'd pop down and see how it was going here. Sophie says I've just missed the children.'

'They were worn out, bless them. They've been playing on the cricket ground all afternoon.'

'As they should, as they should. You must be tired too.'

'No more than usual.'

'You work too hard, both of you.'

Oskar beamed at them. Alice suspected the party had been a good one for his warm voice was louder than usual and his athletic frame less coordinated.

'Did you drive down, Oskar?'

'I did. Lovely run. People out celebrating in every village.'

'Perhaps you should stay the night?' He raised an eyebrow at her and she felt herself flush again. 'In the spare room,' she said hastily. 'I'm sure you're, er, tired too.'

Goodness, she was making a meal of this. She'd never been very good with men; something about their strutting self-confidence made an instant dent in hers.

'As it happens,' Oskar said, 'that might be a good idea

because I brought us a little something.'

He reached into a bag and produced a bottle. 'Ta-da!'

Sophie snatched eagerly at it. 'Is that champagne?'

'It certainly is.'

'Hurrah! I'll get glasses.'

'Not for me,' Alice said.

'We won the war, Alice!' Oskar cried. 'You have to have champagne.'

'I don't normally drink alcohol.'

'And this isn't normal, is it? We won the war!'

Alice swallowed. 'Technically, Oskar, as Germans we lost the war.'

'For heaven's sake! As Jews, Alice, we very much won. Today is the liberation of our people from the most hideous oppression in modern history. We don't know the scale of it yet, but it's not going to be good news. If the Nazis had won, Alice, they would have hunted down every last one of us, you and I included, so please, have a glass of champagne and enjoy this historic day.'

Sophie gave Alice a knowing look and Alice groaned at her own caution.

'Very well. You're both right. Thank you.'

She held out her glass and, as Oskar let the cork fly exuberantly loose, she laughed with Sophie and tried hard not to look at where it hit the ceiling. Given the damage wrought on Europe in the last five years, one cork-mark was nothing.

'To victory,' Oskar proposed, and they lifted their glasses and chinked them together.

'To victory!'

Alice took a cautious sip and, my, but it tasted good. It was soft and buttery with hints of vanilla, and the bubbles popped deliciously against her tongue. She took another sip.

'Nice?' Oskar asked.

'Very nice,' she agreed. 'Thank you, Oskar.'

'You deserve it, Alice. You too, Sophie. Anyone can see how stable and happy you've kept these children.'

'Thank you, Oskar,' Alice said again, not quite sure what to do with herself.

The psychologist was rather close and waving his champagne glass so expansively that drops were falling onto her skirt. Not that that mattered – the skirt was a tatty old thing – but it seemed a shame to waste the lovely wine.

'Cheers,' she said, using the English word with a smile.

'Cheers,' he agreed and, thankfully, took a deep drink, dropping the level in his glass to a far safer one. 'To the Hampstead War Nurseries!'

Alice smiled and drank more champagne, feeling the bubbles pop not just against her tongue, but all around inside her head. It was really very pleasant.

'I love New Barn,' she confided.

'Good, good. Delighted to hear it, though I suppose the question now is, what next?'

Alice froze, her glass halfway to her mouth. 'Sorry?'

'Well, these are the Hampstead *War* Nurseries. With no war, there'll be no need for the nurseries. It'll take a month or two but they'll be disbanded. So – what next?'

Alice looked to Sophie but she, too, had frozen, her usual sunny smile nowhere to be found.

'I'm not sure,' Alice stuttered. 'I suppose... I suppose I'll have to go home.'

'And where is home?' Oskar asked.

It was a good question. It had once been in Berlin, but who knew what state that poor city was in, or what people were still alive within it. Alice thought of Max and her heart contracted. Her parents were dead, her one aunt too; if Max, Lilli and Ruthie hadn't made it, what was the point of going on?

'Where is home?' she repeated quietly and set down her glass. 'That, I'm afraid, I really don't know.'

THREE

TASHA

Tasha turned into the rough square before her dorm and gasped to see the violent scene before her. Four children had thrown an old piece of rope over a branch and were preparing to mock-hang a fifth.

'Suzi, Judith!' She rushed forward. 'This isn't nice. Moishe, Ernst, no! We don't play like that.'

'It's just a game,' Suzi objected. 'We're the guards and Marta is a prisoner and we're going to hang her.'

'Why?'

They looked blankly back at her.

'Because we're the guards and she's the prisoner.'

'But what's Marta done wrong?'

They frowned.

'She's a prisoner.'

Tasha looked to the skies for help. It wasn't their fault. They were only seven years old and the ghettos and camps were all they knew. Justice was arbitrary and power everything.

'When there's no war,' she said carefully, 'we only punish people who've committed a crime.'

They drew around her, intrigued.

'What's a crime, Tasha?'

'Something that's against the law of the land. Like stealing.'

'The Germans stole all our things and they didn't get punished.'

'Not then, but they will be now.'

'Are they being gassed?'

Tasha bit hard on the inside of her mouth to stop herself from crying.

'No. It's not normal to gas people. It's not right. In the real world, if we suspect someone has committed a crime, there's a trial where a judge and jury decide if they're guilty and then determine a punishment.'

Moishe stared disbelievingly up at her and she didn't blame him. That sort of fairness seemed almost impossible for Tasha to remember, let alone for these poor kids who'd never known it at all.

'How long does that take?' Ernst asked.

'Weeks. Months maybe. You have to be sure it's fair.'

The word clearly puzzled them.

'Fair?'

'Just. Proven. Right.'

'Hmmm. So, the Germans will have a... a trial?'

'I believe so, those that we catch.'

'But everyone knows they're guilty,' Ernst put in. 'They killed my mama. I saw them. They put her in the left queue, and they sent her into the gas chamber and her smoke came up the chimney. I know cos the other boys pointed it out to me.'

It was such a calm statement of fact, but Tasha heard the crack in his young voice and bent down to put her arms around him. He squirmed away at first but then suddenly gave in and pressed himself so tight against her that she had to brace against the tree to take his weight.

'That was very, very wrong, Ernst,' she told him. 'And they will be punished.'

'By hanging?'

'Maybe. I don't know.'

'I think hanging,' he said, pulling back as suddenly as he'd given way. 'Tell you what, Marta, you be a Nazi guard and Suzi, Moishe and Judith can be the trial and then I'll hang you.'

'I don't want to be a Nazi guard,' Marta objected.

'Someone has to be.'

'No, they don't,' Tasha said firmly as Marta's lip wobbled. She took the girl's warm little hand, quivering at the memory of her sister's grasp. Amelia was gone, but these kids were here and she had to do her best to help them. 'The war is over and there are no more Nazi guards. Why not play at dragons, or princes and princesses, or, or...' Tasha cast around her mind for the games she'd once played but could see why they would seem futile to these camp children. 'Hopscotch,' she suggested.

'What's hopscotch?'

'Here.' She reached for a chalky rock and drew squares on the street. 'I'll show you.'

A few minutes later, the kids were happily counting their hops and jumps on her rough little track and she was able to take the rope down and spirit it away before their evil game got too realistic. Poor kids. At least Tasha had a happy childhood to look back on, with a swing in a green back garden and storybooks full of fairy-tale monsters instead of real-life ones with guns and whips and slavering dogs. At least she'd had Tata to throw her in the air and Mama to tuck her up at night and a sister to argue over dollies with. She'd even had a maid to make fresh biscuits for tea and look after them when her parents had gone out to parties and dinners in fine clothes. True, it now felt like another life, but she knew it had been hers and the warm glow of it was deep in her bones, however much it had been tainted.

An image came to Tasha of her father being dragged out of the half-buried shed in which they'd all hidden when the Germans had finally retaken Warsaw after the failed uprising, and, legs wobbling, she sank onto a low wall. For sixty long days last summer, the people of Poland's capital had fought the occupiers, waiting for the promised arrival of the Soviet troops to help liberate them. The Soviets had never come and in the end hunger, thirst and disease had broken the people's resistance to the incessant tanks and guns, and the city had collapsed.

Civilians had, in theory, been allowed to vacate peacefully, and soldiers to surrender as POWs, but Jews had still been summarily shot, especially prominent ones like her father. A lawyer by trade, Szymon Ancel had been one of the leaders of the previous Jewish ghetto uprising in 1943, and had hidden his family in the city when it had been disbanded so that he could try again in the general uprising a year later. This time, Szymon had known there would be no escaping Nazi retribution and had urged them to leave without him. Lydia had refused.

'If you die, we all die,' she'd told him, as if it were a final picnic, but it hadn't quite worked out like that.

Tasha's heart beat faster, remembering the sound of jackboots coming down the path towards the shed. The big padlock had been no obstacle for German rifles, the door useless against the fury of their kicks, and the pile of summer furniture pointless as cover. The soldiers had simply torn it apart and then pulled them all out into the open. It had been early October by then and the few trees still clinging to life in Warsaw had shed their leaves, blood-red across the ruins of the city. The Germans had forced Szymon to his knees among them and shot him, just like that, with no warning. Tasha could see him now, falling flat on his face in the leaves. Then they'd all been hustled away, without a moment to cry or kiss his lifeless face. There had been no final picnic, just a single shot, a cruel march to the Pruszków camp and from there, a train to Auschwitz. There had been no time for mourning, just for shock and then a battle for their survival that had led Amelia to God, Tasha to Theresienstadt, and Lydia…

Tasha closed her eyes and fumbled inside her leather bag, touching her fingers to the lock of her mother's hair in the foolish hope it might somehow convey her love – every drop of it – to Lydia, wherever she might be.

'Stay strong, Tasha,' she'd urged her as she'd been shoved out of Auschwitz. 'And we'll find each other. We'll meet in—'

But whatever she'd been going to say had been snatched away by snow and dogs and press-ganged people. Tasha had to assume her mother would head back to Warsaw, but that was hundreds of kilometres from here and she had no idea how to get there, and no money with which to do so. The Red Cross kept telling her to stay safe in Theresienstadt while they 'sorted it all out' but she was sure no one else would hunt as hard for her mother as she would.

She sighed and wiped a tear from her eye. The kids had abandoned hopscotch and gone off, doubtless in search of more violent pursuits, so she pushed herself up to check on them. It wasn't her job, but it wasn't anyone's job, and at least watching out for them stopped her dwelling on herself.

In the main square she was relieved to see them crowding around a set of visitors, clamouring for the innocent treat of chocolate. Her mouth watered and she headed over, curious to see who these new people were. They looked official and if they were from the UNRRA – the United Nations Relief and Reha-bilitation Administration – or one of the other growing search organisations, she might be able to ask after her mother. Many people were starting to compile lists of those separated by the war, and with every new list came the hope that the name you were longing to see would be on it. She elbowed her way to the front.

'Are you with UNRRA?' she asked a young man in a beautiful suit.

'No,' he said in English. 'The Central British Fund.'

She looked at him, unable to understand the language.

'The Central British Fund for World Jewish Relief,' he repeated in Yiddish and, although she was far from fluent, she'd been through enough synagogue schooling to understand. 'We're a charitable organisation in England to help the Jewish people.'

'What are you doing in Theresienstadt?' she asked.

He shot back a reply in Yiddish and when she squinted, repeated it in German. She understood immediately. German had been the violently enforced language of the camps and, much as they might hate it, the Poles had all learned to speak it well. So now she understood the man's words, but they still didn't make much sense.

'You're here to take orphans to England?'

'I am.'

'Why?'

'To give them a new start.'

'In England?'

'Why not?'

'Yeah, why not?' a voice said behind her, the German spoken, like hers, in heavily accented Polish. Georg threw an arm around her shoulder. 'England is green and rich and safe.'

'It's not rich,' the man said warningly. 'The war has bled her dry, but there's enough to welcome those that need succour.'

'Which we do – right, Tash?'

Tasha looked at him. 'Who's we?'

'You and me, of course. We're orphans.'

Tasha yanked away. 'I'm not.'

Georg looked at her with pity. 'She thinks her mother is still alive,' he told the smart young man.

'She *is*,' Tasha said. 'I know she is. She wasn't ill when they pushed her out into the snow. Thin, yes, and cold, but she was a strong woman, stronger than a lot of them. We'd only been in Auschwitz for a few months, you see, so we weren't as wasted as—'

'Auschwitz?' the man interrupted her. She nodded and he eyed her with dramatic sorrow. 'I'm so sorry.'

'Why?'

'That was a death camp?'

'Yes.'

Tasha looked at Georg and he stepped up at her side.

'It *was* a death camp,' he told the man bullishly, 'but, as you see, we are not dead.'

'No,' he spluttered, fighting to compose himself. 'No of course not. Well done, you. That is...'

Georg tutted impatiently. 'How do we sign up? For England, I mean. Where do we tell them we want to go?'

'I don't want to go—' Tasha objected.

But Georg placed a soft finger over her lips. 'Let's find out a bit more about it, hey? Maybe your mother can come too?'

'Not if it's for orphans, Georg.'

'Translation problems,' he said airily in Polish, before flicking back to German for the man from this mysterious Central Jewish Fund. 'Where?'

He looked flustered. 'I'm not sure. You'd have to ask Mr Montefiore. He's in charge.'

'Excellent. And he is where?'

The man pointed into the town hall.

'Thank you very much. Come on, Tasha, this way for England.'

Taking her arm, he led her up the steps, but she pulled back.

'Georg, I'm not sure about this. I don't want to go to England.'

'And no one will make you, but, think about it – if you're on the list, you can always pull out; if you're not on the list, it'll be hell to get added.'

That had a certain logic but Tasha still wasn't sure this wasn't one of Georg's scams. The other day, he'd come running to say that the authorities had opened the food stores for everyone to help themselves. It was a new, more egalitarian system, he'd said, and although it wasn't meant to be launched until later in the day, he'd overheard the guards talking about it and reckoned if they got there first, they'd get all the best stuff. He'd been so convincing that she'd gone with him and, sure enough, the door to the stores had been open and they'd stepped inside to see a paradise of food supplies.

'And we can take what we want?' Tasha had asked, gazing around.

'The door was open, wasn't it?'

'Well, yes...'

'And we've been deprived for so long that it seems only fair, doesn't it?'

'It does, but...'

'And you're hungry, right?'

'Always.'

'Come on then.'

She'd followed him inside and had been reaching for a can of condensed milk, anticipating the rich sweetness running down her throat, when a Red Cross official had marched in behind them rapping, 'What the hell do you think you're doing?'

As it had rapidly emerged, the authorities had not thrown open the doors to their stores. Rather, Georg had expertly picked the lock and invited Tasha in entirely on his own initiative. What had been unclear was how he'd thought he'd get away with it, but Tasha was rapidly discovering that with Georg it was a matter of act now, deal with problems later. Tasha, however, wasn't so keen on getting into trouble and didn't want to get sucked in again.

'I don't think normal people are meant to come in here, Georg,' she protested as he led her into the grandly pillared atrium of the town hall.

'We're not "normal people", my dearest Tasha,' Georg shot back. 'We are victims of war and are entitled to "restitution".'

'We are?'

'Apparently. I was reading a leaflet about it the other day. It means "the restoration of something lost or stolen to its proper owner", which sounds only fair to me.'

Tasha thought of Moishe, Suzi and Marta staring uncomprehendingly at her as she'd tried to explain fairness to them earlier and figured Georg had a point. Even so, she couldn't help feeling apprehensive as they approached the desk.

'Can I help you?' a well-groomed woman asked, her German holding the softer lilt of a Swiss citizen.

'We're looking for the list for England,' Georg told her confidently.

'Which list?'

'Mr Montefiore's list, for the orphans.'

'Ah.' She looked him up and down. 'Word's out about that already, is it?'

'It's true then?' Tasha asked.

The woman turned to her. 'I believe so, dear, but I honestly don't know all the details. I do, though, know that it's for unaccompanied children. How old are you?'

'Sixteen,' Tasha told her.

'Then you'd just qualify.'

'Me too,' Georg said promptly.

Both Tasha and the woman looked at him sceptically.

'What? I'm sixteen. I'm just big for my age.'

'Unusual in the camps,' the woman said mildly.

'So I'm told,' Georg agreed, without blinking an eye.

Tasha thought about him claiming to be nineteen to get into a man's house and marvelled at his unflinching flexibility. 'I can be whatever I want to be,' he'd told her and now, it seemed, he wanted to be sixteen.

'Do you have any papers?' the woman asked.

'Sadly not. Taken from me by the Nazis, like everything else I owned.'

The woman sighed. 'I'm so sorry. Look, put your names down on this paper and I'll see what I can find out.'

Georg took the pen and wrote in large, bold letters: *Georg Lieberman, 16 years old.*

'Here, Tash.'

He held the pen out to her but she hesitated.

'I'm not sure, Georg. I have to find Mama.'

The woman leaned over the desk. 'Do you know where she is, dear?'

'If she did,' Georg shot back, 'she wouldn't need to find her, would she?'

'No need to be rude, young man.' She looked straight at Tasha. 'Do you have any clues?'

Tasha leaned forward too; perhaps this woman could help her.

'Her name is Lydia Ancel and she left Auschwitz on the death marches in January. That's all I know, but she was strong and tough so I'm sure she must have made it. And she has red hair. Like mine.' She pulled on her ginger tufts and the woman gave her another smile.

'That should help then.'

'I think so. She can't be that hard to find, can she, which is why, you see, I can't go to England.'

'Where are you from?'

'Warsaw.'

'Ah.' The woman's face fell, taking Tasha's fledging hopes with it. 'Warsaw is a mess, I'm afraid. So much bombing in the uprising and then, of course, the retribution... The Nazis razed it to the ground.'

'The whole city?'

'More or less. I'm told there are bold plans to rebuild, but at the moment...'

'At the moment?' Tasha pushed.

'There's really not much there and people are being asked not to try to go back. I'm so sorry.'

Tasha thought about the Warsaw of her childhood with its colourful baroque buildings and open squares, its fashionable walkways along the grand Vistula River, its theatres and markets, busy restaurants and cafés. She could not bear to think of all that life and beauty reduced to ugly, barren rubble, especially when her home was amongst it.

'We'll meet in—' she heard Lydia call and the missing final word was a torment.

'What can I do then?' she wailed.

The woman placed perfectly manicured fingers over Tasha's. They were warm and soft and for a painful second it could have been Lydia reaching out to her from before this damned war had torn everything apart.

'It's not my place to say, dear, but I'd suggest that your mother is more likely to find you than the other way around. There is going to be wide advertising of this England project. The names of the travellers will be published, the press will get involved. There will be photos, articles, radio broadcasts.'

'There will?'

'I'm sure of it.'

'So you see,' Georg said, grabbing her hands, 'this is the best possible way you could tell your mother where you are.'

'But if I'm in a different country...?'

'Then I'm sure someone will help her to get there too and you can start a new life, together.'

'In England?'

Tasha didn't know much about the place, apart from that it rained a lot and everyone drank tea with milk in it and played football. Plus, despite being a tiny island, they were best friends with America and could fight like the biggest power on the planet. If everyone there was like that Churchill man then she supposed it had to be as good a place as any to start afresh. But it wasn't home.

Then again, where was?

Tasha took the pen from Georg, drew in a deep breath, and wrote her name below his. She'd just have to pray that when word of this project got out, Lydia would hear of her and find her long before she got on any plane. Then she and her mother could make a life together in Poland, and England could disappear back into its own mist where it belonged.

FOUR

NEW BARN, ESSEX | JUNE 1945

ALICE

Alice looked out at the unusually glaring sunshine, then peered hopefully into the motley collection of outdoor goods in New Barn's old-fashioned porch. What she needed was an elegant parasol but there was nothing more than an ugly black umbrella. It would do little to enhance her dowdy look but there was no help for it. Her skin, paled by the endless clouds over Britain, would be blotched red by the time she reached Hampstead if she didn't shade herself, so, with a sigh, she lifted it out.

The warmth in the air, at least, was welcome and it was nice to be wearing her lighter coat. It would be even nicer to not be wearing a coat at all, but she was on her way to London and it wouldn't do to be too casual. Anna Freud was always so smart and she didn't want to meet her looking unkempt.

Drawing herself up, she started down the path but then a voice called 'Alice!' and eight-year-old Edward came running down the stairs.

'Are you going away?' His face turned up to hers, eyes swimming with worried tears.

'Only for today, Teddy,' she assured him. 'I'll be back by teatime.'

'Promise?'

'Promise.'

He still looked uncertain.

'Everyone else is going away and *not* coming back.'

'I know and you will do too, when your daddy returns from the war.'

Teddy nodded solemnly. 'He'll come and get me and take me home and we'll live happily ever after.'

Alice smiled. 'I hope so, Teddy.'

'When will he come?'

'Very soon. His ship has sailed from the South of France but that's a long way away so it will take time. Remember, I showed you on the map?'

'I remember. He has to go through the plates of Gibraltar, then all the way up the side of France and in past Cornwall where we went on holiday one time, only I don't remember that, but I have a photograph.'

'Exactly right. Very well remembered.'

Alice considered correcting 'plates' to 'straits' but he'd got close and the mistake made her smile, which was what she needed today. Anna was almost certainly going to tell her that she was closing New Barn, and who could blame her with just three children remaining, but that left Alice high and dry.

'Go and find Sophie, Teddy,' she said, prising him gently away from her legs. 'Maybe she'll make buns with you?'

'Currant buns? Yeah!'

Teddy let go and was off, calling to the two other children that they were going to be baking. Alice crossed her fingers that Sophie had the necessary ingredients then, glancing at her watch, set off for the bus stop at pace. She had an appointment for kaffee und kuchen with her boss at 11 a.m. and she didn't want to be late.

The branch-line station at Dunmow was surprisingly busy, notably with young women in pretty summer frocks, some of them clearly new and with wider skirts than Alice had seen in a long time. Fabric was still rationed so she had no idea how they'd managed it, but they certainly looked beautiful.

The train was approaching and one young woman seemed especially excited at its arrival, jumping up and down like a child as it drew up. Almost immediately, a door flung open and a man in uniform jumped down. The girl flung herself into his arms, wrapping herself around him, and, as their lips met, Alice looked away, embarrassed. So much passion! And right out here in front of everyone! How did they dare?

'Because there's been a war on,' she chided herself under her breath. 'They could so easily have lost each other and when you've been facing guns and tanks and bombs, what's so embarrassing about showing how much you care?'

She meant it, she really did. She was pleased for that young couple and all the others who were, thankfully, being reunited, but still... She didn't think she'd be able to be like that.

'Because you're not in love,' she told herself and sidled around the canoodling pair to board the train.

She wasn't in love, hadn't ever been in love, and wasn't likely to ever be in love. She'd had a sweetheart once, back in 1917. Well, he hadn't been a sweetheart as such. Maybe a beau? A suitor? A would-be suitor, if she was honest. All she and Heinz had ever really done was chat shyly at a few parties and, once, danced a waltz. He *had* asked her out for dinner, but then his unit had been called up early and he'd had to cancel. There had never been another chance. Poor Heinz had been killed in Flanders within days of arriving at the front. He'd never taken Alice to dinner and neither had anyone else. Well, there'd been a shortage of men after the first war so they'd had their pick of girls, and no one had been going to pick Alice.

She hadn't worried about it. She'd been busy working in the

orphanage and, with so many people in terrible economic circumstances, they'd been run off their feet. Many was the time a mother had brought her child to their door, weeping and begging Alice to look after the little mite until they could earn enough to feed him or her, but with money losing worth even as the women stood on the doorstep, that had rarely happened.

No wonder people had fallen for Hitler's lies when he'd talked about German pride and prosperity. Alice shuddered at the evil plans those seemingly fine ideals had concealed, remembering the day the authorities had come to the orphanage and told her she was no longer deemed a 'desirable' person to be influencing young German minds. The children had cried, her boss had pleaded, Alice had simply stood there, stunned. She'd been born in Berlin to Berliner parents who could trace their German lineage back centuries, and suddenly she was being deemed Untermensch – under-person.

She should have fought back. They all should have fought back. Could they have? Not knowing if there was anything they could have done to stop Hitler in his tracks in 1933 was unbearable sometimes. But then, she thought bitterly, it had suited so many people in so many countries to attack the Jews, and the evil Nazis had channelled that and turned it into mass murder. They'd never stood a chance.

'Are you all right, ma'am?'

It was only when the gentleman opposite leaned over in concern, that Alice realised how heavily she was breathing.

'Fine, thank you. I'm sorry. It's very hot, isn't it?'

'Very hot,' he agreed, clearly relieved this was about no more than the weather, an Englishman's favourite preoccupation.

He retreated behind his newspaper and Alice looked out the window, focusing on the meadow flowers and the lambs to try to remind herself there was still good in the world. Even so, she couldn't stop her mind straying back to her homeland.

What did Germany look like these days? She'd heard Berlin had been even more badly bombed than London and, of course, it was now an occupied city, carved up amongst the Allies like a victory cake. She couldn't imagine going back but couldn't see how she was going to stay here. Who'd want a German nursery teacher in post-war England?

Then there was Max.

'I'll send for you,' she'd promised when her brother had seen her off on the train to safety back in 1939. 'As soon as I have a job and somewhere to live, I'll send for all three of you and we'll be together and safe.'

'I'll save,' Max had told her. 'Whatever it costs by then, I'll have it. I'll get to England.'

Did that still hold true? Since the war had ended, she'd sent several letters to both her and his old addresses with ways of contacting her, but she'd had nothing back and had no idea if those addresses still stood.

Or if Max did.

Every time Alice came to London, she went to all the aid agencies to ask after him, Lilli and Ruth-Gertrud, and last week she'd had a breakthrough of sorts. Lists of current Theresienstadt residents had made it to London and none of her precious family were listed as living there. She could only pray that meant they'd made it to the end of the war, had left together and were trying to get home. She'd written to every agency in Berlin and ran to the post every morning, hoping for news. So far, nothing.

'Don't give up hope,' she muttered as the fields gave way to the crowded streets of London.

Standing up to gather her tatty briefcase and ugly umbrella, she couldn't help noticing a couple two seats down, talking away to each other with intensity, their eyes locked, their hands intertwined. A diamond shone on the girl's finger and it was clear they couldn't get married soon enough. Or had, perhaps, moved their relationship onto a marital level already.

Alice scolded herself for her lewd thoughts. She'd never known that side of life and likely never would. It hadn't seemed to matter when she'd been busy with work and, of course, no one had had a man around for the last five years so Alice had felt pleasantly normal for once. Now, though, romance seemed to be everywhere and she had to admit, it hurt. She wasn't going to find love herself, that much was certain, so she had to do the next best thing and find a job.

'Alice! So lovely to see you. Come in, come in. Dorothy has found us some apfelstrudel, isn't she a darling?'

Anna Freud ushered Alice into the pretty Hampstead home she shared with Dorothy Burlingham, an American from the high-society Tiffany family and almost as talented a psychoanalyst as Freud herself. A table was laid with fine crockery and a strudel sat on a fancy plate in the middle, freshly dusted with icing sugar. Alice's mouth watered. She had a terribly sweet tooth and had not enjoyed sugar rationing, so this was a welcome treat.

She noticed there were four settings laid and asked, 'Is someone joining us?'

'Shortly,' Anna said, waving an airy hand, 'but it needn't stop us tucking in. Ah, Dorothy, tea. Lovely!'

Alice almost laughed at the sight of this famous Austrian woman sitting down with her American friend to what had been promised as kaffee und kuchen but, despite the strudel, was far more of an English morning tea.

'I'm sorry,' Anna said, as if reading her thoughts – which she might well be doing – 'good coffee is still so hard to get that I thought tea would be better.'

'Tea is lovely,' Alice assured her, looking again at the fourth place. Who was coming? She hoped she knew them; she was terrible with new people.

'So, New Barn is nearly empty,' Dorothy said, patting Alice's hand. 'How does that feel?'

'Strange,' Alice admitted. 'I'm delighted so many of the children have relatives to go back to, but the place is very echoey without them.'

'And, of course, it leaves you without a job.'

Alice jumped. She knew the American was straight-talking but that was very on the nose.

'Dorothy!' Anna chided. 'Go softly. Poor Alice. Have some strudel, Alice.'

Alice accepted the generous slice but her appetite was gone. 'Do you have any suggestions?' she forced out.

Anna leaned forward. 'I'm setting up a Child Therapy course to help more people qualify in our field. It will take some time to get going but I'll need secretarial help.'

'Secretarial?' Alice said weakly. She did office work because she had to but it was far from her strong point. She preferred being out there with the children, caring for them and organising things for them.

'It won't be much fun,' Anna conceded, 'but it might do until...' She trailed off, picked at her strudel. 'Will you stay in England, do you think?'

'Will *you*?' Alice asked, ducking the question.

'I will. I like it here and I think Dorothy and I can do valuable work. Austria is occupied, which means home won't be home for a long time, so I'm making a new one.'

'Very wise.'

Alice couldn't help being jealous of Anna's certainty. But then, she had Dorothy, and it was so much easier to make a home when you had someone to make it with.

'The Dann sisters are talking about setting up a nursery,' Dorothy said. 'Maybe they'll want help?'

Sophie and Gertrud Dann had looked after the infants and toddlers in the two War Nurseries here in Hampstead. They were nice women and good at their jobs, but Alice wasn't one for babies. She preferred children you could communicate with.

'Maybe,' she agreed noncommittally. 'You're not going to keep the day nurseries open then?'

'I'm afraid not. The funding from the war board will run out next month and all my energy will have to go into setting up the course. But I'm sure other people will. I can ask around.'

'Thank you,' Alice said weakly.

'I *will* ask around. We don't want to lose you, Alice – you're exceptionally good at your job and I'd love to see you taking my course eventually.'

'Me?!' Alice stuttered, astonished.

'I could think of no one better.'

'Am I not a bit old?'

Anna laughed. 'You're younger than me, Alice.'

'But so much further behind in my career.'

'That can change,' Anna said firmly. 'You're in your prime.'

'Hardly!'

Alice had to admire her boss's enthusiasm, not to mention her blind optimism, but it was no use unless she had a job. Perhaps she'd have to be a secretary for a while after all. She took a sip of her tea and reached for her cake fork but, just as she put a spoonful of strudel into her mouth, the doorbell rang, making her jump up and spill icing sugar all down her cardigan.

'Oh no!' she cried.

'It'll brush off,' Dorothy consoled as Anna went to the door, but the cardigan was dark wool and clung to the sugar so that Alice was still brushing desperately at it when her hostess returned with a tall, suave man in a beautiful suit.

'Good morning, ladies.' He swept a smart hat from his head and gave a small bow.

'Leonard!' Dorothy cried, going to kiss him on both cheeks.

Alice stood there, covered in sugar and frantically trying to swallow pastry, as he turned her way.

'You must be Miss Goldberger. I've heard so much about you.'

'You have?' she spluttered.

'Please, let's sit down.'

His manners were impeccable and she gratefully took a seat, seizing the chance to wash down the troublesome pastry flakes with a sip of tea.

'And you are?' she asked when she'd composed herself.

'Gracious, how rude of me. I'm so sorry. I'm Leonard Montefiore, one of the board of the Central British Fund for World Jewish Relief.'

'Pleased to meet you,' Alice managed, feeling shyer than ever. If she was bad with strangers, she was even worse with important ones.

'Not as pleased as I am to meet you, Miss Goldberger,' he replied heartily. 'I believe you may be the answer to my prayers.'

Alice flushed and looked to Anna for help, but Anna didn't seem to know any more than she did.

'I'd be happy to help you in any way I can, Mr Montefiore.'

'Leonard, please. And I'm delighted to hear that. You've been recommended to me by Oskar Friedmann.'

'Really?' Alice squirmed at the thought of New Barn's eminent psychologist discussing her with this man. The morning was getting more astonishing by the moment.

'He tells me that you've run New Barn with efficiency, kindness and composure. He says you know exactly what makes each child tick and how to keep that tick, erm, ticking.' He laughed at himself. 'I think I'm losing my metaphor here, but the point is, you're very good with children.'

'I'm flattered he thinks so.'

'You should be. Oskar knows what he's talking about, which is why he's recommended you for my new project.'

A jolt of excitement ran through Alice, as if she'd eaten the whole strudel and the sugar was jigging its way around her bloodstream.

Leonard Montefiore looked around at them all. 'I'm very pleased to tell you that I have persuaded the British government to allow us to bring one thousand Jewish orphans to England for rest and rehabilitation. Many of them have been in ghettos and camps.'

Dorothy gasped. 'Concentration camps?'

Leonard nodded solemnly. 'Death camps even. There are children out there who have survived Auschwitz and Belsen. They've seen their parents and siblings killed. They've been worked like slaves and barely fed. They've endured terrible sanitation and rampant disease. They've slept with corpses and lived, day and night, with the scent of human flesh burning in the crematoria.'

Alice felt nausea rise in her throat and put a hand to her mouth. Those poor, poor children.

'I'm sorry,' Leonard said. 'It's no topic for this delightful tea-party, but it's a hard reality for these orphans and I want to give them a new start.'

'In England?' Anna asked.

'In the Lake District, to be precise. There's a flying-boat factory on a beautiful lake called Windermere, and a large estate beside it, built to house the workers. Many families still live there, but with production scaled back the single workers have dispersed and there are several hostels free for us to use.'

Alice's head spun. Jewish orphans in factory housing by a lake in leafy England? Was this man mad? Or just incredibly kind?

'It would only be for a few months,' he went on, 'to give us time to find them permanent housing in hostels and homes around the country, but it seems a God-sent opportunity to offer them a little peace, a little beauty even. We cannot, of course, hope to make up for what they have lost, but on the Calgarth Estate we can, perhaps, give them a chance to find something new.'

It was a fine sentiment and Alice looked at him with interest.

'What do you want me to do, Mr Montefiore?' she asked.

'You?' He beamed at her. 'I want you, Miss Goldberger, to head up care of the children's welfare.'

Alice's head swam as if she'd been at Oskar's champagne again. Leonard was mad, definitely mad, but wonderfully so. A hostel in England, a chance to offer abandoned children a new start – it sounded like a real chance to carry on the work she'd been trying to do all her adult life. And perhaps a way to make up for heading to safety when so many others had been left in danger. Alice thought of Ruth-Gertrud's confused face as she'd seen Alice off at the station with her father. She thought of the orphans she'd been forced to leave in Berlin – a hundred pairs of eyes beseeching her for help. She felt as if she'd failed those children in 1939, but perhaps, here, six years later, she could help others in their place.

Sitting up straight, forgetting the icing sugar on her cardigan, the faded dress beneath, and the ugly umbrella-parasol by the door, Alice looked Leonard Montefiore straight in the eye and asked, 'When do we start?'

FIVE

PRAGUE | JULY 1945

TASHA

Tasha stood at the attic window and looked down into the pretty streets of Prague, gaping at the people going about their everyday business. They'd been moved here a few weeks ago in preparation for flying to England and the city continually amazed her. Normal life just looked so alien.

That woman, lugging a shopping bag with two oranges wobbling on top, had no idea how unusual she appeared to Tasha. Those old men sitting chatting on the bench, wrinkled faces turned to the sun as they laughed over some shared joke, had no idea that for Tasha they seemed a relic of a faraway life. Those three boys, swinging from the low-hanging tree branch and egging each other to climb higher, could not know how impossibly innocent they looked.

'Uh oh!'

At her side, little Marta giggled and pointed to the woman's oranges as they broke free of her bag. Tasha looked fondly down at the girl, enjoying the happy sound. She and the seven-year-old had grown close in the last few weeks. Marta, who had spent much of the war being hidden alone in the attic of a brave teacher, before being caught by the SS and sent to Theresienstadt in 1944, had no memory of her family and followed Tasha around like a duckling. Tasha, in turn, drew comfort from the innocent devotion of this new sort-of-sister with a fierce protectiveness that made her feel more human. And more afraid. Attachments felt so fragile since the camps, so fraught with potential hurt, but she knew that was a Nazi persecution and one she had to resist with all her might.

Drawing Marta in against her side, she laughed with her as they watched the oranges roll merrily down the street. One of the boys swooped in to snatch them up but, at a look from the old men, took them meekly back to the woman, who thanked him with a smile and offered him one of the pretty fruits for himself. He took his prize excitedly back to share with his friends and Tasha swore her nostrils picked up the tantalising citrus tang on the air as he split open the skin.

'What's that?' Marta asked, peering down as the boys tore into the fruit with relish.

'It's an orange, Kotka.'

Marta had no documents and did not know her surname so Tasha had christened her Marta Kotka – kitten – for her alert green eyes and button nose.

'Is an orange nice?' she asked.

'Very.'

'Can we have one?'

'Soon.'

Tasha groaned at herself. Despite her best efforts, she was turning into a parent. She could hear Mama's voice whenever she'd plagued her with questions as a child: When can we eat? When can we go to the park? When can we have my friends over to play? 'Soon, Tasha-baby,' Lydia had always said, 'very soon.' Her mother had been a busy woman, she could see that now. She'd run a clothes shop in central Warsaw and, on top of that, been something important in their local synagogue society, so had been forever rushing around arranging charity events, flower rotas and newsletters. Tasha and Amelia had always been the first ones to a coffee morning or games afternoon and the last ones to leave.

'Why can't someone else's mummy clear away?' Amelia would moan, and Lydia would shake back her red hair and quote the Torah: 'The Lord will send a blessing on your barns and on everything you put your hand to.'

'We don't have barns,' Amelia would protest.

'We have metaphorical barns,' would be the crisp answer, 'and, besides, it's good to keep busy.'

She'd held on to that idea even in Auschwitz, helping out in the so-called 'hospital' – a barrack full of sick people with little in the way of medicines or bandages to alleviate their suffering. Tasha had helped too, keen to stay at her side, but her job had been carrying the dead out before they infected the living further and, after a few days, she'd given up. She was sorry about that now. She'd give anything for another day in her mother's company, even if it was with the sick and dying.

Every morning since they'd come to this busy orphanage in Prague to await the planes to England, she'd gone down to the town hall to ask if anyone called Lydia Ancel had turned up on the lists. She never had.

'It doesn't mean she's dead,' a lovely young woman had told her. 'There are many reasons why people might not be listed yet.'

'Such as?'

'Such as being too ill to give their name.' The woman had bitten her lip and hurried on. 'Or quite simply that the lists haven't made it to us yet. It's very hard to centrally collate information.'

That made sense but it had been too late to wipe out the image of her mother wasting away in a blank bed somewhere.

What could Tasha do? She'd wanted to work her way around the hospitals of Europe but the authorities had told her firmly that there were hundreds of them and asked if she had the means to travel. The answer, of course, had been no. Tasha had no money, no contacts and no means to travel anywhere, save, apparently, to England.

Now they had been confined to the orphanage in 'quarantine' so that they could be declared safe to enter England's precious confines when the planes came. Tasha resented the implication of uncleanliness. What sort of country was this England, cut off at the cloudy edge of Europe, its borders entirely marked by seas? They were assured that the 'Windermere Project' was happening, but it had been delay after delay and she was beginning to wonder if she'd ever actually see the place.

'Who's that?' Marta demanded suddenly. 'Why's he allowed out?'

Tasha pulled herself out of her thoughts to look down at the little boy coming out of the orphanage door, holding the hand of the principal. She recognised Andreas, a child who'd had word that his father had been found in a POW camp nearby. As they watched, a car pulled up and Tasha's entire body prickled with jealousy. She put a hand to the window frame to steady herself, accidentally catching the side of Marta's head.

'Careful of my piggy-tails, Tasha,' Marta protested, flicking them out of reach.

Tasha had done them for her this morning, the first time the girl's hair had been long enough to take ribbons, and Marta was very proud of them. Tasha stroked them fondly and together they watched as a man got out of the car and approached Andreas. His legs were unsteady but his arms, as he threw them open to his son, looked as wide and strong as the branches of an oak. Tasha watched, tears pooling in her eyes, as the little boy stepped eagerly into a years-overdue embrace.

'Who's that?' Marta demanded.

'That's Andreas' tata, Kotka.'

'Tata?' She frowned. 'What's a tata?'

Tasha looked down at her in horror. This was way worse than not recognising an orange. The poor child had no concept of family, of being looked after by someone who cared about you above all others. Tasha might miss Lydia with her every fibre, but at least she had her to miss. Shaken, Tasha slid to the floor, clasping Marta to her and letting her tears soak into her pigtails. Outside, she heard the roar of an engine and knew that Andreas was off to some semblance of a home, leaving the rest of them here, in this blank orphanage, to try to show the little ones what a family even was.

'Tasha? Are you crying?' Marta twisted in her arms and touched a fingertip to her cheek. 'You *are* crying! What's wrong? You're safe now. We're all safe now.'

Tasha nodded fiercely. It was what they were told all the time, but what use was safe if you were alone?

'I miss my tata,' she told Marta. 'My mama too.'

Marta looked at her blankly. 'I don't think I have those things.'

Tasha had no idea how to reply and was relieved when someone else said, 'Me either, Marta, but it doesn't matter. We don't need them where we're going.'

'Georg!' Marta leaped up and ran to him. 'Do you like my piggy-tails? Tasha did them.'

'They're very nice, sweetie. Nearly as nice as the piškoty someone's just put out in the kitchen.'

'Piškoty!' The idea of biscuits meant far more to Marta than either Mama or Tata. 'Judith and Suzi will be eating them all,' she cried and dashed off, clattering down the stairs to grab her share.

'Are there really piškoty?' Tasha asked, scrubbing at her eyes.

'Of course. I don't scam kiddies, Tash.'

'Just gullible nearly-grown-ups like me?'

'I don't scam you.'

'The store cupboard?'

'Ah, yes.'

'That time you told us all Russian soldiers wear red underpants.'

'That too. But it was very funny watching Andreas trying to pull their trousers down to check.'

Despite herself, Tasha smiled. 'Andreas just went off with his father.'

Georg sat down opposite her. 'Is that what made you cry?'

'No! Well, not really. Marta didn't know what a tata was, Georg.'

'Does it surprise you?' he asked.

'Does it not make you sad?' she shot back.

He sighed. 'I suppose so, but everything can make you sad if you let it.'

'So, what, you just don't let it?'

'Exactly!' He put his hands on her knees, running them up and down her lower legs in a most distracting way. 'It's about looking forward rather than back, to the future not the past.'

Tasha thought about this, or at least as best as she was able with Georg so close. He'd put a little flesh on his bones in the last few weeks and that flesh was taking on a very handsome form. With his hair growing back into floppy curls and his eyes so full of life, he was really a very attractive boy. If ridiculously optimistic.

'What if what you want to find in your future is from your past?' she asked him.

He sighed and took his hands away; she felt their lack instantly.

'Is this about your mother?'

'Why shouldn't it be?'

'No reason. It's hard, losing her the way you did, not knowing what's happened to her. I understand that.'

'Do you? What about your parents?'

He closed up instantly. 'They're dead.'

'How can you be sure?'

'Because I saw them die, all right?'

She flinched back. 'I'm sorry.' She dared to put a hand on his knee. 'I'm sorry, Georg. That's the first time you've said that.'

'Yes, well, I don't like to dwell on it.'

'How...?'

'I said, I don't like to dwell on it.'

'Of course. Sorry.'

He sucked in a visible breath and placed a hand over hers, warm and firm.

'You weren't to know. We've all been through things, right? All lost people?'

She nodded.

'But at least we have each other.'

He leaned towards her and for one glorious moment she thought he was going to kiss her, but then a bird landed on the windowsill, making them both jump, and the moment was lost.

'It'll be better when we get to England, you'll see,' he said. 'A fresh start in a different place where we can make new memories.'

'That sounds good,' Tasha agreed. 'Although I still hope Mama finds me there.'

'Tash,' he said gently, 'do you know how many people survived the death marches?'

'Plenty. There are three boys in the room along from mine who made it all the way from Dachau to Waakirchen.'

'Are they Polish?'

'Hungarian.'

'There you go then. The Hungarian Jews weren't oppressed

until 1944. Loads more of them have survived because they were, you know, healthier when it all kicked off.'

'True but don't forget, Mama, Amelia and I weren't sent to Auschwitz until October 1944 when the Warsaw uprising failed, so we were only in the camp for three months.'

She grimaced at her own choice of the word 'only' – three months had been more than enough in that hell – but she was well aware that others had had it even worse.

Georg huffed. 'Fair point. I guess she did have a good chance then.'

'Very good. Mama was – *is* – very strong.'

'But why, then, hasn't she found you?'

A scream rose inside Tasha and she leaped up, clawing at the wall in her eagerness to get away from him. Her fingers went for the bag she still wore at all times and it wasn't until she felt the lock of Lydia's hair that she was able to breathe again.

'It's not easy,' she told him furiously. 'The Nazis could have sent her anywhere. It takes time.'

'It's nearly August, Tash. We were liberated in January.'

'*End* of January.'

'That's still six months.'

His voice was soft, kind even, but it grated against Tasha like a hundred knives.

'The Red Cross say that's nothing in this situation. It's impossible getting lists to any sort of central system so millions of people are still out there, lost. Didn't Andreas' tata find him? Didn't he take him away just this minute? If it can happen to him, it can happen to me – but not in stupid England.'

'So you don't want to come now?'

'No.'

'You want to stay here and wait for your precious mama to find you?'

'Yes.'

'Well, you'll be waiting a long time because it's tricky to travel back from the dead.'

Tasha fought for breath. 'How dare you!'

'I dare because it's the truth. Your mother's dead, Tash, and the sooner you face up to it, the better.'

'For who?'

'For you!'

'I decide what's good for me, thank you very much. Why do you care anyway?'

'I don't know!' he shouted. 'You're impossible, Tasha Ancel, but I do care. I do.' He stepped closer. 'I hate it when you hurt. It makes me hurt too and I don't like hurting. I've done too much of it, we've *all* done too much of it.'

He reached out a tentative hand and traced a finger down her cheek. Tasha's breath caught and she bit at her lip, unsure what to do with all the emotion swirling around inside her. She knew he was just trying to protect her but she didn't need protecting; she needed her mother.

'Georg...'

He reached out his other hand, cupping her face. 'Tasha. Beautiful Tasha...'

She stood very still, waiting to see what he'd do next, but then footsteps clattered up the stairs and Marta burst back in on them.

'The planes are coming! The planes for England. We're to pack our bags and get ready for take-off.'

'Now?' Tasha gasped.

'Now! Well, soon.'

Soon – that word again. But Georg had pulled away and was quizzing Marta about what she'd heard and before Tasha knew it, they were heading down the stairs to the crowded dorms, her peace gone, her moment lost, and her mother pushed aside. She could pack her bag – it would take no time to put her meagre belongings into a regulation duffel sack – but how on earth did she get ready to leave Central Europe where, even now, Lydia might be searching for her?

'All orphans to report to the office, all orphans to report to the office.'

The message rang around and children rushed to obey like bees in a hive.

'I'm not an orphan,' Tasha said fiercely.

But everyone was too busy to hear.

Two long weeks later, after admin delays, storm warnings and a whole load of fuss over personnel to accompany them, Tasha found herself standing on the tarmac at Prague airport. In front of her was a line of huge, empty-bellied bombers. Hundreds of Czech soldiers had poured out of them, kissing the runway in their delight to be back home, and now it was their turn to take a trip. The doors were wide open and the soldiers lifted the smaller children inside. Tasha could see Suzi, Judith, Moishe and Ernst being settled on rough wooden planks laid along the curved floor, like little human bombs, ready to be dropped on a new land. She clutched her handbag to her chest, staring around the three hundred England-bound children.

'There are so few girls,' she said to Marta.

'I'm afraid less females survived,' one of the helpers said at her side. 'The Nazis weren't as keen on us for labour duties, so...'

She didn't need to finish the sentence; they all knew what had happened to those who couldn't work.

'How many of us are there?' Tasha asked.

'I believe forty-eight of our band are female.'

'Forty-eight? Out of three hundred?'

'I'm sure you'll make yourselves heard.'

'I'm sure they will,' Georg agreed, sauntering over.

Tasha looked at him. Georg had offered to help get

everyone ready so she'd barely seen him in the last two weeks. She had to admit she'd missed him.

'Can you believe so few girls survived?' she said. 'How did I get to be one of them?'

He laughed. 'If you ask me, it's marvellous that you *were* one of them.' He gave her a peck on the cheek, then darted instantly away.

She touched her fingers to the place where his lips had been as she watched him race across to help lift up the younger children. There were as starkly few of them as there were of girls – maybe twenty or so around Marta's age, and a curious clutch of six tinies who toddled around the place hand in hand, communicating in a wild half-language of their own invention. They'd been in Theresienstadt for the Nazis' wicked promotional films but then been left to their own devices all day every day and were wary of all adults. They seemed to trust Georg, however, and Tasha watched, entranced, as he lifted them into the giant plane.

'Is Georg your boyfriend?' Marta asked, peering up at her.

She flushed and looked away. 'No, no. We're just friends.'

'*Good* friends,' Marta said solemnly, and Tasha laughed out loud and swung her hand.

Maybe this would be all right. Maybe England would be nice. Maybe the articles written by the reporters gathering to film their historic departure would make it to wherever Lydia was and maybe, then, she'd know where to come.

Your mother's dead, Tash, Georg's voice said in her head and a tiny bit of her knew he might be right. But he might be wrong too and she had to hold on to that possibility or all of this was for nothing.

'Hurry along there,' a man called from the front. 'We've word of storms coming in from the west and we need to get into the air before they hit.'

'Storms?' Marta looked frantically to the sky. 'That plane's very big, Tash. What if it gets hit by lightning?'

Tasha looked up too and saw dark clouds gathering over the hills to the west of Prague. What an irony it would be to survive the death camps and be hit by a natural disaster.

'In here please, ladies. Quickly now.'

It was all happening too fast. A soldier was handing Marta into the plane and Marta was reaching out for Tasha's hand and she had little choice but to clamber in beside her and shuffle into a place on the wooden boards.

'Will there be lightning?' Marta asked her urgently.

Tasha resorted to the only thing she had. 'God wouldn't do that to us, Kotka.'

She looked around for Georg but he was up in the cockpit, asking the pilot what all the dials were for, oblivious to any danger.

'Doors closed!'

The hatches slid across with a clang of heavy bolts and suddenly the plane was juddering down the runway and they were sitting, shaking in the darkness, with only a sliver of blue through the cockpit window to tell them the outside world was still there.

'I'm frightened, Tasha.'

Tasha put her arms around Marta, stroked her pigtails and muttered more nonsense about a God she was pretty sure had long since deserted them. But in truth she was frightened too, not of the plane and not even of the lightning, but of the decision she'd taken to leave Europe, to turn her back on Poland and send herself a thousand miles into the unknown. Where she going? And, more to the point, what was she leaving behind?

SIX

DACHAU | 5 AUGUST 1945

LYDIA

Lydia was swimming, swimming inside her own lungs. They were filling with water and every breath was a fight against the rising tide.

'Rest,' a low voice said – a life raft she clutched for. Her hand found another, gentle and soft, and she tried to see who it belonged to but her eyes felt stamped into permanent closure and her head was fugged with the same raging heat that suffused her whole body. Was she alive or dead?

'Not dead!'

The cry burst out of her and again came the voice, this time with a second hand, pushing her gently back onto the bed.

'Relax. Don't fight it, Natasha, let the drugs do their work.'

Her eyes flew open. The pain of the light burst into them and she winced but would not close them again.

'What did you call me?'

'Natasha?' the voice repeated, but less certainly. 'It's the only word you've spoken. Is it not your name?'

'My daughter,' she choked out. Every word was an effort,

gurgling in her lungs, rasping up her throat and pumping fire around her aching limbs, but this was vital. 'Natasha is my daughter.'

'I see.'

'Where is she?'

'What's your name, my dear?'

'Where is she?!' Tasha's face filled Lydia's pain-racked mind and she pictured her red hair, so like Lydia's own but brighter, fiercer, more hopeful. Was Tasha still hopeful? Was she even still alive? She forced herself up and grabbed at the life raft. 'Where. Is. She?'

The words bubbled in her wasted lungs and she cursed them, but the man – he wasn't a life raft, of course he wasn't, a doctor maybe? – patted her hand.

'She's safe,' he said.

'How do you know?'

No answer came.

'Don't lie to me!' she shrieked furiously. 'I don't need lies. I need answers.'

'So do I,' he said calmly. 'If we know who you are, we have a better chance of finding your daughter. So, what's your name?'

She fell back on the bed, too weary to fight further. 'Lydia.' It sounded alien. For so long she'd been Number A87342 that 'Lydia' sounded whimsical, fantastical even.

'We will help you find your daughter, Lydia, but first you must get well. You have pneumonia, a complication of typhus. From the march. Do you remember the march?'

Lydia screwed her eyes shut again. Nodded. Of course she remembered the march – the endless icy miles, the huddle of prisoners, the deep, deep blisters as her wooden clogs rubbed themselves into her frozen feet. Of course she remembered the pain and the hunger and the cold. Of course she remembered people dropping dead at her feet, or stumbling and being shot, or simply lying down in the snow at night and never getting up again. And of course she remembered the agony of leaving Tasha, the excruciating fear for her daughter shut in that barrack to die a slow, frightened, lonely death without even her mother's arms around her.

'I left her,' she wept.

'It wasn't your fault. You had no choice.'

They'd all told her that. They'd told her that when her husband, Szymon, had been shot in front of her in what had been left of Warsaw, and when Amelia had wasted away of typhus. And now Lydia had it too, and pneumonia besides, and Tasha – Tasha was alone.

'She's only sixteen.' A thought pierced through her and she grabbed him again. 'What month is it?'

'August, Lydia. It's August fifth, 1945.'

'August!' Tasha was still just sixteen then – her birthday was in September – but the last thing Lydia remembered, it had been barely spring. 'How long have I been here?'

'Since Dachau was liberated on April twenty-ninth. You've been very ill, Lydia.'

'Dachau?'

More pictures spiked inside her: a freight train from Wodzisław with people crammed inside; the clickety-clack of rails as a percussion to the orchestra of groans and wails – a symphony of misery; and then a building, so like Auschwitz she'd hoped she'd come back to where she'd last seen Tasha. But this entrance had been white, the wrought iron gates more ornate than Birkenau, and *Arbeit Macht Frei* in curlicued letters at the top.

Lydia had spat at it. '*Our* work makes *you* free,' she'd said. 'Bastards.'

But she'd been ill already and the word had died in her clogging throat as her torn feet had stumbled through the hateful gate.

'Welcome to Dachau,' someone had laughed in hard-edged German. 'Welcome to the Third Reich.'

'Not for much longer,' a man behind Lydia had jeered. And been shot for it, shot not-quite-dead so that two hours later he'd still been rasping his last breaths into the melting snow.

Another of the doctor's words snagged on Lydia's struggling consciousness.

'Liberated?' she asked.

'Yes. You're free, Lydia. The war is over. We won. This is a hospital now, a US hospital.' He placed a cool hand on her brow. 'Rest. You're safe.'

She almost did but then she remembered.

'Tasha! I have to find Tasha!'

The words rose up through her, raw in their truth, for there would be no rest until she was with her daughter again. Tasha was alive, she was sure of it. And, somehow, she just had to work out where she'd gone and get to her.

PART TWO

WINDERMERE

SEVEN

CROSBY-ON-EDEN | 15 AUGUST 1945

ALICE

Alice paced the runway of the RAF airbase, looking nervously into the louring sky. Today was her forty-eighth birthday, but that had been quietly lost in the arrival of the orphans, and thank heaven. The last thing she needed was a reminder of how old she was becoming; it was far better to be finally getting down to work. Sophie, who had thankfully joined Alice on the Calgarth Estate as head cook, had made her the most delicious apricot pastry for a quiet breakfast celebration, but then Alice had headed out to the airbase in the bumpy old buses that would bring the children to their new home. Whenever they actually arrived.

They'd been here since midday and with the clocks ticking towards four, no planes had landed. There'd been storms, apparently, and Alice hated the thought of the little ones buffeted by tempestuous clouds after all they'd been through. But she couldn't will them in, so she turned her eyes back to the fields and rolling hills all around.

They were at a place called Crosby-on-Eden, and it was

aptly named – the whole of this northerly corner of England was a paradise. Alice loved it in Windermere, where the green fields, meadow flowers and benign slopes of the Black Fell above the beautiful lake reminded her of happy holidays hiking in the Tyrol. She couldn't think of a better place to bring war-damaged children and just hoped she was ready for them.

She'd arrived here two weeks ago, after saying goodbye to New Barn and spending a heady month in London recruiting staff with Oskar. She'd stayed with Anna and Dorothy in Hampstead, and travelled every day to the grand offices of the Central British Fund in Bloomsbury House, right in the city. There, she'd met many of the fund's members – earnest, intelligent people who'd said confusing things about how 'marvellous' they'd heard she was – and a number of wealthy benefactors keen to open their wallets for the incoming orphans. Alice had been intimidated by the sheer number of lords and ladies coming through the smart doors, but also enthused by their desire to help those Jews still battling to survive in Europe.

'We are facing extinction,' one elderly aristocrat had told her, clasping her hands tightly, despite a clear shake in his own. 'Hitler tried to wipe the Jews off the map and if we don't act fast, he may yet succeed. These children, Miss Goldberger, they are the key to our future.'

It had made her glow with the importance of her task. And quake.

Alice's eyes turned to the clouds once more but the skies were still empty.

'They're big planes,' someone said at her side. 'I'm told they fly very slowly.'

Alice looked gratefully to her colleague, though she had to stretch her neck back to see her fully. Marie Paneth, a strikingly handsome woman, over six feet tall, was one of the people she and Oskar had recruited in Bloomsbury House. A German artist and psychoanalyst, she'd fled their homeland just like

Alice, though she had been far earlier to go, heading for America when Hitler was still gaining influence. And, what's more, leaving her husband to do so.

'You left your husband?' Sophie had gasped.

'He was a rope around my neck, darling,' Marie had told them in a cultured drawl. 'Men just hold you back!'

She'd moved to Britain during the war to run a house for the children of the bombed-out East End, apparently dealing with some of the worst behaved youngsters in England with calm, confidence and much success. They might need her expertise when these young camp survivors arrived, for who knew what sort of wild behaviour they would exhibit.

'They'll be very tired by the time they land,' Alice said.

'Hopefully that will make them more docile.'

'Or the reverse.'

'Also possible. I'd have thought mainly the poor things will be hungry, so let's hope the good ladies of the WVS stay with us.'

She indicated the trestle tables by the control tower where the women of the Carlisle Women's Voluntary Service had set up a tea urn and an impressive array of refreshments for the children. They, too, had been here for hours and were looking worriedly at watches and muttering about their own children who would be out of school and needing their care. Indeed, several of the local youngsters had already arrived and were sniffing eagerly around the cakes and sandwiches intended for the hungry travellers.

'Get away with you!' Alice heard one mother chide her son. 'These poor creatures have had nowt to eat for years, so you're not nicking off with their sarnies.'

Alice smiled. She didn't understand all the words but the gist was clear and the lad slunk off to play with his friends minus his 'sarnie'. He was watched with open curiosity by a group of beautifully dressed ladies, holidaying members of the famous Rothschild family, who'd brought baskets of crisp, fresh apples for the arrivals. They'd been sitting in the shade, upright and elegant, for as long as anyone else and even their aristocratic poise was flagging.

'There! Look! Over there!'

It was the 'sarnie' lad, his young eyes clearly sharper than the adults', for it seemed to Alice that he was merely pointing at a slightly darker cloud over the hilly horizon. As she watched, however, the cloud became more defined and she caught the faint hum of an engine on the wind.

'It's them!' She clutched at Marie's arm then remembered this wasn't Sophie at her side and swiftly let go.

Marie, however, just smiled and said, 'It looks that way. Goodness, I hope we're ready.'

Alice was relieved to see that even she looked nervous. These children were an unknown quantity, all they had to go by were the terrible pictures that had come out of Belsen showing emaciated skeletons, barely human beings at all. All recent psychoanalytic theory, as propounded by Sigmund Freud and, more recently by Anna, suggested that what children experienced in their early years was utterly and inextricably impactful in terms of forming their character, so who knew what the poor mites would be like.

Alice thought of the neat rooms she'd got ready with such care back at Calgarth. Each bed was made up with crisp, white sheets and a teddy bear on the pillow, and each bedside table had fresh flowers, picked this morning. The dining hall was clean and bright, there were lawns to play upon and then, of course, Lake Windermere just a hundred metres away and all the glory of the open hills beyond. It was an Eden, perfect for happy children to play in, but could these poor Nazi victims possibly be happy children?

'All set, Alice?' Oskar strode up next to her, rubbing his hands. 'It's going to be very interesting, don't you think?'

Alice looked at her boss and saw him watching the plane, alert and excited. This was an intellectual challenge for him and he was clearly relishing it.

'I hope they're not too damaged,' she said.

'Is it possible to be too damaged, Alice? This, perhaps, is what we are going to find out.'

Alice frowned. 'And if the answer is yes?' she asked.

He looked at her, confused.

'If they are wild beyond our control, what then?'

'Our study is complete.'

'But the children, Oskar, what will happen to the children?'

'Hmm. Yes. Tricky. I guess we'll work that out when we get there – if we get there. I'm sure that with a few months in this lovely place we can set these youngsters on the path to recovery.'

'I do hope so.'

Alice was wringing her hands again and, to her surprise, Oskar put his around them, forcing her to be still.

'You can do this, Alice. You're a highly experienced professional. I've heard great reports of your work in Berlin and you certainly performed wonders with the children at New Barn.'

'I wouldn't say wonders, Oskar, I—'

'Wonders, Alice. And you will do so again, I know you will.'

'I...' Alice had no idea what to say. 'Thank you, Oskar.'

'My pleasure. Now, stand by your beds, here comes the first plane.'

Alice put a hand up to hold on to her hat as the plane came roaring down to the runway, surely too fast to land safely. The tiny wheels beneath its giant belly hit the tarmac and bounced alarmingly, then the pilot slammed on the brakes with a piercing screech, a cloud of dirty smoke and a sharply hot smell. Alice heard the Rothschilds squeak in horror, saw the WVS ladies clutch their piles of baked goodies and their children leap up and down, apparently unconcerned by the huge plane skewing noisily towards them.

But already, miraculously, it was slowing to a halt and the smoke was clearing. Alice watched, her heart in her throat, as a door in the side was flung back and two airmen jumped out. A curious head appeared in the doorway, big eyes scanned the welcome committee and then, with a broad grin, a young man reached out for a hand each from the airmen and jumped athletically down.

Alice watched, fascinated, as several similar young men jumped down to join him and then they began to saunter – there was no other word for it – across to Leonard Montefiore, who had stepped up to greet them. Alice heard the WVS whispering to each other and knew exactly what they were saying. These weren't the starving waifs they'd been expecting, but gangly youths who seemed closer to adults than children. Some of the boys were taller than her and a few were even sporting beards. She'd known, of course, from the lists provided by the authorities in Prague, that many of them were in the thirteen to sixteen bracket, but these first youngsters looked to be very much at the top end. How was she meant to impose her authority upon them?

'A few might have been creative with their identities,' Oskar commented, as a young man with a mop of curly hair shook Leonard's hand with easy assurance.

The boy turned their way and gave them a wide, open grin. 'Good afternoon,' he said in careful English, 'I am Georg.' Then he lapsed into something excitable in Polish that was almost certainly a form of 'thank you for having us'. He shook their hands with enthusiasm and, spotting the food, made for the WVS who, almost as one woman, patted their windblown hairdos at his approach.

'That one's a charmer,' Oskar said. 'He'll go far.'

But there was no time to dwell on individuals, for another

plane was landing and the runway was crowding with children. To her relief, Alice saw a bright-eyed boy of maybe eight leap down and look eagerly around him.

'Come on out,' he called back in German. 'It's really nice here.'

'Coming, Ernst,' a trusting voice replied and a gaggle of little ones appeared in the door. The airmen lifted them down and Alice watched as the youngsters found their feet on the tarmac and stared in wonder at the green fields and hills beyond. There were even six toddlers, huddled in a tight, frightened clutch, and looking so out of place that Alice instinctively headed their way, but the WVS ladies were ahead of her, swooping on the babies with maternal coos.

Hesitating, Alice caught a conversation between a young woman with short, vibrantly red hair, and a little girl with stubby pigtails. The redhead had taken two apples from the baskets being wafted around by the Rothschilds, but the younger girl was looking at the fruit as if it were a grenade that might explode in her hand.

'What is it, Tasha?' Alice heard the smaller girl ask in German.

The older girl bent down to be heard amongst the hubbub. 'It's an apple, Marta. It's delicious. Try it.'

The girl turned the apple around and around in her hand but still looked suspicious, so the older one, Tasha, took an exaggerated bite.

'Hmm, delicious. Here, Kotka, try mine.'

She held out her apple and the little girl put out a delicate, kitten-like tongue and licked at the juice bursting from the opened fruit. Her eyes widened.

'It's like heaven, Tasha,' she said. 'Actual heaven.'

Alice felt tears spring to her eyes. This place truly was an Eden and, if these poor children had never even had an apple before, they'd got them here just in time. Whatever their age, the new arrivals were still children, and whatever qualifications Alice did or did not have to run this curious little hostel on a lakeside in north England, she had care and she had love and she was going to give it all to them. She could only pray that it was enough.

EIGHT

WINDERMERE | AUGUST 1945

TASHA

'Let it fly, Tasha! Let it fly!'

Ahead of her, Tasha saw Georg release the brakes on his bike and, legs splayed out either side, go shooting off down the hill, laughing to the blue skies above. She didn't feel quite as confident on her borrowed bike but it did look fun so she let the brakes off and felt a rush of air across her body as she picked up speed. My goodness, flying was right! She felt wild and free and at one with the beautiful landscape above and... She hit a pebble in the road and wobbled. Slamming the brakes on again, she skidded but just kept control and, heart beating, went back to a more sedate descent.

It didn't matter. It still felt astounding to be out on a bicycle at all. The last time she'd ridden one had been on her eleventh birthday in September 1939 when an SS officer had ordered her off her brand-new gift and ridden it away, his bulky frame buckling the lovely machine. She'd found it weeks later, broken and cast into a ditch – a precious present wasted to indulge an arrogant whim. It had been her first clash with the Nazis and a dark sign of things to come.

A shiver passed across her body and she had to fight to keep the bike from sliding out of control again. 'Come on,' she told herself crossly, 'what's the worst that can happen?' A little tumble and a scraped knee? That was nothing compared to what she'd been through and it was important not just to live, but to *be alive*. Feeling suddenly reckless, she let off the brakes again and allowed herself to career down the track after the now-distant Georg.

A lady pushing a baby in a pram waved merrily to her and she dared a quick wave back. Everyone at Calgarth was so kind. A few of the residents had even come out to greet the buses on the first night they'd arrived. They'd held up lanterns to light their smiling faces, and rung merry bells. True, it had scared a few of the sleeping little ones, so that they'd arrived white-faced and wailing, but Tasha had appreciated it all the same.

These people could so easily have resented them coming into their peaceful part of the world. Mind you, as she'd found out since, many of them had also moved on to the Calgarth Estate in the last few years, brought in from the bombed-out cities of Liverpool and Manchester to work in the flying-boat factory and live in safer rural surroundings, so perhaps they understood what it was like to have to make a new life here. And, she supposed, if she had to make a new life anywhere, this was as good a place as any.

Not that it had started so well. The people in charge had herded them into a draughty hall that first night, all shadows and echoing footfalls, and asked them to undress and line up for disinfecting. Instantly, Tasha had been back in the hateful arrivals barrack in Auschwitz, standing naked with her mother and sister, poked and prodded towards the tattooing pen that had turned them from people into numbers, then on to the shears that had completed the job in several harsh swipes. When a woman had tried to take her bag, she'd snapped.

'Leave it!'

'It's for your own good,' the woman had said.

But Tasha hadn't been fooled. 'That's what they told us in the camps,' she'd snarled.

The woman had yanked back, horrified, pulling the buckle on her bag loose but at least leaving it in her possession.

She'd still had to undress though, if only to her underwear, and still had to step into a tent where a man had pointed a nozzle at her and she'd honestly, for one heart-stopping moment, thought she'd come all this way just to be gassed after all. She'd laughed so hard when puffs of stinky white powder had come out that it had gone all over him as well, and that had made her laugh even harder.

'I'm doing my best,' he'd said indignantly, and that's when Tasha had realised that these sweet, innocent, kind people had no idea what camp life had been like. They were trying but there was only so much they could comprehend. There was a wall of furious knowledge around the camp survivors, as sharp as any Nazi barbed wire, and nothing anyone on the outside could do would penetrate it. Perhaps that was for the best, Tasha reflected, for there was a hatred inside her that should not be released. All she could hope was that with enough hills, lakes and bicycle rides, it might dissipate to only minimally dangerous levels before anything broke the wall.

The track turned a corner and Tasha had to veer sharply to one side to dodge around a sheep and two lambs.

'Sorry!' she cried in English – one of the few words she'd learned so far, along with 'thank you,' 'yes please,' and, 'more'. She looked back to see the mummy sheep staring indignantly after her, the two lambs bouncing as if they'd like to come along for the ride. They were impossibly white, like the few fluffy clouds in the blue sky, the tablecloths in the dining room, and the covers on Tasha's bed.

She'd been unable to believe it when she'd been shown into her room on the first night.

'I'm sorry they're so small,' the mousy woman – Alice something – had said, as she'd opened Tasha's door. 'We were hoping to get you friendly dormitories but this is what was here, so we had to make do. I hope you at least find it comfortable.'

'It's perfect,' Tasha had told her, and it was. She'd spent the last five years in cramped, overcrowded accommodation so having this private space, however small, felt like the greatest luxury.

Marta was next door and she'd been in to kiss her goodnight before stepping into her own room and reverently closing the door. She had her own bed, with the softest mattress and sheets so crisp and clean she'd barely dared step into them on that first night. There'd even been a teddy bear on her pillow. She'd pushed it aside at first, sitting it on the chest of drawers with the pretty pink and yellow flowers someone had arranged in a glass, but when she'd woken in the depths of the night, disorientated and afraid, she'd pulled the bear under the covers with her. Burying her face in the comfort of its soft, gentle fur, she could almost have been home – her real, childhood home, with her parents down the corridor and her sister snuffling in the next bed – and, comforted, she'd gone back to sleep on a wave of borrowed happiness.

Tasha turned the final corner at the bottom of the hill, to find Georg standing on the track, arms spread wide, ready to catch her. Braking, she slowed the bike to stop right up against his broad chest and he grabbed the handlebars, holding her steady, his face mere centimetres from hers.

'I flew faster than you,' he teased in their native Polish.

'I flew fast enough, thank you. I didn't want to fall.'

'If you fell, I'd have caught you.'

He was looking deep into her eyes; it was most disconcerting.

'No, you wouldn't,' she said, 'because you'd already be off
around the corner.'

He laughed. 'I'd come back.'

'By which time I'd be in a hedge with scraped knees.'

'And I'd rescue you and carry you home.'

Tasha rolled her eyes. 'This isn't a fairy tale, Prince Georg.'

He laughed again but then looked around them and said,
'Are you sure?'

Tasha stepped off her bike and looked too. The track had
brought them down to a small shingle beach on the lakeside.
The sun was sparkling in a thousand diamonds across the deep
blue water, while forest-green hills stood guard all around and
softer blue skies seemed to envelop the whole scene in light.
Out here, with the good food and the rest and the startlingly
fresh air, even her eyes seemed to be regaining their strength
and she drank in the beautiful landscape.

'It does feel rather magical,' she conceded. 'Can you believe
that this time last week we were still crammed into that
orphanage in Prague?'

'Thirty to a dorm with trams rattling past day and night and
endless turnip soup.'

'The food is good here,' Tasha said. 'That bread the cook
makes is manna from heaven. It's so white.'

'So soft.'

'So fluffy.'

'So plentiful!' Georg reached into his bike basket and, with
a magician's flourish, produced a loaf.

'Georg!'

'What? It's ours. They said so.'

'They also said it would never run out so we weren't to
hoard it.'

'This isn't hoarding, it's saving.'

'Same difference.'

'Well, if you don't want any...'

'All right, all right.' Tasha snatched the bread from him and broke herself off a large chunk, sinking her teeth into it with relish. She suspected she'd never, ever tire of the yeasty taste of these Windermere loaves, or their heady softness. Not a stone or a bit of grit or straw anywhere. Unbelievable!

It had been chaos the first morning they'd been presented with this beautiful substance. There they'd been, sitting in rows down long tables, pretending to listen to the rabbi saying grace but every one of them with their eyes fixed on the hatches into the kitchen. The instant they'd gone up and baskets piled high with loaves and rolls had started to be passed out, all hell had broken loose. The first baskets had barely made it two metres down the tables before they'd been emptied, bread disappearing instantly up sleeves and down shorts.

'There's enough for all,' the Alice woman had kept shouting, in both English and German, but it had been impossible to believe her. It was only when the man – Mr Friedmann – had stood on a table and shouted for 'order' that the carnage had stopped. They'd all cowered back, Judith and Suzi even hiding beneath the table, but as soon as he'd had their attention, Mr Friedmann had simply smiled and said, 'There really is enough. And plenty of jam besides.'

The mention of jam had nearly started another riot, but Mr Friedmann had stood there, in the middle of them all, until the helpers had got bread and jam onto every table and only then had he let them sit down and tuck in, a bliss-laden silence descending. Even so, at least as much bread had made it out of the dining room in clothing as in tummies, but they'd been here four days and every day food kept coming so even the hungriest amongst them were starting to trust it would continue to do so.

Tasha sank onto a patch of grass behind the beach and looked out across the water. 'It's hard to believe this place has been here all the time, everyone getting on with life while we were, were...'

Georg leaned her bike against his and sat down at her side. 'People lost loved ones here too. The woman who lent me these bikes told me her son was killed at Anzio.'

'That's sad. But that's war, right? That's soldiers, not torturing innocent civilians.'

'It wasn't torture, Tash—'

'You don't think so?'

Georg slung an arm around her shoulders. 'You're right, it was, but it's over. We're here in Wondermere, right?'

Despite herself, Tasha laughed at the nickname the children had given the lake in their first-ever English lesson.

'In Wondermere,' she agreed. 'Pretty, peaceful and so... so clean!' She leaned into Georg, loving the feel of his arm around her. 'D'you know, I've had two showers every single day.'

'I had three yesterday. I can't believe they're there whenever you want.'

'Although I wish people would stop showering in the middle of the night. There's this one girl, Monika, who's forever getting up to go and scrub herself.'

'Is she the one whose three sisters all died of typhus?' Tasha nodded grimly. 'Well, there you go. Who wouldn't want to keep clean after that?'

Tasha felt sadness, always so close to the surface, tug once more at her heart. Looking down, she spotted a daisy in the grass and plucked it, pulling its petals off one by one, taking pleasure in seeing them scattered forlornly around her.

'Tash?' Georg leaned round, trying to see into her face. 'What is it?'

'Monika could wash all day long and it wouldn't bring any of them back, would it?'

'Of course not.'

'And that's sad.'

'It is,' he agreed.

They fell into silence and she felt him squirm beside her, then he leaned forward eagerly, pointing across the sparkling lake.

'Look, is that a swan?'

'A swan?' Tasha squinted into the sun and saw a white bird swimming lazily in front of them. 'Might be. So what?'

'So what?!'

'The swan is alive but Monika's sisters are all dead. So, yes, so what?'

Georg sighed. 'You could say, Monika's sisters are all dead but at least that swan is alive. Not everything is destroyed.'

Tasha leaped up in frustration. Georg's optimism was impressive but also infuriating.

'Are you not sad, Georg?' she demanded. 'Are you not angry? The Nazis took everything from us. They took our families and our homes. They treated us like animals. They starved us and beat us, they set their dogs on us for fun and worked us into the dirt. And then, as if all that wasn't enough, they shot us and gassed us and burned us as if we were nothing. Nothing!'

He'd risen too and she pushed at him in frustration. 'How does that not make you want to rage and shout and tear up everything that's left because it all feels so tainted and dirty and... and broken beyond repair?' She was battering at him now, raining blows on his chest harder and harder, furious that she couldn't make him so much as step back.

He caught at her fists, holding her tight.

'Let me go!'

'No.'

'Bully. Nazi bully.'

He sucked in his breath but didn't let go. 'I *am* angry, Tash, of course I am. I just... I just...' He looked to the sky, fighting for words. 'They tried to destroy us with their evil and they so nearly succeeded. I don't want to let them do that.'

'What?'

'I don't want to let them drag me into sadness and bitterness and anger. It's there, Tash, I promise you. It's there all the time and the only way I know to fight it is to try to look past it. To focus on the white bread and the white swans and the white clouds and hope that, somehow, they'll keep enough of the black away for me to live and love and beat the Nazi cruelty.'

Tasha stared at him, her hands limp in his grasp, as she tried to take this in.

'So, you *are* angry?'

'So angry I could tear the black hearts out of every single Nazi with my bare hands.'

'That's angry.'

'Yes. But where would it get me? I think it's easier to hate. Loving, that's the tough bit. That's the... the scary bit.' He tugged gently on her hands, pulling her closer in against him.

'Scary?' she whispered, her voice embarrassingly hoarse.

'Very,' he whispered back, 'but I'm willing to give it a try if you are?'

'I... I...'

She tried and tried again but she had no words and when Georg tipped his head towards hers, she reached gratefully up and, before she could think, or analyse, or do anything other than exactly what she wanted, she kissed him. His response was instant, his arms going around her back and his lips meeting hers with tentative eagerness. It felt glorious, like riding a bike across the skies, like swans in flight.

Somewhere inside, a nasty voice nagged at her that this was a sensation that so, so many people had been deprived of forever more, but she pushed it away and pulled Georg closer. He was right, they had to live. They had to cheat the Nazis of their final victory.

It just felt so very hard.

NINE

WINDERMERE | SEPTEMBER 1945

ALICE

'Alice! Alice, you have to come. Miss Bowen is making funny noises.'

Alice looked up from the pile of letters on her desk. On her left sat her laboriously written requests for information for every child in her care, ready to post. On her right were the apologetic replies from the last set. To date, she'd not turned up one relative for the Windermere orphans – or for herself. The letter currently in her hand said that UNRRA were terribly sorry but they'd found no record of a Maximillian, Lilliana or Ruth-Gertrud Goldberger leaving Theresienstadt.

Alice knew more about the place now. Many of the children had been there and they'd assured her that it had remained a ghetto throughout the war, so she had to hope this meant they'd left of their own accord, but the not-knowing was so painful.

She shook herself. Sorrow for what was lost was best dealt with by caring for what they still had, and it seemed she was needed. Three boys were waving frantically at her through the window and a crowd was gathering, the children coming from all over the estate. Alice had to act fast.

In the last few days, the exuberance of the first weeks in the Lake District had given way to something quieter but more unsettled. The tinies were still in a tight knot of six but now actively sought adult attention, following their chosen targets around like wild ducklings. The middle children, their immediate needs met by regular mealtimes and warm beds, had started playing imaginary games of a violent nature that spoke of a horribly skewed concept of reality and broke Alice's heart every time she saw them in progress.

Yesterday she'd caught two innocent-looking Italian sisters, Mirella and Fiorina, making little Judith and Suzi hold bricks over their heads until their arms wobbled horribly and she'd had to rush to grab them before they fell on their heads. None of the four of them had apparently seen anything wrong in the game so, on the recommendation of the red-headed girl, Tasha Ancel, Alice had upped storytime in all languages to provide new outlets for their imaginations.

For the older ones, regular schooling was in progress but it was erratic at best. They were trying to teach them English as fast as possible but had to resort to a combination of German, Polish and Czech to cover geography or history. These classes were met with passionate but fitful attendance. The children would throw themselves into a subject with enthusiasm and object when the lesson finished, but then fail to turn up for its continuation the next day.

'It's simply that they don't want scheduling,' Oskar had said, when Marie had brought it up in their evening meeting. 'They've been battered by routines and demands and need to exert their free will. Let them take things at their own pace and they'll settle. It's clear they have curious minds, so they will come.'

He was right about that at least. Debates in religious studies lessons had intensified as the older ones began to explore their feelings about the condition of a world that had brought them here and there had been arguments, sulks and even a few outright fights. The other day Alice had had to break up a bout over which death march had been the hardest.

'Have you not had enough harm done to you already without doing more to each other?' she'd demanded.

'At least here, one of *us* wins,' had been the retort and, really, there was no arguing with that.

Now, fearing another such fight, Alice hastened outside to the boys, but they looked united. And scared.

'What sort of noise?' she asked.

'She keeps moaning and saying something weird about hems.'

'Hems? Take me to her, will you, Chaim?'

The eldest boy nodded and set off across the lawn towards the outbuilding they used as the clothing store. Many kind people had donated clothing for the children, who'd all arrived with almost nothing, but distribution had not been as simple as they'd naively imagined. A lot of the children, far from being grateful for the smart, clean outfits, had complained about them and refused to wear them. Every boy had been measured for a new suit and every girl a smart dress, but until those items arrived, they were forced to choose from the donated clothes and they seemed curiously reluctant. Alice was trying to find out why, but no one would talk openly about it; perhaps today that would change.

'She's in there,' Chaim told her, stopping outside the store.

'Thank you, Chaim. Please don't worry, I'm sure there's a simple explanation.'

Alice went to go inside but Chaim grabbed her arm.

'I didn't mean to hurt her.'

'Sorry?' She turned back in alarm.

'All I said was that my father would have been disgusted by

these seams.' He tugged at his baggy shorts. 'And that's when she started making the noises.'

'I see.' Alice patted him on the head. 'Don't worry, I'm sure it wasn't your fault. I'll sort it out.'

'Thanks, miss.'

He stood there, still tugging at the shorts, and Alice gave him what she hoped was a reassuring smile and headed inside.

'Glynis?'

It was gloomy in the cramped room and she squinted, trying to see Glynis Bowen amongst the racks and tables of clothing. It was, she had to admit, the first time she'd properly come in here and it looked to her like a treasure trove of outfits but, then, she'd never exactly been stylish so who was she to say?

'Glynis?'

There was a strange noise coming from the far corner and Alice stepped around a table laden with jumpers and saw her fellow carer sitting on the floor in the corner, her knees pulled up to her chest and her face buried between them. She was muttering to herself, the only intelligible word being, as Chaim had said, 'hem'.

'Glynis, liebchen, what's wrong?'

Alice approached slowly, dropping to her knees to be on a level with the Welsh woman who had always seemed such a solid, sensible member of the team. Daughter of a mill owner from Abergavenny, she'd volunteered to man the clothing stores, but it seemed it had been too much for her. Alice reached out a tentative hand to touch her knee and Glynis's head flew up. Her blue eyes were wild and looked enormous in her pale face.

'Hems,' she said to Alice. 'I've got to take up the hems.'

'No, you don't,' Alice told her gently. 'The hems are fine. Fantastic in fact.'

'Really?' Glynis's eyes cleared but then she looked up at the garments looming over them on all sides and the moaning started again. 'Can't stop. Have to take up the hems. Have to make the clothes nice. They've suffered enough.' She grabbed at Alice, her slender hand claw-like. 'They've suffered enough, Alice. They should have nice clothes. It's the least we can do. A pretty dress, a smart pair of trousers – is it so much to ask?'

'Of course not,' Alice agreed, 'but you don't have to do it alone, Glynis. We can all take up the hems.'

'So many hems!'

She was off, moaning again. Alice put her arms around the poor woman and rocked her gently, as she might a child who'd had a nightmare. She felt terrible. How had she not noticed the demands the children had been making on this earnest member of her staff?

'Come on, Glynis, let's get you to bed. It'll all look better with a nice cup of tea and a good sleep.'

It was clear Glynis would need far more than that, but getting her out of the clothing store would be a start.

But Glynis didn't move.

'Sophie's made iced buns,' Alice tried. 'Would you like an iced bun? I know I would.'

Glynis shook her head violently. 'No time, Alice. Got to take the hems up.'

Alice thought fast. She could hear a crowd of children gathering outside, which was all Glynis needed.

'You're right,' she said, crossing her fingers behind her back, desperately hoping this was a good approach. She had no formal psychological training like Anna or Oskar, but Anna was in London and Oskar off meeting a new benefactor, so this was all down to her. 'But we need more thread.'

Glynis's head shot up again. 'We do,' she agreed earnestly. 'We do need more thread. It doesn't match, you see. They don't like it if it doesn't match.'

'Of course not, but it's fine. I have thread in my room.'

'You do?'

'Oh yes, plenty of thread.'

'Do you have burnt sienna?'

'I do,' Alice lied shamelessly, praying she wasn't making things worse.

'Excellent.' Glynis leaped up so suddenly that Alice had to hasten to her feet as she strode to the door. 'Let's get it. Now.'

'Quite right, yes. This way.' Alice put a hand through Glynis's arm, trying to make it look relaxed and casual, although her grip was tight as they stepped out into a gaggle of children. 'Make way, please,' she said firmly. 'We've got thread to fetch.'

'Thread?' Chaim asked.

'Thread,' Glynis agreed, grabbing at his shorts before he had time to pull back. 'Thread to make these nice. I *will* make them nice for you. I *will*. I promise.'

'Of course you will,' Alice agreed crisply, and steered her off towards the main building, leaving the children staring after them in astonishment.

Alice had no idea what to do next, so led Glynis towards the kitchens and Sophie. Already, away from the clothing store, the Welsh woman seemed brighter, looking around at the pretty hills as if seeing them for the first time.

'It's nice here, isn't it?' she said conversationally.

'Very nice,' Alice agreed.

'That's good. They need it nice, don't they? They need it very, very nice, because they've been through, through...' And with that she burst into tears.

Alice hustled her gratefully into the kitchen.

'Goodness me!' Sophie was straight over. 'What on earth do we have here? You poor woman, you look exhausted. Sit down by the stove. Don't mind the cat, she'll move. Ah, there you go. She likes you, see.'

Alice stood back as Sophie bustled around Glynis, tucking her in with a blanket and encouraging her to stroke the cat as she brought tea and buns, all with a steady stream of reassuring chatter.

'What on earth happened?' she whispered to Alice when, at last, Glynis seemed more settled.

'I'm not sure,' Alice told her, 'but I intend to find out.'

Leaving Glynis in Sophie's tender care, she headed back to the clothing store, determined to get to the bottom of its mysteries.

It didn't take long.

'You sorting this now, miss?' Chaim asked, sauntering in bare minutes after Alice had arrived.

'That's right,' she agreed. 'What are you looking for?'

'Shorts. Shorts that actually fit. These ones make me look like I'm in my big brother's cast-offs. If I had a big brother that is. If he hadn't been killed at Chełmno.'

Alice forced herself not to flinch. Some of the children talked of their experiences with cold detachment. Some, who'd clearly been interviewed by reporters eager for dramatic copy, revelled in lurid details. Others never said a word. The carers' job, Oskar told them every evening, was not to judge, but simply to listen. It wasn't easy but the children were here to heal and must be allowed to do it in their own way.

'I see,' Alice said calmly to Chaim. 'It looks as if shorts are over here.'

Glynis had the clothing well-ordered and Alice went easily to the section but Chaim snorted in disgust.

'I've been through all those fifty times. There's nothing there for me.'

'That can't be true. And, really, if they're baggy, does it matter too much?'

'Matter?' His voice sharpened. 'Of course it matters. A man's clothing represents him to the world. Even the Nazis knew that – that's why they put us in stripes. Now you're trying to do exactly the same! It's... it's cruel!'

And with that, he turned on his heel and ran out, leaving Alice staring after him in astonishment. If this was what Glynis had been dealing with every day, no wonder she'd broken down. She looked nervously around the room as the door opened again to reveal the red-headed Tasha and her little sidekick with the pigtails.

'Good afternoon,' Alice said. 'Can I help you?'

'I doubt it,' Tasha shot back.

Alice offered her a smile. 'Why not give me a chance?'

'Do you have any new clothes?'

'No, but there are plenty—'

'Then there's no point in giving you a chance. I've looked through all these. We all have.'

'Perhaps we should look again, together. There are some very smart things here. Look at this dress. It's a beautiful aquamarine, like your eyes.'

Tasha blinked. 'Really?'

'Yes. See.' She turned Tasha to the mirror on the wall, holding the dress up next to her face so the blue-green could bring out the light in her luminous eyes.

'It matches!' Marta cried.

'It does,' Tasha conceded reluctantly. 'But look at it; it's so staromodny – old-fashioned.' She tugged at the slim skirt. 'Everyone's wearing flared skirts nowadays.'

Alice remembered the women she'd seen on the station the last time she'd been up to London, their skirts flaring elegantly around their legs.

'You're right there,' she agreed, 'and I'm sure your new dress, when it comes, will be very fashionable, but in the meantime, this might make you pretty. That's to say, you *are* pretty, but it might enhance that.'

Tasha tossed her head. 'I'm not pretty.'

'You *are*,' Marta said. 'I think you are and Alice thinks you are and Georg definitely thinks you are.'

Tasha blushed and Alice had to turn aside to hide a smile. Romance, it seemed, was creeping into Windermere.

'At least try it on,' she suggested.

'Fine,' the girl agreed reluctantly, 'but it won't look any good. Nothing does.'

Tasha took the dress and shuffled self-consciously through to the curtained-off changing cubicle. There was much humphing and grumbling that made Alice smile again. This girl intrigued her. She was so fierce and bold and she wore her heart right out on her substandard sleeve. Alice couldn't help admiring that, although, Lord help them, it made her very combative.

Finally, Tasha emerged looking self-conscious and very, very lovely.

'That's perfect!' Alice said. 'Isn't it perfect, Marta?'

'Georg will explode when he sees you,' Marta declared.

'It'll do, I suppose,' Tasha muttered begrudgingly.

'Good,' Alice said, forcing herself not to overreact, though what she really wanted to do was run up to the girl, shake her, and tell her she'd give a synagogue's worth of gold to look like her. Not that synagogues had gold in them these days, or that Alice had ever come close to Tasha's raw beauty, even when she'd been the same age and nervously shuffling around the dance floor with an equally gauche Heinz. She shook the thought away; this wasn't about her.

'It's all yours,' she said.

Tasha twisted this way and that, trying to see herself from all angles in the mirror. 'It would be better if it was a bit shorter. Could you take the hem up, Alice?'

Instantly, Alice could hear poor Glynis quivering in the corner: 'Got to take the hems up, got to take the hems up.'

'Tell you what,' she said. 'I'll get you a needle and some thread and *you* can take the hem up.'

'Me?'

'That way, you'll get it exactly how you'd like it.'

'Hmm. I suppose so.'

'You can sew?'

Tasha drew herself up. 'I'm Jewish, Alice, of course I can sew.'

Alice squinted at her. '*I'm* Jewish and I can't sew.'

'Really? Goodness, what did your family do?'

'They were academics.'

'I see.' Tasha did not look impressed. 'Well, you're odd then because most Jews sew beautifully.'

'I see.' Alice set to tidying a pile of shirts, her mind working frantically. Her family had moved in university circles and although she'd been aware that several key people in their local synagogue were tailors, she'd never been intimately involved in the world of workshops and factories and had never thought to ask about them. She felt foolish for that now. 'Because their fathers are tailors?' she said.

'Or their mothers seamstresses, yes.'

Alice thought of Chaim's protest that 'A man's clothing represents him to the world', and the pieces of this afternoon's puzzle slotted into place.

'Is that why they don't like these clothes?'

'Of course! Before the war most of us dressed well, Alice. Beautifully even. We had the finest fabrics, the latest cuts and the most perfect seams. Now... now we're expected to "make do" with someone else's cast-offs. I understand it, I do. There's been a war. No one has much. We should be grateful for anything we can get...'

Alice put out a hand to the girl's shoulder. 'That's not true, Tasha. You shouldn't be more grateful than anyone else, but you shouldn't, perhaps, be *less* grateful either. We're doing our best here.'

Tasha threw her hands wide. 'And is it our fault if it isn't enough? We've lost everything, Alice – our families, our homes, the streets we played on, the synagogues we gathered in, and the workshops and offices where we made our living. We weren't destitute before the war, you know, far from it, so forgive us if we aren't grateful for living one rung above.'

Then she was gone in a flash of aquamarine, Marta running faithfully after her, and Alice was left alone, with only charity clothes and her racing thoughts for company.

That evening, with the children finally in bed, and Glynis put on a train to her parents in Wales, the remaining staff gathered around the kitchen table for their daily debrief.

'It's natural,' Oskar said, 'for us to feel the pressure of helping these children. Every day we're learning more about what they've been through from what they say and the way they behave.'

'And the pictures they draw,' Marie Paneth put in.

'Sorry?' Alice asked, intrigued.

'I've set up a room for them to come and paint if they wish. Many have done and the results are... interesting. Come and see.'

She led them into one of the three rooms they used for classes and meetings. Along the side stood a table with a buffet of painting and drawing materials, and on the walls were pictures, mainly of Lake Windermere and the surrounding hills.

'These don't seem so unusual,' Oskar said, looking curiously at Marie.

'Because those are the only ones I dare put up, darling. Here.' She pulled a large folder from behind a desk and started laying pictures across the tables.

Alice scanned them carefully and what she saw cut to her heart: bold, hard pictures, in solid reds and blacks, showing wires and watchtowers, oversized guns, slavering dogs, and bodies. Lots of bodies. The talent of the artists was variable but the stark contents of their young minds was relentlessly similar.

'It's horrific.'

Marie nodded. 'Is it any wonder they're difficult or demanding or violent in their mood swings?'

'So, what do we do?' Alice asked.

'Give them time,' Oskar said. 'Time and attention and care. Give them other things to think about. Sports...' He indicated Jock Lawrence, the down-to-earth sports coach. 'Languages. Mathematics. Practical skills like dressmaking.'

'About that...' Alice said. They all looked her way and she felt instantly self-conscious but this was important. She told the group about her conversation with Tasha and explained how many of the children had high tailoring standards. 'I don't think this is vanity or stubbornness,' she offered. 'I think it's intricately tied up with family pride, as if they worry that, in accepting poor clothes, they're letting their parents down.'

'An excellent observation,' Oskar said. 'What's your advice, Alice?'

'My advice?'

'Yes, based on your vast experience caring for children, what would be your advice?'

Alice swallowed, but then she saw Sophie's kind eyes nodding her on and she drew in a deep breath.

'I suppose,' she said, 'that we should take care to explain very clearly that these outfits are temporary until clothing worthy of them can be found. And maybe, as you say, dressmaking classes, for both boys and girls, so that they can take ownership of alterations and feel they are drawing on their heritage at the same time.'

Silence met this and Alice flushed.

'But what do I know? I'm not trained. I don't—'

'It's a brilliant idea, Alice,' Oskar said.

'Brilliant,' Marie agreed. 'Both practically and emotionally helpful. I'd gladly help.'

'I've got my sewing machine here with me,' someone else volunteered. 'I'll share it with the kids if they'll take care of it.'

'I'm sure they will,' Alice said. 'They'll understand its value.'

'That's settled then,' Oskar said. 'Great work, everyone. Now, let's get some sleep so we can start the new classes tomorrow.'

They began to file out of the art room and Alice went wearily to follow but Oskar stopped her.

'A moment more, Alice, if you don't mind?'

'Of course not.' She turned nervously back to her boss as the others left. Had she overstepped the mark? Been too forward?

'You're a very perceptive woman,' he said.

'I am?'

'You are. I've noticed it before. Indeed, it's why I recommended you for this post and I'm so glad I did. That was excellent work today. Thank you.'

Alice tugged nervously at her cardigan. 'Anything I can do to help the children.'

'Of course. But it's more than that. Our work here could massively improve the understanding of trauma-management. This is perhaps the most exciting live study of our times and it's important to have intuitive people running it.' He grabbed her hand. 'We can make a real difference, Alice.'

Alice swallowed, unsure how to respond. To her, the project was less a 'study' and more a way of helping the children get over a terrible, terrible loss, but that sounded like a naive thing to say to this earnest scientist.

'I like Windermere a lot,' she managed.

It sounded stilted and awkward but Oskar didn't seem to notice.

'Me too, Alice, me too. I felt so... constricted in London. There's more space here to think, to breathe, to *be*.'

'You don't miss your family?' she asked.

'My family? Not as much as I probably ought to. My son

and daughter are all but grown up, and my wife... Let's just say, we're not as close as we used to be.'

'I'm sorry.'

He gave her a quiet smile. 'Please don't be. We've talked it through and reconciled ourselves to the change. We had a good life raising our children together but we've grown apart and we've both agreed that we will be better stepping into the future unlinked.'

'You have?' Alice stuttered. 'How... modern.'

He gave a little laugh. 'Does it sound terribly callous? I apologise if I've shocked you but we believe it's sensible. We considered the issue from all angles and decided that, in a world in which so much misery is already being thrust upon us, there is little point adding to it ourselves. We still respect each other and we will stay friends, for our children's sake, but we have granted each other the freedom to pursue new paths.'

'I see,' Alice said, although she didn't really see at all. No one else she knew would do such a thing and she had no idea how to react.

It was suddenly feeling very hot in the big classroom and maybe Oskar felt it too, for he turned to stride up and down.

'We're at an apex in history, Alice,' he cried, waving to the harsh pictures littering the tables between them. 'Psychoanalysis has never been needed more and all of us – Anna, Dorothy, me, you – have to step up and show the world what we can do.'

His passion was invigorating.

'We do,' she agreed. 'That is, I will.'

He came back to her with a smile. 'I know you will. That's why I picked you. But I've taken enough of your time. I'll tidy up here and let you get to bed. Good night, Alice.'

To her huge surprise, he clasped her shoulders and kissed her on each cheek. The gesture carried echoes of a past she'd almost forgotten – a time in busy Berlin cafés when everyone would greet each other with such easy intimacy – but also some-thing new. A trust, perhaps, a confidence in their relationship. Their *working* relationship.

'Good night, Oskar,' she stuttered and hurried out.

She paused at the door but he was poring over the children's pictures, fully absorbed. It didn't matter.

Alice headed giddily to her room. 'We can make a real difference here, Alice,' Oskar had said. She was certain that, with all this importance swimming around inside her, it would be utterly impossible to sleep.

TEN

TASHA

Tasha covered her face in embarrassment as three hundred children sang 'Happy Birthday to You' in halting, multi-accented English. What a way to turn seventeen! There was bunting strung around the dining hall, a painted banner, and a great big cake, complete with coloured icing and seventeen candles.

'Blow them out, Tasha!' Marta urged.

'And be sure to make a wish,' Sophie put in.

Tasha glanced at the kindly cook; a wish was easy. Closing her eyes and touching her fingers to her ever-present handbag, she wished with all her might that Mama was alive and well and was, right now, locating her name on a list and canvassing authorities to get to England. Actually, forget that, it was her birthday – she wished that right now, as this terrible singing ground to a halt, the door would open and Lydia would walk in and shout, 'Happy birthday, Tasha!' Then she'd sweep her into her arms, pouring every drop of her love into her, and their red hair would mingle and Tasha would know that this was, against all the odds, the happiest birthday of her life so far.

'Blow them out quick, Tasha,' she half-heard Marta urging, 'or the flames will melt the icing.'

Forcing her eyes reluctantly open, she glanced to the door. It remained resolutely shut and, on a big sigh, she blew out all seventeen candles. The assembled children cheered and immediately the clamour for a share of the treat began.

'You cut it, Sophie,' Tasha said. 'It looks an impossible job to me.'

'Nothing is impossible,' Sophie said cheerfully and began cutting the cake into tiny squares, one for every child.

Behind her, Alice cleared her throat with a noise a bit like a billy goat. Tasha couldn't make Alice out. She looked such a dry old stick in her sensible skirts and baggy cardigans, but then you'd see her playing with the little kids like the silliest clown, or you'd talk to her and find that she was listening – really listening, as if you were the most interesting person in the world, which Tasha knew, for certain, she was not. She had to hand it to her on the clothing front too – this aquamarine dress might be a bit old-fashioned but it did look quite nice. Certainly Georg had thought so, doing his usual over-dramatic nonsense about her looking like a mermaid emerging from the waves. Honestly!

'We have a present for you,' Alice said. 'It's not much but, well, I hope you like it.'

She held out a small package, perfectly wrapped in blue silk held with a red ribbon.

'From you?'

'From all of us carers. It's a big birthday, seventeen.'

'If it had happened much sooner, I wouldn't have been here.'

'And that would have been everyone's loss,' Alice replied, then blushed. 'Open it,' she urged.

Tasha felt Marta lean against her on one side and Georg draw close on the other. She took hold of the bow and carefully untied it.

'Pretty,' Marta said, stroking the scarlet ribbon.

'Isn't it, Kotka? We can use it on your pigtails.'

The little girl squealed in delight and Tasha smiled. Marta would never replace Amelia, of course, but caring for her kept her real sister alive in her heart. And kept that heart working. It was like any other muscle, surely, and needed exercise, even if it felt painful at times.

Marta's nut-brown hair was growing so fast in this rich Lake District air that Tasha loved brushing it out into smooth, tangle-free lines and twisting it up into perfect, symmetrical braids either side of her kitten face. Judith, Suzi and the two Italian girls, Miri and Fifi, had started coming to her to have their hair done too and, although none of them had the rich, auburn tresses of her mother, there was something about seeing their stubbly hair growing long and healthy that symbolised so much about this bittersweet year.

Tasha handed Marta the ribbon and turned back to the parcel, unrolling the silk to reveal a shiny buckle.

'It's for my bag!' she exclaimed delightedly.

The buckle on her precious handbag had been slowly working loose since the woman had first tried to take it off her on arrival in Calgarth. She'd been holding it together with string, terrified Lydia's lock of hair would fall out, but now it would be perfect again.

She looked up at Alice. 'That's so clever, Alice. Thank you.'

'Our pleasure. Jock says he'll help you fix it on.'

The gruff sports coach nodded and Tasha tried to thank him too but felt tears collecting dangerously in her throat and had to content herself with a nod.

'Now,' Alice said, as if seeing her discomfort, 'let's have a dance!'

The younger children screamed their approval and went running to clear back tables as Alice drew out her harmonica.

The first time Tasha had heard her play she'd been struck dumb. 'You're really good,' she'd said, and Alice had winked at her, actually winked, and replied, 'You should see me on a piano.'

She was different around music, more relaxed somehow, and as Marie, the statuesque artist, produced a piccolo, and a little lad called Mattias picked out a beat on a triangle, they put together a passable rendition of 'Chattanooga Choo Choo'. Ernst and Moishe leaped up in a silly dance that had everyone howling with laughter and, as Tasha shooed Marta off to join her friends, she felt Georg's arm slide around her shoulders.

'I have a present for you too, my beautiful mermaid.'

'You do?'

'But I'm saving it for later.'

She giggled. Georg was officially her boyfriend now and she had to admit, it felt good.

'Is it a kiss?' she asked, leaning into him.

'There might be a kiss – or two – but, no, it's a proper present. Well, more an outing.'

'An outing? Where?'

'It's a moonlit outing, so you'll have to wait and see.'

Tasha felt a thrill run through her. She glanced again to the door but it was still resolutely shut. Of course it was. Lydia would not be appearing this evening, birthday or no birthday, and she would do well to focus not on who was missing, but on who was here.

'I can't wait,' she said, but then Marta was back, pulling her into the ring for the 'Hokey-Cokey' and, rolling her eyes, she gave in to the birthday nonsense, skipping around in her blue dress as if she'd turned seven not seventeen.

· · ·

Several hours later, however, when she heard a low whistle outside her window, she felt altogether more grown up. Pushing it open, she squeezed through the narrow gap, her skin tingling as Georg's hands went around her waist to help her down.

'Well met by moonlight,' he said in English.

'Sorry?'

'It's Shakespeare. That is, I think he says "ill met" but that wouldn't be right, would it?'

She squinted at him. 'You're quoting English plays now?'

'Why not? They love him here. And that poet too, Wordsworth. What a name for a poet: Words – worth.'

'What?'

He translated into Polish but the joke – if joke it was – lost much in translation and Tasha still didn't get it. It didn't matter though. She had a boyfriend who was quoting plays at her and taking her on moonlight trips and it all felt so deliciously normal. Guilt squirmed into her stomach but she pushed it away.

She'd had a conversation with her mother about this in Auschwitz once.

'When we're out of here,' Lydia had said – it was the way many of their conversations had started in the camp – 'your beautiful hair will grow back and the boys will be queuing up to run their fingers through it.'

'Mama!' she'd protested, squirming.

But Lydia had smiled. 'You won't mind, my sweet, believe me. Love is a gift and you should enjoy it.'

'You have every drop of my love, Mama,' she'd told her.

But Lydia had just smiled and said, 'For now, my sweet, but that will change. *Should* change.'

'I'm trying, Mama,' she whispered to the starry skies and held tight to Georg's hand as he pulled her around the tree-lined mound that separated the houses from the lake.

'Are we going swimming?'

'Much grander than that. Wait here.'

He dropped her hand and, grabbing something from the front pocket of a bulging haversack, crossed the shingle beach to the wooden boathouse. Lifting the lock in his slim fingers, he bent over it in total concentration, then, with a grunt of satisfaction, released it and pulled the door wide open.

'This way, my lady.'

'Georg! Is this allowed?'

'Not as such, but it isn't expressly *disallowed* either. Give me a hand with the boat.'

He grabbed one side of the little craft and, giggling, she helped him pull it out of the boathouse.

'Do you know how to row?'

'Course I do. We had a boating lake near our house when I was a kid. Mama used to take me.'

'She did?'

It was the first Tasha had heard Georg talk about his mother and she was desperate to know more.

'Yeah. She was from fisherfolk out at Gdynia, knew her way around a boat. And she was strong. Once, she let me take one oar while she had the other. My goodness – we went round in circles however hard I pulled. I got so mad!'

'It sounds fun.'

'It was. But then...' He shook himself. 'Doesn't matter. Jump in the boat, birthday girl, and I'll push us out.'

'You'll get wet feet.'

'Hardly the worst thing that's happened to me this year. Jump in!'

There was little to do but obey. Why, Tasha wondered, did every conversation she and Georg have seem to bump up against ruts and boulders in their past? She longed to ask more about his childhood, but didn't dare and, besides, he was pushing them out into the lake and it was far too much fun scrambling for the oars as he jumped in, spraying her with water, to worry about anything other than right now.

'So, księżniczka – princess,' he said, once the boat had settled, 'you lie back and relax and I shall take you wherever the moon dictates.'

He indicated the silvery path opening across the water and Tasha tried to do as he suggested. If anyone had told her as she lay praying for salvation in the dirt and cold of abandoned Auschwitz, last January, that by autumn she'd be on a moonlit picnic on an English lake, she'd have assumed they were dying of some crazy fever.

'Penny for them...?'

'What?'

'It's an English expression – penny for your thoughts.'

'Do you have a penny?'

'No,' he admitted, setting down the oars and lifting the haversack. 'But I do have a picnic...'

'Really?'

She leaned forward, making the boat rock dangerously so that Georg had to grab hold of her to stop her tipping out. He pulled her closer, kissing her long and slow until Tasha might happily have tipped into the lake as long as he came with her. Eventually he pulled away and opened the bag.

'I have bread, cheese, biscuits and even an orange.'

'Delicious!'

'Plus...' He pulled out a bottle. 'Sophie's home-made elder-flower champagne.'

'Georg! Did you steal it?'

'No!'

'Fine – did you liberate it from the unfair confines of the pantry?'

Georg gave her a sly grin. 'You know me too well, Tasha Ancel.'

'What if Sophie notices?'

'She won't. She's made loads. Next year, I promise you, I'll buy you real wine. French stuff. From a proper, posh shop.'

'Next year...?' She raised an eyebrow.

'Yes, next year and the year after that and the year after that and—'

'I get it!'

Goodness, this was just as embarrassing as all those children singing to her! And just as nice.

Georg pulled her onto the bench next to him, his arm warm and strong around her shoulders.

'I'm going to get a good job, Tasha, earn proper money. Two of the boys in my block landed apprenticeships at a textiles factory in Manchester last week. They start in October. Accommodation in a hostel for the first six months and a wage of three pounds a week – an actual wage, Tasha, imagine that.'

Tasha tried but failed. She'd barely seen any coins in the last five years, let alone had a chance to earn them. Jews had been slaves with no right to own anything.

'It sounds good,' she admitted.

'It does. I want that, Tasha.'

'You want work in a textiles factory?'

'Maybe not *that*. I'd prefer machines. Mr Friedmann says they make cars in a place called Birmingham, so maybe I'll go there.'

'And me?'

'You can come with me. A new life, Tasha, together.'

Tasha couldn't stop the niggling thought that she wasn't ready to give up on her old life, but she pushed it away and kissed Georg hard.

'Goodness, Tash,' he said when they surfaced. 'You make me as bubbly inside as this champagne.' He flushed and covered his confusion by toying with the cage around the cork. 'Come on, let's open it up.'

He passed her a metal cup and, with a flourish that sent the boat tipping wildly once more, popped the cork. The buttery liquid frothed up, covering them both as Tasha battled to catch it in the cup, but finally it was full.

'To you, my beautiful, flame-haired mermaid. Happy birthday.'

'Thank you, Georg. This is so lovely.'

'As are you, kochanie. Now – drink!'

Tasha laughed and lifted the cup, feeling the bubbles explode against her lips as the moonlight danced in the sparkling liquid. She'd spent her last birthday cowering beneath the ruins of Warsaw and now here she was, picnicking on a beautiful lake with a wonderful boy.

'Thank you, Georg,' she said. 'I didn't think life could ever be like this again.'

'Worth holding on for, hey?'

She nodded, tears clogging her throat, and bent to her glass for another sip of the delicious liquid.

'Oi, you, what do you think you're doing?!'

The harsh voice ricocheted across the lake like a Nazi whip-crack and, jolting instinctively away, Tasha tipped the drink all down herself.

'What the hell was that?' she demanded, but Georg was already on the floor of the boat, pulling her down, despite being trapped helplessly in the moon's glistening searchlight.

'Looks like the game's up!' he groaned.

On the beach a man was jumping up and down, waving furiously at them. It was Oskar Friedmann, the psychologist, but what was he doing here? And what right did he have to order them in? It made Tasha's blood boil. For a few blissful minutes, life had felt settled, happy, forward-looking, and now he was dragging them back to the world of orders and control. Why did someone always think they could tell them what to do?

'Forget him, Georg,' she said furiously. 'Let's row the other way. What can he do to stop us?'

Georg bit his lip. 'That's Mr Friedmann, Tasha.'

'So?'

'So... I don't know. He's in charge.'

She looked at him, astonished at his unusual caution. 'When did you ever care about that?' she demanded.

'He's the one finding us apprenticeships, Tash.'

'You think you haven't blown that already?'

'I think I'd better do what he says.'

Georg picked up the oars and began rowing, with some speed, back to shore. Furious, Tasha poured more champagne into her glass and drank it fast, barely tasting it in her rush to keep a hold of her birthday treat.

Some treat!

They hit the shingle with a bump and Tasha glared mutinously at Oskar Friedmann as he came running to the boat.

'What on earth do you think you're doing?' he demanded. 'You could have been killed.'

'Hardly,' Tasha retorted. 'It's a great big boat on a flat little lake. And, besides, Georg is from fisher-stock.'

'Tasha, hush.'

Georg seemed curiously cowed before the psychoanalyst as if, she thought furiously, Mr Friedmann's opinion mattered more than hers. It made her mad.

'Honestly,' Mr Friedmann said, handing her roughly out of the boat. 'We've brought you to this lovely place, provided you with all we can to make you feel safe and happy, and you repay us by stealing.'

'We were going to put it back,' Tasha said.

'And the wine too?'

She thrust the bottle behind her back, then, cross with herself for succumbing, brought it out again and took a defiant swig. She was starting to feel more than a little giddy but so what? She was virtually an adult and Georg certainly was, so why on earth was he acting like the little kid Mr Friedmann was treating him as?

'I'm sorry, sir,' he apologised in halting English. 'I wanted to give Tasha a birthday treat.'

'And you didn't think to ask if you could take the boat out?'

'Would you have said yes?'

'Not at midnight I wouldn't. If you'd fallen in, you might have died.'

'We might have died a thousand times in the last few years,' Tasha shot back, 'so forgive us if this didn't feel like much of a risk.'

Oskar Friedmann looked at her and drew in a deep breath. 'A fair point, young lady, but we're not at war any more and if you pair want to be treated like adults you need to behave like them.'

Georg hung his head, Tasha kicked unhappily at a stone. He had a point, she supposed, but did he have to lord it over them quite so gleefully?

'I think you'll find...' she started but then ground to a halt as another figure tumbled onto the beach, a thick dressing gown clutched around a flannelette nightie and greying hair trussed up in a hairnet. 'Alice?'

'What's going on here? Are you all right, Tasha? Georg?'

'We're fine, thank you,' Tasha said. 'We were taking a boat trip for my birthday, but Mr Friedmann doesn't think we're up to it.'

'It *is* rather late,' Alice said, looking uncertainly to Oskar.

'But very bright.'

Tasha indicated the moon and Alice turned her face up to it and smiled.

'That's true. A beautiful evening.'

'Alice!' Mr Friedmann barked. 'That's beside the point. These children took an unauthorised vessel out on the lake.'

'They're hardly children, Oskar. Tasha is seventeen and Georg, whatever he might have told the authorities, is at least eighteen. They are, perhaps, flexing their right to self-determination?'

Tasha felt like cheering. Goodness, Alice really was a curious woman.

Oskar frowned. 'Self-determination is one thing, Alice. Breaking and entering is quite another. We're not here to shelter criminals.'

That got to Georg at last.

'I'm *not* a criminal,' he said indignantly. 'I'm just good with locks.'

'Come on now—' Oskar started.

But Alice cut him off. 'Are you, Georg? They interest you, do they?'

Georg turned eagerly towards her. 'Oh yes. They're so clever, the way each key has a different pattern that opens up a different lock. I think it's fascinating.'

'It is,' Alice agreed. 'There are several world-renowned locksmiths in this country, you know. Perhaps we could find you an apprenticeship with one of them.'

'Really?' Georg's eyes lit up. 'That's a job? A real job? That would be perfect!'

'I'm not sure locksmiths take thieves,' Oscar said repressively.

'Quite right,' Alice agreed. 'You will need to work hard to prove yourself, young man.'

'I will,' Georg agreed. 'I really will. I'm sorry, Mr Friedmann. I didn't have a present for Tasha and I wanted her birthday to be special and this seemed... romantic.'

Mr Friedmann gave a tight smile. 'Romance can be overrated,' he said sharply. 'Tomorrow, Georg, you will scrub the bottom of this boat until it shines.'

'Yes, sir.'

'For now, though, off you go to bed – separately.'

'Sir! I would never—'

But Tasha had had enough of all this apologising. Handing the half-empty wine bottle to Alice with what she hoped was a nod of thanks, she stalked off up the path. Georg ran after her.

'Sorry, Tasha.' He spoke Polish now, trying to appease her.

'It wasn't your fault.' She meant that, but she'd had enough of today and she reached her door with relief. 'Goodnight, Georg. And thank you.'

'Tash...'

'Goodnight.'

She kissed him and tumbled into her room, leaning back against the door, thankful to be alone. Her head was spinning and she was desperate to sleep. If she was really lucky, she might dream of being seven again, blowing out the candles on a cake made by her mother, surrounded by easy love and care, with none of the tangles of being a nearly-adult orphan stranded on an English lake.

'I'm not an orphan,' she said fiercely, then threw herself onto her crisp, white bed and cried herself to sleep.

ELEVEN

FELDAFING, BAVARIA | 23 SEPTEMBER 1945

LYDIA

Lydia sucked Bavarian air into her ailing lungs, tasting pine, fresh water and oxygen with every breath. She looked out across Lake Starnberg, mirror-still on this special September day, and tried to revel in the hills beyond. In the sky above the highest peak, an eagle swooped, reclaiming, perhaps, the heights that Hitler had seized for his mountain lair. The world was slowly righting itself, but Lydia's little part of it still felt horribly skewed. Today was her daughter's seventeenth birthday but she had no idea where she might be spending it, or if she'd made it to seventeen at all. It was so desperately, infuriatingly sad.

What was the point in her lungs mending if they couldn't draw in the same air as Tasha?

What was the point in looking on God's beauty if Tasha could not see it too?

And what was the point of standing up and fighting to be alive if she stood up without Tasha?

'Because,' she reminded herself sternly, 'you *will* find her.'

Will, however, had less to do with it than bureaucracy.

Food, the Allied forces could manage, with the help of thousands of German POWs to bring in Europe's harvest. Beds, they could cobble together; medicines, they could fly in; but documents... They were as rare as diamonds, and just as precious.

Lydia had been transferred to a 'displaced persons' camp at Feldafing, south of Munich, a week ago, when she'd finally been well enough to walk unaided. It was the first all-Jewish DP camp, created because of the many instances of violence against Jews in the general camps. The Nazis weren't the only ones who hated God's people, it seemed, but in Feldafing they were safe. And the odds of finding family here were, surely, increased?

'We'll meet—' she'd cried to her daughter that terrible day when she'd been ripped from her in Auschwitz, but then she'd hesitated, unsure where to specify, and had been swept forward with everyone else, their potential meeting place yet another victim of Nazi cruelty. Now, somehow, she had to pray she'd find a clue to her daughter's whereabouts and here seemed as good a place to start as any.

There were over four hundred youngsters in the sprawling forest camp and on her first days, she'd scoured them all, eager for a beacon of red hair, but found nothing more than a tawny-haired boy and two ginger twins. It was, sadly, little surprise. Mrs Leibowitz, the efficient camp administrator, had told her there were more than three hundred displaced persons' camps between here and Denmark, so the chances of Natasha being in this one had been small.

Even so, you had to take every chance you could get.

That's why Lydia was now standing in a long line to talk to the representatives from the newly established UNRRA Child Search Team, who'd set up their stall at the lakeside. There were three of them, all middle-aged American women with tweed suits, pearls, and leather-bound notebooks but, she suspected from the disheartened faces of those who made it to the front, little idea of how to go about the gargantuan task of finding any of the forty thousand lost people roaming Europe.

Lydia gritted her teeth and prayed for patience as she edged slowly forward, trying to hold in her wretched coughs. She'd be fully convalesced by the time it was her turn, she thought ironically, but at last she was ushered into the tent. One of the women introduced herself with a kind smile as Mrs Barrington and took down Lydia's name in her book.

'And you are looking for?'

'My daughter, Natasha Ancel.'

'Last seen?'

'In Auschwitz.' Images crowded in of snow and ice, of blood and dogs and a press of impossible fear. Lydia looked back to the calm blue lake behind to steady herself and wondered what Tasha was looking at right now. She tried to picture her somewhere as pretty as this and that gave her the strength to carry on. 'I was marched out to Wodzisław and she was left behind because they deemed her a child.'

'How old is she?'

'Sixteen. That is – seventeen. She turns seventeen today. If she's still...' She caught herself. 'She's seventeen,' she said firmly.

'And she was left in Auschwitz?'

'Yes. The bastards shut the children in and, I assume, left them there.' Lydia leaned over the desk and grabbed at the woman's arm. 'Were there children in the camp, when it was liberated, Mrs Barrington?'

The woman flinched back, clutching at her pearls. 'I don't know.'

'You don't know?! You're the Child Search Team.'

'Yes, but we're very new. And children were left in many, many places.'

'But this was Auschwitz. It was vast. There must be records.'

Mrs Barrington gave her a tissue and a patronising smile. 'I'm sure there will be, and as soon as we get a chance to access them, we will obviously be in touch.'

'When might that be?'

'I'm afraid, I...'

'Don't know,' Lydia finished dully. 'And in the meantime, what do I do?'

'You wait,' she said. 'I'm sure the rest will do you good, my dear, and don't worry, you'll be safe here in Feldafing.'

'Safe?!' Lydia threw her arms up in fury. 'As if I care about safe! Do you have children, Mrs Barrington?'

'I do,' she said primly. 'My daughter is working with UNRRA in Frankfurt and my son fought at Omaha. Many died there.'

'And we are very grateful,' Lydia said, because that was clearly what was expected of her. 'But imagine, if you can, what you would feel like if he had been lost on that beach, if you had no idea where he was, or who he was with, or if he was even alive. Would you just wait, Mrs Barrington?'

Mrs Barrington picked at the edge of her notebook, then looked up at Lydia with sudden steel. 'I would not, Mrs Ancel. I would move heaven and earth to find him.'

Lydia nodded. 'Me too,' she said softly.

But heaven and earth were so vast and she had no idea which parts of them to move first, if she could even find the breath to do so. Turning sadly away, she went back to the lake.

'I'm here, Tasha,' she said to the pretty skies mirrored in the blue waters. 'I'm here and I'll find you. Wherever you are, I'll find you.'

TWELVE

ALICE

Alice poured her heart into her harmonica. It might only be 'Twinkle, Twinkle Little Star' but playing the precious instrument always soothed her. Closing her eyes, she pictured her brother's excited face as he'd handed her the present back in 1938. She'd had another letter yesterday from one of the many organisations she'd written to, offering polite sympathy but no news. The organisation would keep her name and address on record, they'd assured her, so that if Max turned up, he would be able to find her. They all said that and the thought of her contact details on boards across many European cities was something. On a deep in-breath, Alice drew out the final notes of the nursery rhyme as if the twinkling star might, somehow, call her brother to her.

'More!' Miri and Fifi cried in English when she finished. 'Play more, Alice.'

Alice smiled. The easy pleasure of the smaller children was soothing too. She'd found it very hard to sleep last night after the altercation by the lake and her mind felt fogged. She'd heard the whole argument as she'd hurried down the path and Tasha's furious words had gone round and round in her head: 'We might have died a thousand times in the last few years, so forgive us if this didn't feel like that much of a risk.'

She'd had a good point. Alice had heard noises and been on her way to investigate, but had paused on the knoll overlooking the lake when she'd seen the pair happily bobbing around together in the silver of the moon. She couldn't help but be cross with Oskar for interrupting them and had felt compelled to go down and speak up on their behalf. He'd been afraid for their safety, she saw that, but them drowning hadn't been very likely. Now they were embarrassed and angry and that seemed every bit as dangerous to Alice.

Even so, Oskar must be furious and she was annoyed at how much that bothered her. Anna Freud was arriving for a visit today and she was scared that he would complain and Anna would be disappointed. Alice was too soft, that was the problem. Oskar was absolutely right that the kids needed discipline as well as love, but they'd had so much of the former and so little of the latter that it was very hard to deprive them of anything.

Tasha had slunk off somewhere this morning and Marta, deprived of her company, slid onto Alice's lap as Sophie led the children in another rhyme. All the younger children sang happily and, in the corner, the tinies were playing their usual self-absorbed games. Those six weren't making much progress in terms of language, or socialisation with the other children, but they were clean and safe and that, surely, was a good start.

Breathing in the sweet smell of Marta's soft hair, Alice wondered what it might have been like to have children of her own. To have had a house and a husband and babies born of her womb that she could bring up her way.

And who might have been stolen from her by the Nazis.

She shook her head again. Why did her brain forever steal down dark paths, even in the sunny uplands of the Lake

District? There were a million might-have-beens haunting their little camp and they had to build a strong, loving present to keep them at bay. If the children could do that, surely Alice could too? Lifting her harmonica again, she played 'Edelweiss' – a song of simple joys with a melody so sweet that even the tinies came tottering over to listen.

'Bravo!'

Alice came out of the reverie of the song to see Anna Freud standing in the doorway, clapping heartily. Behind her stood Oskar. He was also clapping but he avoided her eye and her heart sank.

'Marvellous music,' said Anna, as she swept into the room, gathering children around her skirts as others might dust.

Sinking down to the floor with an enviable ease in her fifty-year-old knees, she started chattering away to them in a relaxed mix of German and English. Even Marta slid off Alice's knee to join the crowd around the psychoanalyst, and Alice got up awkwardly, feeling defenceless without her. Oskar hovered in the doorway and Alice wanted to go and talk to him but found herself, instead, edging over to Sophie.

'They flock to her,' she said, indicating Anna.

'She has an inspiring energy,' Sophie agreed. 'But she lacks your staying power.'

'Sorry?' Alice squinted at her friend.

'Anna comes and goes. She's caring, yes, but first and fore-most she's a scientist. Like Oskar. They're interested in the general study of children's minds, not the specifics of these actual children. That's *your* speciality.'

'It is?'

'Absolutely. You see the individual in every child. I admire it constantly.'

Alice batted self-consciously at her friend's arm. 'Enough, Soph.'

Sophie laughed. 'I tell you, Alice Goldberger, you've landed in the right country because you're as diffident as any Englishwoman!'

Alice squinted at her, unsure whether to be touched or offended, but already Anna was getting up and coming over.

'Alice!' She kissed her on each cheek. 'Lovely to see you. Might I trouble you to give me a tour of this lovely place?'

'Me?'

'Yes please.'

Alice's heart sank again. Oskar had clearly told Anna about her disrupting his authority last night and she was going to get a talking-to.

'It would be my pleasure,' she agreed tightly and, to a clamour of disappointment from the children, led Anna from the room.

'They seem very happy,' Anna said conversationally as they stepped outside.

It was a crisp, bright day. From what Alice had gathered talking to the locals, they'd been blessed with an unusually good summer and the luck was holding into autumn. There had been very little of the rain that presumably supplied the lakes characterising this beautiful part of the world and Alice liked to think God was giving them every help He could to recover. Quite why He had not stopped the Nazis sooner, Alice didn't like to think about too closely, but was it His fault if man messed up His creation so consummately? Isn't that what free will was all about, like Tasha and Georg having the right to take a boat out at night?

Alice looked uncomfortably to Oskar, who was hovering behind.

'Don't worry, Oskar,' Anna said. 'I know you have much to do and Alice and I will be fine just the two of us.'

Oskar's eyes narrowed slightly but he had little choice and, with a tight nod, he turned towards his office, leaving them to go on alone. Anna tucked a hand into Alice's arm and smiled at her, but it did little to calm her nerves. Her boss was, surely, softening her up for a 'chat' about her suitability for looking after these children, especially the older ones.

'What a place,' Anna said, waving around the Calgarth Estate. 'It's perfect.'

Alice nodded agreement. Beneath an oak tree in the middle of the lawn, a group of kids were having a lesson with Marie Paneth, debating something in a tumble of languages. On the sports field, two teams were playing a boisterous game of football with Jock Lawrence, and near the family houses, some children were sitting around a local woman who'd agreed to teach them mathematics.

'They're enjoying learning?' Anna asked.

'Mainly,' Alice agreed. 'Their concentration span isn't high and attendance can be... sporadic. But they're very aware of all they've missed and we've tried to be patient and let them come to lessons in their own time.'

'Very wise, Alice.'

'It is?'

'Of course. I imagine that any attempt to force these young people will be met with the utmost resistance.'

'That's true,' Alice agreed, thinking of Tasha bristling with rage at being made to come off the lake.

'Free will and self-determination are vital,' Anna went on.

Recognising her own words from last night, Alice braced herself for a reprimand.

Her boss, however, simply said, 'Which way to the water? I can hardly come to the famous Lake District without seeing an actual lake, can I?'

Alice turned them down the track, wondering why Anna was dragging this out. It was probably some psychologist's game but, frankly, she wasn't up to playing it. Swallowing a giant lump in her throat, she said, 'I assume Oskar has spoken to you about last night?'

'Last night?' Anna looked at her in surprise. 'Not that I recall. Did something happen?'

Alice avoided her eyes. 'Erm...'

'Alice?'

'Nothing bad. We just caught two of our older children out on the lake in a boat.'

Anna laughed. 'A moonlit boat trip? Hardly wicked. We all did a bit of that in our youth, didn't we?'

Alice had never had an assignation as romantic as the one she'd witnessed from the knoll last night, but she forced out a laugh as if, like her attractive boss, she'd been inundated with such offers. It sounded horribly false but Anna didn't seem to notice.

'Is that our courting couple?'

They'd reached the lakeside and Anna pointed along the beach to where Georg was scrubbing the boat as Oskar had instructed, Tasha working hard alongside him. Alice nodded.

'Then let's go and say hello.' She strode over. 'Good morning. That looks hard work.'

The youngsters looked up, Georg openly smiling, Tasha, as ever, more guarded.

'Punishment,' Georg told her easily. 'For an illicit trip.'

'It seems apt,' Anna said lightly. 'And you're doing a very good job.'

'It's better than mathematics,' Georg said with a grin.

Tasha went on scrubbing.

'It's good of you to help Georg,' Alice said to her.

'Why?' The girl looked up, her eyes flashing ice blue beneath her fiery hair. 'Don't you think girls can work, Alice?'

'I didn't say that.'

'Because we worked in the camps. We worked very hard. We had to.'

'I know that,' Alice said as calmly as she could manage. She could feel Anna's eyes on her and hated it. She was at ease with the younger children but these teenagers with their fiercely protected hurts and their aggressive independence left her stranded. 'I simply meant that the trip was, I imagine, Georg's idea, so it is good of you to share his punishment.'

'It's only fair. Anyway, I like doing things with my hands. We aren't all satisfied sitting around singing nursery rhymes.'

Alice stepped back, stung, but to her surprise Anna faced Tasha down.

'You say you like to be fair – Tasha, is it?'

Tasha nodded.

'Interesting, because I don't think you're being very fair to Alice.'

Tasha blinked, surprised.

'Let me tell you about her,' Anna went on, switching easily into German to be more clearly understood.

'I don't think that's a good idea,' Alice squeaked.

Anna ignored her. 'Alice trained as a youth-worker and, in the years after the first war, she became the head of a state-run shelter for disadvantaged children and their families. Germany was in a mess then. I don't expect you to feel sorry for them, but perhaps spare a thought for the thousands of families who were trapped in abject poverty. Alice certainly did. Her work saved many from misery, but when Hitler came to power, being Jewish – like yourselves – she was forced out of her post. For several years she worked with the children of the Jewish community in Berlin as they were increasingly oppressed by the Nazis, but in the end, at great personal risk, she was persuaded to emigrate to England.'

'At least she got out,' Tasha muttered.

'She was lucky,' Anna agreed, 'but the instant she arrived in England she was interned as an enemy alien and put into a camp. She wasn't allowed to bring her family over—'

'Family?'

Tasha looked at Alice, who avoided her eyes. She wasn't

ready to talk about her brother with anyone, least of all this bolshy young woman.

'And she was trapped,' Anna pushed on. 'Did she let that get to her? No! On her own initiative, she set up a kindergarten for the children of the internees – a kindergarten so impressive that it attracted the attention of the local press and, by a round-about route, myself. I fought to get her released as I knew she was the perfect woman to run one of my War Nurseries, and I was right. Alice is the kindest, most generous and hardest-working person I know. Don't let her soft exterior fool you – under that is a relentless, iron will.'

'I don't know about that,' Alice protested.

Anna shook her head. 'Just take the praise, Alice. It's deserved. As,' she said, looking back at Tasha, 'is our admiration and respect.'

Tasha stared. 'I didn't know all that,' she said to Alice. 'It sounds tough.'

Alice swallowed. 'Not as tough as you had it.'

'But still tough.'

'Still tough,' Alice agreed, feeling ridiculously tearful. Really, she must make sure she got some sleep tonight.

'But we're here now, in Windermere,' Anna said, falling back into English. 'So let's look to a happier future.'

'Hear hear!' Georg agreed.

Anna laughed. 'You sound like a native, Georg.'

'I hope so. I'm going to get an apprenticeship, aren't I, Alice?'

'Hopefully, Georg.'

'And then I will be able to look after Tasha and she won't have to do any work ever again.'

'I can look after myself, thank you,' Tasha objected, but she was smiling dopily at the young man.

Alice remembered them, silvered on the lake last night, and marvelled that love had found its way into their bruised hearts.

The young, it seemed, healed fast, but it would be a long road yet and she prayed they could make it together.

'Don't scrub too long,' Anna said lightly. 'That boat looks clean to me and I'm sure there are things you'd rather be doing.'

'Certainly are, ma'am,' Georg agreed with a wink and, as Tasha splutteringly hushed him, Anna led Alice tactfully away.

'Quite the pair.'

'They're two of our... stronger-willed children.'

'So I see. And barely children at all.'

Alice shook her head. 'Young adults really. I find them harder to deal with,' she admitted.

'Don't we all?' Anna took her arm again. 'Give them a little of yourself, Alice.'

'Sorry?'

'They're learning to empathise, to watch others and decide how they wish to form themselves. Some of that is superficial – their clothes, hair, speech – but they're also working out core values and behaviours. They need to know about their role models to figure all that out.'

Alice laughed. 'I'm no role model for Tasha Ancel.'

'I think you'll find you are. Now, it must be time for luncheon and it's been an age since I had one of Sophie's delicious meals. Let's go!'

She bounded back towards Calgarth, with Alice following dazedly behind.

Sophie and her team had pulled out all the stops with a corned beef hash, broccoli fresh from their kitchen garden, and fluffy cheese scones made by her team of nursery-rhyme singers. They were a bit wonky and had faces poked into them, but they were smiling faces and added to the fun of the meal. The three hundred children ate noisily but with none of the frantic possessiveness of their first week here in Calgarth, and Anna, seated between Alice and Oskar, seemed impressed.

Afterwards she sat on as the children filed out to their afternoon pursuits and Sophie fetched coffee to go with the choco-lates their visitor had brought from London – a rare treat. Not that Alice could quite face them because it looked as if, finally, Anna was preparing for a serious conversation.

'I have some news,' she said.

Alice glanced to Oskar but he returned her look with a surprised grimace that had her daring to hope he wasn't holding a grudge for last night.

'As you know,' Anna went on, 'the Dann sisters were looking at setting up a nursery near London.'

They both nodded.

'Well, they now have a property and some funding so will be opening in the next few weeks.'

She paused, and Alice muttered, 'Lovely,' trying to work out why this mattered.

Anna cleared her throat. 'And what we'd like to do, what we think would be best, is to take the six infants there.'

Alice gasped. '*Our* six infants?'

'The six who are currently living here,' Anna corrected gently. 'Yes. As you are aware, it's rather big and noisy for them to truly develop here. Bulldogs Bank is a smaller, more intimate environment.'

'Bulldogs Bank?'

'It's the name of the house. It's very nice. Peaceful.'

'Close to London?' Oskar asked.

'Yes. Which might help us find them adoptive families.'

'And to study them in the meantime?' he challenged.

Anna drew herself up. 'Correct. This is a unique opportu-nity to study children who have been raised without any direct adult influence.'

'I'm aware of that. I have been making a number of notes myself.'

'Which I would love to discuss with you. And you are, of course, very welcome at any time.'

'Because it's a such short hop to London from here...'

Alice looked from one psychoanalyst to another, fascinated by the barely reined-in spat between them.

'And because all the children will be moving on in the next few months,' Anna countered.

Oskar sighed. 'You're right. And the tinies do need their own place. It's simply that they've become a part of the set-up here, so we'll be sad to see them go, won't we, Alice?'

'We will,' Alice agreed.

'It doesn't do to get too attached to your charges,' Anna said gently.

Alice picked at her chocolate. She knew that, of course she did, it was a core rule of all training for work with children, but that didn't mean it was an easy one to follow.

Later, when Anna had gone for her train south, the younger ones had been put to bed, and the older ones were chatting in the common room, Alice set to tidying toys in the storeroom. She was arranging building blocks – a curiously satisfying pursuit – when there was a knock on the door.

'Only me,' Oskar said. 'Do you have a minute?'

'Of course.' Alice straightened self-consciously as he came into the little room.

'Interesting visit from Anna,' he said.

'Interesting,' she agreed cautiously. 'I'll be sad to lose the tinies.'

'Me too. Fascinating case study – which Anna will now claim for herself.'

'As long as they're well looked after...'

He laughed. 'You're a good woman, Alice Goldberger.'

'Not really. I'm just not as clever as you proper psycho-analysts.'

'That's not true. You may not have as much training, but

you have an intuitive intelligence.'

Alice tugged at her cardigan. It was very hot in here. She picked up a toy sword and then, feeling unnecessarily aggressive, put it hastily back down again.

'Not with teenagers,' she said.

'Definitely with teenagers. You were right. Last night, I mean. I, er, wanted to say that. I was worried and that made me angry. You were much calmer. It was impressive.'

'It was?'

She was blushing, she knew, and clearly Oskar could see it too for he reached out and touched a soft fingertip to her cheek.

'Don't underestimate yourself, Alice.'

Suddenly, breathing felt a challenge.

'No,' she stuttered. 'That is, I'll try not to.'

'Good.'

There was a pause. She fought for something intelligent to say but her brain had turned to English custard. Oskar looked around the tight space and gave a little laugh. 'Look at us, doing business in a toy cupboard! We really must get some better facilities, mustn't we?'

'We must,' Alice agreed weakly.

'Well then. Goodnight, Alice.'

'Good night, Oskar.'

And then he was gone and Alice was alone. Sinking shakily to the floor, she grabbed a toy dog, buried her face in its soft back, and waited for her heartbeat to return to normal. What did he want from her? She'd had little to do with men since those awkward waltzes with Heinz thirty years ago and had no idea how to interpret his conversation, or how to tailor her own. He'd told her he was separated from his wife, but did that mean he was seeking a new one? It was most confusing. She thought she'd come to the Lake District to help sort out three hundred troubled children, but it seemed they weren't the only ones with a road to travel and, goodness, the journey wasn't easy.

THIRTEEN

TASHA

Tasha fastened the new buckle and looked with pride at her handbag. Jock had fixed the clasp and also strengthened the strap attachments so that it was completely secure. He'd even rubbed wax into the leather so that it gleamed like new. No – *almost* like new. There were still a few marks and Tasha liked them. She had no idea who'd once owned this bag and only dark likelihood to tell her where they'd gone, but she hoped a bit of them lived on in this bag, carrying the memento of her mother.

Tasha bit at her lip to hold back tears and undid the buckle again to take out the lock of Lydia's hair. She had a small box to keep it in these days but, even so, it was horribly matted. A couple of times, she'd tried to comb it out but that always resulted in shedding far too many of the precious hairs and she'd felt, foolishly she knew, as if every one lost diminished the chance of Lydia finding her again.

Lifting the lock up against her face, Tasha looked in the mirror and was horrified to see how faded and pale it was against her vibrant hair. Hers was nearly to her chin now and was growing back far stronger and thicker than before. There was probably a lesson in that, the sort of brimmingly optimistic sign that Georg was always going on about, but Tasha didn't want to see it. She just wanted her mother here, at her side to hug her and tease her, and tell her what they were going to do next.

Putting the hair reluctantly back in the box, Tasha went to the window. It was a dull day, heavy clouds hanging low over hills which were turning red, orange and brown as the increasing cold nipped at their stems. Tasha shivered. The last time the leaves had fallen, her tata had been shot amongst them and it was hard not to see blood in the rich colours. For her, Wondermere did not look so wonderful today and it felt as if their idyll was falling away with the leaves. People were leaving. Calgarth had always been intended to be transitory – a jumping-off point for a new life – but Tasha still hated seeing people moving on.

The six tinies had gone to some baby-house in London and now the older ones were heading off, many to hostels in Manchester, Liverpool and other big cities to work in factories. The kids, most of them boys, seemed so eager to get to work, earn a wage, and become a 'grown-up'. Tasha knew she should want that too, but she still felt as if a chunk of her childhood was missing and couldn't find it in herself to be an adult yet.

Last week a busload of eager volunteers had left for Israel, their travel arranged by a Zionist society from Manchester. The UN were working to partition Palestine in order to recreate an Israeli state for the tormented Jews and a number of young men from the society had toured Calgarth for weeks, ardently trying to recruit everyone to 'go home'. Many had answered the call but Tasha had always thought of herself as Polish first and Jewish second and the Holy Land felt no more like home than the Lake District. She supposed it was good that the world was creating a land for Jews after all they'd been through, but a life of rites and rituals was not for Tasha and she'd waved them off without regret.

But that still left the question of where she was going to go.

Alice had told her the other day that the plan was for everyone to have a home of their own before winter, but she hadn't sounded happy about it and it had crossed Tasha's mind that she didn't have a home either. She wasn't married, had no children and was so old that her parents were surely long dead. Miss Freud had mentioned her family but the only clue to that was a picture in a simple wooden frame on the side in her room.

Tasha had seen it when she'd heard crying in the night and gone to investigate. Alice's door had been open, light spilling into the corridor, and she'd crept along to see Marta sitting on Alice's bed, weeping pitifully. Alice had been stroking her hair and saying, 'There, there, liebchen, it was just a nasty dream,' and Tasha had wondered, guiltily, how often Marta got up like this. In the day she usually came to Tasha if she was upset, so she'd wondered why she chose Alice at night. But then Alice had said, 'Maybe something sweet will chase the nightmares away?' and Marta had nodded eagerly and reached for the toy donkey sitting incongruously on the bedside table. Alice had held it steady and, to Tasha's surprise, Marta had lifted the tail, revealing a secret compartment full of bonbons beneath the saddle.

Taking one, Marta had sucked on it happily and as Alice had stroked her sleepy head, she'd gazed over to her bedside table with a look of such sadness that Tasha had crept closer and seen the photograph. It was of a pretty woman with a young girl on her lap, a dark-haired man standing protectively over them, looking so like Alice that he must surely be her brother. Tasha had stared, fascinated by this glimpse into the private life of the self-contained woman, and it was only Alice saying to Marta, 'We'd better get you back to bed, liebchen,' that had sent her scurrying to her room. But she hadn't forgotten the despairing look on Alice's face. Even their carer, it seemed, had sorrows to bear.

'Tasha! Tasha, over here!'

She was pulled from her reverie by the sight of Georg tearing across the grass, waving his arms and smiling from ear to ear.

'Come outside, kochanie! I've got something wonderful to tell you.'

He was waving a letter and Tasha's heart leapt. Had he got news of Lydia? No. Why would Georg have news of her mother? Someone in his family, perhaps? That would show him people could still be found. That would show him she wasn't stupid to keep hoping. Pushing the box of Lydia's hair into her bag, she fumbled the new buckle shut and ran out to see him.

'What is it, Georg?'

'A letter. From Hobbs, Hart and Co Ltd.'

Tasha squinted at him, confused. 'Who are they?'

He puffed his chest out.

'Master locksmiths. From London. Right in the middle, Oskar says, of a street called Cheapside. He says you can see St Paul's Cathedral from the door of the factory!'

'See what?'

'St Paul's Cathedral. That building Marie showed us in our "culture" lesson the other day.'

Tasha rolled her eyes. 'She showed us a lot of buildings.'

'And most of them in London. It's the place to be, Tasha, and these locksmiths – Hobbs, Hart – they want to interview me for an apprenticeship. Isn't that just the best?'

His eyes were shining and Tasha tried very hard not to be her usual grumpy self.

'It's fantastic, Georg. Just what you wanted.'

'It is. Oskar sorted it all for me.'

'Oskar did?' She stared at him, astonished. 'You remember whose idea it was, Georg?' It was clear he didn't and she tutted.

'It was Alice's idea, that night with the boat, when all Oskar was doing was shouting at us like little kids for breaking into the boathouse. Alice, though, Alice didn't care about the "crime", she simply saw that you liked locks.'

'Maybe she did mention it,' Georg agreed.

'Maybe?!' Tasha felt fury, always simmering below her skin, rise up inside her. 'It was all her idea.'

'Fine!' Georg put up his hands. 'If you say so. It was a good idea and I'll thank her when I see her.'

'Good.'

'But it was Oskar who sorted it out. He knows someone who's the grandson of Hart. Or is it Hobbs? Anyway, he's related to one of them and running the company. So, he talked to them and they offered me an apprenticeship. It's all about who you know, Tasha.'

'It's all about knowing yourself,' she shot back. 'Or those you care for. Without Alice you'd be off to some anonymous textile mill with the others.'

'Instead of which, Oskar is taking me to London on the train. This afternoon. We're going to stay in the Jewish Shelter and we're going to have dinner in his club.'

'What's a club?'

'A fancy building where businessmen get together and...' He searched his mind for the word and produced it like a magic trick: 'fraternise.'

'What about businesswomen?' she asked.

He laughed uproariously.

'What's so funny?'

His laughter stopped. 'You're serious?'

'There are women running businesses – shops and nurseries and galleries and—'

'Those aren't businesses.'

'They make money.'

'But they're small. Private industries. I'm talking about *real* business – big companies that make things happen.'

'And that has to be done by men, does it?'

'Of course.'

'Because...?'

He floundered, but then lifted a triumphant hand. 'Babies!'

'Sorry?'

'Women have babies.'

'And that means they can't run businesses?'

'Well, yes. You can't take babies into an office, can you?'

Tasha could feel herself twitching with indignation and Georg must have seen it too, for he put his hands on her shoulders to steady her.

'I'm not saying women aren't brilliant, Tash. They are. Smart and brave and clever. And beautiful too. My mother was fantastic. Well, mainly she was, but... But that's not the point. The point is, that women have babies and that's the most impressive thing in the world. It's a miracle. An act of creation. The whole purpose of a species. Right?'

'Right,' Tasha agreed reluctantly.

'So, you do that and us humble men, we're here to care for you and protect you and make sure the world works well to keep you safe.'

Tasha thought about this. It sounded good, generous even, but there was a flaw.

'And you have to do that in men-only "clubs"?'

'They just...' He thought again, clearly seeking more Oskar-wisdom, 'oil the wheels of business.'

'Men's business?'

'Exactly!'

'Real business?'

'Yes,' he agreed, but uneasily and rightly so too.

Tasha looked him up and down, fighting to try to stay calm and logical, though her every fibre was bristling with indignation. Her father had gone out to court to hold fancy arguments and her mother had run a shop selling dresses, warm coats and comfortable undergarments. She knew which one had felt more 'real' to her.

'Without shops,' she said, with careful control, 'we would all be naked, hungry and cultureless.'

Georg ground his teeth. 'I know that. I'm not denying that we need shops, I'm just saying its different to the high-level stuff. The big money, the politics, the—'

'Lock factories?'

He glared at her. 'Everything has to be an argument with you, doesn't it, Natasha? Everything has to be a point to make and your point always has to win.'

'Only when I'm right.'

'Which – in your opinion – is all the time.'

'Georg...'

'I came here to find you because I was happy. I'd had good news about a future that excites me and I wanted to share it with you. I wanted you to be happy too, but you can't be, can you? You can't be happy for me. It all has to be about you.'

'That's not true.'

'Isn't it?' He let go of her shoulders and stepped back. 'Think about that, Tasha. I'm off to London for the biggest inter-view of my life. I'll see you when I get back, tell you how it went. If you're interested.'

'Georg...' He'd turned away and Tasha ran after him, seizing his arm. 'Georg, I *am* happy for you, really I am. But—'

'Always a but,' he said, shaking his head. 'See you around, Tasha.'

'Georg...'

But he was gone, off across the grass to his room. Tasha saw him pause as Alice came out of the kitchens. She was holding a letter and looked distracted, unhappy even, but Tasha saw her shake that off as Georg bounded up and listen to him with intent nods and a kind pat on his arm. Tasha was glad he'd thanked her but furious he'd forgotten her kind cleverness in all his fancy male grandeur. 'It all has to be about you,' he'd thrown at her but he was just as bad. Well fine, let him go to fancy London for his fancy job and fancy club. She didn't need him anyway. She didn't need anyone.

Except Mama, a voice said in her head but she pushed it away and, alive with fury, turned and ran from the estate.

'Tasha!' someone called.

She glanced back but it was only Alice so, picking up her annoying, restricting skirt, she ran again.

FOURTEEN

ALICE

Alice laboured up the hill, cursing her ageing legs. She really should have taken the chance to do more hiking while in this beautiful area, but she'd been so busy organising the children and trying to locate their families that there'd been little time for romping around the countryside. She cast around for any sign of Tasha. The girl had raced off with a face like thunder and every limb an angry line. Alice knew how that felt, especially right now.

Fumbling at the letter in her pocket, Alice sank onto a nearby boulder, her legs weak with more than simply exertion as she was poignantly taken back to childhood holidays in the Tyrol. Her parents had been stolid, determined climbers, focused on the end-goal of a mountaintop somewhere far ahead. They'd left her and Max to their own devices and, glad to be free of the usual restraints of hard work and good behaviour, they'd run wild, tracing a merry path between flowers, streams and animal-sightings. If she squinted into the low sun, Alice could almost see the pair of them, laughing and calling to each other, alive with the joys of the abundant nature around them.

Alice's heart squeezed, trying to expand with love for her brother but being constricted by an iron band of fear about what had happened to him. Blinking back tears, she drew out the letter and read it again. The Red Cross had turned up new records of shipments from Theresienstadt to Auschwitz, and Max's name was there – Lilli and Ruthie's too. They'd almost made it through but it seemed that, with the Russians driving the German armies back, Max had been shipped to Auschwitz on 29 September 1944, Lilli and Ruth-Gertrud following him on 4 October. Their names were clear on the Theresienstadt exit list, but, again, the trail ended there.

Alice feared what that meant. She'd seen the newsreels, she'd read the articles, she'd pored over the ever-emerging statistics about the horrific German extermination plans. If her only remaining family's names did not appear on the Auschwitz lists, they had not made it into the camp. And if they had not made it into the camp, they had only gone one way – up the chimney. Alice knew that, but still she could not *feel* it. Her brain told her they were dead but her heart fought that iron band with every single beat and she had to find out more. Lists must surely be missing from that hateful camp, just as they were from everywhere else.

Alice squeezed her eyes shut against the sorrow but, as a soft autumn breeze caressed her face, she drew in a deep breath, opened them again and let the tears flow. Up here she was alone, free from the prying eyes of children, colleagues, or even Sophie, her dear, kind friend but also a Catholic woman, able to understand the fate of the Jews with the compassion of a human but not the gut-wrenching fear of a fellow victim. For once here, on an English hillside, she could stop worrying about everyone else, be herself, Alice – sister and auntie – and just grieve.

'Alice?'

She wiped furiously at her eyes as, in a flurry of flying leaves, Tasha came tumbling down through the heather to land at her side.

'Alice! What are you doing up here?'

'Looking for you,' Alice said, determinedly not looking at her.

'Why?' Tasha leaned forward, peering at her, and lapsed into German. 'Are you crying?'

Her voice was so incredulous that it made Alice wonder what the children in her care thought of her. Was she too distant? She remembered Anna counselling her to share a little of herself with her older charges, but it was hard. What if you released 'a little' and then you couldn't stop it all tumbling out? The last thing these poor children needed was her worries on top of their own.

As if to prove her point, Tasha's hands flew to her mouth.

'It's not Mama, is it? Have you heard something? Is that why you're looking for me?'

'No! Goodness no, sorry. I mean, I haven't heard anything either way. Which is good news, isn't it? I mean, we're getting more lists of the dead. That's to say...' Help, she was making a meal of this!

Tasha, however, let out a sharp laugh. 'That's my sort of optimism, Alice!'

Alice shook her head and dared to look at her young charge. Her auburn hair was whipping around her head in the rising wind and her eyes were almost translucently blue and as red-rimmed as she knew hers were.

'What's wrong, Tasha?'

Instantly the girl clammed up, pulling her knees to her chest and staring out across the blue water below them.

'Is it Georg?'

'Georg! Pah.'

It was then.

'You've fallen out?' Alice asked tentatively.

'We very rarely fall *in*,' came the terse reply. 'He's off to London, you know, to an interview with some locksmiths with a silly name.'

'Hobbs, Hart. Yes, I know. That's good, isn't it?'

'It's very good. It was a genius idea.'

'Well, I don't know about—'

'*Your* genius idea, Alice. But do you know who that ignorant boy is crediting? Mr Friedmann. Mr kretyn Friedmann, who was far too busy calling him a criminal to show an actual interest in him.'

'He was worried—'

'But because Mr kretyn Friedmann has "contacts" and "a club" and a great big schlong—'

'Tasha!' Alice protested at the crude word.

The girl flushed but stood her ground. 'Sorry, but it's true. Georg thinks Oskar sorted being a locksmith out for him and totally forgot it all came from you until I reminded him.'

'That was kind of you.'

'But should not have been needed.'

Alice looked at the girl, bristling with passion, and reached out to pat her knee, glad of the distraction from the painful letter she'd stuffed back into her pocket.

'I agree, but at least the interview has been secured and Georg may be on his way to employment he can really throw himself into.'

Tasha pulled back, staring at her in a most discomfiting way; it seemed she'd said the wrong thing. Again!

'Doesn't it bother you?' she demanded.

'That Georg can't remember whose idea it was to become a locksmith? Not really. It's finding him the work that counts.'

'But he should value your contribution. He should see what you're doing for him. He should see *you*.'

Alice batted this away. 'No one sees me.'

Tasha let out a furious yelp. 'And you're happy with that?'

'I—'

'You should *not* be happy with that.'

'I'm not sure I matter that much, Tasha.'

Tasha grunted. 'It's up to you if you want to see it like that, but don't *we* matter, the few girls in this great big group of boys?'

'Of course you do.'

'So shouldn't you be standing up and making sure you're heard, so that we are too?'

Alice gaped at her. Should she? It had never occurred to her.

'You'll always be heard, Tasha.'

'Because I'm stroppy and bolshy and angry?'

'No. Because you're fierce and proud and full of passionate ideas.'

'Oh.'

The girl lapsed into silence and together they looked out across the lake.

'Why were you crying?' Tasha asked a few moments later.

Alice dug her fingers into her skirt pocket, feeling the letter crackle beneath them. 'I was thinking about my brother,' she admitted. The words felt barbed coming out of her throat and made her physically cough.

Tasha laid a quiet hand on her back and Alice felt it there, an unexpected rock against her aching spine.

'Where is he?' the girl asked.

'I don't know.' She sucked in an unsteady breath. 'I've just had a letter telling me that he was sent to Auschwitz.'

'Auschwitz? Like me!'

Alice looked at her, stupidly making the connection for the first time.

'Like you, yes. When did you go, Tasha?'

'October 1944,' she said promptly. 'When the uprising failed.'

Alice clutched at her sleeve. 'My brother was sent there on the twenty-ninth of September, and his wife and daughter a few days later.'

'So I could have arrived around the same time?'

They stared at each other as this sank in.

'What were their names?' Tasha demanded.

'My brother was – *is* – Max. The others are Lilli and Ruth-Gertrud.'

'Lilli and Ruth-Gertrud Goldberger?'

Despite herself, Alice looked at the girl with hope. Was it possible that she'd been in the Lake District for the last two months with someone who knew the answers she was seeking?

'That's right,' she said, her voice hoarse with longing. 'Did you know them?'

'No. I'm sorry.'

'Scheiße.'

The bitter disappointment knocked the swear word out before she could stop it and Tasha blinked.

'You don't half surprise me sometimes, Alice.'

Alice gave a sharp laugh. 'You surprise me all the time, Tasha.'

The girl's hand rubbed up and down her back, warm and surprisingly gentle.

'It's horrid isn't it, the not-knowing?'

'Horrid,' Alice agreed. 'Would you tell me about your mother, Tasha? Could you?'

Tasha chewed on her lip and Alice saw her hand go instinctively to her handbag.

'Do you have a keepsake in there? Might I see it?'

Still Tasha didn't speak but she undid the buckle and slowly, uncertainly, withdrew a battered box, set it on her lap and lifted the lid with nervous tenderness. Alice leaned forward, expecting a jewel or a photograph, but instead saw a matted lump of hair.

'Is that your mother's?' she asked softly.

Tasha nodded.

'She gave it to you?'

Tasha shook her head.

Alice sat waiting and suddenly words were tumbling out of the girl.

'They took it. The Nazis. They lined us up and they took shears to us and they took it. All of it. From everyone. I heard the other day that they sent it off to make carpets. How sick is that?' She didn't wait for an answer. 'I was behind Mama, with Amelia – that was my little sister – in between us. I was watching out for Amelia. She was only twelve and we kept worrying that they'd pull her out of the line and send her to... to... the other line.'

Alice nodded and tentatively put an arm around Tasha's shoulders, trying to focus on her charge and not think about Max and Lilli and little Ruthie being sent...

'And then suddenly,' Tasha went on, 'there was this hideous buzzing noise and I looked up and there was Mama's hair, falling to the floor. It was such beautiful hair, Alice, like a curtain of flame. People noticed it wherever we went and those bastards were hacking it off. And her scalp – so white and bare and bleeding where the razor had nicked it. It was like watching her core shorn away.'

Alice felt the hurt in Tasha's young voice and instinctively pulled her close. Tasha leaned on her shoulder and cried, as Alice had cried earlier. Alice stared out at the lake and hated the shake of the child's grief against her but knew, too, that this was a much-needed release. For them both.

'She was still your mother though,' she said gently.

Tasha nodded. 'That's what she said. She was so brave in there. She worked so hard in the day and then, in the evening, she sat and told us stories and talked to us of times past and took us out of those horrible, dark, dirty barracks into other, happier places. I swear that's what kept me sane in there, even when Amelia died.'

'I'm sorry.'

Tasha gave a harsh bark of a laugh. 'Not as sorry as I am. But that's past, right? That's what Georg says anyway.'

'It's a past event, but that doesn't mean it isn't still present in your heart.'

Tasha pulled away to look at her. 'That's wise, Alice.'

'Hardly.'

'No, it is. It... it helps. The future, it's, you know... tricky.'

Alice smiled at the understatement. 'Very tricky.'

'It's all right for Georg, bouncing off to London to make locks, but what am I meant to do? Where am I meant to go?'

'Where would you like to go?'

'Home,' Tasha moaned. 'I'd like to go home to Warsaw, to my house and my family and the life I had. It wasn't anything special. It was a normal, ordinary life but I want it back. I want it back so badly.'

'I know,' Alice agreed, picturing her little apartment in Berlin and Max's happy family home just a few streets away. 'It's hard when your life is taken from you.'

'The Nazis cut everything away,' Tasha moaned. 'Everything. First they bombed and burned our city and then they went after us. I knew they were going to the instant I saw those damn shears make their first swipe of Mama's hair. I knew it. I pounced and I grabbed some and I kept it scrunched up so tight in the palm of my hand that they never noticed. Then I hid it in a gap in the wall so that sometimes I could look at it and remember what it used to be like. What it could, maybe, be like again. That was the hope, Alice, in there. That was always the hope. It kept us going, the dreams. But now... Now we're out and the dreams haven't come true. Life is easier, yes, and I'm grateful for that, truly I am, but where's the hope?'

Alice closed her eyes, thought of her and Max picking edelweiss on a Tyrolese mountain, and felt the painful truth of Tasha's wail. But surely, if Tasha had made it out of Auschwitz, then Max might have too.

'Maybe your mother and my brother are sitting in a refugee camp somewhere working out how to find us,' she suggested.

Tasha rolled her eyes. 'Maybe,' she said. 'Or maybe they're both dead.'

Alice winced and the girl gave an exaggerated sigh.

'Sorry. I'm sorry, Alice. You're right – we have to have hope because what else, in the end, is there?'

'The future?'

Tasha groaned. 'The future feels so exhausting. For me anyway. Georg doesn't seem bothered. He can't wait to move forward. He never speaks about the past. He never even speaks about his parents.'

'How did he lose them?' Alice asked.

The girl plucked at the grass. 'I've no idea,' she said. 'Which is precisely my point. Who doesn't even speak about their parents?'

'Someone who's hurting?' Alice suggested tentatively.

But at that Tasha leaped up. 'We're all hurting,' she shot back. 'I'm hurting, you're hurting. At least we're talking about it.'

'Only just,' Alice said, but Tasha was already gone, off down the hill, taking her hurt with her and leaving Alice alone, once more, with her own.

Tasha was uncharacteristically helpful the next day, dusting and sweeping the communal rooms as if she might clear out all their emotional mess with the household dirt. Around teatime, however, she slunk off, and was nowhere to be seen when Georg came bouncing back, brimming with life.

'I did it, Alice,' he cried in English.

'You got the apprenticeship?'

'I did. I start in two weeks' time. They said that I seemed a very "enterprising" young man. I didn't know the word but I asked Oskar and he says it means you take any opportunity presented to you and so I think, yes, I am "enterprising" and I'm going to take this opportunity and... and knock its socks off.'

Alice laughed out loud. The boy had been working hard on his English and was clearly trying to master the country's more peculiar phrases.

'Good for you,' she said.

He looked eagerly around the dining room. 'Is Tasha here?'

'She's disappeared. She's been very... busy. I think she's missed you.'

'I doubt it,' he said gruffly, but he raced off to look for the girl all the same and Alice wished him luck. 'Oh, and Alice...' He turned back at the door to shout down the hall. 'Oskar said to ask you to come to his office. He's got someone there who'd like to see you.'

The faces of the remaining diners turned her way and she flushed.

'Very well, thank you, Georg.'

She rose and made herself tidy up her place at the table with studied calm. What she really wanted to do was race out as Georg just had – though whether towards the office or far, far away she wasn't quite sure. Was this about Max? Had they found him? Or, worse, had they found records of him? Records, she was rapidly discovering, were rarely good news; she trod slowly towards Oskar's office.

As she approached the open door, however, she saw that the visitor was none other than Leonard Montefiore. Mortified at having kept their prime benefactor waiting, she rushed forward.

'Mr Montefiore, I'm so sorry I'm late.'

'You're not late at all, Alice. I'm sorry for interrupting your work. Come in, come in. A whisky?' He waved to the decanter sitting between the two men.

Alice shook her head vehemently.

'A sherry, perhaps? Do we have sherry, Oskar?'

Alice put up a hand. 'Nothing for me, thank you. Did you want to see me?'

'I did, Alice, I did.' Leonard sat forward, resting his elbows on the table and steepling his long fingers. 'As you know, we are moving children out of Windermere as fast as we reasonably can.'

Alice nodded and glanced to Oskar. 'Georg tells me he secured his apprenticeship,' she said to him. 'That's wonderful news.'

'Isn't it?' Oskar agreed. 'Such an apt position for him. I knew immediately I saw his prowess with a lock that it would suit.'

Alice frowned. She thought of Tasha up on the hillside yesterday raging about women not being heard. The girl was absolutely right and she opened her mouth to remind Oskar that it had been her idea but could find no way to say it without sounding petty. She closed it again.

'He seems very excited,' she managed. 'And I'm delighted he has a future to look forward to. I wish I could say the same for the younger children.'

'But you can,' Oskar said, beaming at her. 'Leonard has a new project for us.'

'Us?' she squeaked.

'Of course. We're a team, aren't we? I couldn't have achieved half of what I've achieved here without you.'

What *we've* achieved, Alice heard Tasha say in her head, but that was semantics. Oskar was praising her, giving her her due – *hearing* her.

'Or I without you,' she said. 'We have, as you say, been a team.'

Oskar didn't look quite as keen on the idea when she said it, but he kept smiling and now Leonard was talking again.

'I'm delighted to report that my good friend Sir Benjamin Drage has offered his home to house the four- to nine-year-olds, and I would very much like you to consider running it.'

'His home?' Alice stuttered, fighting to catch up.

'Well, half of it. He'll move into the east wing with his wife, and you and the children can have the west wing.'

'West wing?'

'It's quite a big house.'

'It must be.' Alice couldn't quite take this in. 'Where is it?'

'Lingfield. That's in Surrey, south-west of London.'

'And only about an hour away from the city on the train, so I can continue to be involved,' Oskar said. 'If you'll have me, that is.'

'Of course I'll have you, Oskar,' Alice told him and then, feeling absurdly suggestive, fought for better words and lost them in a cough. 'Perhaps I will have a small whisky,' she choked out.

Leonard leaped to pour it, sloshing the amber liquid into the glass and adding a splash of water from a crystal jug. 'Bottoms up, Alice!'

She raised her glass weakly, and took a tiny sip. 'Surrey?' she said, testing this newly presented version of her future on her tongue and finding it almost as heady as the whisky.

'Surrey,' Leonard confirmed. 'The house is called Weir Courtney and it's a lovely old place. See?' He took a photograph from his top pocket and passed it across the table.

Alice stared at the beautiful country house with ivy-coated walls leading up to decorative gables and a great stretch of garden, paradise for growing children. There was even a swing already dangling from a big oak in the foreground.

'It's perfect,' she gasped.

'Glad you think so, Alice. Welcome to your new home.'

Home: that word again. *I'd so like to go home,* Tasha's voice moaned in her head – as if the damned girl had actually crawled right in there – and that gave her an idea.

'Can I take Sophie?' she asked.

'Of course.'

'And maybe a few of the older girls, to help out. To be, you know, big sisters to the little ones.'

'Sounds a capital idea to me,' Leonard said. 'If you think they'll be happy.'

Where's the hope? Tasha asked, back in her head once more. Well perhaps it was here, between these ivy-covered walls in Surrey.

'I hope so,' she said, touching a fingertip to the swing, sitting there waiting for someone to take to the skies on its wooden seat. 'I truly hope so.'

FIFTEEN

TASHA

'Sophie, you'll never guess what!'

Tasha – hunting for a snack in the pantry, and, purely coincidentally, avoiding Georg – looked out curiously as Alice burst into the kitchen at surprising speed.

'What?' she heard Sophie ask her.

'We've got new jobs.'

Tasha stiffened. She recalled Alice yesterday, putting her arm around her on the hillside and telling her she understood about her fears for the future. She'd sounded so sympathetic but it seemed that, all along, she'd been plotting something. She huddled further back in the pantry, listening hard.

'Where?' Sophie asked.

'Surrey. It's in the south of England, not far from London. Sir Somebody-or-other is donating the use of his house for the kids and we're to run it.'

Tasha's heart skipped a beat; perhaps this wasn't as bad as it seemed.

'Which kids?' Sophie asked.

'The younger ones.'

Tasha gasped, then clapped a hand over her mouth. Alice only wanted the little kids, the sweet, pig-tailed ones like Marta, not the bolshy, older ones like her.

'It'll be perfect for them,' Alice was going blithely on, 'like Bulldogs Bank for the tinies. They can go to the village school with the locals and start getting some routine back into their lives. Start looking to the future.'

'The future?!' The English word burst from Tasha in a fury, releasing a spurt of tears that she batted angrily away as she launched herself into the middle of the no-longer-so-cosy kitchen.

Both women jumped and looked at her in concern.

'I'm not crying,' she said in furious German. 'That is, I *am* crying, but it's anger. I'm angry. Not sad. I don't care what you do, either of you. You waltz on to Surrey and have fun. See if I care. I hate you all anyway, with your do-gooder ideas and your pretend care and your, your...'

She ground to a halt as Sophie stepped up, wrapped her large arms around her and held her so closely against her ample form that there was no way to escape.

'I'm not fooled,' Tasha wept against her. 'This isn't a hug, this is control.'

'It's a hug, silly,' Sophie said calmly, squeezing her even tighter and releasing a cloud of icing sugar from her apron that made Tasha sneeze violently. Still Sophie held on.

'You'll have to let go when you leave,' Tasha protested. 'When you *all* leave, like everyone leaves. Like Tata left when the bullet hit him, like Amelia left with typhus, like Mama left on the march, out into the snow while I was shut in the barrack.'

'That wasn't any of their fault,' Sophie soothed.

'But they still left!'

Tasha wrenched away and stormed to the door but Alice was blocking it. She was slight enough for Tasha to push aside but something about the set of her body and the flash in her dark eyes made her hesitate.

'I'm not leaving you, Tasha.'

'You are. You're going to Surrey.'

'So are you.'

'Rubbish. I heard you. I'm not a "younger kid", am I? I'm an adult. I can take care of myself.'

'Are you sure about that?'

'No!' Tasha screamed. 'But I don't have much choice, do I? I'm as much a prisoner here as I was in Auschwitz. Let me pass, please.'

'No,' Alice shot back. 'Not until you listen to me. I want you to come. I asked Mr Montefiore if you could come.'

That stopped Tasha.

'You did?'

'And he said yes.'

'He did? Why?'

'Because I told him that you – and any other girls – can help me look after the littlies.'

'Look after the...?' She'd thought Alice actually wanted her along, but no, she was simply seeking cheap labour. 'Is that the future you envisage for me, Alice? Because if so, I'd say your talents as a job-finder have deserted you. I'm not being a nurserymaid.'

She spat the word out. How come the boys were invited to factories and businesses and she was only fit to look after babies?

'What's wrong with being a nurserymaid?' Alice asked, her voice cold.

A little late, Tasha remembered Anna Freud telling her all about Alice setting up nurseries in Berlin and in her internment camp and somewhere else she couldn't quite remember, and felt ashamed of her comments. But so what? Alice was fine, in her own way, but Tasha didn't want to be like her. And she didn't need her charity either.

'Didn't you ever want your own children?' she demanded.

'Tasha!' Sophie admonished.

But Tasha was past caring. Everyone was disappearing – again – so why should she pussyfoot around them? She stared Alice down but Alice had gathered herself and stood her ground.

'I did want children, but that chance passed me by and I don't see the sense in mourning something I can't have, especially not when there are all you children to love as my own.'

'Oh no!' Tasha put up a hand. 'You can't do that. You can't claim us just because some rich kretyn put you in charge. We're not your children. *I'm* not your child.' Alice tried to say something but there was a buzzing in Tasha's ears and a darkness crowding in on her sight and she pushed blindly to the door. 'I have a mother,' she shouted back into the kitchen. 'But everyone is too busy soothing their guilty souls with "caring" to help me find her. Well, I don't need caring for, not by all you dried-up old spinsters. I just need my mother, my own warm, kind, brave, bold, funny mother. The rest of you can go to hell!'

She stumbled out, ready to run back up the hillside and right on until she reached the boundaries of this do-gooding island where she could get on a boat and find her way back to Lydia, but she ran smack-bang into Georg.

'There you are, Tash. I've been searching for you.' His smile faded as he looked into her face and he slid into Polish. 'What's happened?'

'Everything,' she flung at him. 'Everything has happened and everything *is happening*. People are leaving. You're leaving. Alice is leaving. Sophie's leaving. So, I'm leaving. Right now.'

'Fine.'

To her surprise he let her go and, wrong-footed, she had little choice but to head on out of the Calgarth Estate. She looked around her. On reflection, the hills were probably not a good choice. It was getting dark, the sun cowering behind louring clouds as it crept towards the Black Fell, and the first droplets of rain were forming in the leaden air. The road would be a wiser choice. There would be a bus sometime, to somewhere.

'You've got money of course?'

She glanced back to see Georg sauntering behind her.

'Of course,' she said, tapping her handbag, though it was empty of all but her mother's lock of hair, as well he knew.

'That's good then. Buses aren't expensive but the trains can be.'

'I'll manage.' She reached the road and turned right, making for the wooden bus shelter.

'I got the job, by the way,' Georg said, still from a few paces behind her.

'Congratulations. I'm sure you'll be a brilliant locksmith.'

'I will,' he agreed. 'The man said I was enterprising.'

'Good for you.'

She reached the hut as the rain began to fall in earnest and ducked gratefully inside to scan the timetable. The buses in this direction went to somewhere called Kendal, though only once an hour and only until 7 p.m. What time was it? She glanced at the sun, almost behind the hill.

'It's five to seven,' Georg supplied, looking at his wrist.

Tasha stared. 'Is that a new watch?'

'It is. Oskar bought it for me, to help me keep time for work.'

'Delightful. Well, good luck and all that.'

She sat down on the bench, willing him to leave, but, to her annoyance, he leaned on the side of the shelter, apparently oblivious to the rain.

'Bus is coming.'

Tasha's heart pounded but she refused to show it. 'Bye then.'

'I'll just see you on safely. And you've got money for the fare?'

'I said so, didn't I?'

She could hear the bus rumbling towards them, its wheels churning up the puddles on the road. Her stomach tightened.

'And for a hotel in Kendal? Unless you're going to sleep rough. Are you going to sleep rough, Tash? It's really not a good night for it.'

'What's it to you?'

'Just curious.'

'Right.'

The bus drew up and the door slid open, orange light spilling onto the wet pavement. Tasha's heart pounded and she had to physically force herself to stand up.

'And, of course, because I'm madly in love with you.'

She froze.

The driver said something unintelligible about 'hopping on board'. She gave him an awkward smile but did not hop anywhere.

'And because I want you to come to London with me and marry me so we can make a home together and try, somehow, to make the most of the life that we clung onto so desperately in Auschwitz.'

'You... you do?'

'I do. I haven't got a ring because I wanted to, you know, do it properly, but sometimes you make that impossible, Tasha. But I mean it, truly. I must be mad, as you're an irritable, grumpy, infuriating—'

'You getting on, duck?' the driver asked.

'—impossible pain in the whatsit,' Georg went on, 'but you're also sparky and fun and exciting and, my goodness, Tash, I don't want to live without you.'

'Last chance,' the driver said.

That, Tasha understood and thought he might be right, though not in the way he meant.

'Sorry,' she muttered and stepped back.

The bus pulled away and she turned to Georg, standing there in the rain, his curls plastered to his head, his eyes looking intently at her and his hands held out.

'I love you too,' she said. The words surprised her. A few moments ago, she hadn't loved anyone bar a red-headed woman who might, or might not, be alive somewhere in Europe, but as she took Georg's hands, she knew that, scary as it might be, it was true. 'You're insufferably optimistic, painfully energetic, and infuriatingly naughty, Georg Lieberman, but I'd never have got this far without you and I don't want to get any further without you either.'

He pulled her close and dropped a kiss on her forehead.

'London then?' he whispered.

'London,' she agreed.

Her lips found his and she wrapped herself tightly in against him. She loved Georg, truly she did, and she longed to give herself to that love and turn it into a life. If going to London was what that took, then she had to give it a go. But even as he kissed her, her mind was skidding around thoughts of leaving dear little Marta, of doing without Alice and Sophie and her tentative pseudo-family, and, above all, of departing the sort of place where Lydia, if she was still alive and still looking, might one day find her.

LYDIA

'Where do you think you're going?'

A dark-eyed young woman with a well-practised saunter stepped in front of Lydia, blocking the entrance to the girls' dorm. Lydia sized her up with a quiet smile. She'd survived rebellions and deportations, she'd survived a concentration camp and a death march, so there was no way she was going to let some jumped-up youngster stop her now.

'I'm told there are new arrivals in this dormitory, Miss...?'

'Markowitz. Evalina Markowitz.'

'Well then, Evalina, I need to see these new arrivals in case one of them is my daughter.'

More girls were gathering around their leader and Lydia sighed. Even in a refugee camp people had to play their petty power games. Had they not had enough of that from the Nazis?

'Her name?' Evalina asked.

'Natasha. Natasha Ancel.'

'Nope. Sorry. No Natashas here. Where was she?'

'When?'

Evalina rolled her dark eyes at her acolytes. 'When the war ended, of course.'

'Of course. Erm, I don't know. I left her in Auschwitz.'

'*Left* her?'

The kids crowded round, shocked, and Lydia threw her hands up defensively.

'I had to. They forced me. Pushed me out and shut her in. I tried. I—'

Evalina put up a hand to stop her, her eyes kinder now. 'Don't worry, stara, we understand. We were in it too.'

'In Auschwitz?'

'No, but one camp is much the same as another. They herded us like cattle.' She leaned in, her dark eyes gleaming like jet. 'But we aren't cattle, are we, stara? We aren't stupid. And we'll find each other again, despite their best efforts. You'll find your daughter.'

'You think?' She was pathetically eager for the assurances of this cocky young woman.

'Certainly,' she said, adding, 'Palestine.'

'Sorry?'

'Is she a smart girl?'

'Oh yes, she's—'

'Then she'll be in Palestine, that's where all the smart kids are going. Adults too. It's Zion, stara – the promised land, given to Moses and restored to us at last. Our own land for our own nation of Israel.'

'Ah,' was all Lydia could manage. She'd heard of Palestine of course but it had sounded impossible that it would actually happen. 'I thought that was just a dream.'

'A dream reality. And no less than we deserve.'

'True.'

'So, your girl, your...?'

'Tasha.'

'Yes. Your Tasha, she'll be on her way there, you mark my

words, just like we all are. You should sign up as soon as possible.'

'Sign up?'

'For transport. Over here, come on.'

She hustled Lydia over to a stand where she could apparently put her name down for the next bus to Zion. Lydia looked at the long list, then around the other stands that had sprung up in Feldafing over the last couple of months. There were people canvassing refugees to go everywhere. The Polish government were offering food bribes to lure them back to Poland but few were falling for that given the reports of violence to Jews. There were people promising tickets to America, and even a group canvassing for orphans to go to England, but this list for Zion was by far the longest. Is this what Tasha would do? Lydia wondered. All the stands promised new homes, but this was the only one claiming to be the original Jewish home. Would that tempt her daughter?

'When does the next transport go?' she asked nervously.

The mood darkened instantly.

'Who knows,' Evalina said. 'Could be days, could be weeks, could be months.'

Lydia thanked her and moved away, feeling even more lost than before. She'd missed her chance to tell Tasha where to meet her back in the swirling ice of Auschwitz and now there were so many choices – most of them bound to be wrong. Feeling horribly weak, she sank onto a rough bench and fought a fit of coughing.

'Did you sign?' Mrs Leibowitz, the camp administrator asked, sitting down at her side.

Lydia looked up. 'No, but I might do yet.'

'You want to leave?'

'I want to find my daughter and I don't think waiting for lists which never arrive will help me do that. I need to go out looking myself, but how do I work out where she's gone?'

Mrs Leibowitz grimaced. 'If you ask me, that's a hopeless task. There are a million routes across Europe and a million people on each one. Better to consider where she was.'

'Sorry?'

'Lists can only be made of those in front of us. We're trying to collate them into a central system, but it could be years before that's possible. Our priority is moving people not paper, so if you want to find your daughter, I suggest you start where you know she was.'

'Auschwitz?' Lydia gasped.

'If that's where you last saw her, then yes.'

'How far away is it?'

The administrator grimaced again. 'It's about eight hundred kilometres, I believe, all the way through Czechoslovakia.'

'I see.'

Lydia felt panic rise like an all-too-familiar-tide in her wasted lungs but fought it back. She should have thought of this herself, she should have known. She couldn't just sit here by a pretty lakeside and wait for someone else to do the work. To find her daughter, she had to go back to the beginning. She had to go back to Auschwitz.

PART THREE

WEIR COURTNEY

SEVENTEEN

ALICE

Alice stared up at her new home, so distracted by its beauty that she almost fell off the steps of the bus.

'Steady there!'

Oskar took her arm and she smiled gratefully at him.

'Thank you, Oskar. I was just... Well, it's so grand, isn't it?'

'It is rather nice,' he agreed, looking around. 'It certainly won't be any hardship to visit you lovely ladies here.'

He gave her a broad smile and, flustered, she turned back to the bus.

'I'd better be sure the kiddies are all off safely.'

'Allow me.'

Oskar stepped keenly forward, though the first person off the bus was not one of the children but their new helper, Manna Weindling. Oskar handed her down and she thanked him and looked around, clearly as dazed as Alice had been a moment before, though far more charming in her disbelief. Manna had been sent to them by Anna to replace Marie Paneth, who was moving on to a different hostel. Manna was kind and efficient and she played the violin in a way that made even Alice's old feet twitch to dance. She was also, at only thirty years old, bright, fresh and bursting with energy. Now, she clapped her hands and turned to tell the emerging children that they had woken up in a fairy tale.

They came, eyes wide and sleep-fugged, and very ready to believe her as they gazed around. It was only six o'clock but the nights drew in early these days and a number of them had fallen asleep on the long journey down from the Lake District. Suzi and Judith stared around, hand in hand, while Mirella and Fiorina Bellucci huddled together, gazing up at the imposing house. Young Mattias refused, for some time, to get off the bus and even Moishe and Ernst, the oldest and liveliest of the boys, were subdued. With Marta clinging desperately to Alice's skirts, she felt guiltily aware that the poor kids were having to adjust to a new home yet again.

But what a home!

The dark was chased away here at Weir Courtney by several large gas lamps burning on a small roundabout at the top of the drive, as if waiting to light up carriages from another age arriving at a grand ball. In their flickering light, Alice could see the ivy-clad house with its pretty gabling and grand front door. She could see the edges of long lawns to the right and the oak tree with the swing, creaking slightly in the winter wind.

A glass-walled building that might be an orangery – not that Alice had ever seen such a thing outside story books – was also lit up and in front of it she could make out the covered rectangle of a tiny swimming pool. Windermere had been stunning but the Calgarth buildings had been pre-fabricated huts, a little too like the camps for comfort, whereas this was a real house. A big house, yes, but a real one.

Alice began hustling everyone towards the front door, wanting to get this arrival just right. A week or two after they'd first settled the children into the Calgarth Estate, one of them had related the arrival procedures in camps like Belsen and Auschwitz. They'd described being stripped of their clothing and lining up to be disinfected, not knowing if they'd ever come out, and the carers at Windermere had looked at each other in horror, realising that they'd unwittingly given the children similar treatment. Alice was desperate for that not to happen again.

It was Hanukkah tonight and they'd travelled with baskets of Sophie's finest goodies, as well as all the candles they could find for the festival of light. It had been extra work on top of the usual packing and, if she was honest, Alice would be happy to crawl straight into bed. But this time last year, the children had been huddled in camps and ghettos with only darkness around them and they were determined to mark the change for this most joyful of Jewish ceremonies.

'Mrs Goldberger?' A tall man pulled open the door, arms spread wide and a broad smile on his friendly face. 'Welcome to Weir Courtney. I trust you and the children will feel at home here. Come in, come in.' He ushered her inside, shaking her hand heartily. 'I'm Sir Benjamin Drage and this is my wife, Lady Phoebe. We're so very glad to have you all here, truly we are.'

'You're very kind, Sir Benjamin.'

'Least we could do. Absolute least. Only the two of us here these days and what's the point in us kicking around the place with half the rooms empty when there are children in need, what?'

He spoke in a richly rounded accent and Alice wasn't quite sure if he was asking her a question, but it seemed not as he was already moving on to shake the hand of each and every child, bending his tall frame to stand at their level and chatting away as if he welcomed European orphans every evening of the week.

'You must be very tired,' Lady Phoebe was saying to Alice,

'but we took the liberty of preparing a little welcome party. It is Hanukkah, after all.'

'It is,' Alice agreed gratefully, 'and we've brought— Oh!'

Her words were sucked out of her as Lady Phoebe opened another door into a large drawing room that was glowing with the light of a hundred candles, set in gracious silver candlesticks.

'Sparkly!' little Marta cried in easy English, darting around her and running into the centre.

Lady Phoebe laughed. 'Happy Hannukah,' she said.

Alice watched, delighted, as Marta skipped about in the centre of the room with Suzi and Judith. Poor Marta had been very quiet and withdrawn since she'd discovered Tasha wasn't coming to Weir Courtney with them and it was good to see her happy again. If she was honest, Alice had been feeling rather quiet about that herself.

'I'm going to London with Georg,' Tasha had told her the day after her outburst in the kitchen.

'With Georg? But Tasha, you can't—'

'It's not what you think. I'm no prostytutka.'

'I didn't say—'

'He's going to marry me. That is, we're going to marry each other.'

She'd been at her spikiest, standing right up on her toes, poised for a fight, and Alice had done her best to tread carefully.

'That's very romantic.'

'Yes. It is.' She'd stared Alice down. 'Mazel tov, that's the phrase you're looking for.'

'Mazel tov, of course. It's just... Are you sure, liebchen? You're still young.'

'I'm seventeen. It's allowed. And we've got it all planned. We'll live in separate dorms in the Shelter until we can organise the ceremony and then we'll go for it. Seize the future, yes?'

'Yes. Of course. Good for you,' Alice had agreed hastily. 'It's just a big decision. Are you sure you're ready?'

'Of course I'm ready,' she'd snapped. 'And so is Georg.'

'I have no doubt that Georg wants to marry you, Tasha,' Alice had said, stalling. 'I merely thought that, perhaps, you would want to wait until your mother could join you for the happy day.'

It had been a low blow and she'd not been proud of herself when the girl's defiant face had closed in, but had prayed it might at least persuade her to wait before taking on the responsibilities of a wife. Given a choice, Alice would have liked to bundle her onto the coach down to Surrey where she could mother her for a little longer, but Tasha had made it clear that she did not want Alice's mothering, so she'd let her go.

That didn't mean she didn't worry about her though. She'd visited the Jewish Shelter when she'd been working with Oskar in London and hadn't liked it at all. It was cramped and run-down and frequented by some very shady characters. To be honest, she wasn't happy about tough Georg being there, let alone vulnerable Tasha. Frustratingly, she knew Oskar felt the same as he was always railing against its unsuitability for young people, but he had done nothing to stop either of them moving.

'It's London, Alice,' he'd said. 'Property is twice as expensive as elsewhere, so it's bound to be crowded.'

'Crowded is one thing, Oskar, but dirty, noisy and unsafe is quite another. I thought you didn't want our youngsters turning into criminals, so why are you housing them with some?'

'Alice! That's a charitable foundation and the people there work very hard.'

'Including the one you showed me dealing opium out of a back room?'

He'd squirmed then. 'Did I show you that? How indecorous of me.'

'How truthful of you. It's no place for our children.'

He'd taken her hand. 'They're not *our* children, Alice.'

He'd said it kindly but it had felt patronising and had, besides, been so wrung through with overtones of Tasha's words – 'I'm not your child, Alice' – that she'd backed off immediately. How much of her work was genuine care and how much simply satisfying her own need to be loved? A picture of Max, Lilli and Ruthie being herded into Auschwitz flashed painfully across her mind and she had to put a hand to the wood-panelled wall to steady herself.

'Well, this is rather nice,' Sophie said, coming up behind her.

Alice gave her friend a grateful squeeze. It *was* nice and if Tasha didn't want to be here, that was up to her. Two teenage girls, Mina and Golda, had chosen to come to Weir Courtney and were playing with the little ones with a sweetness that would certainly have been missing from Tasha's response. She'd probably have said something snide about the curtains, or pointed out that the candlesticks were not all the eight-candle menorahs prescribed by the most observant – not that Tasha was even that observant and—

'Stop thinking about her,' she chided herself.

The girl was right, she was not her mother and the sooner she stopped thinking of herself that way, the better for both of them. She could write to her perhaps, check that she was well, as was her duty as the supervisor of her care here in England, but that was as far as it should go. Soon, Tasha would be Mrs Lieberman and she should make her way in the world as she wished.

And yet...

If Alice tried to picture Tasha as a bride, all she could see were her big eyes, beautifully blue but filled with pain, and that old handbag crossed over her thin chest holding a scrap of her mother's hair as if it were the greatest treasure in the world.

She should have another push to try to find Lydia Ancel,

she thought, staring into the flickering light of the nearest candle. Her letter-writing had dropped off with all the organisation of the move but now she was in Surrey, she could try again. In this lovely house she could find the energy to contact more organisations about the Auschwitz records for Max, Lilli and Ruthie, and while she was at it she could try to find Tasha's mother. It would be the best possible bride-gift for the girl, one that might make her smile in a way Alice had seen her do far too rarely.

Smile at you, you mean, a voice – probably Tasha's – said in her head and she tutted at herself. She was in pretty Surrey, in a gracious new home with kind hosts and happy children. She should stop worrying about those who weren't here and make the most of those who were.

'Isn't this lovely?' she said, determinedly loud, as she stepped into the centre of the room. 'Let's all say a huge thank you to Sir Benjamin and Lady Phoebe for welcoming us to our new home.'

The children obligingly clapped, then Sophie opened up one of her baskets of goodies, Manna lifted her violin, and the cosy room was filled with music and light and sweetness. Alice sent up a prayer of thanks to God for all she had, and tried, for once, not to think about all she had not.

EIGHTEEN

THE SHELTER, TOWER BRIDGE | DECEMBER 1945

TASHA

'Bitch!' The shrieked obscenity pulled Tasha from an uneasy slumber and, with a groan, she squashed the pillow over her head and prayed for this morning's dispute to be over quickly. 'You took all the hot water!'

'I did not,' came the equally high-pitched reply. 'It was barely tepid when I got in.'

'You put up with it for long enough. You were in there ages.'

'Can I help it if I have so much hair to wash?'

'Oww! Do you hear that?'

Tasha's bunk shook as the first woman prodded at a friend in the bed beneath.

'Beth's taunting me. She knows why my hair's still short. And we all know why hers is so long and shiny, Nazi cocksucker.'

'That's not true, Aliza, you bitch.'

The bed shook again, to more shrieks, and Tasha reluctantly emerged from her pillow to look down on the two women, kicking and slapping each other between the bunks.

'Grow up, why don't you?!' she shouted.

They both froze and looked up at her. Aliza folded her arms and Beth extracted her fingernails from her opponent's skin and stood at her shoulder, all disputes apparently forgotten.

'What did you say, new girl?'

Tasha sat up and folded her own arms; she'd seen enough bullies in the camp to know not to show any fear.

'I said, "grow up". It's only a shower and we're lucky to be alive to take one at all.'

There were a few murmurs of agreement from around the dorm.

But Aliza looked mutinous. 'And we're expected to be grateful for that for the rest of our lives, are we?'

It was exactly the protest Tasha had made on several occasions, but that had been in the safety of Windermere. Here at the Shelter, life felt gritty and hard, and that made Tasha conversely keener to make the most of it.

'Surely our arguments should be with other people, not ourselves?' she said carefully.

'The girl has a point,' Beth said, adding, 'though she should learn her place if she's going to get on in here.'

With that, the pair of them thankfully flounced off, and things settled in the dorm. Tasha lay down and willed herself to go back to sleep. She'd been awake half the night, disturbed by the grunts and snores of fifteen women, reminded uncomfortably of camp life and then feeling cross with herself for the association. No one was imprisoning her here. She'd come of her own free will and she could leave of her own free will too.

Some days she almost did.

'Just a few months,' Georg would promise whenever they had time together, which wasn't often enough.

He was out at his lock factory for hours every day. He insisted he was saving for a ring and a home of their own, which was very good of him, but it left her horribly lonely.

'What's the point in me being here if you don't come back until nearly bedtime?' she'd protest, and he'd apologise and kiss her and she'd forget all about it – until the next night.

London was sort of fun, she supposed, and it was certainly an imposing city. Some days, if the sun was shining, she'd head down to Tower Bridge to walk along the River Thames. There were many bomb holes in the city but in between them were some striking buildings and a real sense of life. It still didn't feel right though. If the war came up with the Londoners, they all spoke about something called 'Blitz spirit', which seemed to involve sitting in underground stations drinking gin and singing around a piano. The Warsawians had hidden from bombers underground too, the entire city cowering as building after building was knocked down around them until there had been no water, no electricity and no food and they'd been forced to surrender to the vicious Nazi soldiers.

It hadn't been easy in London, even Tasha could see that when she looked at the many ruined houses, but no one had ever actually met a Nazi in the street here. No one had faced the barrel of his gun, or the vicious end of his hateful ideology. The war, for the 'plucky Brits' had been lived at one remove and Tasha couldn't help but resent their rose-tinted experience of victory.

'That's mean,' Georg had told her when she'd tried to explain. 'They didn't have to fight, you know. They could have sat on their island and stayed out of it. They could have done a deal with the Germans and avoided having their houses bombed and their sons and husbands slaughtered on the battle-fields of Europe. The Americans too. We should be grateful.'

It was true, Tasha knew, and that made it worse. She wasn't good at being grateful and absolutely understood Aliza's complaint. Not that she'd tell her so. Being nice got you nowhere in a place like this. Which was fine. Tasha was tough. But she was tired too. And lonely. She'd spent far too much time since she'd been in this bustling city fretting about Alice and Sophie and the children. One in particular.

'Why are you leaving me?' Marta had asked when she'd explained she was going to London with Georg.

'I'm not leaving you.'

'You're not coming with me.'

That had been hard to refute.

'I'm a grown-up now and I have to get a job,' she'd told her, 'but you'll still be my kotka. When Georg and I get married you can be my bridesmaid, and when we get a home of our own you can come and live with us. But that will take time and until then we can write to each other.'

'It won't be the same,' Marta had said unhappily, and she'd been right.

Tasha sent her letters every few days, saving her pennies to buy picture-postcards of London to show her sort-of-sister her new home, but she missed Marta's sweet company. Plus, for all her grand explanations, she'd struggled to find work. With so many soldiers back from the war, employers weren't allowing women to 'steal' men's gainful employment. Only the highly skilled were keeping their jobs and Tasha had no skills at all. Her sewing was too basic for factory work and her English wasn't good enough for waitressing, which just left cleaning. Cleaning! She'd grown up with a maid and now she had to skivvy. What's worse, the one job she'd been able to get was at the Shelter, so she had to clean for all those who went out to finer labours. It was not the glamorous future Georg had promised her and, up to her elbows in stinky lavatories, it was hard not to resent it.

The clock on the end wall struck eight and Tasha knew she had to get up. Her shift started at nine and if she wanted a shower – a cold shower, by the sounds of it – she'd have to get in the queue. Heaving herself out of her top bunk, she grabbed her still damp towel and bent to her locker to find that her flimsy padlock had been busted and her soap had gone missing. Again.

'Kradnące krowy!' she shouted in Polish, then 'Diebische Kühe' in German, before finally resorting to, 'Thieving cows!'

No one paid attention in any language and, closing her eyes, Tasha tried to picture her Warsaw home. The images that came to mind, however, were, as so often these days, of her room in Windermere, of her crisp white sheets and her fresh flowers and the silly teddy she'd secretly loved. She remembered her seventeenth birthday, with cake and dancing and everyone singing her name. She remembered the buckle the carers had bought her – a small present, perhaps, but one chosen with real care. Here at the Shelter the supervisor didn't let her wear her handbag to work, claiming it was 'an impediment to efficiency', so Tasha had to hide it underneath her blouse and it chafed painfully at her bare skin.

'Just a few months,' Georg had said when she'd showed him, because that was all he ever said.

He meant it, she knew he did. When they did get time together, he would hold her close and talk to her in tantalising detail about the bedsit they'd share when they were married, but Tasha had looked at the prices of bedsits and they'd need more than three pounds a week to get one around here.

A wail from the shower cubicles jolted Tasha out of her thoughts.

'What's up?' someone called.

'Water's off,' came the reply to a general groan and, as Tasha turned back to her bunk, she couldn't stop herself thinking about the endlessly plentiful showers at Calgarth. She'd known that was a holiday camp; she just wished, now, that she'd made the most of it.

Reaching into her locker for the rough skirt and blouse the Shelter had given her for work, her fingers brushed up against a letter she'd stored at the back, wrapped in her underthings in the hope of keeping it from prying fingers. It had arrived a few days ago and at first, staring at the unknown writing on the envelope, Tasha had thought it might be from UNRRA with news of her mother. When she'd turned it over, however, she'd seen the sender's details straight away: Alice Goldberger, Weir Courtney, Surrey. Alice had put them there to spare Tasha her imaginings, she knew, but it had hurt in a different way.

Weir Courtney! What sort of a name was that for a house?! Marta had written too, drawing pictures of a cosy kitchen and a huge playroom with dolls' houses and rocking horses, of dorms with pink frills on the pillows, and of sprawling gardens with flowers in a hothouse and swings beneath the trees. It all looked like a crazy fantasy from the grime of central London but, knowing Alice and her kind band of helpers, Tasha suspected it was largely true.

'True,' she told herself fiercely, stuffing the letter to the back and tugging her blouse over her handbag, 'but not real. This is proper, grown-up life and I can cope. After all, it's only for a few months.'

Even to her ears, though, that sounded hollow, and it was with a heavy heart that she headed down for work.

NINETEEN

ALICE

'Line up in the hall, please, holding hands in pairs. That's super!'

Alice smiled encouragingly at the children, hiding her nerves beneath an English jollity that sounded horribly fake even to her. Today was the day the children were starting at the village school and she was desperate for it to go well. She'd been planning this to get them back into something approaching a normal routine, but now the day was actually here, she was worried. She'd barely slept for fretting about whether the children would be teased for their accents, for their lack of parents, for their heritage.

Her continued letters had, at least, found relatives – one aunt and two grandparents – for two of her charges, but the other nineteen were having to get on with life as orphans. They were sweet, cheery kids, but she was aware that they were something of an exotic curiosity in sleepy Surrey and did not want them targeted for it. The teachers had been very encouraging, especially the headmaster and his kindly wife, the junior teacher. That was reassuring for the younger ones, but there were still the other children to contend with. In Weir Courtney, Alice could keep her charges safe and loved; at school they were beyond her protection.

It was an icy cold January day and even in the hallway of Weir Courtney, the children's breath was forming clouds in front of them. They were dressed in their warmest coats, with the hats, scarves and gloves Sophie had knitted for Christmas, and most of them looked eager for their new adventure. No wonder – Alice had been telling them for the last month how much fun it was going to be. Sixteen of them were lined up neatly, hands held, ready to go; three were not. Little Marta was very hesitant and, as she didn't have a partner, Alice took hold of her hand herself. That left the oldest two boys.

'What's wrong Ernst? Moishe?' Alice asked them as Manna began marshalling the others out of the house.

'We don't want to hold hands, Alice. That's for little ones.'

'Yeah. And girls.'

Alice hid a smile. Recently this pair had been exerting themselves to be more, as they put it, 'manly'. It was useful when they offered to chop and carry logs for the fire, or do jobs around the house, and she'd been very grateful to Joshua, Sir Benjamin's gruff gardener and handyman, for letting them help him. Growing boys needed male role models. It was another reason to get them out to school.

'Very well. Just walk calmly alongside each other then, please.' Still the boys shifted. 'What is it?' Alice demanded.

'Can we take our bikes? Please.'

'To school?'

'Yes. Lots of the boys do it. We've seen them. And they play on them at lunchtime too.'

Again, Alice had to hide a smile at the thought of Ernst and Moishe watching the locals for the best way of doing things. They both had good bikes, donated by the kind people of the

West London Synagogue, scions of London's longest-standing Jewish families and their benefactors here at Weir Courtney. Besides, they were going to be late if they hung around much longer and that wouldn't do at all.

'Very well,' she agreed, putting up a hand to forestall their mad cheering. 'But only if you show me that you can ride carefully and safely.'

'Yes, Alice. We definitely can. Stay on the left-hand side, tight to the edge and use your hand to signal. We know how to do it.'

Finally, Alice smiled at them. 'I know you do, boys. Off you go then and we'll see you there.'

'Yeah! Thanks, Alice.'

And they were gone, darting for the bikes kept in Joshua's shed around the side of the house.

'Boys, hey?!' Alice said companionably to Marta, stepping out after them. Or trying to. Marta had dug her heels into the parquet flooring and was going nowhere. 'Marta? Come on – we're going to be late.'

'Don't care.' The little girl stuck out a mutinous lower lip. 'Don't want to go.'

'To school? Why not? It'll be fun.'

'It's fun here. And I do learning. I can read.'

'You're very good at reading,' Alice agreed, 'but school is more than that. It's mathematics and geography, art and games.'

Marta's head went up at the word games, but she forced it determinedly down again. 'We do games.'

'Well, yes, but there aren't many of us, are there? You can play better games with more children.'

'Like what?'

'Let's get going and I'll tell you.'

'No.'

The heels went in again and Alice looked at the open door in frustration. Beyond it, Ernst and Moishe went rushing past on their bikes, ringing their bells in the frosty air, and Alice was desperate to follow. Manna and the other children would be halfway there and she had to catch them up. The teachers had gone to great efforts to get the Weir Courtney children settled and it would be terribly rude not to turn up on time.

'Tell you what,' she said, crossing her fingers behind her back. 'Let's go and see the others in, and if you don't want to go with them, you can walk back with Manna and me.'

Marta looked at her suspiciously. 'You don't mean that.'

Alice thought about it. 'Actually, I do mean it. I think school will be fun but I'm not going to force you to do anything you don't want to do.'

'You aren't?'

'No.' Alice uncrossed her fingers; she wasn't lying. If Marta was uneasy, she could miss today. The head would understand and no doubt once the others came out chattering about the fun they'd had, she'd ask to join them of her own accord. 'I promise, Kotka.'

The nickname slipped out without thinking but, to her horror, Marta's eyes brimmed with instant tears. Hurrying her out into the cold, Alice set off down the road, the little girl's hand held tightly in hers, her mind racing.

'Is something particular bothering you, Marta?'

Marta wiped at the tears with her gloved hand. 'I miss Tasha, Alice.'

Alice felt an instant tug on her heart. 'Me too,' she said honestly.

'She was my sort-of-sister but she didn't come with me. Why didn't she come with me, Alice?'

Alice sighed. 'I'm sure she would have done if she could, but she's a grown-up now and she had to get a job.'

'Does she have a job?'

'I don't know.'

Tasha sent regular letters but they were tight, superficial

accounts of everyday nothings that Alice suspected hid the fact that she was finding life in London hard.

'Is she going to get married then?' Marta demanded. 'She said she was going to get married and she said I could be her bridesmaid. I'd like to be a bridesmaid, Alice.'

'I know, Kotka, and I'm sure as soon as it's organised, Tasha will be in touch.'

'Are you?' Marta kicked at a pebble on the pavement. 'I think she's gone.'

'Gone?'

Alice looked down at the little girl as she marched her into the outskirts of the village. She could hear children in the play-ground and had to get there before the bell called them inside.

'Not gone, gone. Not like up the chimney…'

Alice held in her cry of protest though even now, the chil-dren's callous acceptance of such brutal things took her breath away.

'Just not coming back,' Marta finished.

'Maybe, then, we can visit her.'

Alice regretted the words the moment she saw Marta's face light up. What a fool – never make promises you couldn't keep!

'Really?' Marta bounced up and down. 'Can we really? I'd love that, Alice. When can we go? Today? Can we go today?'

'It's school today.'

The bouncing stopped. 'You said I didn't have to go.'

They turned the corner and there was the school, an imposing red-brick building, softened by the happily shrieking children running around in front of it. Marta stopped dead, grabbing at the branch of a leafless tree to anchor herself, and Alice cursed under her breath.

'And I meant it, Marta. But I can't go to London because I need to be here when the others come back.'

'Why?'

'So I can hear all about what a lovely time they've had.'

Marta's eyes narrowed. 'It won't be a lovely time. London would be a lovely time.'

Alice knelt down in front of her. 'And we'll sort it out as soon as we can.'

She had to go to London every month to report to the ladies of the West London Synagogue. She'd only been twice so far but she'd hated it both times. She'd had to stand there in front of wealthily stern London women, their perfectly manicured hands crossed over their perfectly tailored bosoms as they perused her budgeting in minute detail.

'Does this Mattias child *need* piano lessons?' Mrs Pinto, the imposing chairwoman, had asked last time.

Alice had looked at her, certain that she had a clutch of children who took not just piano lessons but violin and flute too, not to mention riding, ballet and whatever else took their spoiled fancy. Mrs Pinto had no idea how Mattias' little eyes lit up when he heard music, how long he'd spent at Sir Benjamin's piano trying to teach himself the notes, and how grateful he'd been when Alice had shown him the basics. He was naturally talented and with professional input he could go far.

'I believe,' she'd said firmly, 'that offered a choice between bread and piano lessons, Mattias would choose the lessons. He longs to be a pianist.'

Mrs Pinto had shaken her elegant head. 'And that, you see, is the problem. We are here to provide the basics of life for these orphans, Miss Goldberger, not to indulge unrealistic fantasies.'

It had made Alice want to scream. They saw the children as cardboard charity cases, not living breathing individuals to be shown what living could truly be.

'Can I suggest,' she'd said, keeping as calm as she could, 'that when you next visit Weir Courtney we ask Mattias to play what he has learned so far? Perhaps then you will see how much the piano means to him?'

Thankfully another lady, Mrs Reinhart, had agreed that

was an excellent idea and Alice had been allowed money for the
lessons, but every meeting was a fight and already she was
dreading the next one. Visiting Tasha would certainly make that
particular London trip more worthwhile – if the girl wanted to
see them.

'I'll write to Tasha,' she promised Marta.

'When?'

'Today.'

'Good. I'll help you.'

'You don't want to be in school?'

'No.'

It was no use, Alice could see that. Marta had made up her
mind and fair enough. But there were still the others to think of.

'You sit here then, while I go inside.'

'Here? By myself?'

'You'll be quite all right, but I have to see the other children
into their classrooms, don't I?'

Marta nodded reluctantly. 'You'll come back?'

'I will.'

'And we'll go home?'

Alice's heart squeezed again. It was the first time she'd
heard any of the children call Weir Courtney 'home' but it
sounded so natural. 'We'll go home,' she agreed.

'And write to Tasha?'

'And write to Tasha, yes.'

At three o'clock that afternoon, they were back at the school
gates. Marta had been at her most charming once she'd been
safely back in Weir Courtney. She'd made soup with Sophie,
spent an unusually patient amount of time reading with
Manna, and then sat earnestly with Alice to write to Tasha
and ask if she might visit her. All in all, they'd had a sweet
time, but Alice prayed the others had had a good day to tell the

girl about and watched the school doors nervously as the bell rang.

She needn't have worried. The Weir Courtney children were in the middle of the general tumble, several of them chatting away to the local kids. Suzi and Judith came running as soon as they saw Alice, scrambling to tell her about the skipping tricks they'd learned at lunchtime, and Alice was delighted to see Marta listening intently.

'You should come tomorrow, Martie,' Suzi told her. 'We did painting and adding up with pebbles, and we had a really good story about a unicorn.'

'A unicorn?' Marta asked.

'Yes. A unicorn that cried.'

'Why did it cry?'

'We don't know. We get to that bit tomorrow.'

Alice kissed Suzi gratefully. The girl couldn't have said anything better if she'd been primed and Alice reminded herself to bring the unicorn up again at supper to keep Marta curious. For now, though, it was time to gather her charges for the walk home.

'Ernst, Moishe, do you have your bikes?'

'Course we do.' Ernst ran over. 'Jack showed me how to do a wheelie.'

'Did he indeed? That's very clever. But no wheelies on the road.'

'I know! I'll show you on the drive back home.'

There was that word again – home. The children were clearly relaxing into life here in Surrey and that, in turn, made Alice feel more relaxed herself. She mustered her crocodile as the two lads pushed their bikes out of the store at the side of the school, and was glad to see Marta slide in between Suzi and Judith to hear more about their day.

'Off we go then. Sophie's made shortbread for everyone who walks nicely, so let's see your best feet forward.'

The children giggled at the English idiom and set happily off towards Weir Courtney, Alice at their head and Manna at the rear. The sun had come out earlier, chasing away the worst of the frost, but already it was growing dark.

'Watch out for slippy bits,' Alice warned, leading inevitably to several of the children attempting to slide around. 'Not here,' she warned. There weren't many cars on the road but the pavement was narrow and it didn't do to be careless. 'We can maybe make a skid patch on the drive when we get back.'

'A skid patch?!' cried Ernst, shooting past on his bike. 'Brilliant!'

'If you're careful.'

'I'm always careful.'

That wasn't true but Alice was glad to see him turn his attention back to the road, keeping tight to the edge as he headed off, Moishe on his back wheel. She recalled her childhood when, if their parents weren't looking – which they often weren't – Max would pour water onto their terrace so that it would set into a long line of ice that they could shoot down in their gripless indoor shoes. It had been such fun. The children here would love it and—

Alice heard the shriek of the brakes before the engine of the car. An acrid smell filled the air and she instinctively stepped in front of the crocodile of children as the bonnet of a smart Austen came round the corner at a most unnatural angle. The car was slowing, but not fast enough and it was heading straight for Ernst and Moishe, who'd spotted the danger and stopped, flinging their bikes aside and pressing themselves tight against the hedge.

Alice saw the driver wrestling with his steering wheel, desperately trying to pull the vehicle straight, but, although his front wheels turned, the back ones were locked and she watched as the rear slewed round and rammed, with a crunch of what she could only pray was mere metal, into the helpless bicycles.

'Ernst!' she screamed. 'Moishe!' She turned to the children. 'Stay there! Stay right there.'

Manna huddled the children around her, their eyes white in the gathering gloom, and Alice ran to the boys.

'Alice!'

'Moishe, thank heavens.' She swept him into her arms, feeling him shaking helplessly against her. 'Ernst? Ernst!' The second boy was nowhere to be seen. The driver was out of the car, white-faced and babbling, but he didn't matter. 'Ernst!' she screamed and then she saw them – two little legs sticking out from under the smoking car. 'No!'

Pushing Moishe gently aside, she knelt on the ground, the driver with her. A small, pathetic moan came from underneath and she sobbed.

'He's alive. Ernst, it's Alice. I'm here, liebchen. I'm going to get you out.'

'It hurts,' he moaned.

'I know, sweet one. I'll be there in a minute. I'll make it stop hurting.'

The driver was grunting hideously as he pushed against the car but it wouldn't shift. There was more smoke and he looked at Alice grimly.

'I'm going to have to pull him out. We shouldn't move him, but...'

She nodded and glanced back to the others as he reached under and gently took hold of Ernst's legs. Moishe ran to his friends and Alice's heart broke to see Marta throw her arms around him, but they were not her concern right now.

'Ernst, my liebchen.'

The man had lifted him into his arms and Ernst looked so small against his broad chest, and so limp. His eyes were closed and he dangled helplessly as they carried him away from the car and laid him on an overcoat a passer-by had quickly proffered. Others had stopped too and were efficiently closing off the road and sending for help from the village, but Alice heard all this activity through a fug of horror.

'Mutti?' Ernst whimpered. 'Mutti!'

The desperate cry cut through Alice and she sank down to cradle his head in her lap, stroking his hair away from his face.

'I'm here, Ernst.'

It was a lie but it was already horribly clear to Alice that the boy was not going to know that. Not now and not ever. His legs lay at an unnatural angle and his breathing was coming in ragged pants.

'Mutti,' he murmured and smiled, already half angel.

His hand gripped hers with brief, sudden strength and then went limp. Alice pulled him up against her, covering his face in kisses, but it was too late. He was gone; gone to his mother. His tiny life, saved at huge effort from the horrors of war, had been lost to one patch of ice.

'Is he...?' The driver slumped next to her. 'He is, isn't he? My God, I killed him. I killed a child.' He buried his face in his hands.

Alice was torn between hating him and feeling desperately sorry for him. She put out a tentative hand to his knee but even as she did so a fury of small fists came raining in on the poor man.

'Nazi!' Moishe screamed, flinging himself bodily at the man. 'Nazi pig!'

'What?' He looked up, even more horrified. 'I'm no Nazi. I'm an accountant. I go to church, I...'

But Moishe was still screaming and Alice had to let go of poor Ernst's little body to clasp him to her.

'He's not a Nazi, Moishe. It was an accident. A horrible, terrible accident.'

'He's dead. Ernst's dead. Nazi!'

'Why does he keep saying that?' the driver stuttered.

'He was in the camps,' Alice said, fighting to make sense of it herself. 'As far as he's concerned all death comes at Nazi hands.'

The man blinked furiously. 'Good God. This is awful. I didn't mean this to happen. I'm sorry. It was the ice, just the ice. I, I...' He was shaking violently, clearly in shock and rambling.

Alice was relieved to hear the clanging bell of an ambulance arriving. To be honest, she felt rather shaky herself and was even more relieved when Sophie came running and put her arms around her, her broad grasp encompassing Moishe too.

'Holy mother of God, save us all!' Sophie exclaimed. 'My children, my poor, poor children. Let's get you home.'

It was the third time today that Alice had heard their house described that way and this time she leaned into it gladly. The ambulance men were carrying Ernst into the van and now Sir Benjamin had arrived and was imposing his ready authority on the situation, so Alice let Sophie lead her and her terrified charges back up to the road to Weir Courtney. To home.

It took a long, long time to settle the children that night. They had all believed, like Moishe, that only Nazis killed and that, therefore, with the Nazis defeated, there would be no more death. To find out in such a sharp, horrific way that the world was still a dangerous place was a terrible shock and there were many tears. Alice sat in the girls' bedroom playing soft tunes on her harmonica until they all went to sleep, but Moishe was the hardest hit and, in the end, she had to resort to a dash of brandy in hot milk to soothe him to sleep.

She took a far larger dose of it to bed herself but, even so, all she could see when she closed her eyes were Ernst's legs poking out from under the smoking car. He'd been in her care, under her guardianship. Logically she knew it had been a terrible accident but if only she hadn't let the boys ride their bikes, or had made them ride behind her, or push the bikes round the bend. Not that that would have helped either, but it was so hard to believe that death had come to the children in a place she had told them all was safe. Over and over in her head, she could hear Ernst's desperate little voice calling for his mutti and was sure she wasn't the only one. Ernst was at peace now but the others were not and she knew already that there would be cries in the night.

In the end, she got up again and, sitting at her desk, picked up the letter she and Marta had written so innocently to Tasha earlier in the day. She tore it into tiny pieces. There was no way, after today, she was taking an eight-year-old into busy central London, but Marta needed to see her sort-of-sister more than ever. Reaching into the hidden drawer where she kept her savings, Alice drew out a ten-shilling note and slid it into the envelope. Then, picking up a pen, she took a fresh piece of paper and wrote a new letter.

She wrote of Marta's tears, Ernst's death and Moishe's enraged cries. She wrote of the broken hearts down in Surrey and of how a visit from Tasha might help them start to mend. She didn't write of her own heart. She didn't write of the way she missed seeing the flash of Tasha's red hair around the corner, or hearing her fierce voice in a debate. She didn't write of the weight of guilt sitting on her because that was hers alone to bear, but she longed for the girl's company anyway and hoped, perhaps, she would sense it between the lines.

Please come, she signed off. *The children would love to see you.*

She read it back. There was nothing between the lines.

And so would I, she added, then hastily sealed it up before she could change her mind, and headed into the frozen night to send it on its way to London.

TWENTY

THE SHELTER | JANUARY 1946

TASHA

Tasha rolled what felt like the hundredth matzoh ball around in her palms and dropped it onto a tray, ready to go into the great vat of chicken soup that Chef was preparing for the evening meal. She'd branched into helping out in the Shelter kitchens and liked it more than cleaning the toilets, but not by much. The kitchen was cramped and busy and Chef had poor ingredients, demanding customers and a very short temper; not a happy mix.

Tying her apron tighter around her waist, she felt the familiar rub of her handbag beneath her blouse and touched her fingers to it for strength. Inside, as ever, was Lydia's lock of hair but also these days Tasha kept the small amount of her earnings left over after paying for her keep, as well as her letters from Alice. The latest one felt almost hot within the leather and she flushed at the thought of the words within.

> *Please come. The children would love to see you.*
> *And so would I.*

The heat was part pleasure, part guilt. Poor Ernst's death sounded terrible and she hated the thought of her kotka crying and longed to curl up and cuddle her. And yet... She'd written, commiserating with them all in every language available to her and assuring them she'd be down as soon as she could possibly get away, but hadn't yet brought herself to get on the train to Surrey. She was scared – scared that when she saw the fancy house and the happy children, when she saw Alice organising it all and Sophie cooking up warm, comforting food with real, soft, melt-in-the-mouth matzohs, not the chewy things they churned out in the Shelter, she would never want to come back to London. It was a pathetic, selfish reason and she hated herself for it, but she still couldn't quite get on that train.

'Are the matzohs done yet?' Chef demanded.

'Yes, Chef,' she said, nudging the tray forward and pushing thoughts of Weir Courtney away with it.

'Ah.' He was clearly taken aback. 'Well, good. Just in time.'

'A thank you would be nice,' Tasha muttered under her breath – the English coming easily now, even when talking to herself – but she wasn't holding out for it. Not, at least, until everyone was fed, the surfaces were cleaned down and Chef was putting his feet up with a glass of plum brandy. Occasionally at that point she would get a smile or a begrudging, 'You're not bad at this, girl,' but usually she was long gone, escaping for a precious hour or two with Georg.

He came home earlier now that the days were darker and shorter. They'd found a fire escape on the third floor that led out to a small section of roof where, if no other couples had beaten them to it, they could snatch some private time. It was freezing in this dank British winter, but they could cuddle under a blanket, watch the city below them and talk. Or, at least, Georg could talk.

'See that house over there,' he would say, picking out some

fancy three-storey townhouse overlooking the Thames, 'that's where we're going to live.'

'Is it indeed?' Tasha would say, playing along. 'I can see our duck-egg blue drawing room, with floor-length curtains in thick fabric. I can see our utterly impractical cream carpet and our two matching sofas and the cute little chaise longue for reclining.'

'And our grand piano, of course, right in the middle.'

'Of course, because both of us play so well.'

'Because *our children* will play so well.'

She'd always lose patience before him.

'We're not going to have any children if we don't actually get married, Georg.'

'Just a few more months, kochanie.'

That was his theme now – a few *more* months. If pushed, he always had a more specific goal to hand: 'We'll be in by Pesach'; 'We'll book the synagogue for Shavuot.' He meant it. Every time he meant it. But the much-promised engagement ring hadn't appeared and she knew every date would slide past similarly forgotten. Marta wouldn't be a bridesmaid, or come to live with them, and the guilt of that nagged at her constantly. Georg, in contrast, was excited to be getting on with his work, and it was hard for him to see that there was little of merit for her in London.

'What would you like to do?' he'd ask, but she didn't know.

Lydia had always told her that she'd inherit her clothes shop and, while Tasha had never been as interested as her mother in the clothes, she'd liked the idea of running a shop. She still did. She wanted a space of her own to make inviting so that customers would tell her, as they'd told Lydia, that she'd made their day/their daughter's wedding/their bar mitzvah. Making people look (and feel) good wasn't a grand aim, it wouldn't change the world, but it might, in a small way make it better.

Shops in London, however, seemed to either be grubby back-street places or grand, Oxford Street stores. Perhaps there were areas of the capital with more bohemian shops but, if so, they hadn't found them yet.

'First shift's coming in,' Chef called. 'Stand by your beds.'

Reluctantly, Tasha took up her position at the counter, pushing her bag round to her back and picking up a ladle.

'Ooh, our favourite serving girl,' Beth cackled, first in the queue. 'Give us an extra matzoh, bunk-mate. Some of us have been at work all day.'

'Give me strength,' Tasha muttered to the ceiling and, gritting her teeth, began dishing up.

Finally, service was over and she was free. Pulling her bag out from under her blouse, she felt for the letter.

Please come. The children would love to see you.
    And so would I.

She glanced to the window and the streetlamps glittering in a bright frost. Perhaps she should take a walk along the river, find Victoria station, enquire about trains to Lingfield. It need only be a short visit; she would definitely come back. She and Georg had plans here in London and one day they'd make them a reality. Plus, of course, she'd told every search operation in London that she was living here, so if Lydia did come looking...

Tasha turned into reception and stopped dead.

There, standing at the desk, back to her as she talked earnestly to the receptionist, was a woman – a tall, slender woman with shoulder-length hair the colour of flames in a wintertime hearth.

'Mama?' Tasha croaked. Then she was running, skidding

across the tiled reception area and flinging herself at the woman. 'Mama!'

Strong arms went around her, a hand stroked her hair. Someone said 'Tasha', as if from far, far away, and she buried herself in her mother's embrace and felt as if her heart might explode with joy.

'You're here,' she wept. 'You're alive.'

'Tasha,' the voice said again. It didn't sound like her mother but then, she probably didn't sound like herself these days either. 'Tasha – let this poor woman go!'

A hand closed over her arm and Tasha looked up crossly to see the receptionist trying to pull her away. She blinked in confusion.

'It's fine,' a second voice said. 'I understand. That is, I think there's been some sort of mistake, but it's fine. Truly, it's fine.'

Slowly Tasha looked up at the woman she'd so eagerly rushed to. The face that looked back at her was kind, tender even, but it was not Lydia. She leaped away, stung.

'You're not her.'

'No,' the stranger agreed. 'I'm sorry.'

'You're not Mama,' she repeated dazedly. Her body was still singing with the joy of recognition and it was taking an embarrassing amount of time for her brain to catch up to the reality that she'd flung herself into the arms of a total stranger.

'My name is Nicola Grainger. I'm a nurse, here to see one of the residents.'

Tasha stepped away, noticing the smart uniform beneath the woman's simple woollen coat.

'Your hair...' she stuttered.

Nicola Grainger put a self-conscious hand to her head. 'Is it the same as your mother's?'

Her voice was kind, but Tasha didn't want kindness. She wanted her mother. Not this woman posing as her, however inadvertently, getting her hopes up just when she'd been learning to keep them hidden away where they couldn't hurt so much.

They hurt now.

They hurt as if someone had taken shears to them and shorn them down to their most naked, bleeding base. Turning, she fled from the Shelter and ran for the river, tears flowing, ice-cold down her cheeks.

'Tasha?'

It was Georg, strolling down the street with another young man. Tasha looked desperately round for a way to avoid him but there was no means of escape.

'I'm busy.'

She tried to push past but he grabbed her arm.

'You're crying. What's wrong, kochanie?'

'There was a woman,' she said, gesturing back to the Shelter.

Georg's companion ducked inside, sliding around Nicola Grainger, who must have followed Tasha out and was looking curiously at them both.

Georg looked back. 'I see,' he said.

'What do you see?'

'I see what you thought.'

Tasha folded her arms defensively across her chest. 'Yes, well, I was wrong.'

'As you were bound to be, Tash.'

His voice was kind but his words were not and Tash felt filled with anger: anger that the woman in the hostel wasn't her mother; anger that she'd come to London for a new start and it was a terrible one; anger that she was hurting Marta and letting Alice down; anger that Georg wanted life to all be forwards and never back.

'She's not dead!' she shouted at him. 'I know it suits you if she is. I know it means we don't have to worry about the past, though why you have such a problem with that I have no idea because you never, ever talk about it. It's all future with you, isn't it? All rosy future, full of your fancy, utterly meaningless dreams.'

'They are not meaningless,' Georg shot back. 'I'm working, aren't I? I'm getting on, doing well, building the foundations for us to be together. All you're doing is moping around waiting for a ghost.'

Tasha gasped. 'Mama's not dead!'

'She is, Tasha. Of course she is. They're *all* dead.' He grabbed her arms. 'The Nazis killed millions of them; what makes you think she's any different?'

'She just is. I know it, Georg. I know it here, in my heart.' She pounded at her chest, her knuckles knocking against the leather of her bag. 'See this,' she drew out the lock of hair, 'I kept this to keep her alive to me and I won't give up on that just to suit you.'

Georg took the hair from her, lifting it to the light of a lamp-post where it hung, dark and ragged.

'You think this is life?'

'I think it's a reminder of life.'

'A life you'd clearly rather have than one with me. You have to let this go, Tasha, if we're to stand a chance.'

'Why? Why haven't you got room for me to love my mother as well as you?'

'I have!' he cried. 'You can love her memory, Tasha, honour it too. It's just that I can't bear having to put *our* life on hold until she comes back into it. And I hate the hurt that's going to come to you when she doesn't. Let it go, Tasha. For me, for *you*, let it go.'

Then he opened his fingers and, just like that, released the precious lock. The freezing wind snatched it and blew it down the pavement and, horrified, Tasha ran after it, stamping her foot on it to keep it safe.

'Let go of my mother?' she demanded furiously. 'Let go of my family and my roots and all that made me, me?'

'*You* made you, you. Can't you see that? You're your own woman and a glorious, bold, brave, delicious woman too. Please, Tasha, take the bag off, stand up and just be yourself.'

He stepped towards her but Tasha put up her hands. His every word was grating against the reopened wound of her missing mother and she couldn't bear to be with him for any longer. How dare he release Lydia's hair to the wind? How dare he scatter her possessions as if she were, in turn, a possession of his?

'Your future is an empty promise, Georg Lieberman. Your "foundations" are mere money. It takes more than that to make a life. It takes strength and vision and self-knowledge. Ask any damned tree – without roots, you fall over in the slightest wind.'

Georg gaped at her. 'I'm doing my best,' he said, his voice so low, so scared, that she longed to take him in her arms.

But she'd done that one too many times. There would be no townhouse and no chaise longue and no grand piano. There would be no wedding and no babies and that was fine by her.

'It's not good enough,' she told him.

Then she turned from his handsome face and bent to retrieve Lydia's hair from beneath her shoe, thinner and more matted than ever. Shaking, she returned it to her bag, pushing the battered box down where it caught on Alice's letter. She stared at the ten-shilling note peeking from the envelope, beckoning her with simple, openly offered care. Georg had told her he would look after her but he hadn't done so. Only one person, since Lydia had been driven out of Auschwitz into the snow of a bitter Polish winter, had ever actually looked after her.

'Alice,' Tasha whispered.

Clutching her bag with the last shreds of her courage, she turned and walked away from the Shelter, away from Georg, and towards the only sliver of home left. Maybe Georg was right; maybe Lydia was dead. But maybe she wasn't. And until Tasha knew, there was no way she was letting go of either the last tangle of her beloved red hair, or the last strands of hope. If Georg didn't understand that, he wasn't worth being with, however much that hurt.

TWENTY-ONE

LINGFIELD | FEBRUARY 1946

ALICE

Alice paused halfway up Lingfield High Street, her eye inextricably drawn to the bright pink hearts stuck to a big shop window. They were, she assumed, for St Valentine's Day, but they made her want to cry. Ernst had had a great big, warm heart, she thought, and it had been crushed by that wretched car slamming into him across the ice.

'Enough, Alice,' she told herself crossly.

The children were slowly getting over losing their friend and it was doing no one any good her dwelling on it, but something about his death seemed to have brought everything else into sharp focus: the many moves she'd made in the last few years; the lack of news about Max; the loss of Tasha, who still hadn't come to see them. She just felt so weary and so endlessly, mournfully sad.

'Are you all right there, my lovely?'

Alice jumped. A buxom woman in a startling pink tabard was standing in the doorway, looking at her in concern.

'I'm fine,' she stuttered. 'Just, er... looking at your hearts.'

'Pretty, aren't they? Everyone needs a little love, I always say. Did you want an appointment?'

'An appointment?'

'Cos you're in luck – I've just had a cancellation so I can fit you in before closing. Come along in.'

'I don't think—'

But the woman was taking her shopping bags and ushering her inside and she seemed to have lost the will to do anything but follow. She found herself in a warm room, gaudily decorated in cream, gold and pink, with several gilt-framed mirrors on the wall.

'A hairdresser's!' she said out loud.

'That's right, my lovely. Welcome to Beautiful You. I'm Joyce.'

Alice blinked, dazzled. 'It's very... bright.'

'Thank you,' Joyce beamed. 'I modelled it on Elizabeth Arden's salons.'

'Elizabeth...?'

'Arden, my lovely. She's an American, famous for the best beauty salons in the world. Of course, hers are in fancy places like New York and Paris, but I didn't see why our little bit of Surrey couldn't have some luxury too. So, here we are! And for half the price. What's your name? Alice? Beautiful. You just sit back and relax, Alice.'

Alice was certain that wouldn't be possible and as Joyce eased her into a padded chair she stared glumly into a far too well-lit mirror. Her hair, freed from its usual bun, dangled limply around her face, both of them equally grey.

'Has it been a while since your last proper cut, my lovely?' Joyce asked gently.

Alice considered. Sophie took the scissors to her hair every so often to keep the ends neat, but that wasn't what this smiley woman was asking.

'I think the last time was in 1932.'

'1932! That's – heavens! – nearly fifteen years ago.' Joyce picked up a glossy magazine and fanned herself. 'You poor, poor love. How come?'

'Do you really want to know?'

'Of course,' Joyce said. 'How can I make you into your most beautiful you if I don't know who that you is?'

Alice blinked at her in the mirror. It was an interesting idea. No one asked her about herself these days and this bright, cosy salon felt like such a safe place.

'I'm Jewish,' she confided, watching for a reaction. Many people, even here in sleepy England, still did not like Jews, but Joyce nodded at her, wanting more. 'And I used to live in Berlin.'

'Ah. Herr Hitler?'

Alice sighed. So much pain and hurt trussed up in that single, hateful name.

'Herr Hitler,' she agreed. 'He banned Jews slowly and steadily from everything in Germany. My brother and I lost our jobs.'

'No! What did you do, Alice?'

'I ran a nursery for children whose parents were too poor to keep them.'

'What a beautiful thing to do!' Joyce clasped a hand to her ample bosom. 'And how terrible of those nasty Nazis stopping you. Who looked after the kiddies instead?'

'Someone blonde,' Alice said bitterly.

Joyce gave a little laugh. 'There now, he was stupid that Hitler, wasn't he? Even little old Joyce Cherry could have told him that you can change hair colour with the twist of a dye. It's not what you look like that counts, is it? It's how you treat people.'

Alice stared at Joyce in the mirror. So much wisdom in such a sunny package.

'It is, Joyce,' she agreed. 'But they didn't see it that way, so I had to leave.'

'And your brother?'

Alice's heart thudded and she had to fight for the breath to answer. 'They wouldn't let him go until I was settled in England, and by the time that happened, they'd closed the borders.'

'No! You poor dear. How's he doing?'

'I don't know.'

'You don't...? My good heavens, Alice, you've not heard from him?' Alice shook her head and for a moment Joyce was stumped, but then she rallied. 'The post is terrible these days, isn't it? I'm sure a letter will get through soon. Does he have family?'

'A wife and a little girl.'

'There, then, they'll be together.'

'Together somewhere,' Alice said darkly.

'And when you next see them, you'll have beautiful hair.' Joyce put up a hand to forestall Alice's protest. 'It doesn't feel important in comparison, I understand that, but at least it's something you *can* do.'

And with that, Alice could not argue. The endless waiting for news made her feel so painfully impotent and, picturing Max striding up to her saying, 'Hey, sis, I like what you've done to your hair,' she smiled for what felt like the first time in far too long.

Joyce leaned in, gentle hands on her shoulders. 'How would you feel about going short?'

'Short?' Alice put a hand to her hair, and felt it lank and thin around her shoulders.

'It's all the rage. You've got a natural wave that's being pulled out by all this length, so if we took it right up, it would fluff out beautifully around your face. Give you more... body.'

'Make me look less scrawny, you mean?' Alice asked. She'd

learned the English word from a mum at the school gates and thought it very apt.

'There now,' Joyce said. 'We're all a bit thinner than we used to be after this damned war, but things are getting better.'

And, sitting there in Beautiful You with Joyce smiling so kindly at her, Alice thought perhaps they finally were.

'Do whatever you want,' she said recklessly.

'Ooh, my favourite words! Trust me, you'll love it. Now, this way for a wash.'

She took Alice over to the lurid pink sink and, as the hair-dresser began massaging delicious-smelling shampoo into her scalp with gentle assurance, Alice closed her eyes and prayed she was right. She was under no illusions that Joyce could work miracles, but it wouldn't hurt to smarten up a bit. Frankly, in the last three weeks since that car had slewed into poor Ernst, it had been an effort to even get dressed, let alone take care with her appearance. She'd got through it by focusing on the other chil-dren but it had been hard. They'd all been shocked and tearful and she'd understood completely because she'd been exactly the same herself.

Her mind was pulled inexorably back to the boy and she pictured his eager face when he'd leaped out of the aeroplane at Crosby-on-Eden. 'Come on out. It's really nice here,' he'd called back to the little ones and then he'd been off, eager to explore every corner. Even more clearly, she could see him shooting past her on his bike, keen to be a big boy and ride home, she could hear the squeal of brakes and the sickening crunch of his poor body.

She was glad to close her eyes as Joyce rinsed her hair with deliciously warm water. The funeral had been so sad. There'd been no one to notify, that's what had hurt Alice most. There'd been not one person to tell about the loss of this vibrant little boy; not one relative to mourn him. Everyone at Weir Courtney had been there for him, though, she'd insisted on it. Even the funeral director had tried to talk her out of letting the children go to the service, but she'd put her foot down. They were each other's family now and families paid their last respects. Besides, it had been important for the children to see the dead treated with dignity and sadness, not dumped on a heap for callous disposal.

'Are you all right there, my lovely?'

Alice blinked her eyes open and they were filled with the sunrise colours of the salon.

'Sorry. I was just... I lost a little boy a few weeks ago.'

'No!'

'And I can't stop thinking about it.'

'I'm not surprised!' Joyce escorted her back to the cutting-chair with kind hands. 'You've been through the mill, haven't you?'

It wasn't a term Alice knew but it was exactly right – she felt as battered and ground down as if she'd been crushed between ancient millstones.

'He wasn't *my* little boy,' she explained hastily. 'That's to say, he was in my care—'

'So he *was* your little boy, or as good as. You must be the lady from Weir Courtney. I've heard such good things about that place. You're doing a tremendous job there, giving those poor mites a happy life again.'

'We are? Thank you.'

'No, thank *you*. It's folks like you will set the world on its feet again. Look at me, swanning around cutting hair all day, while you look after those poor orphans. I feel terrible, I do.'

Alice smiled. 'Please don't. People need a bit of cheer.'

Joyce tipped her head on one side, considering. 'They do,' she agreed, smiling again. 'Everyone's lost something these last few years. My hubby was killed at Dunkirk.'

'I'm so sorry.'

Alice felt instantly guilty for being caught up in her own sorrows, but Joyce waved an easy hand.

'Don't be. I'm long since over it. Don't get me wrong, he was a nice enough man but nothing special. I only married him cos I got caught with our Betsy and I'm ever so glad I had her. Him, though, I could take or leave. I was sorry he died, of course I was, but I don't, you know, miss him. I'm better on my own. You, love?'

Alice flushed. 'I'm definitely better on my own.'

'There, see.'

Alice wasn't sure she did see but Joyce was lifting her scissors and she was spared having to say more, as the first grey lock fell to the tiled floor.

'This is going to look beautiful,' Joyce cooed.

Alice crossed her fingers in her lap and hoped that was true. Oskar had wanted to treat Sir Benjamin and Lady Phoebe to dinner and had talked Sophie into cooking up a feast tonight. He often stayed for dinner these days, stopping over in the little guest room alongside the boys' dorm, but this was to be a grander affair than their usual kitchen suppers. Manna had bought a new dress and invited Mina and Golda to 'make an occasion of it'. Alice had been dreading any hint of fun after all that had happened but sitting here, in Beautiful You, she could almost look forward to it.

The bell over the salon door tinkled merrily and a girl of maybe sixteen in a skewed school uniform came tumbling inside. She bounced up to Joyce, landing a smacking kiss on her cheek. This, Alice presumed, was Betsy.

'Hey, Mum.'

'Hello, sweetie.' Joyce kissed her back. 'Good day?'

'Nah,' Betsy said cheerily. 'I was bottom at maths and Mrs Turner wouldn't let me in the home economics room cos she said I was an "accident waiting to happen".'

'The cheek of her!' Joyce exclaimed indignantly.

But Betsy giggled and threw herself into the next chair. 'She's right, to be fair. Last week I set light to Audrey's hair with the gas ring.'

'Betsy! You didn't?'

'Only a bit. Audrey didn't mind. Said she wants it cut short anyway, so I told her to come here and I'll do it for her.'

'*I'll* do it for her,' Joyce said repressively. She rolled her eyes at Alice in the mirror. 'Kids – they think they can do anything, don't they?'

'I'm going to be a top hairdresser,' Betsy told Alice complacently.

'Maybe you will, sweetie,' Joyce agreed, 'but only with the right training.'

'Lucky I have the best teacher in the world then, isn't it?' Betsy was up again, giving Joyce another smacking kiss, then she bent down so her fresh young face was next to Alice's. 'Your hair looks lovely.'

Alice blinked. 'Erm, thank you.' She stared at herself. Joyce was still snipping away but the bulk of her hair had gone and the shorter style did make her face look less scrawny. 'It's a bit of a shock.'

Betsy glanced to the piles of hair on the floor. 'I bet! Still, who needs all that hair, right? It just holds you back. Paternalistic repression, you see.'

'Sorry?'

Joyce tutted. 'Get away with you, Betsy.' She leaned in to Alice. 'She's picking up all these new-fangled ideas. Feminism and that. "Why can't girls be as good as boys?" she's always saying. I've told her – we *are* as good as boys and it's our secret weapon that we know that and they don't. She won't have it though. It's all about "equality" these days.'

Alice smiled at Betsy. 'I know someone you'd get on well with,' she said, thinking of Tasha's fierce assertions in Windermere. 'She told me that it was my duty to make myself heard by men so that your generation would find it easier to do so.'

'Quite right,' Betsy agreed. 'She sounds super. Is she local?'

Alice shrank back. 'No. She's in London.'

'London! Lucky her!'

'Not if you ask me,' Joyce said crisply. 'Nasty, smelly, unfriendly place. Now off you pop, Betsy, and let me finish this poor lady's hair in peace.'

Betsy shrugged and bounced off though did not, thankfully, pop.

'Right,' Joyce said to Alice, 'blow dry.'

Alice wandered back to Weir Courtney feeling mildly dazed but happier than she had in ages. Joyce's easy bonhomie had soothed her and she rather liked her new hairstyle. Her neck was naked in the cold evening air and she was nervous about the bottle of something from America called hairspray that would apparently help the style 'keep its shape', but her head felt so much lighter and she was looking forward to the shock she'd give everyone when she walked through the door.

She glanced at her watch. Heavens, it was gone six already. Sophie would be having to cope with kiddie teatime on top of preparing her dishes for tonight's dinner and Alice guiltily picked up her pace. When she made it to the dining room, however, she found Mina and Golda in full charge, their hair in curlers and a surely unnecessary amount of make-up plastered across their faces.

'Alice!' Golda cried. 'Look at you! Very à la mode!'

Alice flushed as all eyes turned her way.

'Cute!' Moishe said, giving her a smile. It was weak but one of the first she'd seen since he'd lost his friend and that alone made the impetuous haircut feel worthwhile.

Behind her she heard the front door open and flushed. Was

that Oskar? Heavens! She hadn't even had a chance to get changed yet. She considered taking the back door out of the dining room and leaving Mina or Golda to entertain him, but then scolded herself. They'd already been holding the fort while she'd swanned off to have her hair done.

'I'll get it,' she said and, swallowing self-consciously, went back into the hall.

The door was slightly ajar but there was no one there. Had she left it unlatched? How thoughtless of her in this cold. She strode forward and pushed it shut but as the latch clicked, she heard a strange noise – something like a whimper.

'Is someone there?'

She snatched the door open again and peered out into the gloom.

'Alice?' a faint voice said, then louder, 'Alice!'

Suddenly someone was flinging themselves at her with as much force as Betsy had flung herself at Joyce earlier and Alice staggered back into the hallway to see a wild-eyed redhead.

'Tasha! Tasha, you're here.'

Tasha stepped back, suddenly stiff before her. 'Is there still a job going?' she mumbled.

'We don't need nurserymaids, Tasha.'

'You don't?'

'Nope.' Alice stepped forward to drop a kiss on the frown-lines across her lovely young face. 'But we do need *you*. Welcome, Tasha. Welcome home.'

'Home?' Tasha murmured, shifting awkwardly from one foot to the other. 'Can it be home without my mother, Alice?'

'Not fully perhaps,' Alice conceded, her heart aching for the awkward young woman before her, 'but I hope we can, at least, hold you close until you find her.'

'Hold me close?' A shy smile broke across Tasha's face and she took a hesitant step forward. 'That sounds nice.'

Alice needed no further invitation and swept the girl into

her arms, but Tasha was taller than her now and as she held her in return, it was hard to know who was holding whom. Alice closed her eyes, drawing in the return of her spiky charge and prayed that somewhere, as she'd suggested to Tasha back on the slopes above Windermere, Lydia Ancel was chatting to Max Goldberger, and that they would someday, somehow, find their way back to them both.

TWENTY-TWO

THE AUSTRIAN BORDER | MARCH 1946

LYDIA

Border, 1km the sign said in German, English and another
language Lydia did not recognise. She peered at it in wonder.
She felt as if she'd been trudging through Bavaria forever.
People had been very kind along the way. She'd been given lifts
in carts and trucks and on a donkey. She'd been offered beds in
barns and outhouses, in hostels, camps, spare rooms and even,
once, in a smart hotel with an owner kind enough to dole out a
little luxury to a weary traveller.

For one precious night she'd lain in a warm bath, eaten a
full meal – with vegetables and even sauce – and slept in silken
sheets. She'd slept so deeply that she'd woken believing she was
home, in Warsaw, in 1939, with a husband, two daughters and a
maid. And then consciousness had slammed into her and she'd
been back to being a 'displaced person' with no home and no
family and nothing but a trip back to hell to get her out of that
borrowed bed.

The days, like her weary footsteps on the long, muddy
roads, had begun to meld into one so it was with something like

excitement that she read the sign. A border was surely progress.

Österreich, the next sign told her – Austria. Of course! She'd seen this on the map before she set out – a tiny patch of Germany's onetime ally poked up between them and Czechoslovakia and it seemed she must cross it. Her heart lifted. Austria, like Germany, was occupied by the Allies. There might be soldiers at the border, British or American military who could help her on her trip, for she was going far too slowly under her own weary steam.

Lydia hitched her bag up her aching back and pushed herself onward. She was close to the border now and could see lights in the gathering dusk, see a big hut and a barrier and guards. Guards with guns and dogs. Her limbs started shaking and she tutted at herself. These were not Nazis. These were the Allies, her liberators. But it seemed she could not tell that to her body and it was only with the fiercest will that she kept herself creeping forward.

'Halt!' a soldier barked.

She stopped, instinctively grovelling low. He walked around her and she felt the steam of his breath, heard the thud of his heavy boots, sensed the butt of his gun hunting her out.

'I'm a refugee,' she stuttered. 'Just a refugee.'

'Refugee,' the soldier repeated, then something that sounded like, 'bezhenets'. His accent was nasal, sibilant. This was no American, no Brit, this was not even a Frenchman. No, she realised with sick dread, this border was patrolled by the Russians.

'I'm sorry,' she said, putting up her hands. 'I don't want to cross. I'm going back. I'm...'

She tried to turn but he grabbed at her arm.

'I help you.'

'I don't—'

'I help you,' he said, more forcibly. 'I ally. Friend.'

She dared to look up and saw a thin face with a daunting scar carved across one cheek. Her body quivered harder but his eyes, at least, were kind and, besides, what choice did she have? He was picking up her bag and his grip on her arm, although not painful, was tight enough to become so if she tried to resist.

'I'm looking for my daughter,' she babbled. 'Just looking for my daughter.'

'Everyone,' he said with a shake of the head, 'is looking for someone. This way please.'

She found herself in the hut. It was bigger than it looked from afar and held several rough desks with even rougher men sitting at them. They wore tightly belted khaki tunics and blue-topped caps and on the wall behind them was emblazoned a silver sword on a red background with a golden sickle in front. Lydia wasn't sure what it meant but it was too reminiscent of Nazi symbolism to feel good.

The guard deposited her at one of the desks and she glanced to the door. Could she make a run for it? Of course not. Her legs could barely walk, let alone run, and even if they could, they'd be shot from beneath her in her final heartbeat.

'I'm looking for my daughter,' she told the new man.

He did not seem to hear her.

'Papers,' he demanded.

'I don't have any. I'm a refugee.'

'Papers.'

He put out a hand and she stared helplessly at it. The guard had set her bag at her feet and she fumbled for the certificate from Feldafing that gave her official displaced person's status. The Russian frowned.

'This German certificate. For Germany.'

'I'm looking for my daughter.'

She willed him to understand.

'Where daughter?'

'I don't know. That's the problem. I have to get to Auschwitz.'

'No one at Auschwitz.'

'No,' she agreed, trying to stay calm, 'but there are records.'

'Papers?'

She nodded keenly. 'Papers, yes.'

'But you – you have no papers?'

'I'm a refugee.'

They were going round in circles. What a fool she'd been to think the border was a sign of hope. Why hadn't she taken the road further north? She'd been wanting to save her aching feet the extra kilometres but instead she'd let them walk her into the Soviet police.

'Please,' she said, 'I mean no harm. I just want to—'

'Find your daughter. Yes. Is no problem.'

'Really?'

'We just need to confirm your identity and you are welcome to cross Soviet Austria.'

Lydia shifted on her chair. 'How long will that take?'

He waved a hairy hand. 'Not long. We just check with Moscow.'

'Moscow?!'

'Of course. This way. We have hostel.'

'No! I don't want a hostel. I don't want to stay. I'll go. I'll go back to Germany. I won't trouble you—'

'No trouble. No trouble for you. And no trouble for us.' He snapped his fingers and a younger soldier ran up.

'Please!' Lydia begged. 'I haven't got time. I need to find my daughter. I need to find Tasha.'

'Why rush?'

'I'm dying.'

He shrugged, reached for a bottle of vodka. 'We are all dying. You go to hostel. You rest. We find identity. Maybe we find daughter. Maybe she finds you.' He lifted the vodka with a thin smile. 'Na zdorovie.'

The last thing she heard as she was hustled away was him pouring himself another glass and then she was being shoved into a room at the back where a handful of other women were cowering between the sort of rough wooden bunks she'd been driven from by the Nazis more than a year ago.

'No!' she wailed, pushing at the guard. 'Let me go. Let me find my daughter.'

He looked at her pityingly. 'Come, lady, you think your little desires are worth more than the security and prosperity of a whole nation?'

'Yes!' she screamed, but it was too late.

The door locked and, again, she was at the mercy of a state machine that thought it owned the rights to her freedom. She sank to the floor, her breath rattling out of her lungs in dry, heaving sobs but no one heard or, if they did, no one cared.

TWENTY-THREE

TASHA

Tasha touched her toes down into the flower-dotted meadow grass and pushed off hard. The swing curved up towards the fresh green oak leaves and the cloudless blue sky beyond and she tried hard to feel the joy of it. She'd been at Weir Courtney two months now and it was a lovely place but life felt paused here and the peace of it was beginning to chafe.

Alice wrote letters to all sorts of people all the time and had encouraged her to do the same but the replies that slapped onto the big house's elegant doormat never held any news. Europe was full of refugees. Tasha had seen them on newsreels in the local cinema, milling around camps and cities, seeking loved ones. It looked like a giant Theresienstadt, but there seemed to be no way to penetrate and find your one person in the millions.

Tasha swung higher, kicking out her frustration. Beyond her, Weir Courtney's gardens were bursting into bloom, and, in Sir Benjamin's orangery, tiny oranges were forming on the lush trees. Sir Benjamin was often in there, tending his plants, and was always happy to show the children around and answer their questions.

'Where did the orange trees come from?' Marta had asked him the other day.

The little girl, after an initial suspicion that had torn at Tasha's heart, had taken her to her bosom again and was with her as often as she could be.

'I brought these ones back from Spain,' Sir Benjamin had told her. 'They were small enough to fit in my suitcase then, but they like it here and they've grown big and strong.'

'Like me,' Marta had said guilelessly.

'Exactly like you. You children are all exotic plants and I love to see you thriving.'

Marta had preened at the comparison and Tasha had understood their host's words to be kindly meant but she didn't feel comfortable as an exotic plant.

'Have you ever been to Poland?' she'd asked him.

'I have. To Krakow once and Warsaw several times.'

'Warsaw?! When?'

'It would have been in the early thirties, when I was trading there.'

'I was there then,' she'd burst out. 'I was born there in 1929.'

Sir Benjamin had smiled at her. 'Well, there you go. We could have passed in the street.'

That had been a strange idea – her young self skipping past a tall, English businessman without ever knowing that she would one day live in his grand house. Reliant on his charity. One of his exotic plants.

'Lovely city,' he'd gone on. 'Or, at least it was before the Bosch blew it to smithereens. That is… Oh my dear, I'm so very tactless. I do apologise. Don't let a bumbling old fool like me upset you. Come and see my orchids. They're coming into bloom and they're very lovely.'

He'd hurried her towards the stunning purple and white

flowers, babbling about their provenance while she'd listened intently, though both of them had been, she was sure, thinking of the coloured houses of Warsaw and the ruins they'd become.

Tasha swung even higher, trying to top out through the leaves, out through the very canopy of this troubling, difficult world. She was an ungrateful cow to feel cross, she knew. It was idyllic in this house and she'd chosen to come here, but it felt empty without Georg. He'd written to her several times – laboured, careful missives assuring her of his continued love and begging her to come back.

I'll come when you get a place of your own, she'd written.

I can't afford it, Tasha, he'd replied, *but I've spoken to the people at the Shelter and if we get married, we can have a room of our own until I can.*

That had been tempting, she had to admit. She'd still be stuck in that stinky place but at least she'd be stuck in it with Georg. She missed him. She missed his teasing, she missed his kissing, she missed his plans and his dreams and his wretched positivity. She even missed their arguments. But she didn't miss the uncertainty of life with him and, until he showed up here with an actual marriage licence from an actual rabbi, she wasn't going to commit to any of his endless ifs.

In the meantime, she was stuck in Weir Courtney like a cuckoo in the nest. The others all called it 'home' without a second thought and ran comfortably around with each other as if they were true siblings. Tasha shared a bedroom with Mina and Golda and they prattled away to her day and night. It was most disconcerting. Nice, Tasha supposed, but it felt like a big game of make-believe – a stopgap family until they could find their real ones again. Or, at least, it did to her.

The one task she truly enjoyed was helping brush the little girls' hair and tame it into pigtails for school every morning. They all had long hair now and, although they were fiercely proud of it, they were less keen on dragging a brush through the tangles and often wriggled and complained.

'Ssh,' Tasha would tell them, 'or I'll take the shears to you.'

It was a bittersweet joke that hurt her every time she made it, but it worked a treat. For the younger ones the memories of the camps were fading fast – and thank God for that – but they still, like her, remembered the fear of that first arrivals room and always stood still if she so much as hinted at it.

Tasha's hair had grown well past her shoulders and every night she would sit and brush it out with a hundred strokes, each one an act of love for her mother. The new, shorter styles did look tempting. Alice's made her look ten years younger and Tasha had been down into the village to stare at the Beautiful You salon a few times but had never gone up close. The way Alice had described it, the crazy pink owner dragged you in off the street and set on you with her scissors, and Tasha wasn't having that. Besides, if she half-closed her eyes and let her brushed-out hair fall across her face in the dim light of the dorm, she could imagine it as Lydia's brushing against her as she kissed her good night, and she wasn't missing out on that for any cut, however fashionable.

Tasha flung her head back, pushing the swing so high that the ropes buckled. She welcomed the jolt; it felt more natural than an easy swoop. It was May now. May the eighth to be precise. This time last year, she'd been living in the heat and noise and misery of Theresienstadt, spending her days hunting for food and trying to avoid disappointing all those searching for loved ones. This time last year, Georg had come running to tell her a horse had ridden through the gates and they'd stood together outside the town hall and heard Mr Dunant announce that the war was officially over.

VE Day they were calling it – Victory in Europe. There was a VJ Day too, commemorating blowing up millions of Japanese civilians with a dirty bomb, and to Tasha this one didn't feel much better. Of course, peace was a good thing. She understood why everyone was going mad with the bunting and the fancy cakes, but for her today didn't feel like a victory. It marked the end of the war, yes, but also the start of the search – the heart-breaking, fruitless search. It marked the day when hope had turned into a list of the dead, and that did not feel like cause for a party to Tasha.

Not one of the children who'd flown to England in those great big bombers had found a living parent. Alice wrote tire-lessly to agencies. Tasha often saw her still at her desk when the rest of Weir Courtney settled into sleep, combing through replies for hope, but it rarely came. A handful had gone to aunts and uncles in America or Palestine and one or two had located a sibling (or, like Mirella and Fiorina never been parted from them), but not one mama or tata had arrived to hold any of them close since they arrived in England. Not one.

So far.

Instinctively Tasha's hand went to her handbag and the swing skewed sideways, so she stopped kicking out and let it slow. Without the rush of air in her ears, the unusual silence at Weir Courtney sounded very loud. Everyone was out. The kids were at a bumptious celebration in the village with Alice and Sophie, but Tasha had had no desire to 'roll out the barrel' with jolly English villagers. Mina and Golda were in London with Manna, who'd been keen to see the grand celebrations outside Buckingham Palace, but Tasha had refused that too. She didn't want to go back to London and she most certainly didn't want to run the risk of bumping into Georg. It would be far too tempting.

'How could I ever miss that idiot?' she muttered to a black-bird that had landed in the oak tree.

It looked curiously down at her, its head cocked on one side as if searching for an answer but apparently it couldn't find one as it upped and flew away again. Tasha watched it enviously.

'Tasha?'

She looked round to see Alice struggling across the lawn, two deckchairs knocking against her knees.

'What are you doing here?' she demanded. It sounded rude but, really, she didn't need checking on all the time.

'I came back for chairs,' Alice said. 'You sure you won't come and join us?'

'To drink warm beer, toss haybales over poles and dance with bells tied to my knees? I'm fine, thanks.'

'Morris dancing isn't so different to Polish or German folk dances.'

'Save that the English are still alive to do it.'

'Except all their young men who went off to Poland and Germany to fight for our freedom.'

Tasha bit her lip; she'd deserved that.

'I'm happy here,' she said tightly, forcing herself to add, 'thank you'.

'Are you missing London?'

'No!'

'The Shelter?'

'Definitely not.'

'Georg?'

God, did the woman never give up poking into other people's business?

'I don't want to talk about Georg.'

Alice set down the chairs, as if she'd heard the complete opposite of what Tasha had said. She was so infuriating.

'It might help, you know. He was a big part of your life after all. You survived Auschwitz together—'

'I recall, thank you.'

She could remember them trying to prise open the door of their barrack, remember sharing a look of horrified disbelief as they realised the Nazis had locked them in and left them to die. But they hadn't died.

'You were in Theresienstadt together this time last year,' Alice said.

Tasha ground her teeth. 'I remember that too.'

The feel of his hand in hers as Dunant read out the armistice, his arms clasping her waist as he whirled her round and round...

'And of course, Windermere—'

'I know, Alice!' The bicycle ride, their first kiss, sitting in a boat beneath a silver moon, before they were hauled in like little kids by Oskar. And rescued by Alice. 'I know,' she said again, more softly. 'And I'll always treasure him for that, but it's not enough to build a life on. Georg is all dreams and no substance.'

'Is he not sticking at his job?'

'Well, yes...'

'Saving money?'

'Some.'

'Making friends?'

'Definitely that.'

'Putting down roots?'

'No! He doesn't care about roots. I told him once that without them, you fall over in the slightest wind, but he doesn't see the need. Roots aren't flashy enough for him. He's all about what's on the surface.'

Alice frowned. 'Is that not a bit unkind, Tasha?'

'Unkind?!'

'Maybe what's beneath is painful?'

'Maybe. But surely, if he wants to share his life with me, he has to trust me with that?'

Alice leaned against the tree. 'I suppose so. I'm not the best person to ask.'

Tasha resisted the urge to point out that she *hadn't* asked; Alice was the one with all the questions.

'Have you *never* had a boyfriend?' she queried.

Alice drew herself up tall. 'I had a suitor, thank you very much.'

Tasha looked at her, intrigued. 'When?'

'In 1917. Heinz, he was called, and he was very nice. Very lovely.'

'You were in love with him?'

Alice visibly squirmed. 'I wouldn't go that far. That's to say, we hadn't had time for things to, to progress that far.'

'Before what?'

Alice looked up at that, staring straight at her. 'Before he died, Tasha. Killed in Flanders, two weeks after he was called up.'

'Ah.' Tasha felt mean. 'I'm sorry.'

'Thank you.'

Tasha thought about it. 'But you weren't, you know, committed? He hadn't asked you to marry him?'

'Does that matter? Georg asked you and I don't see that helping a lot.'

Tasha sucked in a breath and Alice looked mortified.

'Sorry. I'm sorry, Tasha, that was unkind.'

Tasha laughed. 'Good to know you have it in you, Alice.'

The older woman shook her head violently. 'I don't think it is. There's been enough unkindness in this world without adding to it. I don't know why, now the verdammte war is over, everyone can't just count their blessings and be happy.'

Tasha stared at her. It was like listening to Georg all over again, only from Alice it sounded uncomfortably fair and she felt a sudden urge to explain herself.

'The thing is, Alice, that until I find my mother, or until I... I know what happened to her, I'm not sure that the war truly feels over...'

Alice kicked at a deckchair. 'A good point, Tash, but surely today of all days we can at least try?'

Tasha sighed and stood up off the swing. It was impossible to stay cross at Alice; she was too decent a person.

'Come on,' she said, lifting the deckchairs, 'I'll help you over with these. But I'm not staying if anyone tries to put bells on my knees.'

Alice gave her a broad smile. 'Fair enough. Let's—'

But her words were cut off by a shrill cry piercing the baby-blue English sky.

'Nazis! Run! It's the Nazis!'

TWENTY-FOUR

ALICE

Alice panted onto the cricket field to find the Lingfield VE Day celebrations in disarray. The ladies of the WI were watching, distraught, as Suzi and Judith cowered beneath their gingham tablecloths. Marta and others were seeking refuge behind the tombola, the Bellucci girls were scrambling up an oak tree, and Mattias had jumped into hook-a-duck and was trying to splutteringly hide beneath the water. The scene would have been comic if it hadn't been for the utter terror on their faces.

'Save us from the Nazis!' Moishe was begging two men playing skittles. 'Get your guns. You have to get your guns.'

Alice ran into the centre of the chaos and grabbed Sophie.

'What on earth is going on?'

In reply, Sophie pointed to the field beyond the cricket ground. A group of men in striped uniforms were being marshalled to pick stones from the bare ground by uniformed police. They must be prisoners of war earning their keep before they could be returned to their home country, but Alice could see, from what little she knew from the children's passing comments, that they looked exactly like a scene from the camps. The fact that the Germans were now the prisoners had been lost on the children in their immediate, visceral fear.

She looked around, trying to work out how to scoop them all up safely, but her view was blocked by Mrs Smythe, the dour-faced chair of the village committee.

'Miss Goldberger, your children are disrupting the fair!'

Alice drew herself up. 'Mrs Smythe, your committee have allowed a scene that is brutally reminiscent of the concentration camps to be enacted within sight of the children who are trying to recover from them. We adults may see the role reversal as just revenge, but the children are simply reacting to the implicit violence – and who can blame them?'

Mrs Smythe, to her credit, went white. She looked to the prisoners, being poked and prodded by their far from sympathetic guards, then back to Alice.

'My goodness, I'm so sorry. I'll have them removed straight away.'

She strode across to talk to the head guard, watched by the entire cricket pitch full of villagers. At first he looked mutinous, waving a paper that must be his official orders, but he was no match for Mrs Smythe and soon crumpled. With an apologetic glance to the broken festivities, he led his striped prisoners away and the harder job of coaxing the children out began.

Alice went to the hook-a-duck, offering a hand to Mattias, but he was shaking so much she had to step into the water and lift him, dripping, into her arms. Sir Benjamin lured the children from beneath the WI stall with sweet treats, Tasha did the same at the tombola and Sophie coaxed Mirella and Fiorina down from the oak tree. The skittle players calmed Moishe by the unconventional but seemingly effective means of demonstrating how to bludgeon an assailant with a wooden skittle and, as the two fiddlers with the Morris troop began to play a gently lilting tune, peace returned.

Alice sank to the floor holding Mattias tightly in her arms as the others joined her. She was very aware of the villagers watching and could see mothers trying to explain the curious behaviour to their children. She wondered what the local families had told their kids about the Weir Courtney orphans. Part of her didn't want them to know what their new school-fellows had been through, but another, angry part of her felt that it was only fair that the suffering was in some way shared out. Not that it would lessen it for her charges, as was all too evident. They were white and shaken, the sight of the prisoners in their striped uniforms clearly tapping into deeply embedded traumas.

Oskar would be fascinated by this, she thought, and tried to note details to tell him when he next visited, but then felt callous. Scientific study was excellent and would help other children down the line, she was sure, but her concern right now was the quivering little ones sitting in a scared circle around her. She had to help them and the only thing she could think of was stark honesty.

'Some of those men in the next field were Germans,' she told the intent children. 'But they weren't the guards. They were the prisoners. They've been caught and they're locked up and they only come out to work guarded by English policemen. They're being punished for the war and they cannot get to you or hurt you in any way.'

The children stared at her, taking this in.

'Why are they still alive?' Moishe demanded. 'They should be dead, like my mutti and vati are dead.'

Alice swallowed back the instant tears that his pained voice drew from her. She had to stay calm for them, but it was hard.

'Because killing is wrong,' someone else said for her – Tasha. 'Only barbarians kill.'

Moishe looked at her curiously. 'What are barbarians?'

'Wild men and women. Uncivilised, basic, primitive.'

Moishe folded his arms. 'I'd like to be a barbarian to Germans.'

'Now, Moishe—' Alice started but Tasha was still going.

'Me too,' she said. 'Truly, Moishe, what I would really like to do is line up every last one of the Nazis and punch and kick and stab them, like they did to us. I'd like to make them carry corpses on their backs, like they did to our mothers. I'd like to make them run and run until they collapse, like they did to our friends. I'd like to shoot them and hang them and I'd really, really like to herd them into gas chambers and let them die screaming and clawing at the walls, like so many of our families.'

'Tasha, this is too much!' Alice objected.

But Sophie put a hand on her arm and nodded to the children. They were listening, rapt, and Alice realised that these words were not shocking them, as they shocked her, and as they definitely shocked the few villagers close enough to listen. To these poor children, this brutality was simple fact. It was what they had seen day in, day out and they had to be given a chance to process it openly and without judgement. Clamping her mouth shut, Alice listened carefully.

'But if we did that,' Tasha said, 'we would be as bad as them. Who wants to be a Nazi?'

The children shook their heads vehemently.

'Me neither. Nazis were vicious and cruel and mean. We can be better than that. We can be kind and loving and intelligent. We can show that we know how to treat other human beings, even ones who are different from us. And it's hard. It's really hard and it doesn't get much easier as you grow up, believe me, but we have to teach ourselves to be good people because *that* is how we really win.'

Silence. Somewhere behind them the Morris dancers were starting up again. Alice thought of Tasha saying she wasn't staying if someone tried to tie bells to her knees, and felt a rush of affection for the spiky girl. She put a hand on her arm.

'Well said, Tasha.'

Tasha looked at her, slightly dazed. 'I'm not sure where that came from,' she admitted.

'From your heart,' Alice said. 'From your very good heart.'

Tasha gave her a wonky smile. 'I usually hide it well.'

'Pretty well,' Alice agreed. 'But it's there all the same.'

Tasha fumbled for her precious handbag. 'It's nice to be useful for once,' she said sadly.

Alice looked at her curiously but she avoided her eye and leaped up.

'Shall we go home?'

The children all nodded, the celebratory mood drained from them. Alice lifted Mattias from her lap and got up slowly, not noticing her damp dress, so intent was she on watching Tasha as she self-consciously guided the children off the cricket pitch. She'd seemed mainly happy here – save for her obvious pining for Georg – and Alice hadn't realised she was feeling useless. How foolish of her! The girl was seventeen, of course she'd want gainful employment, but what would suit her? She'd made it very clear what she thought of being a nurserymaid and, to be fair, she wasn't temperamentally right for it. So, what?

They left to concerned looks. Some of the local children offered toys they'd won on the tombola. The mothers pressed cakes and biscuits on them and Mrs Smythe rushed across to personally assure them all that she would have 'the bad men sent far, far away'. Alice was grateful for it all, but most grateful for the strong figure of Tasha striding out at their head, the children pressing close behind.

'They've had it hard, haven't they?' Mrs Smythe said, and Alice nodded.

Today the village of Lingfield had seen, first-hand, how much there was to truly celebrate in the war being over – and how long the road to full recovery might still be. They could take the children away from the camps, but the horrors they'd experienced there were deep barbs within them and it was with a sad heart that Alice saw them back into Weir Courtney.

They were listless and distracted. Alice and Sophie tried singing and storytelling but the children struggled to sit. They tried games on the lawn and some of them began to cheer up or, at least, to run off whatever horrors were eating them up inside. Moishe and a few of the other boys started up an exceptionally boisterous game of football and Alice was glad when Sir Benjamin returned from prize-giving duties and gamely took on the role of referee. Some of the smaller children, tired out, were happy to retreat to the playroom and play with their dolls but Marta, Suzi, Judith, Mirella and Fiorina were restless and discontented.

'Tell you what,' Tasha said to them, 'why don't we try out new hairstyles?'

Their eyes brightened and Alice, trying to elicit interest in a game of ludo, sat back as they crowded around Tasha. She'd noticed that the return of their hair had been important to the girls and now their attention was truly caught.

'Like what?' Marta demanded.

Tasha stroked the girl's two plaits. 'My mother used to do this really clever style on me. It was like a plait but sort of upside down, so that the hair was flat on the head and the plait standing up like a challah loaf.'

Mirella and Fiorina clapped.

'Let's do that.'

'It's not easy,' Tasha warned. 'It might take a few goes.'

'We can help.'

One of them ran for a brush as Tasha freed Marta's long hair from her plaits. They all crowded round, tongues between their teeth in concentration as they tried to work out how to get the effect they were looking for. Alice watched Tasha's slim fingers as they slid in and out of Marta's hair, and within ten minutes, saw an 'upside-down plait' begin to emerge. It was messy at first but Tasha undid it time and again until, finally, she got it perfect.

'Yay!' her crowd of admirers cheered, then they were clamouring to have the new style themselves and Tasha was busy on one little head after the other. The girls were totally involved and looked up, astonished, when Sophie rang the bell for tea.

'Come on,' Mirella cried. 'Let's go and show the boys our new hair.'

'They won't care,' Fiorina said but, in fact, when Moishe and his mates came running into the hall, they were most impressed.

'How did she do that?' Alice heard Moishe asking Marta.

'She's super clever with hair,' came the answer and it sparked a flame in Alice's brain. Of course!

She turned to Tasha, sitting quietly pulling hair from her brush. 'You *are* super clever with hair, Tash.'

Tasha laughed. 'It was just a few plaits.'

Alice shook her head. 'No, it wasn't. It was interest and enjoyment, and, and... passion.'

Tasha laughed harder. 'Rubbish, Alice. It was hair!'

Alice thought of Joyce, with her cosy cream and pink salon, her happy manner and her quietly easy philosophy to make her clients into their most beautiful selves. That was what Tasha had done here this afternoon.

'You like hair?' she asked.

Tasha shrugged. 'I suppose so.' She fiddled with the bristles of her brush, then added, 'I used to brush out my mother's hair in the evenings sometimes. It would glow in the firelight and the more I brushed, the more it glowed.'

She dipped her head, the laughter all gone. Alice saw her fingers reach, as ever, for her little handbag and her heart ached. VE Day should have been a happy day, a celebration of liberation, freedom and peace, but it hadn't worked out that way. Weir Courtney was an uneasy place this evening and no one was more unsettled than the girl who had helped, more than she'd ever admit, to keep these poor damaged children as content as it was possible for them to be.

Alice wished she could find Lydia Ancel. She wished she could bring her back to her brave, passionate, suffering daughter, but the world wasn't that kind. Letters arrived at Weir Courtney most days, but they rarely had solid news. She'd found out recently that some ex-prisoners were opening Auschwitz as a museum and were working to collate any records found on site and elsewhere. She prayed every day that those records would include something about Max and his family, and prayed almost as hard that they would locate Lydia. She would keep trying, keep writing, as she did for all their children, but in the meantime, Tasha needed something to look forward to. She needed something to make her into her most beautiful self.

It was time to pay another visit to Joyce.

TWENTY-FIVE

LINGFIELD | 10 MAY 1946

TASHA

'I don't want a haircut.'

Tasha looked from Alice to the boldly coloured salon and back to Alice again. Was the woman mad? She'd told her before that she treasured the way her hair had grown back like her mother's and now she was trying to get her to cut it off. She turned away, keen to get back, but Alice took hold of her arm with surprising firmness.

'I'm not suggesting you do.'

'So why am I here then? Am I not beautiful enough?' She gestured to the sign above the door: Beautiful You. What a silly name!

'You know full well how beautiful you are,' Alice told her.

Goodness, she was in a bolshy mood this morning; Tasha almost admired her for it.

'But no, I want you to meet someone.'

'You do?' Tasha peered in the window, confused. 'Who?'

As if in answer, the door opened and a buxom lady with

bouffant blonde hair (neither wave, nor colour natural if you asked Tasha), stepped outside with a cheery hello.

'You must be Tasha,' she said. 'Alice has told me all about you. Come in, come in...'

She waved them through and there was something so disarming about her ready welcome that Tasha stepped obediently inside. The smell of the salon hit her first – luxurious shampoo and dryer-warm hair, undercut with a hint of intriguing chemicals. She looked around at the cream and gold wallpaper, the pink sinks, the padded chairs and the glossy magazines, and tried to feel scathing of the overt opulence but something about it all made her feel safe, happy even.

'I'm Joyce,' the woman was saying. 'And I'm delighted to welcome you to Beautiful You.'

'It's a lovely place,' Tasha managed.

'Thank you.' Joyce gave her a lipsticked smile. 'It's totally over the top, I know, but so much of life is dull and grey, don't you find?'

Tasha nodded dumbly.

'So I thought, why not give everyone a bit of colour like they do in America?'

'A bit!' Tasha blurted out. She clapped her hand over her mouth, horrified at herself.

But Joyce just laughed, totally unoffended. 'A lot then. But you can't have too much of a good thing, I say. Let me show you around.'

'Me?'

Tasha wasn't entirely sure why she was here, but she had to admit that the place fascinated her, and she went gladly with Joyce as she showed her the washing station, the two cutting areas with their huge mirrors and, far more interestingly, Joyce's box of tools – all sorts of different scissors, clippers and combs.

'Do you use all of these?' she asked incredulously.

'Oh yes. There are so many different hair types, you see, and you have to have the right blade so you don't tear the hair. Then there's the different styles. These clippers are for trimming the back of the neck on the shorter styles. These sideways ones are for a sharp pageboy cut and these...' She held up a curious pair of golden scissors with a run of square teeth all along both edges...' are for thinning out overly thick hair. Like yours.'

Tasha shrank back. 'I wouldn't want my hair thinning.'

'And I would obviously respect that if you were my client, but I'd also suggest that taking the weight out of your glorious hair would allow that lovely natural wave more room to unfold.'

Tasha put her hand to her hair. 'Unfold?'

Joyce laughed. Joyce, it seemed, laughed a lot.

'You think I'm talking a load of guff!'

'Guff?'

Tasha looked to Alice for a translation. Her English was good these days but this word was a new one. Alice, however, clearly had no idea either.

'Nonsense,' Joyce supplied easily. 'I talk a lot of that, but in your case, I mean it.'

Tasha looked accusingly at Alice. 'So you *did* bring me here for a haircut.'

'No,' Alice said, glancing at Joyce. 'I brought you here for an apprenticeship.'

Tasha felt her mouth physically fall open and hastily closed it again. She looked around the pink and cream salon and tried to picture herself working here. Actually working! As a hairdresser! Here! She felt a spike of something that might have been joy, but then told herself she must have misunderstood. Joyce probably wanted her to make the tea or sweep the floor or something.

'An apprenticeship?'

Joyce gave her an open smile. 'That's right. You'd work here, alongside me, learning how to cut hair and do permanent waves and sets and all the other bits and pieces.'

'You'd teach me?'

'That would be the idea.'

'Why?'

'Why not? I'm rushed off my feet with the men back from war and everyone wanting to look nice again. And there are so many new styles coming in, I can hardly keep pace. I need a bit of young blood around the place. Betsy – that's my daughter – is keen to learn but she's got a year at school yet and I'm not having her cut short her education. There's a lot of work to running a salon – doing the books and balancing the rents and all that – so you've got to be smart. Alice says you're smart, Tasha.'

'She does?'

'Yes, and that you work wonders with hair. You can Dutch plait, I believe?'

'I can? Oh, you mean the upside-down ones?' She blushed. 'I can do those, yeah, but I doubt there'd be much call for that sort of thing around here.'

'You'd be surprised, my lovely. I do a lot of twenty-first birthdays, fancy dinners, weddings...'

'Weddings?' Tasha thought of Georg and his promises of marriage, but they'd come to nothing and she couldn't hang around waiting. This smiley, blonde power-force of a lady was offering her an apprenticeship and it suddenly seemed the most logical thing in the world.

'I'd love to work with you,' she heard herself saying, her voice bubbling with embarrassingly childlike enthusiasm. She turned to Alice. 'You did it again, Alice – the perfect job! You really are a clever old stick.'

'Don't! You'll swell my head,' Alice protested, but she looked delighted all the same. 'Right then, I'll leave you to it.'

'Now?' Tasha squeaked. 'I'm starting now?'

'No time like the present,' Joyce said. 'I've a customer due any minute so you can watch your first cut.'

'I... Gosh!'

This was all happening very fast.

'You can start next week, if you'd rather,' Joyce said gently.

Her voice was so kind and motherly that Tasha had to turn away to hide a tear. She looked slowly around Beautiful You and realised that what she'd found here – or what Alice had found – was her chance at a future. She'd be mad to hide from that.

'Today would be wonderful,' she said. 'Thank you.'

Joyce nodded at her and Alice left them to it, the bell over the door jingling merrily as she bounced out like a woman half her age.

'She's a sweetie, that one,' Joyce said.

It wasn't exactly how Tasha would have put it, but she took Joyce's point.

'She's been very good to me.'

'Which must make her rare in the last few years. But hey, let's not dwell. Uniform time!'

Joyce led Tasha into a cosy back room. Down one wall was a kitchen area with a fridge, a two-ring stove and even a Swan electric kettle. 'Lets me easily make drinks for my ladies,' Joyce said, opening a cupboard to reveal both tea and coffee pots. 'Not to mention for myself. Can't get through the day without at least ten cups of tea, me.' She winked at Tasha. 'Now – uniform. It'll have to be one of my spares until I get you one your own size. It might be a little loose.'

She grabbed a tabard and put it over Tasha's head. It hung limply around her thin body as if waiting for someone else to step in and join her, and the vibrant pink clashed hideously with her hair. Tasha glanced in the mirror and cringed.

'Hmm,' Joyce said. 'We might get you a cream one. Nice contrast to me, don't you think?'

Tasha nodded dumbly, praying no one she knew came into the salon. But then, why would they? The only people she knew were the other orphans and they were hardly going to be turning up at Beautiful You.

'I'm not an orphan,' she growled.

'Sorry, my lovely?'

'Nothing, Joyce.'

'Right. Well, let's pop your handbag on this hook, shall we, and— Ow!'

She'd reached for Tasha's handbag and Tasha had instinctively pushed her away. Joyce staggered back, knocking into the kitchen surface opposite, and Tasha rushed forward.

'I'm sorry. I'm so, so sorry. I just... I don't take this bag off.'

Joyce righted herself warily. 'Why not?'

'What's it to do with you?' Tasha demanded fiercely.

'Whoa!' Joyce put her hands on her hips, her smiles gone. 'It's everything to do with me if you're going to work here, young lady. I can't have a rough bag banging against my customers while they're trying to relax, can I now?'

Some part of Tasha could see the logic of that, but the logic was hazed by her ever-ready anger. What did the comfort of some middle-England ladies matter compared to her mother, lost and probably injured somewhere in the chaos of post-war Europe?

'I don't take it off,' she repeated.

Joyce folded her arms. 'Then you don't work here.'

The joy Tasha had felt in her heart not ten minutes before, shrivelled and died. Of course it did. She'd been a fool to think anything in her cursed life would be this easy.

'Fine.' Yanking off the lurid pink tabard, she made for the door.

'Wait!' Joyce called. 'I'm sorry.'

She was sorry? Tasha froze, confused.

'It obviously matters a lot to you. Just, please, tell me why.'

Tasha touched her hands to the bag and turned slowly back round. 'I keep my mother's hair in here. It's the only thing I have left of her and I don't want to lose it.'

Joyce stared at her and then, to her huge surprise, stepped forward and enfolded Tasha in her warm arms.

'I'm sorry,' she said again. 'Did your mother die?'

'No!' Tasha jerked back. 'That is, I don't know. I don't know anything. The last time I saw her was in Auschwitz when she was pushed out into the snow with all the other women. The Nazis locked us kids in so I couldn't go with her. We didn't even get a chance to say a proper goodbye.' Tasha shut her eyes against the treacherous tears but the image was too strong. 'I climbed up to one of the tiny windows trying to see her but they were already being marched towards the gates. I caught a flash of her hair before she pulled a blanket up over it and then that was it – she was gone.'

'You poor, poor dear.'

Joyce clasped her close again and Tasha didn't resist. The hairdresser's arms were so strong and loving, her bosom so soft and, as she let herself collapse against it, she could hear the steady beat of her kind heart against her ear.

'Have people tried to find her?' Joyce asked tentatively.

'Oh yes,' Tasha said. 'There are lots of organisations with lots of lists, but so far... I ask whenever I can, and so does Alice, but she could be anywhere in Europe and there's very little you can actually do. Then I got on this programme to come to England and Georg persuaded me to come...'

'Georg?'

'An idiot boy.'

'I see.'

'So I came, but now I'm so far away and I don't know how I'm ever going to find her.'

Joyce stroked her hair. 'You won't need to, my lovely.'

Tasha glared at her. 'You think she's dead? Like Georg, like—'

'I don't think she's dead. That's to say, she may be, but if she's not, I do know one thing – she'll be moving heaven and earth to find you.'

'She will?'

'Of course. She's your mother.'

'Well yes...'

'So you will be the most precious thing in the world to her.'

More tears quivered in Tasha's eyes but these ones felt softer than her usual bitter weeping. 'I will?'

'Definitely. Goodness, if I'd been separated from my Betsy, I'd be frantic to find her. People must know you're here?'

'They do. We're on public lists and there's been a few articles about us.'

'So, she'll find you.'

'You really think so?'

'If she possibly can then yes, I do. And when she does, Tasha, you'll be halfway to becoming a hairdresser so you can support the two of you, get an apartment together, make a new life.'

It was an enticing idea. Even more enticing than pink chairs, luxury shampoo and twenty different types of scissors.

Tasha wiped away her tears. 'You'll still let me work here?'

'If you want to, absolutely. We can't have you wearing the bag' – she put up a hand to forestall Tasha's objections – 'but I can lock it in my safe while you're here so no harm can come to it.' She indicated a sturdy-looking safe set into the wall behind the hooks. 'Would that be all right?'

Out in the shop, the doorbell jangled and Tasha saw an older woman hobble inside on a stick, then look round and visibly straighten.

'That would be fine,' she agreed. 'Thank you, Joyce. And, er, sorry for, you know, pushing you.'

Joyce was all smiles again. 'Sorry for trying to take your bag. I have a bit of a temper, Tasha.'

'Me too,' Tasha said ruefully.

'Then we're both going to have to learn how to deal with that, aren't we?'

Tasha nodded and, gritting her teeth, took her bag off and handed it to her new employer. Joyce took it with care and, opening up the safe, locked it securely away. Tasha tugged on her overlarge tunic, feeling almost naked without the bag that had come with her all the way from Auschwitz. She had to admit, though, that she felt a little freer without it and it was with a lighter heart that she followed Joyce back into Beautiful You to start her first day of work as an apprentice hairdresser.

She looked at the padded chair as Joyce settled her customer and imagined Lydia sitting in it and looking at Tasha in the mirror, the two of them reflected side by side at last.

'You can do this, my girl,' Lydia seemed to say, and Tasha nodded, tears misting the vision.

'I'll make it work, Mama,' she whispered. 'I'll make a future – for us both. All you have to do is find me.'

TWENTY-SIX

TŘEBÍČ | 10 MAY 1946

LYDIA

Lydia pulled her hair out of the rough string tie and let it fall around her face as she dipped it into the River Jihlava. Freedom! After six excruciating weeks in the Soviet 'hostel' even the mud of the road and the straw of an outdoor bed felt wonderful. Moscow had finally decided she was no threat to the great Soviet machine two weeks ago and she'd been released. The guards had been very surprised when she'd turned back into Germany, but she preferred to go the long way round the tip of their wretched zone than face the border control on the other side. Her ailing body couldn't afford any more delays.

Plunging her whole head into the clear water, Lydia felt it tingle with life. Even with the spring sun shining blessedly down on her, the river was breathtakingly cold and she had precious little breath to spare. Even so, she kept her head there, willing the current to sweep the endless dirt from her growing locks. Czechoslovakia (when she'd finally made it in) had welcomed her with a relentless spring rain that had churned up mud at every turn, and she threw her wet hair back, glad to see a little of her natural red returning.

Restored, she looked around Třebíč, a fairy-tale Czech town of medieval cobbles and whitewashed houses. It was some five hundred kilometres from Feldafing but still three hundred kilometres more to Auschwitz. It had taken forever to get here, but her destination still seemed so impossibly far away, and Lydia sank onto a low wall, fighting for the will to carry on.

'I just want her to be safe,' she moaned to the careless river. 'I just want to know Tasha's safe.'

It wasn't strictly true. She wanted to hold her, to talk to her, to fill her up with every drop of her love and tell her that she hadn't wanted to leave her.

'She knows that,' she told herself sternly. Tasha wasn't a baby and there was no point in being melodramatic. She'd told her to stay strong, promised her they'd be together again. And they would.

It was just taking so long.

Lydia put a hand to her wet hair, regretting her reckless wash. Her lungs were precarious and she worried that they had a finite number of breaths left in them before some part inevitably broke away. And yet, she wasn't a machine but a living thing. Exercise would make her stronger, that's what the doctor had said. Though he perhaps hadn't meant an eight-hundred-kilometre hike.

Lydia permitted herself a wry smile and pushed herself up again. It was dusk and Třebíč was sinking into shadows, but lights were going on in every window, spilling onto the cobbles in puddles of gold. Lydia came to a small square with benches all around it and a few roses blossoming in the centre. On the far side a solid, cream building was glowing with light from high, arched windows and as she drew closer, she sucked in her breath, for there, nailed to an unassuming doorpost, was a mezuzah.

A synagogue!

Lydia stared at it in disbelief. It was like looking at an extinct animal and she hardly dared approach, but then a man came out onto the low steps – a man with a trim beard and a bright white kippah on his head.

'Rabbi?' she queried, hardly daring to believe it.

'Child! Come in, come in.' He led her into the simple, whitewashed synagogue, the walls emblazoned with Torah script, like letters from a beautiful past. 'The Lord bless you, but you're frozen. And, my goodness, you have a cough like a walrus.'

A laugh escaped from Lydia's lips, the first in a long, long time, but it swiftly dissolved into another cough.

'Oh, my dear, we can't have this. Come, eat with us, tell us your tale, let us help.'

Lydia thought she'd never heard more beautiful words.

Later, over delicious home-made chicken soup at the rabbi's table, Lydia finished her account and saw him exchange horrified looks with his wife.

'What did they do to us?' he moaned. 'God help us, what did they do?'

'Nothing that hasn't been done before,' his wife said sagely. 'But they didn't succeed. Not quite. We will rebuild, as we always do, one soul at a time.'

Lydia looked at her curiously. 'How are you still here?' she asked. 'How did they not get you?'

The rabbi smiled. 'The Lord sent us good friends, kind Christians who hid us, and Třebíč is not, you know, the most important of places. We were blessed to remain away from the eyes of evil all the way to the end of this terrible war so that we could restore the synagogue and offer a community to those few others who, like yourself, escaped the monster.' He smiled again. 'Where are you heading, child?'

'Auschwitz,' she said and saw him exchange another look with his wife. 'I seek a record of my daughter.'

'I see.' He steepled his hands. 'Then I think I can help. I have friends in the US army whose Jewish brethren I tend to. They are good men and, more importantly, they have trucks, many trucks, travelling all over the area. I'm sure I can get you a lift to Ostrava if that helps?'

'Ostrava?' Lydia fought to picture the maps she'd drawn on rough paper before setting out from Feldafing back in 1945, but her brain did not retain such things any longer.

'Ostrava is close to the Polish border,' the rabbi provided.

Poland! Home!

'And once over the border, it is a bare fifty kilometres to Auschwitz.'

Fifty kilometres.

Once upon a time, when she'd been a Warsaw shopkeeper with high heels and a maid, fifty kilometres would have seemed an impossible distance; now it was a giddy nothing.

'Yes!' she cried. 'Yes, please.'

In mere weeks she could be there, could find out where Tasha was. If she was anywhere. Fear threaded through Lydia's weary veins and for the first time since she'd stepped out of Feldafing on this long journey, she dreaded its end.

She's not dead, she told herself. She couldn't be dead. For if she was, then this was all for nought, and Lydia might as well be dead too. She just prayed that someone, somewhere, was looking after her beloved girl until she could get to her.

TWENTY-SEVEN

LONDON | JUNE 1946

ALICE

Alice surreptitiously wiped sweat from beneath the band of her smart hat and wondered, for the twentieth time that morning, if she really needed her gloves. No one else seemed to be wearing any and she suspected it was rather an old-fashioned thing to do, but the women of the West London Synagogue *were* rather old-fashioned and she had to impress. There was a lot to ask for.

Checking in her bag for her budgeting file, she tried to remember all that Oskar had said to her when she'd admitted over supper that these visits intimidated her.

'No need to be intimidated, Alice,' he'd proclaimed, waving his wine glass around as he so often did when he was animated. 'You're a smart, intelligent, hard-working woman. What have these Londoners got that you haven't?'

'Style, poise and elegance?' Alice had suggested.

Oskar had laughed. 'You're funny, Alice. And every bit as poised as any of them.'

Alice didn't think that was true at all, but it was nice that he did. He'd been down a lot recently, ostensibly to complete a study on the children for the important-sounding *Journal of Clinical Psychology*, though he seemed to spend just as much time with Alice, Sophie and Manna as with the kids.

'Why not ask the children?' she'd suggested the other day when he'd been quizzing her about ongoing anxieties.

'You're with them day in day out. Your observations are invaluable, Alice – invaluable.'

Which was nice, of course, though she couldn't help feeling that the children's immediate opinions might be even more so. Still, he was the professional so what did she know?

The bus was getting close to the West London Synagogue and Alice gathered her stuff and made her way unsteadily to the front. She could feel her stomach tightening with all-too-familiar nerves and was glad of her gloves to stop her sweating onto the seat-back as they juddered to a halt. She felt again for the file, finding, slid in alongside it, the envelope that Oskar had handed her yesterday.

'A little bonus payment,' he'd said, 'to show you how much we value you. Buy yourself something nice – a new dress perhaps, a pretty floral one like Manna wears.'

Alice hadn't been sure what to make of that. Manna did wear lovely dresses, but Manna was twenty years younger than Alice, with the sort of voluptuous body that looked good in a lovely dress. Alice was more of a skirt and cardigan sort of a woman. Still, maybe she could get a new blouse and there'd be a bit left over for...

'And you're not to spend it on the children,' Oskar had said. That was the problem with these psychoanalysts – they read your mind.

'They're growing fast, Oskar, they need so many things.'

'And always will, but you need things too.'

It had been kind of him and she appreciated it. She'd been keeping her eyes out for shops from the bus and had seen a sensible-looking boutique, tempting enough to give her the boost she needed to get through the meeting.

'Just go into the synagogue, deliver your budget and tell them what you need for the next month,' she told herself. 'What's the worst they can do? Say no.'

Except that it was impossible to be calm about that, because 'no' would mean no swimsuits for the little ones, no football goal for Moishe and the boys. And no special gift for Tasha.

Alice stepped onto the pavement and squared her shoulders. Tasha was doing so well with Joyce. She came home every day full of what she'd learned and last week she'd excitedly reported that she'd been allowed to do her first cut. Just a fringe trim, but it had been as much of a thrill to her as a surgeon making his first incision and Alice had loved hearing her enthuse about it.

'I'm going to get really good, Alice,' she would say. 'I'm going to have my own salon and when Mama finds me, I'll be earning enough money to support us.'

There was still no word on Lydia Ancel, any more than on Maximillian Goldberger, but if Tasha could be optimistic, Alice could too. She also had a plan to help the girl, a plan that required money and, therefore, the cooperation of the women she was about to face, so she gathered herself as Mrs Pinto showed her in.

'How are the children, Mrs Goldberger?' the chairwoman asked once Alice was sitting before them.

On this, at least, Alice was comfortable and she opened her notes and began telling the worthy women about Mattias' piano recital at the local hall last weekend.

'I hope he played some good English music?' Mrs Van Raalte said.

Alice shifted. 'He is working on a piece by Elgar.'

'Lovely. But what did he play at the recital?'

'Bach,' Alice admitted.

'Bach?!' The ladies threw their hands up in horror.

'It's his favourite.'

'It's German, Mrs Goldberger.'

'As am I,' she shot back, stung. The ladies looked uneasily at each other but, really, this was ridiculous even for them. 'Not all Germans are Nazis,' she said, 'as we surely know here? The rescue of the German Jews – not to mention the Poles and Hungarians and Czechs – has been one of the great charitable works of the Central British Fund, of which you are all such kind benefactors.'

'True,' Mrs Pinto said with a condescending smile, 'but, even so, we at the committee believe that the sooner these children are anglicised, the better.'

'I see.'

Alice gripped the side of her chair to stop herself saying any more. Personally, she thought that while it was important for the children to learn good English, it was also vital they kept hold of a sense of their heritage. She remembered Tasha talking to her about how a tree fell over without roots and had to agree, but now was not the time for debate.

'Mattias' piano teacher is working hard with him on Elgar for the next recital,' she said primly.

Let them turn down his lessons after that, she thought, and launched into her budget report. She was careful to detail how many fruits and vegetables they were growing to save money and teach self-sufficiency. She explained the children were learning to sew their own clothes, and slid in that all they needed was fabric – surely not something hard for the Jewish community to provide as half of them had textile factories. She told them about Mirella and Fiorina setting up their own 'business' selling home-made cookies and lemonade at the village cricket matches, not mentioning that they baked Italian amaretti like their mother used to make. Personally, she thought they were the most delicious biscuits she'd ever tasted, but she was sure they wouldn't be English enough for the committee.

'It all sounds marvellous,' Mrs Pinto said when Alice ground to a halt. 'Well done. With such savings, no doubt you have plenty of money to spare.'

Alice looked to the painted rafters for help.

'We can cater for basics,' she agreed, 'but we are stretched on the...' She didn't want to call them extras, because as far as she was concerned, they were essential, 'the additional facilities required to grow the children into rounded adults.'

The committee leaned forward as one.

'Such as?' Mrs Van Raalte asked repressively.

Alice drew in a deep breath. 'Well, Tasha Ancel, one of our older girls—'

'The one who ran away from the Shelter?'

'The one who realised, very sensibly, that she was not quite old enough for life in central London.'

'The superintendent was most concerned about where she'd gone,' Mrs Pinto said.

'I telephoned him personally. The girl was in some distress and needed greater shelter than the, the...'

'The Shelter?' Mrs Van Raalte provided.

Alice groaned but pushed on, 'could provide. Anyway, Tasha has settled into Weir Courtney very well and is a big help with the younger children. Plus, she's secured an apprenticeship to a hairdresser in Lingfield.'

'A hairdresser?!'

The women, all of them perfectly coiffed, did not look impressed.

'She's doing very well and will soon be earning a proper wage, which is, as you know, our aim for all the children, but she needs a pair of scissors.'

'Scissors? Surely at Weir Courtney you have scissors, Miss Goldberger?'

Alice prayed again for patience.

'We have kitchen scissors and craft scissors but not hair-dressing scissors. They are a precision instrument, I'm told, and each hairdresser likes to have her own to fit her particular hand and style of cutting.'

Alice smiled to herself at the memory of Tasha's animated face as she'd explained this in great detail last week. She'd shown Alice a picture from a magazine of the pair Joyce had said would suit her and had taped it to her bedroom wall. She was saving up, she'd told Alice, and had asked for a tin to hold the few pocket-money coins Joyce gave her. It would take a long time to get the funds, though, and Alice longed to be able to present the scissors to her. It would help her develop skills but, more importantly, do her confidence the world of good.

'I see. And how much do these scissors cost?'

Alice girded her loins.

'Fifteen shillings.'

The ladies let out a flutter of protest. 'So much?'

'The Richards company has an excellent reputation and the blades, I'm told, are very sharp and made of an especially durable Sheffield steel that will not need to be replaced for some time.'

'I would hope not. This is a big ask, Mrs Goldberger. Really, you are quite extravagant.'

Alice almost laughed; she didn't think she'd ever been called extravagant before.

'Look on it as an investment,' she tried.

'For who?'

'For Tasha, for her future. It is the most constructive sort of charity possible, giving her the means with which to provide for herself.'

There were a few murmurs of agreement at this but the sum was a large one, at least in Weir Courtney terms. Alice pretty sure every one of these women would eat a dinner that cost more than a pair of even the very best scissors, but their charitable budget was far more frugally considered. Not that she could complain. It was their money and it was up to them what they did with it, including paying her wages.

'Perhaps a contribution to her own savings?' she tried.

To her surprise, Mrs Reinhart stood up. 'It seems a good expenditure to me, if the girl is proving herself dedicated.'

'She certainly is,' Alice assured her.

The others still looked uncertain but Mrs Reinhart gave Alice a broad wink and then turned their way. 'And just think, once she's qualified, she can visit us with Miss Goldberger and demonstrate her new skills. For free.'

A little ripple went around the room. The women were as parsimonious as they were rich and free haircuts were an enticing prospect. Alice looked gratefully to her supporter, who gave her another wink and sank into her chair as the committee begrudgingly voted to permit the funds. Alice could have leaped up and kissed her and, as she moved on to fight for the next items on her modest list, she could already picture Tasha's face when she brought the precious scissors home.

Alice was weary by the time she got off yet another bus a few hours later, but the impressive sight of Tower Bridge opening up to let a large boat through cheered her.

That's like us opening up the gates to our children's futures, she thought, and then told herself off for being fanciful. Not to mention arrogant. The kids were opening their own gates, all they did was ensure they had the strength to wind the handles.

Alice gathered her shopping bags, feeling very grand. In one was her new dress and she glanced self-consciously down, checking she'd really bought it. It was a most un-Alice-like garment – a sweeping dress in a white and blue floral pattern that was totally impractical for a woman who worked with children but which had made her feel so young again that she'd recklessly splashed almost all of Oskar's bonus on it. He'd told her to buy something nice, after all, and she couldn't help but hope he would admire her in it. It was silly, of course. He was far too sophisticated and intellectual to ever be interested in a dull old thing like her, but he'd been most attentive recently and he *had* given her the money for the dress.

In the second bag, far more importantly, were Tasha's scissors, bought from a lovely man who, on hearing the girl's story, had thrown in a comb he'd assured her was 'top notch'. Some of these English phrases really were baffling but his expertise had been beyond question and Alice was sure Tasha would be delighted. For now, though, she had one last job to do in London and she turned her steps away from the grand bridge and down Mansell Street to the Jewish Shelter.

It was not her first visit, but the last time she'd been looking on the hostel as an impartial observer; now she was seeing it as the place Tasha had tried to call home. It did not measure up well. It was crowded and noisy, and the people in there looked so tough. Alice felt quite daunted and thought with panicked fondness of the peace and beauty of Weir Courtney. But Tasha had coped here for weeks, so surely she could manage a single hour to meet someone important?

She made for reception, poised to ask for her contact, but was sideswiped by a bundle of raw, male energy.

'Alice! It's so good to see you.'

'It's good to see you too, Georg,' she cried, delighted. 'How are you doing?'

'Good! That is, work's good. I got promoted last week. The boss says I'm a natural.'

'I'm sure you are.'

'And it's not too bad here, when you get used to it. I like being near the river. It's so big it's almost the sea.'

'You grew up near the sea, didn't you? Do I remember Tasha saying you were from fisherfolk?'

Georg laughed, but it came out strangled. 'She was exaggerating. My mum's family fished at Gdynia, that's all.'

'Right. Well, I'm glad you're doing well.'

Georg scuffed his foot against a loose tile, suddenly looking more like the boy who'd arrived on the plane from Prague than a man making his way in the world.

'How is she?'

'Your mother?' Alice asked, confused.

'No! Tasha. How's Tasha?'

The name was run through with longing and Alice felt stupid.

'I'm so sorry, Georg. Tasha is very well. She's an apprentice hairdresser now.'

'Really?' His face lit up. 'That's wonderful news. She'll love it. She's got this thing about hair. Well, you'll know that, you... It was your idea, wasn't it?'

'It was an obvious idea,' Alice hedged.

'But still yours, like me becoming a locksmith. Thank you, Alice, thank you for helping to make her happy.'

He was so sincere, it tugged at Alice's heart.

'Happier,' she said gently. 'She misses you, Georg.'

'She does? Does she tell you that?'

Alice longed to say yes, but she was a terrible liar.

'Not as such – you know Tasha – but I know from the way she mopes.'

He turned away. 'That'll be for her mother, not for me.'

Alice put a hand on his shoulder. 'For both, perhaps, but definitely for you. She keeps your letters in her handbag.'

'That damned bag,' he said.

But Alice saw his smile and knew he was pleased. 'You should visit, Georg. We'd love to see you.'

'But would *Tasha* love to see me?'

'She would,' Alice asserted and worried instantly about the truth of it. Tasha *would* love to see Georg, she was sure of it; whether the proud young woman would admit as much was another thing entirely. 'Perhaps write first?'

Georg rolled his eyes. 'I write all the time.'

'The course of love never did run easy,' Alice told him.

'Smooth,' he corrected. 'The course of love never did run smooth. It's Shakespeare.'

'Is it indeed? Well, he was a wise man, Georg. Keep at it. You two are meant to be together, I'm sure.'

'Which is more than I am,' Georg said, but he looked happier and, as the supper bell sounded out, he bounded away, energy restored.

'Mrs Goldberger?'

'Miss,' she corrected automatically, turning to see a nurse coming towards her, kind green eyes shining beneath beautiful auburn hair. 'Miss Grainger?'

'Nicola, please. And yes, that's me. Come along in and let's have a cup of tea.'

Alice had rarely heard more welcome words and gladly let the young woman lead her into a side room and make her a drink. London was exhausting! She sat gratefully in a chair and gave Nicola all the details she could recall about Tasha's mother. The nurse had contacted Weir Courtney wanting to help Tasha after she'd fled the Shelter. Now, she assured Alice that she had contacts all over Europe and would do her very best to locate Lydia Ancel. There was no reason to suppose that a lone nurse would find what the might of the American and European search agencies had failed to, but it was worth a shot.

'You're very kind,' Alice told Nicola when, reluctantly, she dragged herself up to head back out into the streets of the capital.

'It's the least I can do. She's been through the wringer, poor kid. And, besides, us redheads must stick together.'

Alice smiled. She had no idea what a wringer was, but she'd take any help on offer. Indeed, she was desperate for it.

'Do you think,' she said shyly, 'that while you're asking about Lydia you might also, perhaps, if it isn't too much trouble, enquire about a Maximillian Goldberger?'

Nicola reached out a hand. 'Your...?'

'Brother. And his wife, Lilliana, and daughter Ruth-Gertrud. I know they were sent to Auschwitz at the end of September 1944, but nothing more...' She saw Nicola's shoulders tighten and put up a hand. 'I know what that probably means but, even so...'

'You'd like to know for certain. I understand.'

Alice didn't think she did. What she really wanted to know was that they were alive and well; that, against all sickening odds, her loved ones had been some of the few to make it out of that hellhole; that she would see them again. But she supposed that if they were dead, as she feared deep down inside they were, then, yes, she wanted to know that too.

'I'm very grateful.'

'Nonsense. I'm the one who should be grateful not to have to go through this. I'll do all I can, I promise.'

'Thank you.'

Alice gratefully shook Nicola's hand and left, heading for home at last with her scissors, her dress and a slightly lighter heart.

Weir Courtney was all but silent when she finally dragged herself through the front door well after nine. All she wanted was a nibble from Sophie's goodie-tin and her bed, but remembering the scissors in her bag gave her an injection of energy. She headed up the stairs, making for the little room Tasha shared with Mina and Golda. A light was shining and, as she turned the corner, she heard most un-Tasha-like giggling. What was going on? She moved closer and saw the backs of the two younger girls clustered around the dressing table they all shared.

'Ooh, Tash, you look gorgeous!' Mina purred.

'Like a film star,' Golda agreed.

'Like Audrey Hepburn,' a third voice said, and Alice froze.

Manna was in there with the girls, expertly brushing eyeshadow across Tasha's lids. She wore an elegant nightgown, topped with a peach silk robe, and looked every inch the film star herself. Alice glanced down at the blue and white dress in her bag and felt foolish. What on earth had made her think she could ever even come close to the younger woman's effortless glamour?

She turned to leave, reluctant to disturb this cosy tête-à-tête, but her foot caught in the edge of the carpet and she clattered into the wall.

'Who's there?' Mina squeaked.

'Maybe it's that gardener's lad spying on us,' Golda said, decidedly hopefully.

'No,' Mina said, 'it's just Alice.'

Alice steadied herself. 'Just me,' she agreed dully.

But Tasha came forward. Her face looked very odd plastered in make-up, but she smiled sweetly all the same.

'It's so late, Alice. Did you have a good day?'

'Very good,' Alice agreed. 'I got you something.' This wasn't quite how she'd imagined the scene, but she'd blurted it out now.

'Me? What on earth could you get me?'

In reply, Alice handed the bag to her. Tasha took it and slowly lifted out the smart black box. Her eyes widened and, fumbling with the ribbon, she lifted the lid.

'What is it?' Mina asked, jealous.

Golda leaned over. 'Just a pair of scissors,' she said scathingly.

They headed back into their room, unimpressed, but Tasha was staring at them as if Alice had brought her the treasures of Tutankhamun.

'My scissors! Alice, you bought me my scissors!'

'Not me,' she said hastily, 'the synagogue committee.'

Tasha wasn't fooled.

'But you must have asked for the money. You must have persuaded them to give it to you. How did you manage that?'

Alice smiled. 'I told them they were an investment for a very special woman who was going to be the best hairdresser in England.'

'Alice! Nonsense.'

Tasha blushed, but then she was throwing her arms around Alice and thanking her over and over, and Alice hugged her gladly back. Tasha wasn't her daughter, she had made that abundantly clear, and Alice could only pray that Nicola would, somehow, find Lydia Ancel to mend the huge hole in her great big heart. In the meantime, however, caring for the prickly girl had become not simply Alice's duty, but her joy. God help her, tired as she was, she'd schlep all the way back to London right this minute if it made Tasha this happy. She had no idea what that meant but so what? She was a carer not a psychoanalyst and, for now, she would just get on with the all-consuming business of caring.

TWENTY-EIGHT

LINGFIELD | JUNE 1946

TASHA

'Morning, Trainee!'

Betsy clattered into the salon from her and Joyce's upstairs flat and gave Tasha a cheery wave.

'Morning, Non-trainee,' Tasha responded.

It was a joke. At least, Betsy thought it was hilarious. Tasha didn't think it was funny teasing Betsy about not being able to work as a hairdresser yet, but the British sense of humour was very peculiar at times.

Sure enough, Betsy roared with laughter.

'One more year. One more boring year of mathematics and silly old books and then I'll be here with you.'

'Books are not silly,' Joyce said repressively, coming in from the back room with steaming mugs of tea. This was one British custom Tasha was getting used to and she took hers gladly.

'Fine,' Betsy said. 'The books aren't silly but they make me feel that *I* am. I can barely understand half of what that Shakespeare goes on about.'

'My boyfriend loves Shakespeare...' Tasha started and then

remembered that Georg was no longer her boyfriend and cut herself off.

Betsy looked at her curiously. 'Georg?' she asked.

She was often in the salon after school, sweeping and helping out and, even more often, gossiping. The pink and cream space seemed to inspire confidences, both in the clients and amongst themselves, and Tasha had admitted far more about Georg to Joyce and Betsy than she normally would.

'Georg,' she agreed heavily. 'He was obsessed with learning good English.'

Betsy snorted. 'Well, blinking Shakespeare won't help him there. He talks nonsense half the time.'

'Not what the literary critics say,' Joyce pointed out.

'Emperor's new clothes,' Betsy retorted merrily. 'Yikes, I'm going to miss the bus if I don't skedaddle. See ya!'

And with that she was off, spinning out of the salon with a clang of the bell, satchel knocking against the door frame and tea mug slammed down so hard that the remaining liquid spilled all over the table. Tasha rushed to mop it up.

'Thanks, my lovely,' Joyce said. 'That girl can never do anything at less than a hundred miles per hour!'

'I like her enthusiasm,' Tasha said.

She meant it. The young girl's energy reminded her of Georg and how he always attacked life. She wished she could be more like that, but she was naturally cautious. She infuriated herself with it; no wonder she'd infuriated Georg.

A picture of him flashed into her mind, red with anger and shouting: 'All you're doing is moping around waiting for a ghost.' Was he right?

'All well there, Tasha, my lovely?'

She shook herself. He *wasn't* right. Look at her, here with an apprenticeship. She was getting on and making the most of herself and if she still prayed daily that her mother was alive, that was her business.

'All well,' she agreed determinedly, taking the tea-stained cloth through to the back room.

'Good,' Joyce said, 'because today I want you to do a perm.'

Tasha gaped at her. 'Me? By myself?'

'Why not? You've watched me enough times, so you know what to do.'

'I do,' Tasha agreed eagerly. 'I do know what to do.' She glanced to the Icall machine in the corner. An impressive contraption, with many electrical curlers dangling from a circular top, it looked like some sort of chandelier from outer space. The client's hair had to be treated with Joyce's special solution and then wound, slowly and carefully, into each roller before the machine could work its magic. The resultant permanent wave was very popular with customers but Joyce had the machine on hire purchase so Tasha was honoured to be trusted with it. 'Thank you, Joyce. I won't let you down.'

'Of course you won't.' Joyce patted her on the back. 'Start gathering the materials so we can mix our solution. Mrs Gifford will be in at ten.'

Tasha gave Joyce a quick kiss on her soft cheek and rushed off to do as instructed.

'If you could see me now, Georg Lieberman,' she muttered under her breath.

She wished he'd walk through the door and do exactly that – and wished it almost as fiercely as she always wished Lydia would – but the only person ringing the bell this morning would be Mrs Gifford, so she put her head down and got on with her job.

The perm went fairly smoothly. The tricky bit wasn't so much winding the hair into the dangling rollers as keeping up cheery chatter, but Joyce always had a stream of questions for her clients and Tasha was grateful to be able to focus. When she'd finally finished, she set the machine running and went off to fetch Mrs Gifford a cup of tea and a glossy magazine with a huge sense of relief.

Meanwhile, Joyce was brushing setting lotion into Mrs Samson's soft white hair. The old lady came in without fail every week for a shampoo and set and, far more importantly, a morning of chat and attention. Tasha offered her a 'cuppa' too and she accepted gratefully.

'You're a good girl, Natasha,' she said, catching at Tasha's heart. Only her mother had ever called her by her full name and it was like an echo out of her past. 'Are you enjoying working here?' the old lady chattered on as Joyce began gently pulling her hair into rollers.

'I am, thank you, Mrs Samson. I'm learning so much.'

'You've got the best teacher. Joyce is a marvel.'

'She is.'

'It's the highlight of my week, coming here.'

'Ah there now!' Joyce said, looking teary. 'We love having you.'

'It's better than any medicine, is a good wash and set at Beautiful You. You know all these new-fangled ideas about "therapy"?'

'I certainly do,' Tasha agreed, thinking of Alice, Oskar and Anna Freud and the way they always seemed to be studying you.

'Well, I'm sure they're very clever and they mean well, but most of the time, all people really need is a bit of care and attention.'

'Am I your therapy, Mrs S?' Joyce asked.

'You are, dear, you really are.'

The two women laughed merrily but Tasha thought they were wiser than they realised. Perhaps she'd mention it to Alice sometime, maybe when she was being especially annoying. She moved to tidy up her workstation as Joyce finished Mrs

Samson's rollers and eased her into the second dryer next to Mrs Gifford.

'Will you have a salon of your own, Natasha?' the old lady asked companionably.

Tasha jumped and turned back.

'I suppose so. One day. I've got so much to learn but, yes, that would be perfect.'

'Lovely. What will you call it?'

'Sorry?'

'Your salon, dear, what will you call it?'

'I've no idea.' It was a thought too dizzying to get her head around. 'I'm not even sure if it would be here, in England, or at, at home...'

She stuttered on the word and Mrs Samson looked at her curiously.

'Where's home, dear?'

Tasha swallowed. 'Warsaw. In Poland.'

'Ah.' The old lady reached and grabbed Tasha's hand. 'That's hard.'

Mrs Gifford leaned in, her metal curlers clinking. 'My grandson was part of a battalion in Poland. He said your poor country was treated terribly.'

Tasha looked from one to the other, feeling exposed. 'I... Yes. I mean, I suppose so. That is – we let ourselves get invaded, so you know...'

'No one could have beaten that Hitler and his nasty dark armies.'

'You Brits did.'

Mrs Gifford gave a funny little laugh. 'Only once we got the Americans on board with all their fancy money!'

'But, never mind about that horridness, dear,' Mrs Sansom said, 'we're talking about salon names. What about calling it Natasha's? That has a nice ring to it in any country.'

'Oh no!' Tasha shook her head. 'I couldn't. It would feel too...' She sought for the word. 'Arrogant?'

'Nonsense,' Joyce said. 'If it's your shop, why not put your name over the door?'

It was exactly the sort of thing Georg would say but it wasn't Tasha's style.

'I couldn't.'

'What about someone else's name?' Joyce suggested. 'What about your mother's?'

'Lydia's?' Tasha tested it out on her tongue and felt a bubble of joy rise inside her. 'Lydia's! It sounds fantastic.'

'It does,' Mrs Gifford agreed.

'And wait until you tell her,' Mrs Sansom said. 'She'll be over the moon, I bet.'

Tasha felt the bubble of joy pop in her gut.

'If I ever find her,' she said miserably.

Mrs Sansom looked panicked. 'Oh, my dear, have I put my big old foot in it?'

Tasha looked down at the old lady's neat feet, her head spinning, but then Joyce put a strong arm around her shoulders and she felt herself steady.

'Tasha and her mother were separated at the end of the war,' she said calmly to the two ladies. 'It's taking time to find each other again.'

'Goodness!' Mrs Sansom looked horrified. 'You poor dear girl. How terrible. But you will find her, I'm sure you will.'

'Are you?'

'Oh yes.' Mrs Sansom nodded so vigorously that her head battered against the side of the dryer.

Tasha was grateful for the kindly old lady's confidence, and horribly aware that hers was waning. It was almost a year and a half since Lydia had been marched out of Auschwitz so surely, if she was alive, she'd have found some way to get in touch? She sought for something to say but was spared by the timer on the

Icall machine ringing out its imperious summons and scuttled gratefully across to attend to Mrs Gifford's hair. This was her first proper permanent wave, after all, and she had to get it right.

The wave, thank heavens, looked really good and Mrs Gifford thanked her effusively and even gave her a tip. Tasha ran to stash the coins in her bag, tucked away in the safe, and came back to find Marta standing in the middle of the salon, fighting for breath.

'Kotka? What's wrong?'

'Nothing's wrong,' Marta choked out but she was still getting her breath back and it was only after a few deep gulps that she could add, 'It's good news.'

'What?' Tasha demanded impatiently.

'Alice came to school to get Mirella and Fiorina.' A pause for breath. 'I ran all the way here to tell you as soon as we were allowed out on morning break.' She sucked in more air. 'They've had a letter.'

'What does it say?'

Tasha was aware of Joyce and Mrs Sansom listening intently and willed Marta to find the oxygen to continue. The little girl, like many of them, didn't have the greatest lung capacity but she was recovering fast – although also becoming aware of her audience.

'It says,' she proclaimed grandly, looking around, 'that their parents are alive and well and together in Italy and they want them back.'

Tasha's knees folded in on themselves and she had to clutch at the sink to stay upright. 'Their parents? Alive? Both of them?'

Marta nodded keenly. 'Their tata was a prisoner and their mama in camps. They both had to get home to Italy and then they found each other and started looking for Miri and Fifi and now, now...'

'They've found them?!' Tasha cried.

'They've found them,' Marta confirmed.

Tasha looked dazedly around the cream and pink salon; it seemed to fill and dance with the news and the bubble of joy fizzed once more inside her.

'You see,' Joyce said softly, 'people *are* still finding each other.'

Tasha nodded and turned back to Marta. 'What camp was their mama in, Kotka?'

Marta smiled. 'Auschwitz, Tash. She was in Auschwitz, just like yours.'

The hated word seemed to dance too. Miri and Fifi's mother had been in Auschwitz and she'd made it out, stayed alive, and found them. If Mrs Bellucci could do it, then why not Mrs Ancel? Tasha glanced sideways into the nearest mirror, again picturing Lydia here, alongside her, and her heart, so battered recently, felt swollen with hope once more.

TWENTY-NINE

AUSCHWITZ | JUNE 1946

LYDIA

Lydia trod the last steps up from the quiet village of Oświęcim slower and slower, but for once it was not her broken lungs holding her back but her pounding heart. Up here, in the stripped-out Polish countryside, lay her worst nightmare and every particle of her body strained against returning.

'All's well,' she told herself over and over. 'It's not a camp any longer. There are no Nazis, no guns, no dogs, no gas.' But her body did not believe her and she had to will her feet to keep moving up the side of the train tracks that, just under two years ago, had brought her, Tasha and Amelia into the jaws of hell.

Then suddenly, there it was and she staggered back, clutching at a lamppost for support. The wires were stretching their barbs into the distance, watchtowers at tight intervals all along them. The barracks were still inside and the long, dark gateway was still before her, looking just as it had that bitter day in January 1945 when she'd been pushed through it in the ice and snow and Tasha had been left behind.

'Tasha!'

The thought of her daughter sent Lydia darting forward and that's when she took in the changes, subtle but utterly vital: the fences no longer crackled with lethal electricity; the watch-towers stood empty; the gates were wide open and two workmen were quietly concreting over the train tracks. Lydia crept closer. Inside, she could see everything was the same save that grass was growing where once there had been only mud, and birds perched on the wire, singing merrily. As she reached the gateway, one of the workmen tipped his cap to her. Embarrassed, she sidled past and there she was, inside Auschwitz once more and it was totally and utterly empty.

A sob rose in Lydia's throat. She tried to swallow it down but it caught on the barbs in her lungs and forced its way back up as a racking cough. The workmen looked over in concern and she hastened further inside, her steps taking her automatically towards the barrack where she had slept with Tasha, right up to the moment when the Nazis had torn them from their bunk – and from each other.

It stood before her, an anodyne wooden hut, scrubbed clean of the mud and blood and pus of camp life. No one who walked in here now and saw the orderly bunks, the central stove and the bright wood would ever believe what had gone on in here. Why was it even still standing? Why had the Allies not just set a torch to the whole, hideous place and wiped it from the surface of the earth, as the Nazis had tried to do to the Jewish nation? This bare hut told no stories. It was empty of women in various stages of decay, empty of lice and rats, empty of any trace of the endless, grinding suffering of every single prisoner. Empty of Tasha.

Lydia stumbled outside, sank down on the grass with her back to the wooden wall, and looked around in fury. Months it had taken her to get here and there was nothing. Nothing! She'd used up far too many of her dwindling allocation of breaths to return, like a dog to a cruel master. For nothing.

'Tasha!' she shouted to the stark camp but the cry bounced off the scrubbed huts and rattled back through her lungs, mocking their fruitless efforts. Exhausted, Lydia buried her head in her hands and wept.

'Stara?' The voice was soft, tentative. 'Stara? Can I help? Are you looking for something? For someone?'

Lydia unfolded herself with an effort and looked up into a pair of concerned eyes.

'I was, but it was a foolish dream. There's no one here.'

'*I'm* here.'

She tried to smile. 'Forgive my rudeness, but you're not who I seek.'

'You *are* looking for someone then?'

'Of course I'm looking for someone,' she said wearily. 'What *things* would a Jew have to seek?'

The man bit his lip but didn't move away. 'I understand your anger.'

'How can you? You weren't here when it was all fear and pain and disease.'

'I was.'

She jumped and he sat down opposite her, a respectful distance away.

'You were in the camp?' she asked.

'Yes. Tadeusz Wąsowicz at your service. Inmate number 20035.'

He pulled up his shirtsleeve and Lydia stared at the tattoo across his lean forearm.

'I don't understand,' she said. 'Why are you here? Why come back?'

'I'm here with a small delegation, sent by the Polish Ministry for Arts and Culture, and tasked with preserving this place to bear witness to the suffering that went on within it.'

'You are?' She gave a dark laugh, then waved a hand around the sanitised camp. 'I don't see any suffering.'

'Would you want to?'

She drew in a rattling breath. 'No. But this... it's so, so bleached clean.'

He nodded. 'True, but what can we do? We cannot leave typhus to rage. It's claimed enough victims, don't you think?'

Her cough was the only answer he needed.

'We're collecting pictures, stories. It will never convey the whole experience, but we will do our best.'

'Why?'

He shrugged. 'So it never happens to mankind again.'

Lydia laughed bitterly. 'You are a good person, Mr Wąsowicz. Better than me. I would like to think of mankind, but have space only for myself.'

'Will you tell me who you seek?' he asked softly.

'Will it help?'

'It will.' Tadeusz smiled. 'For in that bleached-clean barrack over there' – he pointed across the complex – 'we keep the records.'

Lydia's head snapped up at the magic word. 'Records?'

'Entry lists, crematoria books, death certificates. I warn you, the SS burned some in the last days of the camp, but not all.'

'What about after?' Lydia whispered hoarsely. 'Did anyone make a list after?'

'Of survivors?' Tadeusz asked.

Lydia could only nod.

'Yes, the Red Cross did that – all survivors.'

'All survivors?' she echoed wonderingly.

'And where they were sent. Shall we?'

He stood up, offering his arm, and, shaking all over, Lydia took it and let him lead her away from the barrack in which Tasha had been locked, and towards the one in which she would find out if she'd ever escaped. Her legs would barely support her and Tadeusz had to half-carry her the fifty long steps to the answer she had travelled eight hundred kilometres to find.

He settled her in a chair and she sat, gripping the arms with every ounce of her strength, as he opened up a small notebook and set a finger at the top of the neat lines of text.

'What name am I looking for?'

She fought for the oxygen to say it. 'Natasha. Natasha Ancel.'

'A,' he said softly. 'Easy.'

Then his finger began travelling down the page and, just a few lines down, stopped. Lydia held what remained of her breath.

'Here it is. Natasha Ancel. Survivor.'

Lydia's hands flew to her mouth. 'My girl,' she said. 'My beautiful girl.'

And then all went black.

THIRTY

ALICE

Alice surveyed the pile of letters sitting unopened on her bed and reached into the top drawer of her bedside table. Tucked away at the back were her emergency chocolates; there weren't many left. Selecting one at random, she popped it into her mouth and let the delicious sweetness flood down her throat, giving her the strength to face her mail. She should have dealt with it this morning but with the children off school she'd been needed to supervise swimming in Sir Benjamin's pool. The rest of the day had slid by in the same vein so here she was, past her bedtime and still with work to do.

It had been manic ever since news had got out about the Bellucci sisters' parents finding them. She'd been contacted by so many journalists, historians and members of the public wishing to express their happiness for the girls and, while it was very nice of them, it didn't half increase her workload. At least with school over, she could pass the easier missives on to Mina and Golda to answer, but that still left the rest.

The most heartbreaking ones were from other refugees,

desperate to find their families. There were young people who had come to England in the kindertransports in 1938 and were growing into adulthood alone. There were academics and business people who'd fled Europe before the war but lost their networks. There were even a few who'd battled their way here individually during the war and had no idea what had happened to those they'd left behind. All wrote to Alice in the hope that, because two of her charges had been delivered the fairy tale, she had some sort of magic touch.

How did she tell them she was as ordinary and helpless as they were?

I know how greatly you wish to find those you love, she would write back time and again. *I, myself, have family missing in Europe so truly understand your pain.* She doubted it was much comfort but it was all she had to offer.

In the meantime, at Weir Courtney, all was excitement verging on hysteria. Mirella and Fiorina had become minor celebrities and the letter from their parents had been read so often that it was becoming faded and torn. In the end, Sophie – with the girls' permission – had stuck it on the noticeboard, carefully pinned at all four corners so the children could peruse the words of love and hope without smudging them. There was always at least one child peering hopefully up at it, wishing the names at the bottom would morph into those of their family.

Alice was delighted for Miri and Fifi, of course, and she couldn't deny that the injection of hope was welcome for all of them, but every day she had to answer at least three or four pleas of 'when are my parents going to write to me?' from the other children and it was both heartbreaking and wearying. The myriad letters merely added to the speculation and, with the children not at school, Alice would emerge from her office for much-needed coffee to find several of them waiting hopefully outside. The children were happy at their Weir Courtney home, but there was another, more individual home nestled in every one of their hearts and the Belluccis' letter had turned them towards it once more.

Sighing, Alice sliced open the first of the envelopes. It was from a journalist wanting to take photos of the girls. Alice started a pile for Mina and Golda to answer. There would be several of these and each person would have to be told they could be present at Victoria station from whence the girls would take the train south to Dover once a guardian could be found to accompany them.

The next was in a similar vein, but wanting a full, filmed interview. Alice suspected the girls might like that but it was not good for them. They were blessed to be going home to their parents, but it should not set them aside from – and certainly not above – the other children who had been less fortunate. So far.

The third letter was from a young man who'd lost touch with all his family since coming to England in 1938 and was pleading with Alice to 'use her contacts' to find them. She would have to answer that one herself and it went on a new pile. The fourth letter was written on unusual lilac paper, the address in a rounded, confident hand. Alice opened it up and glanced to the signature at the bottom of the second page: Nicola Grainger.

Her heart skipped. This letter was from the red-headed nurse who had promised to try to find out about Lydia Ancel. And about her own, dear Max. Licking her lips for a scrap of chocolate to sustain her (and finding none), Alice smoothed the letter out on her counterpane and began reading.

My dear Alice,

I hope all is well with you and the children in your care in Surrey. I have been making enquiries about Lydia Ancel, and am writing because I believe I may have found a lead. Please do not get your hopes too high as the name Ancel is a common one and I have yet to confirm individual details with UNRRA but we have been contacted about a Lydia Ancel in hospital in Katowice, transferred there from the new museum at Auschwitz-Birkenau. I will leave it to you to decide whether to mention this to her daughter but might personally caution against it for fear of creating heavy disappointment if this does not prove to be the correct woman. Nonetheless, my hopes and prayers are with her and I will be in touch again the moment I've found out more.

Alice stared and stared at the words, unable to believe they were really there. *Please do not get your hopes up too high*, Nicola had said and she was quite right to do so, but how high was too high? If they could find Tasha's mother, the girl would be transformed. Alice brought the letter to her lips and kissed it, then looked guiltily to the door in case anyone had seen. It was slightly ajar but, at gone eleven o'clock, there was no one wandering the corridors, so her sentimentally went thankfully unseen.

She was about to put the letter onto her own pile, determined to reply to it first thing tomorrow, when she realised that Nicola's signature had been on the other side of the lilac page. There was more. Turning it over, she read on.

And then wished she hadn't.

I have more news, Alice and this, I'm afraid, is not so positive. There is no kind way to say it, so I'm going to have to be blunt, but please be assured that it breaks my heart to write this, as I know it will break yours to read it. The name Maximillian Goldberger has emerged on a crematorium book from Auschwitz-Birkenau, smuggled out by a Sonderkommando who escaped the death marches, and recently delivered it into official hands.

There is, obviously, no way of ratifying that this was your brother, but the man in question was cremated on 29 September 1944, having arrived in the camp from Theresien-stadt that day. There are also a Lilliana and a Ruth-Gertrud Goldberger listed in the crematorium book on 4 October 1944, also on the day they arrived in the camp. This evidence, combined, does suggest that they are the people you were seeking and that they, very sadly, went to their deaths in the Auschwitz extermination camp.

I'm so, so sorry, Alice. I can only hope that the knowing brings you a little peace but am sure that will never make up for having your family in your life and offer my sincerest condolences. I would be happy to talk at any time if you feel the need but know that you are with caring, clever people who will be able to help you more than I. Do talk to them, Alice. We all need friends in these terrible times.

Apologies again for being the bearer of such sad tidings.

With all love,

Nicola Grainger

Alice stared so hard at the words that they ran into each other, but that didn't make them come out any better, just encouraged several of them to jump at her, cold and hard: *extermination camp, went to their deaths, crematorium book*. The dates made sense with what she knew already and fitted into one dark, painful truth. A howl grew inside her stomach, sharp and hard and loud enough to echo round every corner of Weir Courtney, and she dropped the letter to stuff her fists into her mouth and keep it inside. She could not frighten the children by waking them with her grief, and she folded in on herself, rocking against the bedhead as the inescapable reality of Nicola's words battered at her.

Max was dead. Her big brother would never smile at her

again, never hug her, tease her or wish her shalom. Her sister-in-law would never roll her eyes at Alice and ask, 'is he always like this', and her niece would never run to her to show off her latest picture or collage. No one, now, would remember her parents or be able to reminisce with her about times from her youth. She was, truly, on her own. The howl tore at her throat and she had to force herself to pant harder than a birthing mother to stop it flying out and cutting the hard-won peace of Weir Courtney.

'Max,' she moaned, one hand still in her mouth, the other clutching at her sides in case the grief physically tore her apart. Her vision was blurred with tears, her head full of them, her very heart drowning in their tide. 'My poor, poor Max.'

She pulled an image of Auschwitz into her head, compiled of photographs from the news and snippets from those children who, like Tasha, had been incarcerated there. She imagined Max pushed off a train, long since separated from his wife and daughter, prodded and pushed into the wrong line. The journey must have broken him badly if the Nazis had not thought him even worth working to death, and she imagined him being shoved, naked, into a chamber, confused and disorientated. Had it been dark in there? He'd never liked the dark. That would have scared him even before they'd piped the deadly gas inside.

'Stop it!' she told herself sharply, but she could not.

He must have suffered horribly, so the least she could do was consider what he'd gone through. And her little niece too, clinging to her mother, asking where Vati had gone. Had they thought they were going for a shower, as some had apparently been told, or had they known? Here in cosy England, the post-liberation photos from the camps had been a total shock and she could only pray that it had been the same in Poland, but somehow she doubted it. Millions did not disappear from ghettos without serious suspicion spreading; her family would almost certainly have gone knowingly to their deaths that late in the war.

'1944!' Alice moaned into her clenched fist.

When Max was rattled off to his death in Poland, the Allies had been marching into Europe. The Nazis had been in retreat but still, hidden behind their own lines, they'd gone on sense-lessly killing people as if it was their right to decide who lived on God's earth.

Her eyes went to the photograph on her bedside table and she snatched it up. With her fingertip, she traced the line of her brother's face, so proud standing there with his arm around his wife and child, smiling at the photographer. It had been taken not long after little Ruth-Gertrud had begun walking, so perhaps in 1937. By 1944 she would have been eight, the same age as Marta or Suzi.

Why not them instead?

The thought crept into her mind but she pushed it right back out again. None of this was the fault of the brave children in her care who were battling their way to a new form of life, just as she must now do. Like them, it seemed, she was without anyone of her very own.

'Aaaah!'

The cry could be contained no longer and she let it fly as she flung the precious photo across the room. It hit the wardrobe and smashed, cracking the wooden frame and sending glass across her carpet.

'Alice? Oh, Alice!'

Alice looked up from her cocoon of misery to see, to her horror, Oskar standing in the doorway. She could not think what he was doing up here at this time of night, had not even known that he'd arrived at Weir Courtney, but somehow here he was and she was curled up wailing like a fool. What must he think of her?

He came striding inside, scooping up the picture in a single, fluid movement. He looked at it and his eyes filled with sorrow.

'You've heard about your brother?'

Alice nodded.

'He's...?'

'Dead!'

It came out on another wail, the grief impossible to stop even with her boss in the room, but he was unfazed. Sitting on the bed at her side, he pulled her into his arms and cradled her.

'I'm sorry,' he soothed. 'My poor, poor Alice, I'm so sorry.' Alice tried to compose herself, tried to resist the wave of grief but it was too great and she sank against him and wept. 'My poor Alice,' he said again, stroking her hair. 'Cry all you want. I've got you. You're safe.'

So cry she did. She wasn't sure when she stopped. She didn't recall crying herself into exhaustion, didn't remember him tucking her under the covers, but he must have done because she woke at dawn, her throat raw, her eyes swollen, and her body broken by grief, but somehow held together for another endless day.

THIRTY-ONE

LINGFIELD | JULY 1946

TASHA

As the train pulled into Lingfield station, Tasha felt an overwhelming urge to turn around and run. This had been a foolish idea. She didn't want to see him, didn't want him to come here, didn't want...

The door nearest her flew open and whatever she wanted became irrelevant, because here he was and it seemed that her body was in stark disagreement with her mind. Every part of her sang at the sight of Georg as he bounded, with the energy she remembered so well, onto the platform. He looked around and, spotting her, did a comic double-take.

'Tasha! You look beautiful.'

Tasha shifted awkwardly, glad she'd made an effort. Alice, who'd been most peculiar these last few days, had pushed her to agree to meet Georg, saying it was 'lovely to have people who care around you', so she'd given in and agreed to this visit and she had to admit that, seeing him now, she was glad she had.

She brushed self-consciously at her dress. Manna, who'd

turned out to be a whizz with a sewing machine, had made several nifty nips and tucks in the turquoise creation Alice had found her in Windermere. She'd also lent her mascara and lip gloss to 'enhance her natural beauty', or some such nonsense. She'd been most animated about the joys and the pitfalls of courting, warning Tasha to 'make sure you're getting what *you* want from the relationship.'

'I know that,' Tasha had told her.

'Good. I wish I did,' had been the cryptic response. It seemed all the adults at Weir Courtney were behaving strangely and Tasha had wanted to ask more but Manna had scuttled away and, frankly, she'd had enough worries of her own to bother chasing her down.

Waking nervously early this morning, she'd spent a long time brushing her hair so that it glowed copper in the summer light. The familiar act had soothed her and she'd almost liked what she saw in the mirror before she came out, but it certainly didn't warrant the open admiration with which Georg was drinking her in.

'How did I ever stay away?' he said, his voice hoarse.

He stepped forward so she thought he would kiss her and wondered if she would resist, but he confined himself to dropping a light peck on each cheek, the second one grazing the corner of her mouth so that she felt the very pulse of him through her veins. They stood there, staring at each other, and it was only a large woman barging past that jerked them apart.

'Shall I show you round?' Tasha asked awkwardly.

'Lovely.'

'Do you have long? Before your train back, I mean? Not that I'm trying to get rid of you. No, no. You can stay as long as you like. That is, I'd like you to stay for a long... Oh, honestly!'

She cut herself off and Georg laughed and nudged companionably at her.

'There's hours till the last train, Tash. And I'm not at work tomorrow so I could stay if... That is, if there's a spare room or a sofa or something. I didn't mean... Which isn't to say...'

Now it was his turn to tangle his words.

Tasha laughed. 'Let's worry about all that later, shall we?'

'Let's,' Georg agreed gratefully.

They headed into Lingfield and Georg looked around him, drawing in gulps of air.

'Are you ill?' she asked, concerned.

'No! But my lungs can't get enough of this fresh air. Goodness, Tash, it's been so muggy and dirty in London these last months. It's roasting in the Shelter at night, especially up on the top floor. Sometimes I sleep on the fire escape, but then you get all the noises of the city and the sun shining down on you not long after it's gone to bed. I never seem to feel rested any more.' He looked down at her. 'Course, that might be my own fault.'

'How so?'

His eyes, when she dared to meet them, were staring at her with such intensity.

'Because I let the woman of my dreams go, and now my dreams are useless.'

Tasha's heart leaped even as her brain struggled to make sense of the words. She'd forgotten Georg's literary tendencies.

'Shakespeare?' she asked.

'Lieberman,' he said. 'Me. I miss you, Tasha.'

His hand found hers and she clutched at it, but couldn't quite bring herself to meet his eye. This had been the problem before. Georg was good with words and dreams and promises but less so with the day-to-day reality of being together.

'Shall I show you where I work?' she suggested.

He gave a tiny sigh but nodded. 'Yes, please.'

They walked down Lingfield High Street in silence, a thousand thoughts and memories thrumming between their linked fingers. This, Tasha thought, was the man – boy, then – with whom she'd been locked into a frozen barrack. This was the man with whom she'd refused to die, and then, once Ana and Ester had let them out, the man with whom she'd fought for life. This was the man who'd hugged her when the Russians had ridden into Auschwitz, the man who'd told her they were free. She'd barely remembered what the word meant and hadn't quite believed him because so much of what she would have freely chosen for herself had been stolen away by the war. Georg had always embraced freedom more easily than her.

His hold on her hand felt sticky suddenly and she was glad to stop outside Beautiful You and let go. It was Saturday afternoon so the salon was closed and that was fine by Tasha. The last thing she needed was Joyce and Betsy – especially Betsy – analysing Georg. He would be bound to turn on the charm and they would be bound to love him and then they wouldn't be able to understand why she wasn't with him. Not that, now he was here again, Tasha was sure she understood that either.

'You work *here*?'

Georg's voice was incredulous and, as he stepped up to the window, cupping his hands to see more clearly into the vibrant interior, she tried to look at Beautiful You through his eyes. The bright cream and bold, bouncy pink were not, she admitted, her sort of colours; she was more of a sludge green and fog grey sort of a person.

'It's not what you expected?' she asked lightly.

'There's a bit of a clash.'

'With my hair?'

'With your everything.'

Tasha laughed. 'I thought that at first too. It's crazy, isn't it? Far too hectically pretty for grumpy old me.'

'I didn't say that.'

'But you thought it.'

'Actually, I thought that I'd love to lie back against that

glorious pink sink and have you run your beautiful fingers through my hair.'

The image sideswiped her.

'I'd like that too,' she admitted.

Without thinking, she reached up and twined a finger in a loose curl at the side of his face. He sucked in a breath and stepped closer, putting a gentle hand to her waist and, when she didn't resist, pulled her in against him.

'I really miss you, Tasha. I miss talking to you, I miss teasing you, I miss arguing with you, I miss kissing you.'

His face was a centimetre from hers. Her fingers tightened in his hair, pulling him across that great divide and then their lips were meeting and her heart was pounding and—

'Oi, you pair – get a room!'

They sprang apart to see a gaggle of local lads catcalling from the opposite side of the street. Tasha was mortified but Georg just slung an arm around her shoulders and gave them a broad grin.

'Jealous, boys?' They flushed scarlet and ran off, and he smiled down at Tasha. 'Shall we find somewhere more private?'

'Erm...'

'To talk, I mean. I really, really want to talk to you, Tasha.'

'You do?' He sounded serious. Tasha wasn't sure she was ready for serious.

'Yes. I've got things to say.'

She definitely wasn't ready for 'things to say'. But what could she do? She looked around.

'If I take you to Weir Courtney, you'll be inundated.'

'Sounds fun, but not yet. I want you to myself.'

She thought.

'We could go to the cricket field.'

Georg burst out laughing. 'Look at us, Tasha – the cricket field! When did we get so English?'

Tasha laughed too. 'When we got on a plane and flew from Prague to blinking Windermere.'

'Wondermere,' Georg said wistfully. 'It truly was paradise, wasn't it? I really thought I'd landed on my feet – and I had – but it turns out you can't just land, you have to walk forward, and that takes a bit more effort.' He squeezed her shoulders. 'Especially when it comes to choosing the right direction to walk in.'

More fancy words.

'Was your dad a poet?' she teased and was surprised when he winced.

'Where's this cricket field?'

She swallowed. She could feel him tense against her now and ducked gladly down the alleyway that led to one side of the big field. There was, thankfully, no match on, though a couple of kids were practising with a bat, and a handful more were climbing the oaks at the far side. Tasha remembered Miri and Fifi shooting up there back in May when the poor children had thought the Nazis had returned. Now the Bellucci sisters were getting ready to head home. To their parents. Both parents.

She sought for the words to tell the whole story to Georg but she didn't have his way with them, so steered him silently to a nearby bench. A brass plaque told them it had been erected: 'To Fred, who loved this field, and Maisie, who loved Fred.'

'That's beautiful,' Georg said.

'Do you think?' Tasha wasn't so sure. 'There's poor Maisie busy loving Fred and he's just loving the damned field.'

Georg shook his head at her. 'Always with the negatives, Tasha Ancel. It doesn't say Fred didn't love her. This is a tribute from Maisie, an open statement of unconditional love.'

'Hmmm.'

'What's wrong with that?'

'It's very sweet, I suppose, but I wonder if unconditional love is, well, a bit stupid.'

Georg squinted at her. 'Stupid?'

'*Unconditional*. What if Fred murdered someone? Would Maisie still love him then?'

'Probably,' Georg said. 'Though she might not like him very much.'

It was a ridiculous thing to say and, despite herself, Tasha laughed out loud.

'You amaze me, Georg. You see the best in every situation.'

'I don't see the best in us being apart.' He was serious again. Sitting on the bench, he took Tasha's hand and pulled her down next to him. 'You said once, Tash, that to grow, you have to have roots, yes?'

'I did, but—'

'It made a big impression on me. You see, I think my roots are... shrivelled.'

Tasha frowned at him. 'Shrivelled, Georg? Hardly. They were cut away, severed by the Nazis and—'

'They weren't.'

His voice was low but firm. She stared at him.

'Sorry?'

'My roots – that is, my parents – weren't killed by the Nazis.'

'But you said—'

'I never said anything. People just assumed. Everyone else's parents were killed by the bastards, so they assumed mine were too. And I... I let them. I let *you*. I'm sorry.'

Tasha's head spun.

'You told me about it. You said you saw them die in front of you.'

'I did. Just not in the war. And not together.'

'Then...?'

Georg looked into the grass at their feet, fiddling nervously with her fingers. 'It's not a heroic story, Tasha.'

'Why should it be?'

'I just… You obviously had a nice family and a nice house and a good life, whereas I…'

'Please, Georg, tell me what happened.'

'Fine.' He drew in a deep breath. 'It won't take long. My father was killed in a bar brawl. I'd been sent to fetch him home, he didn't want to come. The barman was on my side, other people weren't, it all got nasty and he… he was stabbed. He died on the floor of the bar, spitting blue murder.'

'That's awful, Georg. How old were you?'

His fingers twitched in hers. 'I was five.'

'Five! Your mum sent you into a bar when you were five?'

'I told you – it wasn't a life like yours. I mainly lived it on the streets with the other kids.'

'Which is when you got good at picking locks?'

'Only decent thing my dad ever taught me.'

Tasha rubbed his hand. 'I'm sorry, Georg. It wasn't your fault.'

'Not my father, maybe. But Mama…'

The Polish word flared in Tasha's heart, but this wasn't about her now; this was about him.

'Can you tell me?'

He looked at her, his face so bleak she barely recognised him.

'It's not pretty either, Tash. After Tata died, she, well, she took to the drink. Ironic – she'd hated him being at it and then she embraced it like an old friend. I wasn't enough for her, you see. We weren't enough for her.'

'We? You had siblings?'

Georg gave a funny little sound, part growl, part cry of distress.

'Not for long. I had a little brother, Leon, but not long after Tata died, he… he got sick. We couldn't afford a doctor. That's to say, we could have afforded a doctor but vodka was, apparently, a better deal.' The pain tore through the cracks in his voice and Tasha felt helpless before him. 'He died in my arms while Mama drowned her sorrows downstairs. She apologised at the funeral. Wept and begged my forgiveness and then fell into the rough little state coffin and knocked it sideways.' He looked at Tasha, his eyes cold. 'I hated her then.'

Tasha nodded. 'I would have done too.'

'You would?'

'Of course. She killed your brother.'

'I don't know about killed...'

'I do. Death by neglect. The Nazis did it all the time. I saw as many people die in the ghetto as in the camp. Typhus, pneumonia, starvation, childbirth – they kill just as easily as Zyklon B and at half the cost.'

Georg winced. 'Don't, Tash.'

'Why not? You went through it. You saw it too.'

'But my parents didn't. Tata went out in a scrap and Mama simply sank into nothingness.'

'How did you survive?'

He gave a bitter laugh. 'I got canny. I learned that if I wanted to eat, I had to get to her benefit money on a Friday when she'd just picked it up. I'd sneak it out of her purse and hide it in a special hole in my pillow so that by the middle of the next week I'd still have a few zloty for some bread.'

Tasha pictured a miniature Georg sticking a tiny hand into the middle of his pillow for coins so he could eat and wanted to wrap her arms around him and take away all the hurt, but he was so rigid, so unusually pulled in on himself, that she didn't dare.

'D'you know,' he went on tightly, 'I can't even remember when Mama actually died. There was so little difference between coming home to her comatose and when she was actually gone that it barely registered.'

'How old were you by then?'

'Twelve.'

'You lived on pillow-bread for seven years?'

'Give or take, yes. I got better at picking locks.'

Briefly, the lopsided grin that Tasha knew so well emerged and then it was gone again. She missed it instantly.

'I'm so sorry, Georg. But you shouldn't be ashamed.'

He turned on her then, fierce. 'I should! My parents were drunks who cared so little for their children that they couldn't even feed them. When the war came along, I was relieved. Relieved! How awful is that? Suddenly I wasn't the only one having a bad time. When they started shoving Jews into ghettos, my life actually improved. I'm probably the only one that can say that, but I got put into a house with this lovely family who thought my parents had been killed in the transfer and took me under their wing. For the first time in years, I was fed regularly. The mother would give me the food off her own plate – no one had done that for me before. I was cramped and cold and diseased, yes, but I wasn't alone.'

Tasha had no idea what to say. The ghettos had been awful – inhuman cesspits of discomfort and distress – and for Georg, they had been a step up.

'I'm so sorry,' she said again but it sounded more and more inadequate.

'It was terrible, Tasha, of course it was. The Nazis threw us into hell and we were burned. Even those of us who made it out were burned and nothing can mend that. But after the war, everyone was wading in to help the few orphan survivors of the Nazi Holocaust and it was easier to go with that tide, pretend I belonged with the rest, pretend—'

Tasha stamped her foot, unable to bear this. 'Stop there, Georg!'

He looked at her, shocked.

'I'm not having that. You weren't pretending. You did belong. You *do* belong. You're Jewish, yes?'

'Yes.'

'And an orphan.'

'Yes, but—'

'But you were orphaned far earlier than most of the rest of us. So what? It only makes your suffering greater.'

'But I wasn't orphaned by the Nazis. I was orphaned by my own parents' lack of care.'

'Which isn't your fault.'

'Maybe not. But it still makes me a fraud. I'm sorry.'

Tasha thought about this carefully. Not the fraud stuff – that was nonsense – but all that Georg had told her. It made so much sense.

'No wonder you were so keen to forget your past, to "move on".'

'There's certainly not much to go back for. This country, Tasha, my job and my new life, it's such a blessing and I want to throw myself into it.'

Tasha nodded. 'I can see that.'

He spun to face her suddenly, clasping her hands, and a little of the fire returned to his rich, dark eyes.

'I want to make a good life, Tash. I won't be like my parents, not ever. I'll be good and kind and hard-working and I'll look after my family. I'll look after you, Tasha, if you'll let me. And any babies God blesses us with. Will you, Tash? Will you let me?'

Tasha smiled at him. 'If you'll let me look after you too.'

And then she was kissing him and there was no one to call out, no one to bump them or push them apart. Just a soft English sun, Fred and Maisie's bench, and the soft thwack of a children's cricket ball as they found each other again.

'I'm sorry I threw your mama's hair away,' Georg said when they finally parted.

'I understand more now,' Tasha told him. 'You were jealous.'

He frowned. 'I'm not sure about jealous.'

'That you didn't have a mother to miss, I mean.'

'No.' He shook his head. 'No, it wasn't that. It was that you were so obsessed with finding your past that you couldn't see how to make a future.'

'That's not true. I was – *am* – happy to make a future. I just want it to include my mother. Is that so weird?'

'It is when she's dead. That is... when she might be dead.'

'Like yours?'

'Well, yes, but—'

She stared at him. 'That's what you want, isn't it? That's what you're telling me here. We need to be together because we don't have any parents, or siblings, or anything at all. That suits you.'

'No...'

'Yes! But, guess what, Georg, I don't want my past wiped out. I want it all scribbled on with what's happened already – the good and the bad.'

'Me too.' He grabbed at her, holding her tight. 'Me too, Tash. I know we can't wipe Auschwitz away and I don't want to. I was there with you.'

'At the end.'

'Exactly. We were there, together, at the end.'

'And I was there, before, with Mama.'

He froze.

'And that was better?'

'Better?' Tasha gave a bitter laugh. 'Come, Georg, you cannot use that word in any sort of context in Auschwitz.'

'But you preferred it when she was there?'

'Of course I did. Please, Georg – of course I did.'

He shook himself. 'Yes. Sorry. I'm sorry, Tasha. I didn't come here to argue. I came to explain. I came to tell you about my parents, to be honest with you.'

'Thank you.'

'And to ask you to move back to London with me. We can get married.'

He reached into his pocket and her hand flew to her mouth.

'You've bought a ring?'

He coughed. 'Not quite. Sorry. I can't, you know, afford that yet. But I can afford a wedding band, Tash, and I've been to see the rabbi. I've got a licence – look.'

He pulled a piece of paper out of his pocket and Tasha squinted at it, stunned.

'That's...'

'Wonderful? You told me I was too many dreams and not enough action so look – action.'

'Yes. I see. But London, Georg? What about my apprenticeship?'

'At the pink place?'

'At Joyce's salon, yes. I'm getting full training.'

'How long does that take?'

'Two years.'

'Two years?! To cut hair?'

'It's very complex.'

'Is it?'

'More complex than a few locks.'

'There's a joke there,' he said, but there was nothing funny about this situation. 'Can you not learn in London?'

'Maybe,' she agreed, trying to think about it. 'But I bet it's harder to get an apprenticeship there and I'm already a few months in. If I carry on, I can be done by spring 1948 and I can open my own salon.'

'Salon? What about our children?'

Tasha blinked. 'Our children? I'm not sure, Georg. They've not exactly been in my plans recently. All I've been focusing on is getting my training and opening Lydia's and earning enough money to support Mama and me, and...'

'Hang on.' Georg put up a hand. 'You're saying that while

I'm in London working my arse off to try to get a flat for you and me to live in, you're saving for you and your mama.'

'I didn't think you wanted me any more.'

'You gave up easily.'

Was that true? Tasha couldn't think straight.

'I wrote to you,' Georg pushed on. 'I apologised. I told you how I felt. I told you I was working for our future and you, what, didn't believe me?'

Tasha thought about it; the answer wasn't easy.

'I don't think I did. Or, at least, I didn't want to rely on it. I had to make my own plans, so I did. I'm sorry.'

He folded the marriage licence slowly and carefully and she watched the words disappear, her heart in her throat. He slotted it back into his pocket, then looked up.

'I'll wait.'

Tasha shifted. 'I can't ask that of you.'

'But I can offer it. I love you, Natasha Ancel, and I want you to love me too, but you have to do that freely.'

'I do love you, Georg.'

'Then I'll wait.' He took her hands, squeezing them so hard they went white at the ends. 'Come and find me when you're ready. When your mother turns up, one way or another.'

'What does that mean?'

'Exactly what I said. You must allow the possibility that she's dead. You're the one complaining about my optimism all the time.'

Tasha shrugged. 'Maybe all of my optimism is poured into this one thing.'

'Maybe it is.' He looked up to the skies. 'I should go.'

'Go?! Aren't you coming to Weir Courtney?'

'Not like this.' He took her hand and dropped a single kiss upon it, as formal as an old man. 'You know where I am, Tasha Ancel, if finding me ever gets to the top of your list.' Then he was pulling away and running from the cricket field.

She ran after him. 'Georg!'

He was already halfway down the high street but he turned and looked back, held out a hand. Nearly she ran to him, nearly she took it and ran with him to wherever life might take them but out of the corner of her eye she saw the gold and pink of Beautiful You and stopped. Georg sighed, then ran on.

And was gone.

THIRTY-TWO

ALICE

'That's it, children, run towards me. Keep coming, keep coming.'

Alice watched in horrified stupefaction as the sprightly film director encouraged the kids at speed across Weir Courtney's mole-ravaged lawn.

'Watch out for the holes...' she cried, but too late.

Suzi went flying, her summer skirts flapping wildly and her wails sounding out before she even hit the ground. The cameraman kept filming as Manna ran to her, gathering her against her fine bosom and dropping kisses onto her Tasha-perfect plaits.

'Fantastic,' the director oozed, as if this were Hollywood and not deepest Surrey.

'How long is this nonsense going to go on for?' Alice asked Oskar, but he, too, seemed fixated on the pretty scene of Manna cradling a perfectly well recovered Suzi.

On my birthday too, Alice thought grumpily. Not that it

mattered. Not that she was expecting anything. Not that she had any family left to remember it anyway.

Oskar had quietly removed her brother's picture after that embarrassing night when he'd found her flinging it across the room. It had been smashed and probably torn, and he'd spent a lot of time picking up little bits of glass from her rug, which had been very kind of him. She missed the picture though, and was trying to work out how to ask for it back. It was all she had left of her brother.

Alice swiped a hand across her tear-filled eyes, then let it rest there, blocking out the tomfoolery before her. The film was Mr Montefiore's way of marking a year since the children had arrived in England and encouraging people to dip into their pockets and fund the work still ahead. The idea, Alice supposed, was good, but what was the point of such shallow nonsense when there was so much loss in the world?

'I don't think you're getting this right,' a strident voice said, and she forced her eyes open again to see Tasha facing the director, hands on hips. Had someone else had enough of this too? she wondered. But no.

'You should film people looking sad,' the girl went on.

'Why would I do that?' the director asked.

'Because people will be more likely to give money then. No one gives coins to a beggar if they're sitting with a cup of tea having fun, do they? Same here, surely? If they see us with our fancy house and our nice rocking horse and our lovely swimming pool, they'll keep their money for their own children who don't have any of those things.'

'She's got a point,' the director said to his team.

Alice groaned.

'I can look sad,' Tasha pushed on. 'I can sit on the swing and stare into the distance with a tear in my eye. Then your narrator person can say something like, "And yet still, we must remember that these poor children have lost so much – their homes, their families, their countries." Then you cut to some of those pictures of Belsen and, bang – everyone's weeping.'

The crew looked stunned and Alice stepped forward.

'Enough, Tasha! This nice man does not need you doing his job for him.'

Tasha did not look convinced and Alice had to work hard to resist the urge to march her up to her room and tell her to not come back out until she'd remembered how to behave. The girl had been impossible since Georg's visit two weeks ago. They'd been expecting him for tea at Weir Courtney but he'd never turned up and Tasha had whirled through the house like a hurricane to barricade herself in her room until Mina and Golda had complained they couldn't get to bed.

Alice had attempted to talk to her a couple of times but been brushed off with a scathing 'you wouldn't understand' each time. But why wouldn't she? True, she'd never been 'in love', with whatever heady, giddy connotations that seemed to have, but she'd loved. And she knew about loss.

She shook herself. This was no time to be dwelling on her own problems because, to her amazement, the director seemed to have taken Tasha up on her idea and was moving her over to the swing. One of the assistants was busily brushing her hair and another was setting up one of their fancy lights under the oak tree to mimic the sun, which had very inconsiderately gone behind a cloud.

Alice watched as Tasha pushed herself off, head back, red hair streaming behind her, glowing in the fake sun. She was becoming a beautiful woman now that the hollows of Auschwitz were rounded out of her and the shot looked spectacular, but the little ones were standing around disconsolately and Alice felt cross with Tasha for pushing herself forward.

She'd been like this all three days of filming, desperate to be in every shot. It was most unlike her. Plus, the film crew had promised they'd be finished by teatime but now Tasha had marched in from work and started throwing artistic ideas at them, they'd never leave. Sophie had promised Alice chicken for tea and she'd been looking forward to enjoying it in peace. She looked crossly at her watch. Two of the director's many assistants were picking out other children to 'look sad', with Marta being arranged to peer mournfully down at a dolly in her lap, and Moishe being asked to sit on a football, head in hands. This was ridiculous.

She marched into the middle of the lawn. 'Stop!'

Everyone jumped. Leonard Montefiore, waiting to see the crew off, came hurrying across, Anna Freud in his wake, and Alice felt horribly self-conscious, but this wouldn't do.

'Is something wrong, Alice?' Leonard asked.

'Something is very wrong,' she agreed. 'Look at this pantomime.' She indicated the posed youngsters. 'The last thing these children need is to be told that people will only care for them if they look sad.'

Leonard frowned but Anna's hands went to her mouth.

'You're right, Alice. You're so very right. I should have seen that, I'm sorry. Your analysis is superior to mine.'

Alice blinked. 'I wouldn't say that, Anna. I just know the children better.'

'Alice is very astute,' Oskar put in, joining them, and Alice felt her skin flare as the smart, important people around her nodded earnestly.

'This isn't about me,' she said hastily. 'It's about the children. They've had enough filming and need to get back to a peaceful routine.'

'Absolutely,' Leonard said.

'Couldn't agree more,' said Anna.

'We'll get onto it,' agreed Oskar, and went striding off to talk to the director.

Alice was pretty sure the crew had snuck in their 'sad' shots while she was talking to her bosses, but at least now they began packing up.

'Come along, children,' she called. 'Say goodbye to the lovely film crew and then all inside to wash and tidy up for tea.'

'Tea' was still a magic word for the children, and they raced to do her bidding. Swiftly, the lawn was cleared of all but the lurking moles, with only Tasha lingering on the swing, watching the crew load their cameras, lights and clapperboards into a big van. It looked like it would take a long time and Alice went over to her.

'Are you coming inside?'

'Now you've spoiled the film, you mean?'

'Spoiled it?'

'They were filming some really good stuff of me, Alice. Did you see me on the swing? Did you see my hair?'

'I saw it,' Alice agreed dully and couldn't resist adding, 'I never thought of you as vain, Natasha Ancel.'

Tasha jumped as if bitten. 'Vain?' Her blue eyes narrowed. 'You think I want to be in this film for vanity?'

'Don't you?'

'No!'

'So...?'

Tasha threw her hands in the air. 'So, if this gets shown around. If it gets on, say, the news, or distributed to Jewish organisations, then she might see me.'

'She...?'

'Aaahh!' Tasha pushed herself off the swing and stormed off towards the house. 'She. Lydia. My mother. I have to find her, Alice. I keep telling people that. I keep saying but no one listens, so I'm stuck here in idyllic little England and the only thing I can think of to help is this film.' Tears spilled from her eyes and she dashed at them as she stomped on.

Alice grabbed her arm. 'Stop, Tasha. I'm sorry. I understand now.'

Tasha stopped so suddenly that Alice ran into her.

'Do you, Alice?' she asked coldly. 'I'm not sure you do. Georg had a licence, you know. From a rabbi.'

Alice stared at her, trying to follow this sudden change of topic.

'He wanted to marry me. It was very romantic. But, guess what – we argued. Again. Over my mother. Again. He says I'm obsessed. He says I can't plan a future with him until I know what's happened to my mother and he's right. I see that now. So, I *have* to find my mother.'

'I... I see,' Alice said, stunned.

'And no one – no one! – is doing anything to help.'

That stung.

'Now hold on, young lady, that's not true. There are plenty of people working to trace the displaced.'

'The generally displaced, yes, but not my specific one.'

Alice felt angry tears prick her weary eyes. She was tired from three days of chaos and it was her birthday, not that anyone seemed to have remembered. The last thing she needed was a selfish teenager throwing around unfair accusations.

'*I* am trying.'

'How?'

'If you must know, I have Nicola Grainger making enquiries. Specific enquiries.'

Nicola's words came back to her – *I'd advise not talking to the girl yet* – but it had been over two weeks since that crucial letter and Nicola did not have to deal with Tasha on a day-to-day basis so could have no idea of the reserves of patience necessary.

'Who's Nicola Grainger?' Tasha demanded.

'She's a nurse, in London.'

'Why would she be looking for my mother?'

'Because she's the one that you mistook for her in the Shelter.'

Tasha's pale skin flared and Alice knew she remembered. How could she not; it had been very upsetting for her.

'How do you know her?' Tasha stuttered.

'She contacted me. She was concerned about you. As am I.'

'You are?'

'So she's been making enquiries via the hospital networks.'

'And?' Tasha grabbed at her arms. 'And, Alice? Has she found anything?'

Lord help her, there was no going back now.

'She may have traced a woman called Lydia Ancel, but there's no telling if it's your mother. She's trying to find out more.'

'Where? Where is this woman?'

Tasha's eyes had taken on a manic hue, like gas flames, and Alice regretted her impetuosity. The girl got to her every time.

'In a hospital in Katowice.'

'Katowice is nowhere near Warsaw.'

'No. It's near Auschwitz. The woman in question was transferred there from Auschwitz.'

'But... but Auschwitz isn't a thing any more, is it? I mean, it isn't a camp?'

'No,' Alice agreed. 'But I'm told it's opened as a museum.'

'A museum?! Our lives are, are...?' She shook herself. 'It doesn't matter. What matters is that this woman was there. She was looking for someone.'

'Perhaps.'

'Me? Was she looking for me?'

'I don't know...' Alice could see the girl's colour rising, trace her heart beating far too fast against her blouse. 'I shouldn't have told you, Tasha.'

'You should!' She paced before Alice. 'How do I know it's true? How do I know this Nicola woman is to be trusted? She might be making things up.'

Alice thought of the information Nicola had sent her, the

apologetic reporting of the crematoria records, and her heart twisted.

'I pray she is,' she said, her voice breaking.

Tasha stared at her. 'Why?' She grabbed Alice's shoulders. 'Why, Alice?'

'Because she found out my brother died.'

Tasha went very still. 'No?! Oh, Alice. How? When?'

To one side of them a bird was cheeping in the hedge. Somewhere in the background, Alice could hear the shouts of the crew clearing away and, in the house, the children chattering as they got ready for tea. Normal, happy sounds, rushing around her ears on a wave of grief.

'In Auschwitz. That's to say, on arrival in Auschwitz. In 1944.' She could hear her voice, dull and flat, but it was the only way she could force out the words. 'His name is in a crematorium book. And his wife and daughter's names a few days later. They were gassed, Tasha.'

She dared to look into the girl's face and saw all rage and selfish concern gone from her eyes, to be replaced by utter sorrow.

'I'm sorry. Alice, I'm so, so sorry.' Then her arms were around her and she was stroking her back and repeating it over and over. 'I'm sorry. I'm so, so sorry.'

'I'm sorry too,' Alice said, and the words were so hopelessly inadequate that they both shook with a spiked mixture of sorrow and laughter that might have turned manic if they had not been holding so tightly onto each other.

'I'll write to Nicola again,' Alice said. 'I'll push for more. We'll find her, Tasha. We'll find Lydia – for both of us.'

'Thank you, Alice. I really am sorry. I'm a selfish cow.'

'We all are sometimes,' Alice told her.

But Tasha shook her head. 'You're not. Now come on – it's teatime and I think there might be something special waiting for you.'

'There might?'

'Of course. It's your birthday after all.'

'You remembered?'

'How could we forget, Alice – you remember all of ours. Now, come on!'

Then she was tugging her into the house and Alice caught the delicious smell of roasting chicken and didn't think to pause to tidy her skewed hair, straighten her rumpled dress or wipe the tear-smudges from her eyes as they headed for the dining room. None of it mattered, especially when she stepped into the dining room to a roar of, 'Happy birthday, Alice!'

'What?!' she stuttered.

There was bunting around the room, and tablecloths on the tables. There was a huge bunch of fresh flowers at her table-setting and a great pile of home-made cards and presents. There was a cake covered in candles and now there was singing and clapping. She saw Leonard and Anna applauding heartily, Manna leading the singing, and her dear friend Sophie brandishing a cake knife. She saw Oskar proffering a chair and let Tasha lead her into it.

The children presented their presents one by one, each made with such care, Alice thought her heart would burst. There were embroidered hankies, paintings and home knits. Sophie had somehow got hold of some German chocolates, Manna offered a ticket to a piano concert and Tasha gave her a new brush, specially designed for short hair. Alice was quite overwhelmed and then Oskar stepped up holding a small, rectangular package.

'I hope you like it.'

He looked unusually nervous and Manna had to encourage him forward to proffer the gift. Curious, Alice took it and carefully undid the wrapping. It was beautiful paper and well worth keeping but what was inside was even more so, for there, in a brand-new silver frame, was the picture of her brother and his family.

'Oh!'

She was so surprised, she almost dropped it and Oskar darted forward and steadied it, his hand over hers.

'If you don't like it, I can take it away. I wasn't sure, I...'

She shook her head.

'It's perfect, Oskar. Thank you. The frame is beautiful; it preserves Max as he deserves to be preserved.'

'I'm so glad.'

She thought he was going to give her a kiss but then he glanced round at all the children and stepped shyly back.

'Happy birthday.'

And finally it was. Alice's heart still ached with the accumulated losses represented in the beautiful silver frame before her, but she had made gains too and none more so than the warm-hearted people around her now. Exactly a year ago, she had stood on a runway in Crosby-on-Eden waiting for huge planes to come out of louring skies bringing the very children who were now singing to her with love. So much love. She looked around them, each and every one, and felt blessed. She had lost Max, yes, and there would be other hardships ahead but here, in this beautiful house with these beautiful people, she was loved. What better birthday present could she ask for?

THIRTY-THREE

WEIR COURTNEY | 20 AUGUST 1946

TASHA

'Suitcases! Where are the suitcases?!'

Alice came running down the stairs, tearing at her hair, and Tasha shook her head at the fuss.

'They're right here, Alice. The girls brought them down earlier.'

She indicated Mirella and Fiorina's matching cases, waiting by the open door, as eager to be gone as their owners. Barely had the camera crew left Weir Courtney before Alice had received notice that a guardian had been appointed for the sisters and travel was being arranged for their trip to Italy. Their trip *home*, Tasha thought bitterly, away from this funny little stopgap family and back into the arms of their real one. A true miracle!

In the last week of frantic preparations, many of the other children had stayed close to the sisters, as if their unbelievable luck might rub off.

'When's my mummy going to send for me?' they asked Tasha several times a day.

'As soon as she can,' she would always reply.

Alice said boring stuff about logistics and long distances and Tasha knew she was trying to 'manage the children's expectations' but she also knew what it felt like to want something so much it hurt, and logistics was never a satisfying answer.

She was happy for Miri and Fifi, of course she was, but she was jealous as hell too. Every day she waited for a letter or a phone call about the mysterious woman in hospital in Katowice, but it never came. She and Alice had, together, written to Nicola and the pair of them usually met on the doormat as the postman's footsteps crunched up the grand Weir Courtney driveway, but the only communication had been an assurance that the nurse was still talking to the authorities. It was good of her, of course, but everything took so damned long! If she had the money, Tasha would get on a plane and head out there right now, but she didn't have the money and, besides, there weren't any planes. Poland was falling behind something called the Iron Curtain and everyone was getting out, not heading in. If only she'd been born Italian!

Outside, Sir Benjamin pulled up and tooted his horn and instantly the playroom doors flew open and eighteen over-excited children burst out. Mirella and Fiorina sauntered forward, looking adorable in the matching coats and hats that Manna had made for them. Summer was being rapidly blown away and the adults had fretted about keeping the girls warm on their long trip south. From all Tasha had heard of sunny Italy, it was the kids left behind who needed the good wool, but it wasn't up to her.

'Do you remember your mother?' she'd asked the sisters at teatime the other day.

'I remember her,' Mirella had said proudly. 'I remember her when she visited us in Auschwitz. Before she was sent away.'

'Not up the chimney,' Fiorina had put in.

It was, apparently, what they had both assumed when their

mother had stopped visiting them in the children's barrack
next to the science labs and it had taken them ages to absorb
the new story that had gradually trickled through in their
parents' letters to Weir Courtney. They'd all heard of how
Signora Bellucci had been marched from Auschwitz to Lippstadt and then to Buchenwald, where she'd been when the
Russians had liberated the camp. Very weak, it had taken her
months to find her way home to Fiume and locate her husband,
and then months more for them to trace their girls via
UNRRA.

'I remember Mammina used to come to us and hold us and
make us say our names, over and over,' Mirella had told the
dining room. 'She didn't want us to become numbers. She
wanted us to know who we were so that if we ever got separated, we could find each other again. And she was right! We
have.'

The children had listened, agog, and Tasha had been
touched by the idea, until she'd found Marta weeping that she
didn't know her real name and how was her mother ever going
to find her now she'd been named after a cat? Tasha had felt
strangely guilty then, though heaven knows how they were
meant to find out the name of an increasingly self-conscious
eight-year-old with no memory of it herself. Poor Marta was
utterly anonymous and all Tasha had been able to say was that
her mama would know her when she saw her. Neither of them
had believed it.

'Right then, young ladies...' Sir Benjamin's plummy voice
interrupted Tasha's thoughts and she snapped back to Weir
Courtney and someone else's miracle. Their kindly host had
jumped out of his car and was holding the door like a chauffeur.
'Step this way.'

Miri and Fifi giggled and edged forward, waving to the
others who waited respectfully on the steps. Out on the drive,
however, they both stopped and looked up at Weir Courtney

and Tasha saw the uncertainty beneath their gaiety. Clearly Alice did too as she hurried forward.

'You have your letters from your parents?' she asked.

Mirella nodded and patted her coat pocket. Tasha's hand went instinctively to her bag.

'Good. Miss Thomas will meet you in London and will take care of you all the way to Rome where your mother will meet you.'

'Your mother,' the crowd of children sighed.

Tasha knew how they felt. A few evenings ago, she'd snuck into Sir Benjamin's library, found a book with pictures of the Italian capital, and sat for ages picturing the reunion. Sleep tugging at her eyes, the images had blurred swiftly from Rome into Warsaw, and the Belluccis' mother into her own and she had half-slept in a torturous space between dream and reality.

'You'll write to us, when you're safely there?' Alice was asking.

'We'll write,' Miri and Fifi promised, glancing to the car.

Alice visibly gathered herself and, embracing them both, moved back onto the steps between Tasha and Sophie.

'Lovely. We'll look forward to it. Have a wonderful... life.'

Alice looked surprised, even saddened, by her own choice of word.

'They'll be very happy,' Tasha told her impatiently. 'They're going to their *real* family.'

'Of course,' Alice agreed but she didn't sound certain.

Tasha peered at her.

'You know this isn't real, don't you? You know what we have in this lovely, borrowed house is just a stopgap?'

Alice sucked in her breath and Sophie tutted crossly.

'There's no need to be so callous, Tasha.'

Tasha looked at her, surprised. Was that callous?

'Sorry,' she said. 'I thought it was obvious.'

'It is,' Alice agreed. 'Of course it is. It's marvellous that Miri and Fifi are going home. Marvellous!' She was falling over her words and visibly checked herself. 'It's just such a long journey for them,' she finished lamely.

'Not half as long as the one they've already been on,' Tasha reminded her gently.

'True.'

Alice sighed and the three of them stood in awkward silence as the children took turns saying goodbye to their departing friends.

'Manna's hair looks very nice,' Sophie said, indicating the thick plait coiling around the comely carer's scalp as she kissed Miri and Fifi on both cheeks. 'Is that your work, Tasha?'

Tasha nodded. 'I had to try it out for a wedding I'm helping Joyce with next week and Manna volunteered.'

In truth, Manna had leaped at the chance and babbled away most peculiarly about the need to 'look nice' as Tasha had struggled to focus on getting her soft blonde hair into the tricky plait.

'Isn't it better to *be* nice?' Tasha had said, and then felt Alice-prim and shut herself up.

'It's very clever,' Alice told her now.

'Thank you.'

Tasha looked over to Manna, who'd retreated to the steps. She was blushing most becomingly and deliberately not looking over her shoulder where someone was standing, considerably closer than the small crowd on the steps demanded. *Well I never*, Tasha thought, slotting the pieces all too neatly into place.

'Oskar clearly likes it,' she commented.

'Yes,' Alice agreed wistfully. 'Do you think you could do one for me?'

Tasha burst out laughing, then, seeing the hurt in the older woman's face, stopped herself. She was getting nothing right with Alice this morning.

'You do realise...' she started, then stopped herself again. This was hardly the time for gossip. 'I could try,' she said instead.

'But it would look foolish?'

'Not foolish. It just might not be your, you know, most beautiful you.'

Alice huffed. 'What would be?'

Tasha gave her arm a squeeze. 'You're beautiful as you are, Alice.'

Alice huffed again. 'We both know that's not true.'

Tasha fought to think of a tactful answer but was spared when Sir Benjamin tooted his horn again and pulled away down the drive. Miri and Fifi were hanging out of the back window, waving so hard Tasha thought their arms might fall off, and the other children waved equally hard back. Suddenly, at the gate, the car swerved. A few of the children cried out, perhaps remembering poor Ernst's terrible accident at the start of the year, but Sir Benjamin simply drove around the car coming the other way and, with a final toot, was gone.

Tasha stood, transfixed, as the new vehicle pulled up. It was a battered old medical van that had clearly seen service during the war and looked very out of place on Weir Courtney's gracious driveway. The glass was darkened and she could only see an outline of the driver as they peered out at what must have looked like a curiously large welcome party.

'Inside, children,' Sophie said, ushering them all towards the door.

Marta tugged on Tasha's hand but something about the figure in the van was calling to her and she brushed her off.

The driver's door opened and a woman stepped out – a tall, slim woman, in a smart coat and hat and beneath it, blowing in the autumn winds, a mane of bright red hair.

. . .

'Nicola!'

Alice said the name stridently loud, as if Tasha didn't know already, as if she'd make the same mistake twice. Besides, now Tasha looked more closely, the nurse was nothing like her mother. She was far less elegant and not nearly as pretty. But she was here. That could only mean one thing and all Tasha's amusement drained out of her to be replaced by a swirling mix of excitement and dread.

She stood stock-still, grateful for Alice's solid presence at her side as they watched Nicola take forever getting a briefcase from the passenger seat of the van.

'Good morning,' she said, finally coming towards them.

'Is it?' Tasha asked.

Nicola looked uncertainly to the sky. 'I'd say so. A bit cool but you'd expect that in September and—'

'You know what I mean.'

'Tasha!' Alice chided. 'Manners.'

Tasha bit her tongue. 'Sorry.'

'Come in, Nicola,' Alice said, sweeping their guest before her. 'Let's go to my office. Tasha, could you ask Sophie for some tea?'

Tasha wanted to protest but at times Alice had an ice about her that made it impossible to do so. Besides, if she got the tea, she would have an excuse to be in the room.

'Won't be a moment,' she sang out and made a dash for the kitchen. 'Tea for two,' she panted to Sophie, remembering to add, 'please.'

She sank down in a kitchen chair as Sophie bustled about with all the paraphernalia of English tea. Usually, it made Tasha laugh. In Auschwitz she'd had one cast-iron mug that she'd had to tie to her waistband to stop other women stealing it. Not that she'd recommend that, but it was possible to go too far the other way. Especially when you were in a hurry.

'Can't you go any quicker?' she begged the cook.

'If you fan the flames, missy, you might get the kettle to hurry on and boil.' Tasha rolled her eyes but Sophie was oblivious. 'Good things come to those who wait,' she said and that was too tantalising a thought to ignore.

Surely, though, if this Nicola had come with news of her mother, she would have told her right then and there. Perhaps, Tasha thought, she was here with more information about Alice's brother. Poor Alice had been very upset about that. Understandably. It was funny to think of her with a brother, though. Funny to think of her as a child. She felt like one of those people who'd been born middle-aged.

The kettle sang out and Tasha jumped up as Sophie went to pour the water into the pot. The tray was ready, laid with a pretty miniature tablecloth, and Sophie steadied her as she lifted it.

'Slowly, Tasha, slowly.'

Tasha looked at her. 'Do you know who that is visiting Alice?'

'I'm guessing it's Nicola Grainger.'

'You've heard of her?'

'Of course.'

'Then you'll know she could have news for me.'

'I do. And I very much hope it's good news.'

Tasha swallowed, her feet suddenly glued to the floor.

'Perhaps you better get in there and see?'

Sophie nudged her gently out of the kitchen and Tasha went but then lingered outside Alice's office like a neglected butler. She'd always said that the not-knowing was the worst thing but suddenly she wasn't sure. Now the not-knowing felt like a safety net and it was only Moishe coming out of the playroom and staring curiously at her that forced her to knock on Alice's door.

'Come in!'

Alice's voice sounded cheery enough but as soon as Tasha

saw the smile on her face, she knew the worst. It was fixed in place as forcibly as if there were nails on either side of her lips, curving them upwards. Nicola Grainger rose.

'Let me help you with that.'

Tasha wanted to refuse, to say she could manage, but she wasn't sure she could. Her arms felt almost as weak as they had in Auschwitz when Ana and Ester had battered down their door and she'd seen light for the first time in several days.

'Why don't you sit down, Tasha,' Alice said.

'Why?' she stuttered out. 'What's happened?'

Nicola Grainger cleared her throat and half lifted a letter. It was on thick cream paper, Tasha noted, with an official stamp at the top. She sat down.

'This is from a sister in Katowice,' Nicola said.

Katowice! Tasha's heart pounded.

'We believe she nursed your mother, Tasha.'

'It's her?' Tasha gasped. 'The woman who went to Auschwitz? It's really Mama?' She looked excitedly to Alice, but Alice looked back with pure, unadulterated sympathy and the pounding in Tasha's heart turned to a slow, dark tolling. She gripped the arms of her chair. '*Nursed?*' she queried desperately. 'Has she left? Is she better?'

She knew the answer but she had to ask the question; she had to force them to say it. She stared at Nicola Grainger, daring her to do her worst, but Nicola had been a nurse in the war and wasn't to be cowed.

'I'm so sorry, Tasha. She's dead.'

'*Tot,*' Alice supplied quietly in German. Then, in Polish, '*Zmarly.*'

'I understand!' Tasha snapped at her.

She understood, she just didn't want to hear. She wanted to go back outside the door and stand there with the tea tray. She wanted to go back to believing she, too, could be a Bellucci girl, heading for home. She wanted to go back to screaming at Georg that he was wrong, that Lydia was alive. She wanted to go back to Windermere, back to Prague, back to Theresienstadt and, yes, back to Auschwitz. She'd take an empty stomach and blistered feet and endless cold and suffering, not to hear this word, dead, in any language.

'How?' she choked out. 'When?'

Nicola reached out a hand as if she might take Tasha's and then thought better of it.

'I have the hospital records here and she died in her bed on the thirtieth of July 1946.'

Tasha fought to grasp this.

'That's... that's less than a month ago.'

'I'm so sorry.'

Tasha's head swam. Her mother had been alive a month ago. Alive and looking for her. She stared disbelievingly at Nicola, who pushed on, reading from the letter.

'She was admitted several weeks before, brought in by a Mr Tadeusz Wąsowicz, caretaker of the new museum at Auschwitz-Birkenau. She appears to have travelled there from Feldafing, a displaced persons' camp near Dachau, where she was most probably located at liberation.' The nurse was going faster and faster, using report-speak as if it might cushion the blow, but nothing would do that. Nothing.

'It was certainly in Dachau that she was nursed for some period with the severe pneumonia that weakened her lungs and led, eventually, to her, to her...'

'Death,' Tasha filled in, the word tearing its way out of her throat.

July thirtieth. She tossed the terrible date around and around in her mind. All this time her mother had been battling her way across Europe, trying desperately to find Tasha, while she'd been swanning about cutting hair and drinking tea and making silly films that it was already too late for Lydia to see. How could she have done that? How could she have left? She leaped to her feet. A fierce, black wind was blowing through her brain and she put her hands up to ward it off. Staggering, she fell into the chair and turned, picking it up and flinging it furiously against the nearest wall.

'Tasha, stop!' She felt wiry hands on her arms and fought them off. 'Tasha, please, you'll hurt yourself.'

Tasha fought harder. Why was this funny little dark-haired cardigan of a woman here, when her own glorious, bold, brave, colourful mother was not? And never would be. The black wind rose and Tasha staggered in its force and fell to the floor. For so long she'd lived with this stopgap family, been grateful even, but now she could see that the gap was actually a gaping crevasse that had kept her from her real one. It had pulled her to England, far, far away from where she should have been and now she could never, ever go back.

The pain tore her up inside and she flung it in the only direction she could find: 'This is your fault, Alice. All your fault. I hate you.'

THIRTY-FOUR

ALICE

'This is your fault, Alice. All your fault. I hate you.'

Alice staggered as Tasha pushed her away, but found her footing and dropped down next to where the girl had crumpled on the office floor. Tasha resisted, her arms flailing wildly, so Alice sat back, close but not touching, and fought for some way to ease the terrible hurt that was visibly pulsing through the poor girl. This was not the news she'd wanted when she'd asked Nicola to go looking for Lydia Ancel. But she had known it was a possibility. Should she have left it alone? Let Tasha stomp around in ignorance? She'd seemed to hate that so much, but finding out the truth was far worse, as she knew all too well.

'I'm sorry.' Such inadequate words. Someone should invent better ones. Someone should come up with a new language of grief to match the atrocities that had been wrought on these children. On them all. 'I know how you feel,' she said.

Tasha's head snapped up. 'You do not. You only lost a brother.'

'That's not fair, Tasha,' Alice protested.

But Tasha was way past being fair. 'A grown-up brother, with his own family. It's sad, but it's not the same. Mama – she was everything to me. She kept me together in Auschwitz. She... It doesn't matter.' She scrabbled across the carpet, further away from Alice. 'None of it matters now. She's gone.'

'That doesn't negate your memories, Tasha.'

'No, but it locks them in the past, doesn't it? It shuts them into the darkness where they can only be kept alive with hard work. What's the point of remembering her telling me stories if she's never going to tell another? What's the point of recalling her arms around me if they'll never hug me again? What's the point of remembering brushing out her hair if I can never, ever, ever...'

She burst into tears and put both arms up over her face like a wounded animal. Alice glanced desperately to Nicola but the poor woman looked lost, and no wonder. She was a nurse. She could heal cuts and breaks of skin and bones, but not of the heart. That was the psychoanalyst's job, but Alice was not a psychoanalyst. She was just an old spinster who'd made a life caring for other people's children and she had not one tool at her disposal to salve a hurt like this.

'She's at peace with God,' she tried.

Tasha slowly removed her arms and Alice thought she might have helped but as soon as she saw Tasha's eyes, hard and dark, she knew she had not.

'At peace? You think so? You think she's reclining on a fluffy cloud saying, "Phew, at least that's all over"?'

'No, I—'

'You think perhaps she's skipping through meadows with my father and my sister, all hurt and pain gone—'

'Tasha, no—'

'And not one of them looking round to see where Tasha is?'

'Of course not.'

Tasha tossed her head. 'You think, maybe, she's relieved not to have to suffer pain any more?'

'I think she is *not* suffering pain any more,' Alice said carefully.

Tasha gave a high, bitter bark of a laugh. 'True. That's true. Because she's nothing now. But she *was* suffering and she *was* fighting. All this time.' She scrabbled to her feet, pushing herself up against the wall and looking at Nicola. 'She was ill all the way from January 1945 to July 1946 and all that time she was searching.'

'Yes,' Nicola agreed nervously. 'She fought hard.'

Tasha howled. 'So hard. For so long. And do you know what would have helped her? Me. That's what would have helped her. If I'd been at her bed in Dachau, I could have talked to her. I could have told her how much I loved her, how much I needed her. I could have nursed her. Instead, she had to travel halfway across Europe, as if she hadn't been through enough already.'

'But she found you,' Nicola said.

Tasha glared at her. 'What?'

'I'm told she found the Red Cross records, she knew you'd survived.'

'Even worse,' Tasha cried. 'She knew I was alive and I still wasn't there, wasn't at her side to give her love, hope. Instead, she lay in a hospital bed alone, fading away without me there to hold her, to feed her, to stroke her hair.' Tasha's voice rose and she paced up and down the room as if her limbs were as frantic as her thoughts. 'She died without me telling her that I love her!'

The tears returned and Tasha leaned weakly back against the wall. Alice tried, again, to approach her, but again she put up hands to ward her off.

'Stay away from me, Alice. It's your fault, you and your fellow do-gooders. "Come to England, Tasha", "Make a new life, Tasha." It sounds so perfect, doesn't it? So idyllic, like all the cosy teacups and lakes and fancy lawns. But I didn't need a new life. I *had* a life and while I was over here playing orphans, that life drained away, alone and unloved.'

'Lydia would have known you loved her, Tasha. She was your mother. She would have held that in her heart and—'

'She still needed to hear it!'

Tasha was pacing again, pushing herself off any wall she came up against. Alice wished Oskar were here, or Anna. They would know what to do to help the poor child. She cast desperately around for something – anything – to help.

'What was the last thing you said to your mother, Tasha?'

The girl glared at her but did, at least, stop her crazed movements.

'In Auschwitz,' Alice pushed on, already doubting the wisdom of this. 'When she was pushed out into the snow.'

'Alice...' Nicola objected.

But Tasha's eyes were locked onto hers and Alice dared not break the contact.

'You must have tried to go with her?' she said.

'I did. I did try but a guard pushed me back, went to hit me with his gun.'

'She must have seen that.'

'She did.' Tasha's eyes were looking into the distance, into a past only she could see. 'She said, "Don't hurt her."'

'She would. And you, Tasha, what did you say?'

'I said... I don't remember.' Her hands went into her hair, clawing at it. 'I'm not sure. It was so confused.'

'I know,' Alice soothed. 'I know it was, but can you remember?'

Tasha's brow furrowed and her eyes seemed to roam the air, seeking purchase, while her hands twitched at her side. Alice held her breath and suddenly Tasha half-smiled, her pained eyes focused on something far away.

'She said, "You have every drop of my love, Natasha." And I said... I said, "You have every drop of mine too, Mama."'

Alice let out her breath. 'There. See – you *did* tell her. She *did* know.'

Tasha's eyes focused back in on the room, on Alice. They narrowed. 'And then she said, "Stay strong, Tasha, and we'll find each other." She said exactly that, but we didn't, did we?'

'Because the Nazis tore you apart.'

'No! Because you lot tore us apart. You do-gooding lot, thinking you know best, running around with your precious charity to feed your own empty lives.'

'Tasha!' Nicola protested. 'That's not fair.'

But Alice said nothing, because maybe it *was* fair. Maybe all this – the grand lakeside, the Surrey mansion, the birthday parties and the dolls' houses and the games on the lawn – was more for her benefit than for theirs.

'I'm sorry, Tasha,' Alice said. 'I'm so, so sorry.'

'Too late,' Tasha flung at her, then she was yanking open the door and running wildly out of the door of Weir Courtney and away.

'We have to stop her,' Nicola said. 'She might hurt herself.'

'No! She has to do what she wants.'

'She doesn't know what she wants.'

Alice sank wearily down in a chair. 'I think she does.'

'So what do we do?'

'I have no idea. I'm going to call Oskar and Anna – my bosses.'

'Psychoanalysts?' She nodded and Nicola sighed. 'I don't envy you lot your job. Bodies mend far more easily than brains.'

Alice smiled sadly. She thought of Tasha with her strong limbs, her beautiful face, her glorious hair and her poor, scrambled mind.

'Could you, possibly, see if there's any more to know about Lydia's death?' she asked. 'Ask the nurse who wrote to us if she spoke to her?'

Nicola stood up. 'Of course.'

Alice forced herself up too and held out her hand. 'Thank you.'

'For what? Bringing sorrow?'

Alice shrugged. 'Bringing truth. It's hard now but we have to pray that, in the long run, it will help.'

Nicola clasped her hand tight. 'We do. And Alice, it's not true, what Tasha said about charity. You're doing tremendous work here. Your brother would have been very proud of you.'

Alice's heart thudded. She tried to summon a smile for the kind nurse but it refused to come and she showed her out with her every fibre aching. Was anything they did here really helping? Were they healing these children? Or were they merely sticking a plaster over gaping, oozing wounds that would inevitably, as today, burst out of them as they battled to create themselves the future the Nazis had tried so hard to wipe out? Alice longed to fight those battles for her precious charges but it couldn't be that way. All she could do was work to give them the care they needed to come back stronger each and every time. She just prayed it was enough.

THIRTY-FIVE

TASHA

Tasha didn't so much wake up as drag herself out of restless night and into agonising day. She rubbed gritty grief from her swollen eyes and reluctantly prised them open. She was in the room she usually shared with Mina and Golda, but they were gone, their beds neatly made and the girls removed to wherever Alice had managed to stash them. It had been like this when she'd crept in late last night. Weir Courtney had been blessedly quiet and there had been a single light on in the corridor and another in her room. Finding it empty, her bed waiting with the edge of the cover turned back and a cheese sandwich and glass of milk on the bedside table, had almost made her cry with gratitude to Alice. Before she'd remembered how furious she was with her.

Now, though, she looked around the room and felt trapped. She hated the lurid floral curtains with a visceral disgust. She hated the softness of her covers and the comfort of her mattress and the view out over the lawns and the pool and the classy orangery of Weir Courtney. She curled up tight around the pain at her centre. Georg had been right. The wretched man and his 'scrap the past and look to the future' attitude had been right – Lydia was dead.

That word again, hooking into Tasha and tugging mercilessly at her guts. She burrowed beneath her pillow, but there was no avoiding it.

'He *wasn't* right!' she screamed into the feathers. 'He took me to England. He told me she'd find me but how could she when she was fighting pneumonia? How could she when she was travelling Europe, weak and in pain? It should have been me finding her. I knew that. I said it but no one listened and, in the end, I let myself forget.'

There was no escaping that. Sure, the do-gooders had been convincing. Sure, Georg had been full of plans, but at the end of the day she, Natasha Ancel, had signed the forms, got on the plane and left.

'I'm sorry, Mama!'

The pillow absorbed the words but not the grief and, restless again, Tasha flung it away and leaped up. Her eyes cast frantically around the room and fell inexorably on the cream tabard hanging from the back of the door. It was Monday. She had work. Her heart tore again at the thought of the salon she had been going to build to keep her and Lydia, but she couldn't think about that now. She had to go to work. She had to pick up her scissors and cut hair and turn people into their most beautiful you. It was facile and pointless but at least it was something to stop every part of her spiralling in on herself.

It was early yet so the house was still, thankfully, quiet. Tasha dressed and crept down the corridor to the bathroom. She looked hideous, her eyes dark holes rimmed with a raw red that clashed with her hair. Automatically she fumbled for her handbag, then remembered that the scratty few hairs still clinging on in there were truly all she had left of her mother and threw it furiously at the mirror. It hit with a dull thud and flopped pathetically down into the full basin. Tasha draped it, still dripping, back around herself and borrowed Manna's fancy make-up to try and paint some normality onto her face. She was no expert and feared she'd made herself look like Frankenstein's monster but that felt apt, so she turned her back on her image and made for the door.

'Tasha!'

It was Alice, of course it was. That woman followed her like a shadow – a slightly stooped, greying shadow in a flannelette nightie.

'I'm going to work.'

'Right. Good. Well done.'

Tasha pushed past, not gracing this with a reply. She didn't need the woman's approval any more than she needed her nightlight or her cheese sandwich. Though it had been a good sandwich.

Tasha's stomach rumbled but she ignored it and let herself out of the main door. It was raining. Good. She couldn't have borne sunshine. Even so, it wasn't much fun when the damp crept unpleasantly into her clothes and dripped into her face, doubtless taking Manna's make-up down it in streaks. Certainly Joyce exclaimed in horror when she let herself into Beautiful You.

'Goodness, Tasha – you'll scare the clients! Where's your coat?'

'Forgot it,' Tasha mumbled.

'Honestly! You girls would forget your heads if they weren't screwed on. Get yourself tidied up and wear one of the spare tabards while yours dries.'

'The pink ones?'

'Yes!'

'I look ridiculous in them.'

'Not as ridiculous as you'll look dripping onto the floor. Off you go.'

Tasha wanted to protest but getting here seemed to have sapped all her energy and she dragged herself into the back room. For the second time that morning she had to face herself in the mirror and she looked, if possible, even worse. Throwing cold water onto her face, she scrubbed the make-up away, leaving only the grief behind. Her hair, given added wave by the rain, looked so like her mother's that she searched for her scissors to hack it all off but they were out with Joyce, so instead she grabbed a band and scraped it back into the harshest, flattest ponytail she could manage.

'Tasha? Are you all right?'

Joyce was behind her, concern in her warm eyes. Tasha tensed. She longed to fall into her boss's arms and weep her sorrow into her soft bosom, but that felt like a betrayal to the mother she'd lost, so she stiffened her spine and gave a tight nod.

'Didn't sleep very well. Sorry.'

Joyce looked at her more closely and Tasha turned away and made for the kettle.

'Just need tea,' she muttered, which seemed to satisfy her boss.

The routine of warming and filling the pot was distracting, but the tea was no help at all. Tasha thought, suddenly, of the elderflower champagne Georg had stolen for her out on the lake back on her birthday last November. She remembered how it had rushed through her body on a happy giggle and wished for that now, then hated herself for wanting relief from the pain she surely deserved.

The doorbell jangled and she jumped and looked to the clock.

'It's an early one,' Joyce said. 'Mrs Manion is going up to London to meet her daughter and new son-in-law and wants her hair doing fresh.'

Tasha blinked, trying to imagine a day ahead that involved nothing more troubling than impressing your relatives. It was impossible; she had no relatives. This new grief struck her in the stomach and she had to hastily bend to a perfectly tied shoelace to cover it.

'You sure you're all right, Tasha? Women's troubles?'

Tasha nodded, grateful for the excuse. Joyce patted her back and her kind touch felt like sandpaper on burning skin.

'There's some aspirin in the cabinet. A couple of those with your tea and you'll soon feel better.'

Then she was gone, out to coo around Mrs Manion. Tasha reached for the aspirin bottle. It was large, with lots of the little white pills sitting inside and she rolled them around, listening to the rattle and wondering how many it would take to send her after her mother.

'No way, Tasha Ancel,' she told herself. 'That's not what Mama would expect of you.'

She took two, swallowing them down with her rapidly cooling tea, and went through to the salon. At least tidying the workspaces would give her something to do. Joyce looked sideways at her but Mrs Manion was fussing and she had no time to send her back.

'Tasha!' Mrs Manion called her over. 'What do you think – my tired old shampoo and set or a nice, sharp new cut?'

Tasha glanced to Joyce who gave an urgent nod to the clock. There was no time for a cut.

'I think a set will be a classic choice for going uptown,' she managed.

Mrs Manion tossed her head. 'Classic, maybe, but boring. My Elsie's Peter is in the City, you know. He takes her to all these cocktail parties. Cocktails, if you please! She had three new dresses last month.'

'Lovely,' Tasha said faintly.

The words were hammering at her: cocktails, dresses, parties. What did any of this nonsense matter? She tried to move away but Mrs Manion grabbed her arm.

'I can't turn up looking all... provincial.'

She shuddered in distaste and it was too much for Natasha.

'There are worse problems in the world, Mrs Manion.'

The woman recoiled. 'Well, of course. I know that. I've had my share, you know. I lost my whole kitchen to a bomb. Ripped the wall right off and took my Belling up into the air.'

'Belling?'

'My oven, dear. Only a year old it was and a lovely thing. Integrated grill.'

'Really?' Tasha could not believe this woman. Millions had lost their lives and she was fretting over an integrated grill. 'Perhaps it would have been better if the bomb had taken you instead – spared you the hairstyle agonies at least.'

'Tasha!' Joyce cried but Tasha was gone, flinging herself into the back room, leaving her boss to soothe her furious client.

'Let's do you a lovely pageboy, like Bette Davis,' she heard her trill and knew she had about forty minutes before her boss was upon her, spitting fury. But really, the woman had asked for it.

She looked through the door into the gaudy salon and felt blinded by the pointlessness of it. Why did she want to make people beautiful? There was nothing beautiful about people, nothing at all. At least Georg's job made sense – locks, to hold things in and people out. Tying up the world, that was the only way forward.

'Morning, Tash. Budge over and let me get the kettle on. I'm parched.'

Tasha sank into a chair as Betsy bustled past. She wasn't sure she could take the girl's mindless cheer this morning; it was far too much like Georg. Georg who had made her come to England, who had told her she couldn't search all the hospitals of Europe. That might have been true, but she could have started with Poland. How many hospitals were there in Poland? She'd had over a year to get round them all and then... Even if she'd only got there to hold her mother's hand while she'd died, it would have been enough.

'Did I hear Mother tell Mrs Manion she was doing her a pageboy? What a joke. She's far too old for that.' She put bread into the toaster and fetched jam from the refrigerator. 'Isn't she, Tash? Isn't she too old?'

'Hmm?'

'Mrs Manion.'

'What about her?'

'She's too old for a pageboy cut.'

'I don't know about too old,' Tasha said, 'but she's definitely too ugly.'

Betsy giggled wildly and the sound sawed across Tasha.

'You're wicked, Tash.'

'I am,' she agreed morosely.

Betsy bent down and peered at her. 'What's up with you this morning? Get out the wrong side of the bed?'

'The wrong side of bloody Europe,' Tasha shot back.

Betsy recoiled. 'What's that meant to mean?'

'Nothing. Your toast's up.'

Betsy sniffed and went over to spread her jam, but she wasn't to be put off.

'What's wrong with England?' she demanded. Tasha shook her head wearily, but Betsy came towards her, brandishing her toast. 'Don't you like it here?'

'No.'

'Ooh!' She clutched a hand to her bosom, smearing jam all down her school uniform. 'There's ungrateful for you!'

'Ungrateful?'

'We've welcomed you in, given you a job, made you part of the family and—'

'You have not!' Tasha leaped up, her heart burning. 'You have not made me part of the family. You don't need to because it's perfect already. You and your mother have each other.'

'That's mean!' Betsy flung the toast down. 'If you don't like it here with my mother, why don't you bugger off to your own?'

'I would,' Tasha screamed. 'I'd bugger off there right now, but I can't, can I? I can't because she's, she's... she's dead.'

She forced the hated word out of her, hearing the English term as flat and lifeless as her mother. Then she was turning to fight for the door but something was in her way, something big and warm and annoyingly, impossibly soft.

'Oh, Tasha, why didn't you say?' She kicked in Joyce's grasp but the woman's damned arms were far too strong for her. 'When did you find out?'

'Yesterday,' she said. 'I found out yesterday. She died. She died a month ago, in pain and agony and all alone. She didn't find me, like you said she would, and I didn't find her, and now she's gone and there's no point is there – no point in tea or hair or cocktails or, or life.'

Still Joyce was holding her and, goodness, Tasha's legs were so weary and her eyes so sore, that it was easier to give way against her.

'Is that what she would have said, your mother?' she asked quietly.

'No,' Tasha snapped. 'She would have said live life to the full. But she didn't, did she?'

'She didn't,' Joyce agreed. 'And that's a great tragedy. But she'd want you to.'

Tasha groaned and Joyce stroked her hair, pulling it gently out of the fierce ponytail and smoothing it down, her fingers running expertly across Tasha's scalp as if seeking the knots of grief and anger and teasing them out.

'I don't think I can, Joyce.'

'Of course you don't, not right now. You need time. You're right – in the face of what you're dealing with, hair is silly. You need to rest, to eat and to sleep. You need to go home.'

'Home?' Tasha queried, but Joyce was bustling around her,

sending Betsy to fetch a coat and pulling an umbrella from the rack as she ushered her out of the door. 'I don't want to,' Tasha tried to say but her kindly boss mistook her protest.

'We can manage without you for a few days, my lovely, for as long as it takes. Go home. Go on home.'

Before she knew it, Tasha found herself outside, rain battering on the umbrella above her head and running down the big window behind which Joyce, Betsy and Mrs Manion would be wringing their hands and saying 'poor girl' and thanking God that all they'd lost to the war was an integrated grill.

She set off up the high street on autopilot but soon faltered. She remembered standing in Theresienstadt on 8 May 1945 when Mr Dunant of the International Red Cross had told them they were free to go home. She'd had no idea where 'home' was then; and even less now. She remembered Georg standing at her side, an arm around her shoulder as he cheered with the rest and, through the pain vibrating around every part of her body, she felt one solid, warm beat in her heart: Georg.

'Come and find me when you're ready,' he'd said. 'When your mother turns up, one way or another.' Well, she'd turned up – turned up on a hospital death roll – and right now Georg was the only thing that felt true in this whole, battered world. Turning on her heel, Tasha moved away from Weir Courtney and, instead, towards Lingfield train station.

Two hazy hours later, the Shelter loomed before her, dark, dirty and run through with unpleasant memories. It took all her courage to push open the door and step into the murky reception area and she was relieved to see that the girl behind the desk was new. She wasn't in the mood for being recognised.

'Is Georg Lieberman here please?'

'Who's asking?'

'I'm his, er, his friend, from Windermere.'

'I see.' The girl looked her up and down. 'Was it nice there? I heard it was nice there. I came on a different plane, to Southampton. It was quite nice there but not like everyone talks about that Wondermere place.'

Tasha was thrown. 'It was very nice,' she admitted.

'Lucky you.'

'Erm, yes. I guess. Georg Lieberman?'

'He's at work. Saw him go myself.'

'Of course.' Tasha felt foolish. It was Monday. She'd be at work if it wasn't for Joyce's kind heart. 'Where's his factory?'

She should know that. She should have been with him to see it, should have asked him more about it. She'd been so resentful of his job that she'd avoided it. Something else she'd done wrong.

'It's on Cheapside,' the girl told her. 'Just by the St-Mary-Le-Bow church. You can't miss it. Big factory with cast iron gates.'

'Yes. Of course.'

'Are you quite well?'

'Fine.' She backed away. 'I'm fine. Thank you.'

She spun on her heel and raced back out. She had no idea where Cheapside was, but she knew the direction Georg had always come from and knew it only took him about ten minutes to get to work, so how hard could it be? Sure enough, she located the factory with its distinctive gates easily; the nerve to go in, however, was harder to find.

'Come on, Tash,' she chided herself. 'What have you got to lose?'

The answer was a scary nothing, so she steeled herself and pressed on the button.

'Who is it?' The voice was cut from glass and about as welcoming.

'My name is Natasha Ancel,' she said, keeping her own

accent as neutral as she possibly could. 'I'm here to see Georg Lieberman.'

'Who?'

'He works in the factory.'

'Ah, the factory!' The disembodied voice drew out the word as if examining it for lice. 'You'd better come in.'

A buzzer sounded, then the gates clicked loose and Tasha pushed on them, feeling disturbingly as if she were heading into a camp. There was a big yard inside, with absolutely no indication of where to go.

'Top left corner,' the voice rapped through the speaker, making her jump, but the gates were closing behind her and she had no choice but to cross as instructed.

There was a door there and Tasha pushed on it to find herself in a very smart office. The glass-voiced woman was behind a shiny desk, tapping imperiously on a typewriter, and she stopped to look over half-moon spectacles at Tasha.

'We can't fetch people from the factory unless it's an emergency,' she said without preamble. 'Is it an emergency?'

Tasha hesitated.

'Are any of Mr Lieberman's family injured or dead?'

Tasha recoiled. 'He doesn't have any family.'

'Well then...'

'But...' Tasha had no weapons against this woman's superciliousness. 'I'm his fiancé.' The woman looked to her ring finger, bare and unadorned. 'I *am*. That is, I was...' This was no good. 'I need to see him. Please.'

The woman sighed loudly. 'You can leave him a message, miss, and I will make sure he gets it when he comes out on his break.'

'Right. Or I could wait?'

'I don't think that would be a good idea. We don't like unauthorised personnel in the buildings. Rules, you know.'

'Rules!' Tasha scoffed, adding before she could stop herself, 'My mother died.'

'Heavens!' The woman's hand went to her smart bosom. 'I'm so sorry. When?'

'July thirtieth. I found out yesterday.'

'You only...? I mean, I see. I'm sorry. Here...' She shoved a piece of paper across the desk at Tasha, and then a pen. 'Write a message for Mr Lieberman. Perhaps wait in the Lyons Corner Shop down the road? You'll be warm there and I'm sure he'll come as soon as he can.'

'Right.' It wasn't enough but it was all she was going to get. 'Thank you.'

She wrote the note in her best hand.

Georg,

It's Tasha. I'm here, in London, in the Lyons Corner Shop down the road. I'd love to see you. To talk to you.

It was far from eloquent. She tried to find the words to explain that her mother was dead but they were too hard to say, let alone to commit to paper. *I miss you*, she added. *Please come and meet me.* It didn't seem enough.

'Do you have an envelope?' she asked the woman.

She looked at her as if surprised she even knew what an envelope was, but handed one over.

'Thank you.'

Tasha slowly opened her handbag. She took out the dirty, matted lock of hair and looked at it. The shears flared in her mind's eye, big, jagged teeth biting into Lydia's scalp as they ripped the beautiful auburn curtain from her head. Now they had taken her life too so what use was any of it? Biting her lip to stop the tears falling onto the note, Tasha slid it into the envelope and, fingers shaking wildly, pushed the hair in with it.

Licking frantically at the seal, she closed it down before she could change her mind and pushed it across the desk.

The woman took it in her fingertips. 'I'll see he gets it.'

'Thank you.'

'Let us escort you out.'

She pressed a bell and a blank-faced security guard materialised to walk Tasha back across the yard. Behind the walls she could hear the clank of machinery and longed to see inside, but the guard was relentless in his pace and, before she knew it, she was outside and alone once more. Now all she had to do was wait.

He didn't come.

She sat there all afternoon nursing a single cup of tea with the waitress glaring at her as better-dressed, more affluent customers arrived looking for a table. At four o'clock she spent her last pennies on a currant bun and ate it one crumb at a time. It got her to closing at five, but still Georg did not come. She sat in the street outside, all pride gone, but still no one arrived.

She thought about going back to the Shelter but the woman had assured her he would get the note and she'd been the efficient type. There was only one conclusion – Georg didn't want to come. She could hardly blame him. He'd tried so hard to love her, tried so hard to make a life with her and she'd refused. Now, she was too late. She'd lost her past and she'd lost her future too.

There was only one place to go and it was with heavy feet that she trudged back through the drizzle of London to the station and to Weir Courtney.

THIRTY-SIX

ALICE

Alice paced up and down outside Tasha's room, with no idea what to do for the best. The girl had been in there for two days, coming out only to go to the bathroom or accept the plates of food Alice left outside.

'Don't feed her,' Manna had counselled. 'She'll come out when she's hungry.'

'She's grieving, Manna, not sulking. It doesn't seem fair.'

'Everyone here is grieving,' Manna had retorted. 'What's not fair is that the whole house is dancing to Tasha's tune. Mina and Golda are having to share with the little ones and Marta is very upset the girl won't let her in to see her. Everyone here has known loss, Alice.'

'But not, perhaps, quite as recently as Tasha?'

Manna had tossed her pretty head. 'You're just soft on that one.'

Was she? Alice wondered now. She was pretty soft on all of them. She gave sweeties out for nightmares, had a strict no-hitting policy and believed a cuddle went a lot further than a telling-off. She had rules, of course, and routines, but she wasn't one to use the rod. She'd rarely seen it produce more than fear.

'What do you think I should do?' she'd asked Sophie.

'Not stop feeding her,' Sophie had said stoutly. 'These children have known enough hunger to last a lifetime.'

Alice had thanked her kindly friend and decided to ask Oskar's advice. He'd arrived flatteringly fast after her telephone call this morning and been most understanding. He had, she had to admit, been a little disconcerting about the 'fascinating opportunity to study delayed grief,' but he'd expressed himself keen to help draw Tasha out of herself and that, at least, Alice felt, would help. Now she just had to convince Tasha.

Lifting her hand, she knocked on the girl's door. No reply. She frowned. There were no locks in Weir Courtney bedrooms but Alice made it policy not to enter without permission. Usually.

'Tasha? Tasha it's me, Alice. Can we talk?'

Still nothing.

The reason there were no locks, Alice reminded herself, was in case of emergencies. Those were usually silly things like the boys discovering Manna's best talcum powder to 'turn themselves into ghosts', but the underpinning principle was one of welfare. Alice's stomach churned. She'd checked the room for anything dangerous that first day Tasha had gone out, removing belts, stockings and her precious hairdressing scissors, so it should be safe. But...

'Tasha! I'm coming in.'

'Oh, honestly!'

The relief at hearing the bolshy reply was enormous and Alice stepped inside to find Tasha sitting on her bed, knees pulled up to her chest, tiny nail scissors in her hand, and little strands of red hair all around her, like sparks from a bonfire.

'Tasha! What are you doing?'

'Split ends,' the girl said absently.

'You don't have split ends.'

'I do now.' She lifted a single strand and began fidgeting at it with her nails.

Alice shivered. 'It's cold up here, Tash. Why don't you come down to the living room? We have a fire going for when the children get back from school.'

'No, thank you.'

'They'd love to see you.'

'But I would not love to see them.'

'Not even Marta?' Tasha flinched and Alice pressed her advantage. 'She asks after you every ten minutes.'

'She's very sweet.' Tasha lifted up the nail scissors and snipped off the torn-up hair-end. It fell to join the others.

'Oskar is here,' Alice said, edging closer. 'He'd really like to talk to you.'

Tasha's head sprang up. 'Would he? Why's that then? To make notes on orphan grief?'

It was dangerously close to the mark.

'To help you. Grief is a terrible thing.'

'Not if you're a psychoanalyst I wouldn't have thought. Then it's fascinating.'

'Tasha, that's not fair. Oskar wants to help you.'

Tasha tilted her head on one side, looking at Alice with disconcerting directness. 'I don't think you have any idea what Oskar wants, Alice.'

'I think you'll find—'

'Do you think he likes you?'

Alice coloured. 'What do you mean? We're colleagues, friends.'

'Yes, but do you think he wants more?'

Alice felt her neck flush and put a hand to it. 'Of course not.'

'I do.'

Alice jumped. 'What on earth do you mean?'

'I know men, Alice. I went to find Georg, you know, the other day.'

Alice leaned in. 'When Joyce sent you home?' Alice had been very worried when Tasha hadn't come home from work and had gone straight to Beautiful You. When she'd found out Joyce had sent her home in the morning, she'd been even more worried. It had been a huge relief when Tasha had slammed into Weir Courtney that evening, but this was the first she'd heard of where she'd been. 'How did it go?'

'Dreamily,' Tasha said. 'He swept me into his arms and we got married there and then – which is why I'm currently sitting all on my own in Weir Courtney.'

Alice cringed. 'Fine. It didn't go well.'

'No. It did not. I left him a message and I waited for him and he never came.'

Alice stared at her. 'Really, Tasha? I thought I was the naive one around men?'

'You are.'

'But even I can see that many things could have gone wrong with that scenario. He might not have got the message, he might be ill, he might—'

'Not want to see me ever again.'

'It's possible, but you don't know that.'

'Just like I didn't know my mother was dead?'

Alice flinched again. She'd known this wouldn't be easy but, as usual, she'd underestimated her spiky charge.

'Why not talk to Oskar, Tasha?'

'Your boyfriend?'

'He's not my boyfriend.'

'No, but I bet you'd like him to be. I bet you dream about him coming into your room at night and—'

'Tasha! This is not appropriate. Oskar is my colleague and visits in a purely professional capacity.'

'He's here remarkably often for that.'

Alice's flush grew. This was ridiculous. Tasha was taunting her, as she so often did. Though, it was also true that, despite her tender years, she knew more about men than Alice ever had.

'He enjoys the atmosphere down here,' she hedged.

'The atmosphere! That must be it.' Tasha shook her head. 'Grow up, Alice – he's here for romance.'

'With me?'

Tasha looked at Alice and Alice saw cruelty in her eyes and braced herself for the blow, but just too late.

'Oh no, not with you.' With a sly smile, Tasha picked up another strand of hair, lifted the nail scissors and, with great deliberation, snipped.

Alice stood up, straightened her skirt, and left. She fled down the corridor, her mind racing and one word – one very unpleasant word – banging loudly against her skull: Hündin. Bitch. She would not say it out loud. She had more control than that, more dignity, but it exploded inside her. That little madam had deliberately lured her in and then taken open pleasure in upsetting her. Manna was right. She was too soft on her. Far too soft. Spotting the door to Manna's room up ahead, she felt the urge to tell her, to apologise.

Giving a quick knock, she called, 'Only me,' and went inside. Then froze. There, as if God was laughing at her along with Tasha – along with, it seemed, everyone in Weir Courtney – was Manna, her lipstick smudged across her face and Oskar Friedmann leaping guiltily off her bed.

'Oh!'

Alice clutched her hands to her face and then, catching sight of herself like an idiot cartoon in Manna's big mirror, turned and ran. This was why Oskar came to Weir Courtney so often. This was why he charmed them all, and brought wine and stayed the night in the little guest room at the end of the corridor. Or didn't.

Tasha was right – Alice was blind and foolish and naive,

nothing but a dried-up old spinster, adrift in a foreign country with not a gram of training in how to deal with these poor, damaged children. She could hear Manna calling her name but didn't want to face her, especially not up here where Tasha could listen in to her discomfiture. Turning tail, she fled downstairs, aiming for the kitchen and Sophie's easy company but, to her horror, as she came into the hall, the front door opened and Anna Freud stepped through.

'Anna!'

'Alice? Is all well? You look... uncomfortable.'

God, that woman knew everything!

'Quite well, thank you,' she said. 'Just in a bit of a hurry to... to talk about tonight's dinner with Sophie.'

'I see. Well, I hate to interrupt house routines, but I've brought a guest.'

'A guest?'

'For Miss Ancel.'

'Tasha?'

Alice looked in confusion at the middle-aged woman Anna was ushering through the door. She was wearing a nurse's uniform and had the competent, no-nonsense attitude of her profession. What was this about?

'Sister Devizes is newly returned from prolonged war service in Poland.'

'Poland?'

'Katowice, to be precise.'

'Lydia?' Alice whispered, Tasha's childishly vindictive behaviour forgotten instantly.

Anna nodded. 'Sister Devizes started work at a hospital I was consulting with yesterday and mentioned that she'd been in contact with a Nurse Grainger about a child at Weir Courtney. Naturally I was intrigued and offered to bring her down myself.'

'That was very kind.'

'I had an ulterior motive, but we can come to that later.

Sister Devizes nursed Lydia Ancel at the end and believes she might bring comfort to her daughter.'

'Comfort?' Alice stared at the woman. 'Are you certain? Because she is in sore need of it.'

Sister Devizes smiled and her whole face softened. 'I spoke to Lydia Ancel about her daughter before she died and what she said will, I believe, offer some solace.'

'Goodness, I hope so. I'm at my wits' end with how to help her.'

Sister Devizes patted her hand. 'Allow me.'

Sophie had come out of the kitchen and Alice turned gratefully to her. There was no way she was going back up those stairs.

'Sophie, would you be a dear and fetch Tasha for me? Tell her there's someone here to see her about her mother.'

Sophie gaped comically and then scuttled up the stairs. Alice showed Sister Devizes to the living room, glad of the lit fire. There was half an hour until the children were due home and she prayed this doughty nurse could use it to bring warmth to a sad young woman who had buried herself in ice.

Tasha came hesitantly down the stairs and, seeing Alice, bit her lip. Alice wanted to reach out and tell her it was all right, that she forgave her for lashing out, but then Sister Devizes appeared in the doorway and Tasha's jaw dropped. What Alice felt was unimportant right now.

'Go ahead, Tasha,' she urged.

Tasha still looked uncertain and she gave her an encouraging nod as Sister Devizes drew her into the living room and closed the door. Alice stared at it.

'Shall we have some tea?' Anna suggested behind her.

It was, frankly, the last thing Alice wanted but she nodded meekly and let her boss lead her into her own office next door.

'Are you well, Alice? If you don't mind me saying, you don't look it. I hope you're taking care of yourself?'

'I do my best,' she stuttered, leaning back to try to hear what might be being said in the next room.

'You do your best for the children, of that I don't doubt, but what about you? A carer has a duty to her own care as well as those she tends. Is Oskar looking after you?'

Alice gave a strangled squeak and Anna looked at her curiously.

'I have no problem with my colleagues,' she said stiffly. 'But I confess, I'm no longer sure I have the qualifications to do the best by these children.'

'Nonsense!' Anna's reply was brusque. 'You're the finest carer on my books.'

Next door, Alice was sure she could hear crying and could barely concentrate on what her boss was saying.

'That cannot be true. I only—'

Anna put up a hand.

'Who's the expert here?'

'You are, Anna.'

'So, if I say you are the finest, you are.'

It was going to take more than that to convince Alice, but it was hardly important. It had gone quiet next door and she was desperate to know what Sister Devizes was saying to poor Tasha. The woman had been very certain of her ability to give comfort. Solace, was that what she'd said? Alice wasn't sure of the English word but it had sounded hopeful.

'Alice? Are you listening?'

Alice snapped guiltily back to her boss. 'Sorry, Anna. I was wondering if Tasha was all right.'

Anna smiled at her. 'Which is precisely my point. You are a natural carer, Alice, and I think that will make you perfect for my new course in Child Therapy.'

'Child Therapy?' she stuttered, totally confused.

'That's right. That was my ulterior motive in coming to

Weir Courtney. I'd like you to be one of my very first students, Alice. I have every confidence in you.'

Alice stared. Course? Student? Confidence? The words made little sense.

'Will you think about it?' Anna pushed.

Alice nodded dumbly because it would be rude to do anything else, and because right now it was impossible to think about anything but Tasha. The girl might be spiky and rude and even downright mean at times, but Alice couldn't help loving her and was desperate to help her through her grief. What was going on in the room next door?

THIRTY-SEVEN

TASHA

'Take a seat, my dear.'

Sister Devizes waved to the armchairs near the fire and Tasha perched nervously on the edge of one and stared into the flames. The fire in Weir Courtney was far more elaborate than the one she remembered at home in Warsaw but the flicker of the flames was the same, as was the glow of the embers around the edge and the occasional flare of blue or green as impurities in the wood caught. Her fingers twitched for a brush and then remembered that there was no mother's hair to brush and there never would be.

Never.

A heartbreaking word in any language.

Tasha pulled her eyes from the fire and looked at the woman in front of her. Sister Devizes was tall and strong-shouldered with no-nonsense, short hair. It would look much better with a permanent wave, Tasha thought, but didn't say so out loud. It didn't feel like a hairdressing type of a conversation. Quite what sort of a conversation it was, however, she had no idea. All Sophie had said was that there was a nurse here with some details about her mother.

Were there forms to sign? Was Lydia not, perhaps, buried? The thought of arranging a funeral was both comforting and exhausting. Would it have to be in Poland? Did that mean she'd have to go back? Did she want that? Of course she did. Poland was her home, her language, her people. She'd had enough of England with its lakes and fields and wretched lock factories.

'How are you, Natasha?'

She jumped at the use of her full name.

'I've been better.'

'I can imagine. You've suffered much loss.'

'We all have.'

'True, but I tend to find that other people's suffering does very little to ameliorate our own.'

Tasha squinted at her. 'Amelior...?'

'Sorry. Improve. Soothe. Change. A thousand mothers could die—'

'*Have* died.'

'Have died, yes, but it makes the death of your own no less painful.'

Tasha thought about this.

'If anything,' she said, 'it makes it worse – you don't even get to be unique in your pain.'

Sister Devizes smiled. 'Absolutely true. You're a smart girl, Natasha.'

'Tasha, please. Only... only my mother ever called me by my full name.'

'I see. I'm sorry.'

This woman was very calm. She sat neatly, her hands motionless in her lap and a gentle smile on her nondescript face. And she took her time over every word. It was disconcerting.

'You're a nurse?' Tasha asked.

'Yes. Have been for many years. I worked in field hospitals

through the war, mainly in Africa. Then I went into France behind the Allied Expeditionary Force in June 1944 and followed them all the way to Berlin.'

'That sounds hard.'

'I saw some terrible sights, but I was always well behind the front line so never in danger. When the war ended, I was due to go home but I looked around me and saw people still ill and suffering everywhere. But you'll know that.'

She was talking to Tasha like a fellow grown-up and it was enticing.

'I was in Theresienstadt,' she told her. 'It was chaos, so many people coming and going.'

'And everyone looking for someone?'

'Exactly! I was shown a hundred photos a day.' Tasha closed her eyes and was back there, in the narrow streets of the strange little city. 'All people asked all day long was, "Have you seen this woman?" Or, "Have you seen this man?" It was terrible.'

Sister Devizes nodded. 'It's still going on. Plenty of people are still searching.'

Her voice gave nothing away and Tasha looked at her narrowly.

'You think they're mad?'

'No! Heavens, no, I think they're wonderful.'

'You do?' Tasha really couldn't work this woman out. 'My boyfriend – that is, he was my boyfriend at the time – said I was mad to believe my mother was still alive.'

'Well, he was wrong. We're uniting plenty of families, particularly those who were only separated towards the latter stages of the war, like yourself.'

Tasha shuddered. 'It didn't feel like the "latter stages".'

'I'm sure, and I don't mean to belittle your experience, but the first people were incarcerated in Auschwitz in January 1942. The only ones who made it to the end of the war were the original criminals who became the kapos.'

Tasha flinched and Sister Devizes gave a funny little tap on her own knee, as if warning herself. 'I'm sorry. I find life works best with facts, but I know that not everyone feels the same, so tell me if you do not want to hear this.'

'It's fine,' Tasha said. 'Facts work for me.'

'Good. You, I believe, were sent to Auschwitz in October 1944, so only – and I appreciate "only" may sound callous here – had to survive four months. As did your mother. Your chances of being strong enough to survive were, therefore, statistically higher.'

Tasha leaned eagerly forward. 'That's what I said. My mother was strong and she was bold and bolshy – just like me. I didn't die, so why should she have done? And she hadn't!' The last came out in a sob that felt all wrong in the quiet room and Tasha put a hand to her mouth to catch it. 'Sorry.'

'Please don't apologise. You are grieving. It's permitted.'

'Right. Thank you.'

'This brings us, I think, to Katowice.'

Tasha's breath caught.

'I joined the International Red Cross, you see, and instead of going home, I was posted to Poland to help in the hospitals. In May 1946, I went to Katowice.'

'Where my mother was?' Tasha asked hoarsely.

'Correct. That's to say, she arrived in June. I remember her well.' She smiled. 'You don't forget hair like that.'

Tasha felt tears building in her throat.

'Was she very ill?'

'She was, I'm afraid. Her lungs were badly wasted and her body weak. She'd had pneumonia in Dachau and recovered to a certain extent but her trip across Europe had weakened her beyond repair, as had her time in a Soviet border hostel.'

'Soviet?! They hurt her?'

Raw fury propelled Tasha to her feet but Sister Devizes leapt up too, holding her arms firmly at her side.

'They didn't hurt her, just delayed her.'

'Stole her time,' Tasha spat.

Sister Devizes nodded wryly. 'You could say that. The life of a refugee is plagued by bureaucracy, I'm afraid. The rest at the Austrian border may actually have done her good, but the onward trip sapped her strength.'

'Her trip looking for me,' Tasha choked out. 'Looking for me killed her.'

But at that Sister Devizes put up a stern finger. 'No, no, my dear. She was dying anyway and it's quite possible that looking for you – the purpose and strength that gave her – kept her alive for longer.'

'But not long enough for me to get to her.'

'No.'

The tears swelled, seeming to leak right into Tasha's lungs, and she gulped for air.

Sister Devizes pushed her gently back down into the chair. 'Most of the time she was asleep, Tasha. She didn't suffer, not in Katowice. We fed her through a drip and we gave her morphine if she was in pain. She was peaceful, and all because she knew her daughter was still alive.'

The tears burst from Tasha and Sister Devizes took a perfectly laundered handkerchief and handed it over, but did not stop.

'Many a day the only word she would say was "Natasha". I could lie to you of course but, as I said, I deal in facts.'

'I should have been there,' Tasha wept. 'I failed her, I—'

'No!' Sister Devizes put up a firm hand. 'That was not it at all. I suppose it might have been nice for her to have you holding her hand, and it would certainly have been nice for *you* – so many people feel guilty and it's a most damaging emotion – but it was not what she wanted. Quite the reverse. When she was strong enough, she would tell me she prayed you were somewhere beautiful, that you could live the life she'd given you.'

'She did?'

'She did. I don't lie, Tasha. And then, about three weeks after she'd arrived, we got word. Someone in UNRRA, that's the—'

'I know what it is.' Tasha's tears had dried up and she was desperate to know more.

'Good. Well, Nurse Grainger had talked to UNRRA and they'd put together the Tasha Ancel on their list of the children who went to England, and the Lydia Ancel in hospital in Katowice. It should have happened sooner but, so many people... I'm sorry. Anyway, they came to me and told me, and I told Lydia.'

'You did?' Tasha sat so far forward that she almost fell out of the big armchair. 'You told her that I was here?'

'I did. I quizzed the UNRRA rep in some detail – I like facts, as I said – so that I knew everything and they confirmed that you had been in the Lake District for several months and were now residing in a country house in Surrey. They even reported that you had an apprenticeship with a hairdresser.'

'They did? You knew that? You told Mama?'

Sister Devizes smiled a broad smile that transformed her face. 'I told her and, Tasha, she was delighted. I assure you. "She's safe," she kept saying. "She's safe." Then she asked me to tell you to be happy and to make the very most of life.'

'She did?'

'I promise you,' Sister Devizes said. 'She hadn't much breath, you understand, but what was left to her, she used to ask me to give you every drop of her love – that's how she put it, "every drop".'

Tasha's hands went to her mouth as she heard her mother's words echoing to her across time and space, still as vibrant and meaningful as ever. This, she now knew for sure, was the truth.

'She was happy that I was in England?'

'Very. Poland is not a pleasant place right now, Tasha. The Russians are taking charge and, well... I think you are better off here. Your mother thought that too. "England," she said, when I told her. She said no more but there was a joy to her tone. She said it' – Sister Devizes permitted herself a small smile – 'as one might say "chocolate" or "kitten" or "angels".'

They were curious choices, but she was a curious woman and, besides, Tasha knew exactly what she meant. She wished she could have heard it for herself. She wished she could have held her mother's hand and told her that she was going to a new life, but hearing it from this strange, stiff, kind woman was the next best thing.

'Thank you,' she said.

Sister Devizes nodded, then leaned in with sudden urgency.

'You must believe me, Tasha. Guilt is a most damaging emotion, especially when it has nowhere to go but in on itself. Your mother was dying when I met her. Indeed, I believe she was dying from the moment she was pushed out of Auschwitz, or at the very least from a few days later. She held on for one thing – news of you. She drank it in, taking every snippet I could offer her with every gram of strength she had. And then, finally, she could let go.

'She loved you so very dearly, Tasha. She would have got to you if she could, but her poor body was too ravaged to carry her brave soul any longer. Hearing that you were alive and prospering in England was the greatest blessing we could have offered her, and she died with a smile on her face. She died at peace.'

Tasha's tears were flowing again but this time they felt soft, soothing. Not the bitter sting of regret and anger, but a wash of pure grief.

'There, there,' Sister Devizes said. 'You cry, my dear. You

cry all you want. It is hard, to be the one left behind, but you can do it, I am sure you can. You can grieve and you can hurt and then – then you can be happy.'

And, looking up at the curious nurse through a wash of emotion, Tasha thought that perhaps she was right.

'I've been a cow,' she spluttered.

Sister Devizes gave a little chuckle. 'I think that's allowed, given all you've been through. The key, perhaps, is to know when to start being human again.'

Tasha laughed through her tears. 'Maybe I can make a start now. I don't want to accept she's gone but knowing she went at peace makes it easier, thank you.'

'It will take time,' Sister Devizes said, 'and courage and care. Above all, care.'

Tasha nodded and stood up. 'Alice,' she said. 'I need Alice.'

THIRTY-EIGHT

ALICE

'Alice!'

Alice started as her name rang around Weir Courtney. Leaping up, she raced into the main hallway to see Tasha standing in the middle, calling so loudly it seemed to bounce through the whole house: 'Alice, Alice, Alice!'

'Tasha?'

'Alice!'

She was upon her in a whirl of long arms and red hair, hugging Alice so tight she feared her ribs might crack.

'Is everything all right?'

'No,' she said, 'everything is all wrong, but I can see now that one day, maybe, it will be right again. Thank you.'

'For what?'

'For everything. For being there for me, for looking after me, for not taking offence when I'm awful to you. You're wonderful.'

'I am?'

'Of course. And I – I am a mean cow. A wredna krowa, a gemeine Kuh.'

Alice laughed at her tumble of multilingual insults. 'Maybe a bit of a confused cow, Tasha, but a loveable one all the same.'

Tasha threw her hands in the air. 'God, Alice – do you never get angry? I've been horrible to you, horrible. And you're always so nice back.'

'I haven't been through all that you have.'

'You lost your brother.'

Alice sucked in her breath at the reminder and then Tasha was hugging her tight again, squeezing that breath right back out of her, and she put her arms around the girl's slim back in return.

'Sister Devizes says my mother was happy to hear I was in England,' Tasha told her. 'It made her smile and she wanted me to make a good life here.'

'That's marvellous,' Alice told her.

'It is and I bet your brother would feel the same way too.'

Alice's heart tore with her own, private grief. She glanced to Anna, hovering in the office, and remembered her counselling to share a little of herself with her charges. Looking straight at Tasha, she said: 'I think you're right. When he saw me off at Berlin railway station back in 1939, Max said to me, "Just do your best, Alice. And if it doesn't work, at least one of us will have made it out."'

'There then!' Tasha kissed her. 'You and I, Alice, and everyone here at Weir Courtney, have to live on for those we left behind. It's hard but we can do it.'

'We can,' Alice agreed. 'At least, you can. You *will*. You'll complete your training and open Lydia's and—'

'And it will be in her memory,' Tasha agreed. 'And all thanks to you.'

'I don't think—'

'Shh, Alice. Take the compliment for once.'

Alice heard Anna chuckle but Tasha was still talking.

'I'm sorry. I've been caught up in myself and it's not good enough. I'm seventeen, eighteen next month. I'm meant to be a grown-up.'

'I think you lost a few years of childhood, Tash. You're allowed time to catch up.'

'Yes, well, I'm going to do my best. I've got a job. I've got responsibilities. I've got Kotka. Mama would like that, I think, that I have a new sort-of-sister.'

Alice smiled. 'I think sort-of-sisters are a very good thing. Not as simple, perhaps, as actual sisters but this war has taught us to be adaptable, to find new ways.'

'New families,' Tasha said softly. She swallowed. 'D'you know, Alice, I've been thinking of Weir Courtney and everyone here as a sort of stopgap family, but the gap is permanent, isn't it? So, perhaps the family can be too.' She looked straight at Alice, tears in her eyes. 'No one will ever, ever, *ever* replace Mama, but might you, Alice, maybe, consider being my sort-of-mother?'

'Oh, Tasha!' Now Alice was crying too. It wasn't professional and it wasn't dignified but it felt so good. 'It would be my absolute honour.'

'It might not,' Tasha warned. 'I'll probably still be a cow sometimes, but, well, we'll work it out, yes?'

'Yes!' Alice agreed. 'Yes, we most certainly will. I'm so glad Sister Devizes was helpful.'

'Sister Devizes is also wonderful,' Tasha said. 'She told me all about Mama in a clear, truthful way. She only deals in facts, don't you?' She turned to the woman, who'd come to the doorway of the living room.

'Only facts,' the nurse agreed. 'Lies hurt more in the long run.'

'You see,' Tasha said. 'I mean...' She stopped suddenly. 'It would be better, obviously, if Sister Devizes had come here to say that Mama was alive and recovering and could come to England to be with me...'

Alice swallowed but Sister Devizes stepped calmly forward.

'It would be better,' she agreed, 'but it is not how it is. What matters, now, is that you live the life she wanted you to live and that you carry her forward with you in your heart.'

Tasha looked to Alice. 'She's good, isn't she?'

Alice nodded. 'Very good. Have you considered getting into psychoanalysis, Sister?'

Sister Devizes visibly shuddered. 'Good Lord, no. The mind is a most mysterious organ and not one for the likes of me. Which way is the kitchen? Might I fortify myself with a cup of tea?'

'Let me,' Alice said.

But Sister Devizes waved her away. 'You have far more important matters to attend to. I shall find it myself.'

Then she was gone, sailing imperiously through exactly the right door, as if picking up the very scent of the tea leaves. Alice and Tasha watched her go together.

'Probably best if she doesn't go into psychoanalysis,' Tasha whispered. 'She's quite blunt.'

'Maybe that's what it needs.'

'Maybe, but I think your way of listening to everyone and thinking carefully about them is better.'

Alice looked at her, startled.

'Hear, hear,' Anna Freud said, and Alice and Tasha both turned as the famous psychoanalyst clapped. 'You may be a "mean cow", Tasha Ancel, but you're an astute one too.'

Tasha looked embarrassed. 'Miss Freud. I didn't know you were here.'

'Whereas I couldn't miss you! And that's how it should be. I'm so glad Sister Devizes was able to ease your pain.'

Tasha considered. 'I'm not sure it's eased, but perhaps I can bear it a little better now.'

'Wisely put. I'm afraid that there has been far too much pain in this war, and none more than for us Jews, but with kind people like Alice in charge, we will find joy once more.'

'We will,' Tasha agreed. She looked to Alice. 'I'm going to work so hard, Alice. I'm going back to Joyce tomorrow. First thing. I'm going to slave and slave and one day I'm going to open Lydia's Hair Salon and frame her lock of hair and... oh.'

She dried up and looked to the floor.

'Tash?' Alice asked. 'What's wrong?'

Tasha kicked at a loose tile. 'I gave Georg Mama's hair. I put it in the envelope with my note to him to show that I was putting him first, but... but he hasn't been in touch.'

'Yet,' Alice said gently.

Tasha smiled at her sadly. 'Who's the optimist now?' She shook herself. 'It doesn't matter. It's only hair.'

'It was a keepsake,' Alice said carefully, 'and that can be vital. But look...' She lifted Tasha's hair. 'You have it growing from your own head – Lydia is alive in you, and that counts for much, much more.'

'It does! Thank you, Alice. You shall have free haircuts for life in Lydia's. I shall keep you gorgeous forever.'

'I doubt that,' Alice said drily.

'Gorgeously caring and clever?' Tasha offered.

Alice snorted but Anna Freud nodded.

'Clever enough to take my Hampstead Child Therapy course, for sure.'

'Your what?' Tasha demanded, her eyes sharpening.

'It's for people who want to qualify as full psychoanalysts.'

'Young people,' Alice said repressively, before they got carried away. 'I'm far too old to be studying.'

'It would be *on-the-job* studying,' Anna said.

'And you're not old,' Tasha told her stoutly. 'You're mature.'

'Mature!' Alice scoffed. 'Nice try, Tasha.'

'Mature, Alice, though, perhaps, a little scared?'

That shook her.

'I...'

Tasha took her hands. 'I'm scared too, Alice. I'm scared that I'll never get over losing Mama. I'm scared that I'll be a rubbish hairdresser and won't be able to open Lydia's. I'm scared that I've been horrible to Georg and now he doesn't want me any more and I'll never find anyone else like him, ever again.'

'Tasha...'

She put up a hand. 'I might be right, or I might be wrong. All I'm saying is, I'm scared, so I understand that you're scared too, but surely we have to try – or else what was the point of surviving?'

That, Alice could not dispute. Tasha was right – she had to get on and live the best possible life, for herself, for the children she was encouraging to do the same, and for Max, Lilli and Ruthie, who would never have the chance.

'I have to try,' she said, hearing the quake in her voice.

'We both have to try,' Tasha corrected her. 'We both have to try together.'

And somehow, that way, it felt a whole lot more possible.

THIRTY-NINE

LINGFIELD | SEPTEMBER 1946

TASHA

'So, my sister said to him, "I know you think she's the bee's knees, but you wait till you try her steak and kidney pudding, then you'll know what a mistake you've made!"'

The two women sitting under the dryers cackled wildly and reached for their teacups. Outside, autumn rain was blowing leaves against the window, but in the gold and pink salon all was warmth and laughter.

Joyce smiled over their heads at Tasha. 'Ready to do your first pageboy?'

Tasha grimaced. 'I'm not sure. What does my client think?'

Betsy looked up from the chair with a broad grin. 'I think I couldn't be in better hands. Get cutting, Tash!'

Tasha took her comb and carefully brushed out Betsy's long hair, assessing it for kinks or waves, as Joyce had taught her. She pointed to the double-crown on top of her scalp.

'We'll need to cut with this, right?'

Joyce patted her fondly on the back. 'Exactly right.'

'Here we go then.' Biting her lip in concentration, Tasha began clipping the outer layers of Betsy's hair.

'Your sister should throw him out,' one of the ladies under the dryers was saying. 'He's a fool.'

'Aren't they all?'

'Men? Right enough. Mine only behaves because he's scared of my mother.'

'We're better off without them, I say.' The woman leaned forward. 'Did you hear that, girls? You're better off without them.'

'Depends on the man,' Betsy shot back. 'Have you seen that Harry Jessops from down the garage?'

The women whistled.

'He has a fine figure, that one.'

'Very fine.'

They looked at each other and then back at Betsy.

'You have a crack at him if you think you can, girl. Only don't let him talk you into anything too serious, like marriage.'

More cackling.

Betsy caught Tasha's eye in the mirror and winked. Tasha smiled but was glad to dip her head and concentrate as she made the first cut across Betsy's blonde locks. A curl of hair fell to the floor and she paused to watch it, seeing darkest auburn against a dirty camp floor, then blinked the image away. She was in control now. She chose the cuts, she worked the style, she made the women beautiful. It was the antithesis of what she had stood and watched that fateful day in Auschwitz and she was turning it into her future.

For a time, the salon hummed quietly with the patter of rain on the window, the rise and fall of the women's chatter, and Joyce's murmurs of approval as Tasha cut with absolute care and attention around Betsy's head. She saw the girl's slim neck emerge and felt the joy of the transformation she was affecting.

'It's going to look beautiful,' she assured her friend.

Just then the doorbell rang and a young lad sidled in, dripping water onto the floor.

'Moishe?' Tasha exclaimed, her heart skidding. 'What's wrong? Has something happened?'

'No!' Moishe looked around him. 'Cor, it's bright in here, in't it?'

'Pretty,' Betsy corrected him.

'S'pose.'

Tasha bit on a laugh at his easy English. The children who went to the village school were fluent these days, complete with local slang.

'Did you want something, Moishe?' she asked. 'Your hair cutting, maybe?'

'Lord no! I'm not a girl.'

'We cut boys' hair too.' He gave a dramatic shudder and all the women laughed. 'Then...?'

'Sorry, yeah, I've got something for you, Tasha.'

'For me?'

'Yeah. Someone paid me to bring it in. A whole penny.' He pulled a box from his pocket and held it out.

Tasha looked at it suspiciously. 'What is it?'

'I dunno, do I.'

'Who paid you?'

'Not saying.' Tasha went to the window but there was no one in the damp street. 'Are you gonna open it?'

'What if it's dangerous?'

'It's not dangerous. Did it hurt me?'

'He has a point,' Betsy said. 'Looks like jewellery to me.'

The other women gathered around and Tasha had little choice but to untie the ribbon and lift the lid. There was a layer of tissue paper on top and she took hold of it with her fingertips and lifted it slowly.

'Oh!'

Inside, nestled neatly in more tissue, was a lock of auburn hair, perfectly washed, combed out and tied with green ribbon.

'Mama!' Her fingers shook and she looked around at the others. 'It's my mother's hair. The piece I gave to, to...'

'Georg?' a deep voice said.

The door had opened again and there he was, tall and handsome, his curls wet against his face and his dark eyes staring right at her.

'Georg,' she agreed dazedly. She blinked several times but he was still there, large as life amongst the gold and pink of Beautiful You. 'You're here?'

'I am,' he agreed, adding, 'don't throw anything at me.'

The two women chuckled.

'Maybe these young 'uns know how to deal with men after all.'

Georg looked at them. 'My Tasha could deal with anything,' he said. 'Not that she is *my* Tasha. Not that I deserve her, I mean. But a man has to try, right?'

They nodded cooing agreement, all scathing comments about the male of the species apparently forgotten as Georg came further into the salon.

Tasha put her hands on her hips. 'I left you a message.'

'I know, I—'

'Four weeks ago.'

He coloured. 'I know. That is, I didn't get it that day. Melanie – that's the stuck-up one on reception – went off early to meet some equally stuck-up friend and didn't give me it until the next morning.'

Tasha sucked in her breath. 'The cow! I told her how important it was. I told her I'd be waiting and she said she'd definitely get it to you. Definitely.'

'Well, she didn't.'

He held his hands out and Tasha instinctively took a step towards him, then remembered herself.

'That was still three weeks and six days ago, Georg.'

'Yes. I'm sorry. I had... things to do.'

'Things?'

'To, er, to buy. Goodness, Tasha Ancel, you never make anything easy, do you?'

He stepped forward, but Tasha put up an uncertain hand to hold him off.

'Wait a minute, you—'

'Sssh, please. Just sssh. I'm nervous enough as it is.'

'Nervous? You?!'

'Yes! Do you like your mother's hair? I cleaned it extra carefully, Tash. I didn't lose a single strand, not one. It looks better, I think, more like... like her. Like you remember her, I mean, like you described her to me. And like she will look when you find her again.'

'I won't do that, Georg.'

'You will. I believe you will. I was too cynical before. You were right. My parents were gone and the world, frankly, was a better place without them, but I was far too ready for yours to be gone too.'

'Georg—'

'It was unfair. I've thought about it a lot and I want to help. I'm thinking if we save up, we could maybe go to Poland and—'

'Georg! She's dead.'

'What?' He went white. 'How do you know?'

'I've spoken to a nurse who was with her at the end. In Katowice. She died in July.'

'This July? No.' Georg clasped his hands to his mouth. 'I'm so sorry, Tasha. I took you away. Just like you said, I took you away and—'

'And brought me to England, yes.' She looked out the window. The rain had stopped but grey clouds still hung low over Lingfield High Street. 'Lovely England.'

'I'm sorry,' Georg said again. 'I thought it was for the best.'

'Hmm. Well...' She gave him a little smile. 'It was. The nurse says Mama was glad I was here. That she died with a smile on her face when she found out.'

'She did? That's good. I mean, not good that she died, but good that she was at peace.'

'I know what you mean. So, you see, getting on the plane was the right thing to do.'

'And you're not mad at me?'

'Not for that, no.'

'What for then?'

He was so handsome standing there, head on one side, looking at her with those melting brown eyes.

'I'm not sure yet, but I'll think of something.'

'There now, girl, that's a bit unfair,' one of the women said.

'You should give him a chance,' the other one agreed.

Tasha rounded on them. 'I thought you told us we were better off without men?'

They shuffled, patted at the rollers in their hair.

'Yes, well, as young Betsy here said, it depends on the man.'

Tasha rolled her eyes. 'He's not as cute as he looks,' she warned.

'He does look very cute though.'

She threw her hands up. 'You two are hopeless.'

'I think they're very wise,' Georg said. 'Not the cute thing, of course, but you *could* give me a chance? Do you like the gift?'

'It's hardly a gift, Georg – I gave it to you.'

'Yes. True. You did. But, well, I'm giving it back. So, do you like it?'

'I told you I did.'

'Have you studied it properly though? From, er, from all angles.'

Tasha looked at the women, gathering like a coven around her.

'See,' she said, 'this isn't a gift for me, it's all about him – how well he's done.'

'It really isn't,' Georg said. He put a hand to his head and glanced back to Moishe, hovering, fascinated, near the door. 'This felt like such a good idea in my head,' he complained to the lad then he turned back to her. 'Please, Tash, take a good look.'

'Fine.'

Tasha picked up the lock of hair and, despite herself, felt emotion choke her. This was the last thing she had of Lydia, of any of her family. He'd done a lovely job. It would look perfect in a frame in her salon and...

Something chinked against her nail and she jumped.

'Ooh,' her coven cooed and, looking disbelievingly down, she saw, suspended from the ribbon around the top of Lydia's hair, a shiny ring, set with a small but gloriously deep-red ruby.

'Ooh,' she echoed.

Georg dropped to one knee before her. 'Natasha Ancel, will you please, please marry me and make me the most insane, most terrified, most ecstatic man in the world?'

Tasha looked down at him. He looked so healthy, so handsome, so full of the life that had nearly drained from both of them in the last bitter days in Auschwitz. She looked at the auburn hair in her hand and the ruby ring attached to it. Outside, the sun broke through the clouds, and winked into Beautiful You, bouncing off the mirrors and glinting, like fire, through the jewel and down Lydia's hair as if she were, somehow, offering her blessing on this match.

'Yes,' Tasha said. She'd had enough of sadness, enough of anger, enough of going it alone. She grabbed Georg, pulling him up and pressing her lips to his as the women whooped and cheered. 'Yes,' she whispered against them. 'Yes, yes, yes.'

EPILOGUE

LONDON | SUMMER 1950

'Can I come in?'

'Of course!' Tasha pushes herself up in bed and smiles as Alice slides into the room. 'The door is always open for Granny Alice.'

'Granny Alice!' Alice scoffs, colouring in the way Tasha knows so well, but there's a question in her voice and Tasha waves her forward.

'Definitely Granny Alice, if you don't mind?'

'Mind!' Alice looks down at the baby boy nestled in Tasha's arms and her eyes fill with joy. 'I can think of nothing I would like better than to be granny to little Szymon.'

'That's settled then.' Tasha pats the bed and smiles fondly at Alice as she perches on the edge of it. 'You're staying the night?'

'I wouldn't presume—'

'It isn't a presumption, Granny Alice. We'd love to have you. You can share with Marta. She's very excited. She's made up a truckle-bed for herself so that you can have hers. And she and Georg have been making matzoh soup specially so, you see, you have to stay.'

'Well in that case...'

'Good! Of course, Szymon might cry in the night, so sorry if he wakes you.'

Alice laughs. 'It will be nothing new.'

'No.' Tasha leans forward, the baby snuffling against her in his sleep. 'I remember once, in Windermere, hearing noises in the night and seeing you comforting Marta. You had this donkey and when Kotka pulled the tail, the saddle lifted and there were sweeties inside.'

Alice laughs again.

'I still have it. Maybe when Szymon is older, he'll be able to lift the tail too.'

They look at each other then, caught in a time-loop neither of them could have possibly expected on that first day when Tasha flew into Crosby-on-Eden to find Alice nervously waiting on the runway. They all live in London now, Tasha and Georg in a small flat in Shoreditch over Lydia's Hair Salon, and Alice out in Isleworth. She and Sophie moved there with the remaining Weir Courtney children two years ago, the committee ladies keen to give them opportunities for 'development' (by which, they meant employment) not available to them in rural Surrey.

That was when Tasha and Georg celebrated their second wedding anniversary by adopting Marta and giving her the 'real' surname, Lieberman, although she'd always be Kotka to them. The girl, now thirteen years old, is doing very well at the local grammar school and speaking English with a cockney twist. It has been a long road to bring her from stranger to sort-of-sister to daughter, but Tasha embraces the unusual relationship, as she embraces all her jumbled family, with every drop of her love.

'Tea!'

Georg walks into the room, proudly bearing a tea tray complete with miniature tablecloth and the teacups Alice gave them as a wedding present. He looks every inch the English gentleman, save that an English gentleman would have little idea how to make tea. From the start of their marriage, with Georg working his way up to floor supervisor at Hobbs, Hart, and Tasha establishing Lydia's Hair Salon, they have shared the chores at home.

'We both worked in Auschwitz,' they tell anyone who questions this 'bohemian' arrangement; they are rarely questioned further.

Georg pours the tea and hands a cup to Alice, placing Tasha's on the bedside table as he sits himself next to his wife and child.

'Is he not the most handsome baby you've ever seen?' he asks Alice.

Tasha rolls her eyes but Alice does not hesitate.

'He is, Georg.'

'He feeds like a little demon and he sleeps so well.'

'He does not!' Tasha protests. 'You're the one who sleeps well – right through him crying, right through the feeding and the nappy changing.'

Georg kisses her. 'What can I say? It's a talent.'

'Could you pass it on to your son, then?'

'All in good time, kochanie, all in good time. Here, let me take him and you can drink your tea.'

He takes the baby, nestling him easily into his strong arms. Tasha sips gratefully at her drink, enjoying the moment of peace, but then the bell rings out downstairs and they all hear the unmistakable tones of Marta saying a cheery hello to Betsy in the salon below. Tasha can picture the girl bouncing around the tasteful cream and Wondermere-green salon, passing the framed lock of Lydia's hair between the big mirrors, making for the stairs up to their little home.

Joyce's daughter came to Lydia's last year and Tasha knows the salon is safe in Betsy's competent hands until she can get back to work herself. Betsy is living with three other single young women (to Joyce's declared horror and, Tasha suspects, secret envy) and having a rare old time in London's burgeoning bars and clubs. But Betsy is sharp, reliable, and a talented hairdresser and, if she sometimes looks bleary-eyed first thing in the morning, the clients don't seem to mind.

'Alice!'

Marta flings herself at Alice so hard that her cup rattles, sending tea slopping into the saucer. Alice simply tips it back into the cup and hugs her close.

'How was school?' Georg asks.

'Fine.'

'Any exam results in yet?'

'Oh. Yeah. Physics. I came top.'

'Top? In physics?' Georg looks proudly to Tasha. 'Hear that, Tash – our girl, top! In physics!' They look at each other wonderingly. 'It must be in your blood, Kotka.'

There is a pause, a heartbeat, where they all look at each other and sense, standing between them, the many people lost: Marta's blood parents that she cannot even remember; Georg's brawling father and drunken mother, gone before the war began; Alice's brother, sister-in-law and niece, sent to the gas without even a chance of survival; Tasha's father, shot dead in Warsaw, her sister, lost to Auschwitz, and her mother, Lydia, who battled to stay alive long enough to hear of her daughter's safety.

The ghosts between them in this homely room are too many and too tragic to count without dissolving into bitter tears, so they try not to count too often. What matters is that the unseen web of families has come down to this – a couple saved from the camps, an adopted daughter, and a co-opted grandmother. They are thin threads but, woven strongly, will form the nest for baby Syzmon and all those like him, to grow out of the remains of the killing. New life, new hope, new roots.

'Have you seen?' Marta says to Alice, lifting her brother from her father's arms and dropping a kiss on his downy hair as he stirs from sleep and looks up at her with bright blue eyes.

'Seen what?' Alice asks.

Marta strokes the little baby curls. 'He's ginger!'

'Flame red,' Alice corrects.

'The best colour of all,' Tasha agrees.

For a moment there it is – the flash of Lydia's re-growing hair disappearing beneath a blanket – and then Baby Szymon is wailing for a feed and Tasha has to set down her teacup, take him into her arms and latch him to the breast. Stroking the auburn strands as he feeds, she knows that this, not the biggest guns or the greatest armies or the deadliest bombs, but this continued thread of love, is the true victory, the true peace, the true future. The true home at last.

A LETTER FROM ANNA

Dear reader,

I want to say a huge thank you for choosing to read *The War Orphan*. It was while working on *The Midwife of Auschwitz* that I began researching the fate of those few who made it out of the concentration camps, and when I read that some youngsters had been sent to Windermere, I was hooked. This was a story I had to tell.

If you want to keep up to date with all my latest releases, just sign up at the following link. Your email address will never be shared and you can unsubscribe at any time.

www.bookouture.com/anna-stuart

It's hard to imagine more disparate landscapes than the stark, enclosed Auschwitz and the gloriously open, beautiful Lake District and I so admire the visionary people who worked so hard to make this extraordinary project happen. The true stories are available online and, especially, in the BBC documentary, *The Windermere Children: In Their Own Words*, but I hope my fictional interpretation goes a little way to capturing something of the experiences of the kind carers and brave children as they worked to correct the worst possible start in life.

If you enjoyed this novel, I'd be very grateful if you could write a review. I'd love to hear what you think, and it makes such a difference helping new readers to discover one of my books for the first time. I also love hearing from my readers – you can get in touch on my Facebook page, through Twitter, Instagram or my website.

Thanks for reading,

Anna

www.annastuartbooks.com

 facebook.com/annastuartauthor

 x.com/annastuartbooks

 instagram.com/annastuartauthor

HISTORICAL NOTES

This story is, like all my Second World War stories, based on real happenings and features a number of real people. As always, I feel the responsibility of doing them justice in my fiction and hope that these additional notes will help people to understand more about them, and to point them to places for further research if they wish.

Real people

Alice Goldberger: Alice is not as well remembered as she deserves to be. A quiet, self-effacing woman, she never sought to claim a place in history but, rather, to give the orphans in her care the best possible chance at weaving happy stories of their own. As many of the details about her as possible in this novel are true. For example, Alice did keep a donkey on her bedside table with sweets inside, revealed when you lifted the tail. She also kept a photo of her brother's family and – as testified by Sarah Moskovitz, who wrote the fascinating book *Love Despite Hate* and personally interviewed Alice – she was haunted by guilt that she'd got out of Germany and they had not. In a novel about trying to find family and home, this seemed tragic but a vital detail in her story. Max, Lilli and Ruth-Gertrud are also real people and their names and the dates of their deaths can, sadly, be found on the amazing Auschwitz database today.

Alice never married, devoting herself instead to the care of various children throughout her life. Her great friend Sophie Wutsch was, as shown in the novel, a kind-hearted Austrian cook, and the two women lived and worked together for the rest of their lives, latterly in a cosy apartment in London at which they hosted wedding parties for five of the children who'd been in their care – a testimony to their importance in their lives. There is no suggestion they were ever more than very good friends and romance does not seem to have really featured in Alice's life. I confess, I have taken a little creative licence in imagining a sweetheart killed in the First World War and the possibility of a frisson between her and Oskar, a man who, while brilliant, had a certain reputation as a flirt, but I hope it matters little in the scheme of Alice's life. She carved herself out a huge family of children, grandchildren and great-grandchildren, many of whom kept in touch with her throughout their lives and did, as shown in the epilogue, call her Granny Alice.

The greatest testimony to the loving achievements of this extraordinary woman can be found in an episode of *This is Your Life* from 1978, in which many of those she'd cared for in Windermere and Weir Courtney travelled miles to celebrate her part in making them feel loved and prepared for a world that had treated them very badly in their first years. Sadly, the episode itself is no longer in the public domain but there are clips and pictures online that, along with the amazing Alice Goldberger papers on the US Holocaust Museum website (www.ushmm.org) give a true sense of this most selfless and loving of women. I hope this novel goes a little way to giving her the place in Holocaust history that she deserves.

Anna Freud (and Dorothy Burlingham): Anna Freud is a fascinating figure – a revolutionary woman who carved herself out a career almost as prestigious as that of her more famous father and did groundbreaking work in children's psychoanalysis. She was Sigmund Freud's sixth and youngest child, born in Vienna in 1895, and perhaps the closest to him, taking a precocious interest in his work from a young age.

Her own start in psychoanalysis came from translating other people's studies, as well as acting as secretary and, increasingly, spokesperson for her father after he was diagnosed with cancer of the jaw in 1923. However, she presented her first personal paper to the Vienna Psychoanalytical Society in 1922 and became a member in her own right. She opened a practice working with children, and published her first book in 1927. From her father, Anna absorbed key ideas about troublesome behaviours having their root in childhood experiences, but she applied it practically, working to make those experiences positive to avoid later problems. She believed strongly in playfulness and learning through fun and was, I gather, an inspirational person to be around.

Back in the late 1930s, however, with the Freuds as a prominent Jewish family, their life in Austria came under threat. In 1938 Anna was taken in by the Gestapo for questioning and although she, thankfully, survived the ordeal and was released, the family fled to Britain that June. They set up home at 20 Maresfield Gardens, Hampstead – a building that was to become Anna's first war nursery and is now the Freud Museum. Sadly, Sigmund Freud died just over a year later in September 1939, but Anna held up the family name with her groundbreaking work, including setting up the Hampstead Child Therapy course to train new psychoanalysts – of which Alice Goldberger was, as shown in the novel, one of the first graduates.

Anna met Dorothy Burlingham, an American psychoana-

lyst and member of the New York Tiffany family, in the early
1920s when Dorothy moved to Vienna specifically to seek help
for her son's psychosomatic skin disorder. Anna took all
Dorothy's four children into analysis and the women soon
became fast friends. She always denied a sexual relationship
between them but admitted to 'intimate relations resembling
those of lesbians'... Certainly, Dorothy separated from her
husband and she and Anna bought a cottage in 1930. Whatever
their personal relationship, they were a brilliant working part-
nership and lived together for the rest of their lives.

Anna was one of a number of Austrian and German
psychoanalysts, both male and female, on the vanguard of a
new, analysis-based approach to treating the mind. With many
of them of Jewish heritage, they found themselves as part of a
fascinating and vibrant mini-diaspora, largely living and
working in Britain and America. They do not seem to have
suffered any prejudice for it – on the contrary parents were
hugely grateful for their work – but it must have been hard
being a German in wartime and post-war Britain and I chose to
show Alice – interned as an 'enemy alien' when she arrived – as
very aware of that.

As far as I'm aware Anna Freud did not ever visit Calgarth,
being far more London-based, but she was involved with all the
psychoanalysts and it seemed a good way to introduce and
involve her to bring her up to Windermere so I hope readers
will forgive the liberty.

Oskar Friedmann (and Manna): Oskar Friedmann was
a complex character. He was, by all accounts, a brilliant psychoanalyst and a driven member of the Windermere team, but he
seems to have been either loved or hated by the children and I
suspect he had the slightly abrasive personality of an intellectual, so chose to write him that way. I do not mean to do him a
disservice as he did excellent work and was devoted to the chil-

dren's care, but he was first and foremost a scientist and I wanted to mark the difference between Alice, always driven by the children, and his slightly more distanced approach. His resentment when the six 'tinies' are taken away to Bulldogs Bank is imagined by me, but Anna Freud did publish a ground-breaking study on these children, raised almost entirely without adult influence for their first two years (her book, *The Bulldogs Bank Story*, co-written with Sophie Dann, is fascinating) and I strongly suspect he was jealous of that scientific opportunity.

Oskar's path to Britain had not been easy. In 1932, working as the director of an institution for juvenile delinquents in Wolzig near Berlin, he was arrested and he and all the boys in his care were sent to Sachsenhausen where he was badly beaten, suffering an ear injury and permanent paralysis to the face. He had to undergo significant analysis himself later to overcome the psychological damage and was driven to help others recover from Nazi atrocities. Thankfully he made it out and in 1938 he was invited to take a group of Jewish children to England as part of the kindertransport programme. He originally intended to return to Germany, but the situation was becoming more volatile so thankfully he stayed to work with the Jewish communities in London and his wife, two children and sister joined him, so were also saved.

Oskar seems to have had something of a reputation as a ladies' man – probably more from enjoying flirtation than from actual affairs – and separated from his wife at some point during the war. With Alice, I tried to show him being his naturally flirtatious self and her, naive in the ways of the world, being unsure how to take it, but his relationship with Manna Weindling is based on facts. There is no evidence as to when it started but, although she went to Israel for three years in 1952, she returned and married a now-divorced Oskar in 1956. My authorial imagination assumes that they were attracted from early on, that she hoped moving away would remove the temptation of this married man, but that true love won out and she returned to him. Sadly, he died just two years later so they had little time to enjoy their hard-won togetherness.

Marie Paneth: Marie was another powerhouse of a woman. As shown in the novel, she was a strikingly handsome woman of 6′ 2″, who had left her husband – and children – to pursue her career. She reportedly dazzled New York society for the few years she was working out there, but truly made her mark in psychotherapy when she came to the East End of London during the war and, with extraordinary kindness, resilience and courage, ran a house for some of the most deprived and worst-behaved children in Britain, transforming many of their lives in the process.

Ahead of her time, she developed herself as an art therapist, very much in the way we would understand that now. In Windermere, her work with the children painting pictures of their times in the camps – as briefly shown in the novel – offered real insight into all they had been through. This is also shown well in the film *The Windermere Children* although, to my annoyance, they cast her as a young woman whereas she was in fact, like Anna Freud and Alice Goldberger, into her fifties at this time and doubtless all the more confident and assertive for that.

There is room for a whole novel about Marie Paneth (maybe I will write it myself one day), but if anyone is interested in her war work, I'd highly recommend her own fantastic books: *Branch Street: A sociological study*, about the East End and the recently discovered and published *Rock the Cradle* about her work in Windermere.

Sir Benjamin Drage: Sir Benjamin was a wealthy Jewish owner of a large furniture store in High Holborn who, along with his wife, Lady Phoebe, opened up his beautiful house at

Weir Courtney to the younger Windermere orphans. The house was exactly as described in the novel, complete with orangery and swimming pool, and I believe it still exists as a private residence. A solid, gracious mansion house, it was the place where the children settled into school, village life and regular routines, and they are documented as calling it 'home' in a way they never did of the more hostel-based, transient Calgarth Estate.

The story about the children seeing the POWs nearby and being terrified that the Nazis were back is recorded fact, although it didn't take place at the VE Day celebrations. Also, sadly, a young lad called Ernst really was knocked off his bike by a car (although a little later than shown in the novel in October 1946) and killed, and the children's shock at finding out that it wasn't just Nazis that caused death is also recorded fact. The traumas embedded in these children from their times in ghettos and camps is unimaginable and it is all credit to Alice and her team that most of them grew to be happy, well-adjusted human beings with families and good lives.

It should also be noted at this point that I took small licence with the personnel at Weir Courtney. In reality, only nine children moved there from Windermere in November 1945. A second group of nine girls and five boys arrived in early summer 1946 – mainly from Auschwitz – and Manna Weindling was recruited at that point to help deal with the greater numbers. The Bucci sisters, on whom Mirella and Fiorina are based (see below), arrived in that 'shipment' so were never actually at Windermere, but explaining the logistics of the various transports slowed the narrative so I hope readers will forgive me for simplifying it by placing all children in this novel there from the start.

The Bucci sisters: The story of Mirella and Fiorina Bellucci in the novel is closely based on the wonderful true tale of Tatiana and Andra Bucci. Raised in Fiume – part of Italy in the post First World War era, now Rijeka in Croatia – to a Jewish mother and a Catholic father, both girls were christened in 1938 to try and avoid the persecution coming the way of the Jews. It didn't work. Their father, Giovanni, a sailor in the Italian merchant navy, had his ship, the *Timavo*, sunk by its commander just off the coast of South Africa to stop it being requisitioned by the British. He was arrested and, despite not being military, was taken to Koffiefontain, a POW camp near Johannesburg, where he was imprisoned, in relative comfort, for the whole war.

Meanwhile, in September 1943, Fiume, as part of northern Italy, was occupied and incorporated into the Reich when the Italians went over to the Allies, spelling disaster for Jews. In March 1944, the girls' house was stormed by the Gestapo and they were shipped to Auschwitz with their mother, Mira, their nonna Rosa and other aunts and cousins. Mira threw a note out of the window at one station with their names on it and where they were going and somehow this got back to her hometown so friends could write and tell Giovanni they had been deported. It must have been terrible reading.

On arrival in Auschwitz, half of their train of two hundred people were chosen to work, while the other half were sent straight to the gas, including Nonna Rosa and Aunt Sophie. It's unclear how the girls, then aged six and four, escaped death. It's possible their part-Catholic heritage helped, and also possible that the Nazis thought they were twins as they were assigned to Barrack 1, used to house children taken for horrific experiments by Josef Mengele. Thankfully, arriving in spring 1944, they were never chosen and made it to the end of the war alive.

Their mother, as shown in the novel, snuck visits to them when she could and repeated their names to them over and over until she was sent away in November 1944. They believed her to be dead but in fact she'd been transferred to Lippstadt, a subcamp of Buchenwald, and then to Buchenwald itself where she was at liberation. She fought her way back to Fiume and found her freed husband there towards the end of 1945, but the area was being absorbed into Tito's Yugoslavia and they moved up the coast to Italian Trieste where they finally found out their daughters were still alive and in England.

The process, in a world of cross-Europe letters, took a long time and it seems the girls were first told their parents were alive in autumn 1946 and left for Rome that December. My own Mirella and Fiorina work on a slightly different timeline, with news of their parents arriving at Weir Courtney in June 1946 and them leaving in August, but I hope the joy of someone finding their happy ending – and the hope and envy that aroused in others – is conveyed. For anyone interested in the Buccis' story, I recommend their autobiography, *Always Remember Your Name*.

Significant places

Windermere: From the moment I heard that Jewish orphans had been brought to the Lake District after the war, I was fascinated. I am not the first to the story, however, and would guide any interested reader to the moving film, *The Windermere Children*, and the excellent accompanying BBC documentary, *The Windermere Children – In Their Own Words*. It seems that, as time went on (though not while they were in Windermere) the group became known as 'the boys' and, although that term happily includes the 48 girls in the 300-strong group, I was intrigued more specifically by the female side of the story. That's what set me on the trail of Alice Goldberger, Weir Courtney and the move on from Windermere, and I sincerely hope my novel works as a complement to the film and documentary and does credit to the true stories.

Europe after the war: As shown in the opening scenes in Theresienstadt and in Lydia's sad experiences, Europe after the Second World War was chaos. Many thousands of people were 'displaced' – a rather cold term that incorporates those who'd been in POW camps, in exile, in hiding and, of course, in the variety of labour and death camps across the merciless Third Reich. In an era of no real computers, few telephones and an overloaded postal service, everything took more time than we can possibly imagine and so many people were roaming the continent trying to find missing loved ones and get home.

This will perhaps be especially surprising for the British reader used, as we are, to the idea of Churchill declaring the war over, soldiers gradually coming home, and life slowly returning to normal. There were the privations of continued rationing and, of course, the wounds – both physical and mental – of those who'd fought, as well as the terrible loss of the many who did not return. I do not wish in any way to diminish that suffering, but the core fabric of life remained intact in Great Britain, whereas for so many in the far more fluid European zone, it did not. Homes, indeed whole cities, had been destroyed, millions killed and hundreds of thousands uprooted. For many years, families remained torn apart. Few had the happy ending of the Bucci sisters and, although it broke my heart to do so, I chose not to have Tasha and Lydia reunited to stand testimony to the reality for so many poor people.

The Warsaw Uprising: Tasha, as originally shown when she first appears towards the end of *The Midwife of Auschwitz*, is from Warsaw. This poor city suffered hugely during the war, at the forefront of Hitler's bitter hatred of the Poles. Warsaw was occupied in September 1939, after a bitter three-week-long fight that saw many buildings bombed and many people killed. Their occupation was brutal. The Germans had a plan to elimi-nate all Poles from the capital and turn it into a German city (complete with wooden Alpine-style housing!) and moved the 'Volksdeutsche' (people with German roots) into the city in huge numbers, taking locals' homes and businesses and designating many areas as Nur für Deutsche (Germans only). They were utterly ruthless to the native population. At least ten thousand of Poland's intellectual, political and cultural elite were murdered in the early part of the war and the hounding of the population continued to 1944, with groups regularly and randomly rounded up for mass public executions.

The Poles, however, attacked by the German and Russian powers either side of them for centuries, have a long and proud history of insurrection and set up an astonishing underground army and state which made wide-ranging and highly professional preparation for an uprising when the moment was right to help liberate their own capital.

The first resistance came from brave Jews, shut within the huge ghetto at the centre of the city. Knowing it was to be liquidated in April 1943, they set up an armed fight-back that was ultimately doomed, but meant they went to their deaths with freedom and pride instead of in a cattle cart and a gas chamber. Some of them – like Tasha's family – escaped to hide in the city until the wider uprising a year later, but this one, tragically, was not going to fare any better.

The people of Warsaw, under the forty thousand trained troops of the Home Army, rose up on 1 August 1944 as the Soviets were attacking the eastern outskirts to aid in their own liberation. Sadly, despite their immense courage and fighting spirit, the lack of help from either the Soviets, cruelly content to sit back across the Vistula River and let the Germans and Poles destroy each other, or the British and Americans – stationed at a long reach from Warsaw – left them isolated. Bombed constantly so that everyone was living underground, eventually without water, electricity or food, they had to capitulate at the start of October. The city, on Hitler's express orders, was razed to the ground and the people were driven out, largely to either POW or labour camps. Some of them, especially any Jews, were sent to Auschwitz and this is the journey I chose for Tasha, her mother and her sister.

The Warsaw Uprising was a truly inspiring and tragic point in history and if you want to know more, watch this space for my next novel. It will take readers into the heart of the doomed capital and will feature a little of Tasha and her family, and a little more of Bronislaw and Bartek Kaminski – husband and son of Ana, the eponymous Midwife of Auschwitz...

ACKNOWLEDGEMENTS

On a windswept day in April 2013, my good friend Brenda stood on a beach in Wales declaiming aloud for curious passers-by one of the best emails I'd ever received – an offer from a young editor called Natasha Harding to publish three of my novels. I was thrilled and even more so when I met Natasha and found her to be passionate, articulate and commercially switched-on about the fascinating world of book publishing. We had an amazing journey together with that first novel and, even when Natasha was promoted and moved to another company, we would meet up if I was in London. Every time she would say to me, 'Would you like to write Second World War fiction?' and every time I would say I didn't think it was a good idea. As it turned out, it was a *very* good idea and when I finally gave in to Natasha and started investigating the history of that astonishing period, I was hooked.

I honestly don't think I would be writing the books I so enjoy writing today without Natasha, or having half the success in reaching readers. I love working with her. She's not afraid to tell me if I've had a stupid idea (or at least, as she would gracefully put it, a commercially unviable one) and she's endlessly encouraging and engaged if I have a half-decent one. What's more, many of the best ideas – writing a novel about Auschwitz, for example – come from Natasha, and I so enjoy how we can toss concepts around and, between us, find the best way to carve them into a story readers might appreciate. She is sharp, patient, efficient and kind, not to mention fantastic fun. She's a brilliant editor and I consider myself endlessly blessed that she's *my* editor. Thank you so much, Natasha, and here's to the many future stories we have yet to uncover together!

Natasha is part of a fantastic team at Bookouture who always go the extra mile to encourage, help and promote their authors and this time round I owe especial thanks to the fabulous Peta and the very patient Mark for their assistance in the business side of being an author. And, of course, thanks to my lovely agent Kate Shaw for her work, her editing brilliance and for introducing me to genuinely tasty vegan food!

I owe a debt of gratitude to several other important people for this book. Several of the 'orphans' who came to England are still alive and I was lucky enough to meet two of them, both inspiring people. I had a fascinating chat with Jackie Young and his lovely wife, Lita, to whom he will have been married for sixty years this year! Jackie was one of the Bulldogs Bank children, who went on to make himself a wonderful family life in England. He told me all he remembered about his early years in England, notably about his time at Weir Courtney. He also gave me a real sense of what it was like to grow up in the knowledge that your birth family had been taken from you so cruelly, and some of the trauma of trying to find out who they were that really helped in capturing the feel of Tasha's quest for her mother.

I was also honoured to meet Zdenka Husserl, who came to Windermere aged six and went on to Weir Courtney and then the London 'Lingfield house' with Alice and Sophie. She gave me a real flavour of life in Weir Courtney and shared her very fond, vivid memories of Alice – a huge help in crafting her for this novel. After some consideration, I did not name any of the girls in the novel Zdenka, for fear of doing an injustice to her own direct experiences but she, and those who were there with her are, I hope, represented in Suzi, Judith and Marta.

I was also lucky enough to link up with Trevor Avery, the

amazing historian on the Lake District Holocaust Project, who was kind enough to give me much of his time and wisdom. Trevor has worked on this project since 2005 and is a mine of information about the Calgarth Estate and the children who came there. He was the consultant historian for the beautiful film, *The Windermere Children*, and the excellent accompanying BBC documentary, *The Windermere Children: In Their Own Words*, which I would recommend to anyone wanting to know more. Trevor was incredibly helpful with some of the smaller details of life in the Lake District for the orphans which really helped me picture their world and, I hope, bring it to the page for readers. Thank you, Trevor.

Thank you also to those involved in running the lovely exhibition about the Calgarth Estate in the Windermere library. *From Auschwitz to Ambleside* is a fascinating (and free!) insight into this amazing story of regeneration and if anyone is in the area, do pop in and take a look.

I must also give my thanks to the '45 Aid Society. This group, formed in 1963 by some of the survivors, has a wonderful mission to preserve and honour the stories of the orphans who have, over time, become known as 'the boys' (including the few girls!), and their descendants. Their website is a mine of information, not just on the orphans who came to the Lake District, but also those who arrived subsequently on flights to Southampton and other parts of the UK. The society holds annual reunions and in 2019 six of the survivors and some two hundred and fifty of their relatives recreated the photograph taken of the original orphans in Prague before their flights to Crosby-on-Eden – a moving memorial, also available to view on the internet. The Society were very helpful with offering me information and putting me in touch with Jackie and Zdenka and I would especially like to thank Julia Burton for her time and assistance.

Another website that proved invaluable was that of the

United States Holocaust Memorial Museum (www.ushm-m.org), who hold the Alice Goldberger papers – a fascinating collection of documents about Alice and, even better, copies of letters sent to her by the children which clearly show the love they held for her. I urge any interested readers to take a look.

I must also pay tribute to the website of the Auschwitz-Birkenau museum (www.auschwitz.org) for the myriad tragic stories they share and the detailed records of inmates. It was there that I found the entries for Max, Lilliana and Ruth-Gertrud Goldberger, as shown in the novel, and seeing their names starkly recorded, amongst so very many others, really brought the tragedy of these senseless losses home to me. I hope this novel goes a little way to honouring them.

PUBLISHING TEAM

Turning a manuscript into a book requires the efforts of many people. The publishing team at Bookouture would like to acknowledge everyone who contributed to this publication.

Audio
Alba Proko
Sinead O'Connor
Melissa Tran

Commercial
Lauren Morrissette
Jil Thielen
Imogen Allport

Contracts
Peta Nightingale

Data and analysis
Mark Alder
Mohamed Bussuri

Editorial
Natasha Harding
Lizzie Brien

Copyeditor
Anne O'Brien

Proofreader
Liz Hatherell

Marketing
Alex Crow
Melanie Price
Occy Carr
Cíara Rosney

Operations and distribution
Marina Valles
Stephanie Straub

Production
Hannah Snetsinger
Mandy Kullar
Jen Shannon

Publicity
Kim Nash
Noelle Holten
Myrto Kalavrezou
Jess Readett
Sarah Hardy

Printed in Great Britain
by Amazon

44218351R00223